Righteous
KILL

Righteous
KILL

Norma
Enjoy Sarah's
1st ADventure

JIM DAHER

Jim Daher
5/7/06

HH
HARBOR
HOUSE
Augusta

RIGHTEOUS KILL
By Jim Daher
A Harbor House Book/2005

For information address:
      HARBOR HOUSE
      111 TENTH STREET
      AUGUSTA, GEORGIA 30901

Cove and book design by Renee Conaway

Library of Congress Cataloging-in-Publication Data

Daher, Jim.
Righteous kill / by Jim Daher.
   p. cm.
ISBN 1-891799-59-2 (alk. paper)
I. Title.
PS3604.A3375R54 2006
813'.6--dc22
                        2005035990

Printed in the United States of America

10 9 8 7 6 5 4 3 2 1

DEDICATION

To the memory of my parents, John and Stella, who demon-strated the value of love and family throughout their lives.

Also, to my brother, Johnny who led the way while we were growing up and was always there when we needed him.

ACKNOWLEDGEMENTS

Thanks to my wife, Betty, the love of my life, for your continued support and encouragement while I've chased my dreams. Chris, I could not have asked for a better son or friend. Both of you were and are answers to my prayers. This one is for the two of you!

Judy, sis—you're the best; You, Jeff and Susan will always be special. Mike Daher, your friendship and our golf games mean more to me than you'll ever know. Jerry, I hope you enjoy my novel. Also, thanks to Inez & Therese, my Detroit connection.

I would be remiss if I didn't mention Bouvier, the first English-Springer Spaniel to bound into my life, and Colby, my current "Best of Breed."

The comments and suggestions from those who read the early drafts were a great help. Thanks to Mike Crews, Anna Stroud, Charlene James, Chris and Betty.

Sharon Smith-Henderson spent countless hours helping

me understand the best way to put a story on paper. The good writing skills and techniques exhibited are due to her efforts; the poor one's are all my own.

Thanks to Carrie and the crew at Harbor House for taking a chance on a new author. May *Righteous Kill* be the first of many.

A special thanks to William Rawlings, Jr. for his advice and introductions.

Finally, I thank God for his forgiveness, for answering my prayers and for picking me up and dusting me off when I've fallen.

"Trust in the Lord with all your heart and lean not on you own understanding; in all your ways submit to him and he will make your paths straight;" Proverbs 3, 5&6.

CHAPTER 1

AFTER EASING THE BLACK 350Z into her reserved slot, Sarah cut the engine and put the keys in the side pocket of her tote. She took a moment to mentally review the questions she planned to ask at the bank, before slipping the dated, black and white photo into her jacket pocket. She was confident the tellers would identify the man in the picture as the customer the Bank of America knew as Gary Allen. But, if not, nothing was lost. It would simply confirm that the other Gary Allen was, in reality, Gregory Alan Hawkins, Jr. — the man she intended to kill.

The day of reckoning was near and considering her career, her reputation and possibly her life were at stake, Sarah was amazingly calm. Why shouldn't she be? She had spent the past thirteen years preparing herself — mentally, physically and emotionally — for the confrontation. She was ready.

Opening the car door, she swung her long legs out and looking up, caught two men staring as her skirt slid up her thighs. Tugging it down, she pulled herself out of the low slung sports car, closed the door and pushed the remote to lock it. One of the gawkers stopped in mid-stride to get a better look and the other, who also had his attention focused on her, walked right into him.

Chuckling, she winked, flashed the red-faced duo a dazzling smile, casually slung her tote over her shoulder and with an exaggerated swing of her hips headed for the street exit, muttering, "Men, every one of them has a one-track mind."

Feeling the cold of the gray Atlanta morning, she tightened the belt of her Burberry coat and stepped out of the parking garage into the mist. She crossed Peachtree at mid-block and zigzagged around and between cars idling in six lanes of bumper-to-bumper traffic. When she reached the other side of the street, she lowered her head against the blustery wind and hurried up the short flight of steps to the main entrance of the bank. Her long stride took her to the top step just as one of the smoky glass doors flew open, missing her by inches. The man coming through the door was preoccupied with turning up the collar of his overcoat and didn't notice Sarah until his briefcase banged into her leg. Without comment, he moved to his right to go around her.

Sarah took a step to her left and blocked his path. "Excuse me," she snarled.

He responded with an arrogant, annoyed look that told her he had no intention of apologizing. Then he took a half step back and his expression slowly changed as his gaze dropped to her legs and moved up her body, to her face, and finally her damp, shoulder length strawberry blonde hair.

"Nice," he growled in a voice that rumbled from deep within his chest. His lips curled, baring his teeth, reminding Sarah of a painting of a ravenous wolf moving in for the kill.

Like an electric shock, a shiver ran through her as recognition registered in her mind. His voice, the comment, and the predatory stare brought it all back. Greg Hawkins. She was looking into the eyes of a demon — her demon.

Her first rational thought after getting over the instantaneous anger at herself for being caught off guard: *Does he recognize me? Am I the reason he's here—in Atlanta?*

The answers came just as quickly. *No, I came here, this morning, looking for him. The fact that he's here is pure coincidence. Besides, he wrote me off years ago, and he probably doesn't even know I exist.*

As if confirming her assessment, Hawkins started down the steps without a backward glance.

SARAH STEPPED INTO THE BANK and watched through the smoked glass windows for a few moments before moving back through the doors. With her eyes locked on the back of Hawkins' head, she moved down the steps and into the crowd.

Unlike everyone else on the sidewalk, Hawkins didn't seem to be in a hurry, which made it easier for Sarah to keep him in sight. And, the other pedestrians sidestepping and dodging around him made her less conspicuous as she followed.

People of all shapes, colors and sizes hustled to get wherever it is they had to be on a Friday morning in downtown Atlanta. Many wrestled with umbrellas and fought gusts of wind, carrying briefcases, totes or gym bags. Others clasped sacks from fast food chains—Mickey D's, The Bagel Shoppe or Krispy Kreme. Sarah's eyes zeroed in on the white sack with green lettering and crown. Her mouth watered as she thought about the warm, glazed donuts inside, and for a split second she thought of snatching the bag out of the woman's hand and making a run for it. Envisioning herself dodging around pedestrians while stuffing donuts into her mouth, she laughed.

The woman on her left gave Sarah an odd look. Sarah shrugged, giving her a friendly nod, and pulled her cell phone out of her pocket and punched the auto-dial code for her office.

"Hi Darcy, this is Sarah. I'm going to be late this morning.

I'm not sure when I'll be in but I'll get there as soon as I can. Tell Scott for me, okay? Oh, and reschedule my ten-thirty…Yes, I know it's the district attorney. I even dressed for the occasion. Hey, come to think of it, try to reschedule it for this afternoon, so I won't waste the effort…No. Dressing up two days in a row won't hurt me, thanks…No, no, everything is all right. I've just got a couple of things I need to take care of this morning…Thanks, Darcy, see ya."

Oblivious to the wind and the frigid drizzle, she followed Hawkins south on Peachtree, and was at the intersection of Peachtree and Houston streets before the realization settled in; her quest was almost over. Soon, she would be able to put the past behind her and begin living for the future.

She had kept up with Hawkins for more than a decade, periodically monitoring his career and whereabouts. Two weeks ago, one of her routine checks revealed he had resigned his job and left Nashville. The only lead she had picked up from his former office was that they thought he had moved to Georgia — maybe Atlanta.

Busy with a high profile case, Sarah hadn't had time to do a detailed follow up, but she did discover two Gary B. Allen's had moved into the Atlanta area recently. Both had purchased homes and established bank accounts; one at the downtown branch of the Bank of America and the other at the Alpharetta branch of Trust Company Bank. So far she had uncovered nothing to indicate which man was her target, and decided the best way to do so was to visit the banks and talk to the tellers. Neither man obtained a Georgia driver's license, so a recent photo wasn't available. Improvising, she retrieved a five-year-old photo from a Nashville newspaper and used the Bureau computer to enhance the image, planning to use it. Now, fate had intervened and saved her the trouble.

This was the first time she had actually seen Greg Hawkins since the last day of the trial, more than a dozen years ago. Seeing him in the flesh gave her a sense of fear and determination, mixed with the excitement of the hunt — the same feeling she got just before confronting a criminal with all the evidence needed to put him or her away.

Only this time, there would be no arrest, just an execution. A well deserved, meticulously planned "Righteous Kill."

THIRTEEN YEARS WAS a long time to carry a grudge, but referring to Sarah's obsession for revenge as a grudge was like calling a rattlesnake an adorable critter. This was the man who had taken away her innocence and her best friend without a tinge of guilt. A wealthy, powerful father made justice turn a blind eye to his son's transgressions and a monster was set free without so much as a slap on the wrist. Since then, every life decision Sarah had made was directed toward vengeance — a final confrontation.

Through the years, he had been an image haunting her dreams, and now, he was walking just ahead of her on the wet, crowded Atlanta sidewalk. Watching the rain drip off the back of his head and the tail of his trench coat flapping in the breeze, she remembered Greg the person — the paradox. He had been arrogant and cruel, yet handsome, charming and without a hint of a conscience; a deadly combination for a man who preyed on women. He was wealthy, or at least his father was, and he indulged his son's every whim. Greg wore designer suits, drove expensive cars, and had a presence that made him seem bigger than his lean, five-foot-eight-inch frame. The kind of man who could have any woman he wanted, which was the irony of his life.

Walking along in the misty cold, she recalled the horrible things he had done to her and her best friend, Callie. The abduction, the captivity, the physical and sexual abuse, and the humiliation of the trial — it all came rushing back. In the case of North Carolina - v - Gregory Alan Hawkins, Jr., justice had turned a blind eye to the plight of two innocent teenagers, ignoring their rights and proving the system was susceptible to money and power.

The girls had suffered through a trial filled with humiliation only to see their tormentor set free, and their reputations tarnished. The system sold them out.

Unable to live with the humiliation and shame, Callie committed suicide. Devastated, Sarah vowed at her friend's grave she would get even. One day Hawkins would pay. Determined to do so within the boundaries of the law, Sarah spent the next thirteen years attending college and law school, practicing law, learning self defense, and becoming adept with firearms, all within the system.

If you can't beat 'em, join 'em, became her modus operandi. As a trial attorney, she defended the victims. Now, an FBI Agent, she captured and helped prosecute the guilty. Using her experiences and training to learn the rules and regulations of the system: the laws and, most importantly, the loopholes. One day she would use it all to attain personal justice.

When bouts of conscience caused her to question whether using the system to seek retribution against Hawkins would violate her oath to the Bureau or the Bar Association, she put aside those nagging doubts by remembering the torture and abuse she and Callie suffered at his hands. She was merely righting a wrong overlooked by the judicial system.

Sarah used the library, and later the internet, to monitor Greg's life. After graduating from Georgia Tech, he was appointed Vice President of Engineering at the Charlotte office of his father's corporation. Being the chairman's son kept his name in the company's press releases and its annual reports, making it easy for her to follow his career and his relocations. From all indications, Greg Hawkins was on a fast track to the top.

Conversely, local newspapers where he had lived painted a different picture of his personal life. Brief, hidden articles reported accusations of sexual assault or harassment.

But, there were never any follow up articles; no indication of arrests or indictments. She believed this was due to the Hawkins' money and the shenanigans of their high-powered attorneys.

She lost track of Hawkins only once, five years ago. While living in Denver he was arrested for abducting and brutally abusing a young woman. Since this was his first arrest since the incident in Charlotte, Sarah flew to Denver to attend the trial, only to discover the charges were dismissed and the record expunged. The dismissal didn't surprise her, but the press coverage did. For the first time, Greg got front-page exposure. The Hawkins' name, the judge and the district attorney were all attacked by the media. Within weeks, the judge resigned, the district attorney was fired and Hawkins disappeared.

He literally vanished. Sarah, who by then was with the FBI, used its system to try to locate him, but there was no trace of his existence. Greg Hawkins was gone. After months of frustration, it finally dawned on her that she was looking for the wrong person. Like JJ Johnson, Greg Hawkins had ceased to exist. If Janet Sarah Johnson, JJ, could legally change her identity and become Sarah James to escape the past, Hawkins could have done the same.

Guessing he had changed his name shortly after leaving Denver, she began studying printouts of calls to his father's home and the private line at his office, searching for previously nonexistent patterns, series of calls from one area code, one number. She methodically cross-referenced the phone numbers, narrowing the field, until she discovered a Gary B. Allen in Nashville, Tennessee. Perusing microfich back issues of the Nashville Star, she found an announcement with a picture indicating Mr. Allen had been appointed vice president of sales and development for a local computer company. The picture confirmed her suspicions, Allen was Hawkins. The only surprise was that the company had no affiliation with Hawkins Enterprises. Sarah surmised Daddy had finally had enough and Junior was on his own.

Hawkins stopped at a crosswalk. Mentally reliving the past, Sarah had momentarily forgotten her surveillance training and gotten too close to her quarry. Fortunately, she caught herself at the last second and fell back among the knot of people waiting to cross the street. Sarah realized she had made a careless, rookie agent's mistake. Mentally admonishing herself, she vowed to keep her mind on the task at hand.

The light changed and Hawkins stepped off the curb and started across the intersection. Sarah followed at a safe distance, determined to stay focused. But even the most disciplined mind is a willful creature, and with Hawkins in sight, she couldn't keep hers from drifting. Thirteen year-old memories kept forcing their way into her thoughts. After all, he had taken away her innocence, altering the entire course of her life. Changing Sarah from a carefree teenager to a woman driven by one objective — retribution.

CHAPTER 2

SHE WAS CHRISTENED Janet Sarah Johnson at the Concord United Methodist Church, but she had grown up being JJ to her friends and family — fun loving, easy-going JJ. In her final semester of high school she earned scads of honors; class president, co-captain of the basketball team, voted most likely to succeed and vital to every seventeen-year old, she had a really cool date for the prom.

Her dream was to follow in her father's footsteps and become a pediatrician. Study pre-med at the University of North Carolina, attend Duke Medical School, and complete a pediatrics residency, before joining her father's practice in Concord, North Carolina. Father and daughter would care for the children in their little community outside Charlotte.

That was the plan, before Greg Hawkins forced himself into her life.

The icing on her dream was that Callie planned to go to UNC, too. No one was surprised at that. After all the girls had been best friends, forever. Callie Thompson and JJ Johnson, their names, like their faces, were always linked. You rarely saw one without the other. The girls were next-door neighbors, best friends and sisters at heart. They had shared secrets, comforted one another, celebrated and cried together, and as they got into their teens, gossiped about boys. Callie was prettier with long dark hair, big china-blue eyes, a great figure and was pursued by most of the guys in their class. JJ was stronger, more determined, a natural athlete. She was pretty, but not yet beautiful, tall and thin, with a body that hinted at the curves to come.

During basketball season, they ran three miles every morning to give them an edge — the endurance needed for a burst of energy at the end of a game — and it worked. More than once, the girls had led their team to victory in the final minutes. Both had been named to the All Region Team and were front runners for all-state honors.

They ran at six o'clock every morning to avoid traffic, maintain a good pace, and finish in time to cool down and shower before school. That Thursday morning in early February, they were less than a mile from home when they stopped at an intersection. Jogging in place, talking about the boy who called Callie the night before, they barely noticed the Lincoln Town Car pull alongside them, stopping at the light.

"Excuse me, I seem to be lost..." The girls turned to see the driver peering from the open window. "I'm trying to find Getlins' Restaurant."

"Look at those blue eyes," Callie whispered to JJ with a giggle before leaning toward the window to give the man directions.

Suddenly, the car door swung open, bashing her shoulder and knocking her off balance.

"Run JJ, Run!" Callie screamed as she fell backwards.

Instead of running, JJ grabbed Callie to steady her.

"What is it? What's wrong, Callie?"

Before Callie could answer, the man was standing over them with a gun in his right hand.

"Get in!" he ordered, in a gruff, menacing voice.

The Lincoln's trunk popped open.

Callie was frozen in place, rubbing her shoulder, her eyes wide with fear.

"No! No way!" JJ screamed.

The man slapped JJ across the face with his free hand and then grabbed her arm, his fingers biting into her flesh as he dragged her toward the rear of the car. She dug in her heels, resisting. JJ could taste the blood flowing from her busted lip as her head swiveled from side to side, looking for help. Not a car, not a single person was in sight.

"Help!" Callie's blood-curdling scream pierced the morning silence.

The man released JJ long enough to hit Callie with a blow that knocked her to her knees.

"Shut up!"

Crying, Callie called, "Daaaddeeee."

He kicked her in the side. "I said be quiet."

Remembering JJ, his eyes swung in her direction. "Don't move!" He pointed the gun at her.

He grabbed Callie, yanked her up off her hands and knees and then herded the two girls to the back of the car.

He pointed with the gun. "In there!"

JJ looked around, frantic, seeking help — no one. Her eyes misted over and her throat constricted in fear as she realized it was too late to run. They had to do as he said.

Inside the trunk, she looked into the coldest, most terrifying eyes she had ever seen. "Comfy?" he snarled before slamming the lid shut.

The dark was suffocating. Crunched up in the darkness, the girls hugged each other, shivering in fear.

They were tossed to the back of the trunk when the car pulled forward. Every time it turned, they rolled into each other, until, groping around, they found handholds and managed to brace themselves. Even though it was cold outside, the heat in the confined space and their fear soon had their warm-ups damp with sweat.

"What is he going to do to us?" Callie asked in a voice

that sounded like a child's.

JJ didn't respond. She was afraid of the answer.

The terrified girls cried and prayed as the car bumped and swayed along the city streets, and every time it stopped they screamed for help at the top of their lungs. Finally, the darkness and the stifling air inside the trunk got the best of them and panic took over. They began murmuring incoherent baby prayers.

After what seemed like an eternity, the car stopped. JJ recognized the grinding sound of a garage door closing. The engine cut off. A car door slammed. The trunk opened and the sudden light was blinding. Squinting to focus, JJ saw the man standing there, gun in hand, his eyes shifting from her to Callie.

"We're home girls, let's go in the house." He motioned to a door.

Prodded with the barrel of the gun, the girls stumbled up the single step into a dimly lit kitchen. Hesitating, JJ looked around. There were dark cabinets, Formica counters, a white linoleum floor, and floral wallpaper. A refrigerator stood next to a doorway leading into a hall. The only furniture in the room was a round, wooden table with four ladder back chairs.

The man shoved JJ. "Keep moving this isn't a tour."

Their footsteps echoed on hardwood floors as they tentatively moved down a long, narrow hallway painted a pale yellow.

He motioned toward the first door on the right. "In there."

JJ looked through the doorway into a small bedroom. She looked behind her and saw another bedroom directly across the hall. Both were small, stark white with dark, pile carpet. A ceiling fan was centered over a four poster, queen sized bed. A small night table and a straight backed chair sat by the head of the bed. The girls moved slowly into the room. Once inside, the man shut the door and looked from

Callie to JJ. He glanced at JJ. "You seem to be the leader, you'll be first." He nudged Callie. "You, get in the closet."

Callie backed into the small closet, her eyes wide with fear. The closet was bare and didn't even have a rod for hangers. Callie squatted down, wrapping her arms around her knees.

He closed and locked the closet door and turned to JJ. "Take off the shoes and socks," he demanded.

JJ hesitated, slowly shaking her head no. The look in his eyes made JJ kick off her shoes and bend down to take off her socks.

"Take off the warm-ups. Then get on the bed," he growled.

JJ froze. "No!"

His fist moved at lightening speed connecting with the center of her chest. JJ's feet flew out from under her as breath gushed out of her lungs and she fell backwards onto the bed.

"Sooner or later you're going to learn to do what I say. Take them off!"

Tears streaming down her cheeks and struggling to catch her breath, JJ reluctantly obeyed. Her fingers fumbled with the zippers on her jacket and pants. Shaking uncontrollably, she slipped them off. She felt vulnerable and exposed lying on the bed in the North Carolina blue running shorts and white jogging top she had worn under the warm-ups.

"You can leave those on, for now!" He grabbed her right arm and looped a rope over her wrist then tied it to the post at the head of the bed, stretching her arm out straight. Circling to the other side of the bed, he reached for her left arm. JJ tried to resist and was rewarded with a blow to her ribcage. She grunted in pain as he tied that arm to the post.

"Why are you doing this?"

"She was stupid enough to stop, you're just a bonus," he said.

Moving to the end of the bed he repeated the process

with her legs.

He looked down at JJ spread-eagled on the bed and smiled.

"I'll be back sugar. Don't go anywhere," he said with a smirk.

He unlocked the closet door and grabbed Callie. When she saw JJ, Callie screamed, jerked free and lunged for the open door leading into the hall. He grabbed her hair and yanked her to a stop.

"You just earned the right to be first. Come on, now" he demanded.

Twisting his fingers through her hair, he dragged Callie out of the room. Tilting her head up, JJ could see him push her into the other bedroom. He closed the door.

JJ heard muffled thumping and an occasional cry and guessed Callie was being tied to the bed. A few minutes later, she heard him walking down the hallway, whistling. JJ tugged on the ropes, struggling to get free, but they wouldn't give.

"Callie! Are you okay?"

"I...he hasn't hurt me...You okay?"

"Yes...Are you tied down, too?"

"Yes. I'm so scared. What's he going to do to us, JJ?"

"Shut up you two," the man yelled from a distant room.

The girls did what they were told and the silence was deafening. JJ closed her eyes trying to block out what was happening and what she feared was going to happen. She silently prayed that they would be found, before it was too late.

Sometime later, JJ heard footsteps coming down the hallway. They stopped outside her room then she heard him go into the other bedroom.

"Why are you doing this? No, don't cut me. Please, don't hurt me. What are you doing? No, please!" Callie screamed.

Moments later, a loud slap caused JJ to jump. Callie

screamed. The slapping continued until Callie began begging. "Stop! Please stop! Don't hit me again, please."

Then there was silence, again.

"Callie. Are you okay? Answer me Callie, please."

A scream knifed through the stillness. JJ jerked against the ropes, almost pulling her arms out of their sockets. "No...don't...please. Please...please...please...don't!" Callie pleaded.

Then all JJ could hear were the bed squeaking and Callie's muffled whimpers, punctuated by the man's grunts and foul language. JJ knew Callie was being raped, and she was next. JJ jerked on the ropes until her wrists bled. It was no use.

At last the whimpers stopped. The man laughed again, a wild cackling sound, like an evil, diabolical cartoon character. After he stopped laughing, JJ heard the bedroom door slam and the man's footsteps echoing down the hall. She heard a refrigerator door open and close. Next, she heard the sound of a bottle or can being placed on a table and a chair scraping on the floor, then, nothing, no sound at all. The silence that followed was terrifying and JJ's imagination ran wild.

"Callie? Callie, answer me, please. Calleeee..." The silence was deafening.

LYING IN THE QUIET, tied to the bed, JJ tried to think of good things — her mother's hugs, her dad's laugh, the smell of her mom's cooking. She wasn't sure if she dozed off or was simply lost in her thoughts, but it seemed like hours had passed when JJ suddenly realized she wasn't alone. She turned her head and saw him standing in the doorway, leering at her. A shiver ran down her spine. Her body tensed and fear seized her.

His icy blue eyes seemed to be consuming her. His lips were curled up in a sneer, and he held a long, curved knife in his right hand.

"Oh, God, help me," she prayed.

"Please, don't kill me," JJ pleaded, her eyes wide, panic clearly visible in them and tears streaming down her cheeks. "Don't...don't hurt me...please!"

He walked to the bed and touched the inside of her right thigh with the point of the knife. She shuddered uncontrollably as he slowly slipped the blade under her shorts and slid it along her thigh. JJ froze. She was afraid to move. Roughly, he jerked the knife upward, slicing through her shorts, the blue fabric tearing cleanly. He cut the other leg of the shorts and yanked them out from under her. Then he trailed the point of the knife up her stomach, between her breasts and cut the white sports bra open, leaving her body exposed. The faint breeze stirred by the ceiling fan felt cool and chill bumps appeared on her exposed body

"Nice." His barely audible voice rumbled from deep within his chest. His eyes seemed to be dancing as he lifted his right hand and slapped her right thigh hard with an open palm. He methodically slapped her legs, her stomach and her shoulders, punishing her.

She pulled on the ropes, twisting and turning to avoid the blows but there was no escaping the pain. Just as she felt herself slipping into oblivion, he stopped. JJ opened her eyes and saw him standing by the bed unbuttoning his shirt. His teeth were bared in a half smile as he stared down at her naked body. He reached down and cupped one of her small, soft breasts. A few drops of saliva dripped of his lips and fell on her other breast. He bent down and licked it off.

"You'll do," he growled as he undid his pants and began sliding them down.

JJ turned her head away. He grabbed her hair and jerked her head toward him. He backhanded her across the face.

"Open your eyes!! Look at me!"

When he was naked, he climbed on the bed and positioned himself between her legs. She squeezed her eyes tight and shut down her mind, attempting to block out what was happening to her. She bit her lip to keep from crying out from the pain.

When he was done, he rolled off the bed. JJ was no longer a virgin.

THE NEXT FIVE DAYS were a nightmare. He assaulted Callie each morning and JJ every afternoon. The silence between his visits would be broken by the sound of his footsteps echoing in the hallway. Then one of the bedroom doors would swing open and the abuse would commence.

Beginning the second day and each day thereafter, following her "session," as he called his visits, he would dress, pick up the gun and with his free hand, untie her.

"Change the sheets, they're filthy," he'd order.

She would get out of the bed and her legs would be so shaky and unsteady that JJ was afraid she would collapse. But she welcomed the chance to get the circulation moving in her arms and legs, knowing that if she ever got the opportunity to escape, they would be useless unless she kept the blood flowing through them.

When the bed was changed, he'd tell her, "Let's go to the bathroom. You need to clean yourself up. You're nasty."

He followed her, gun in hand, keeping his distance and always staying out of reach. Once she was in the bathroom, he stood in the doorway, blocking any chance of escape. He allowed her to use the toilet and take a shower, always watching her, devouring her with his eyes.

When she was finished showering, he wouldn't give her a towel. "No towel, honey, don't know what you might try to do with it. You'll just have to drip dry. Go to the kitchen." She led the way down the dim hallway to the small kitchen, water dripping off her wet hair, running down her back and her legs, creating small puddles on the wood floor with each step.

A peanut butter and jelly sandwich sat on the table with a bottle of water. JJ always stood while she ate and drank, to keep her legs steady. As soon as she was finished eating, he took her back to the bedroom and tied her to the bed.

I've got to get away, Sarah continually told herself. *Sooner or later he's got to let his guard down. When that happens, I've got to be ready.*

Each time she made the trip to the bathroom and kitchen, she memorized the layout of the house and looked for anything to use as a weapon. There was nothing. But, on one of the trips to the kitchen, JJ spotted the car keys hanging on a hook beside the refrigerator.

Alone, tied to the bed, she would mentally walk from the garage to the kitchen to the hallway and finally to the bedroom, then she'd reverse it and go the other direction. Knowing the details would make the difference between getting caught and escaping.

When JJ wasn't planning, she prayed, and occasionally, the what-ifs tumbled through her mind. *What if we'd skipped our run? What if we'd started ten minutes later, ten minutes earlier? What if Callie hadn't tried to be helpful? What if I'd run when he let go of my arm? What if, What if, What if?*

The what-ifs could go on forever, but JJ knew they changed nothing. She was trapped — a hostage to a crazed stranger, in a bedroom torture chamber.

CHAPTER 3

THE BLARING OF A CAR HORN snapped Sarah's mind back to the business at hand. Now in her element, she could focus on several things at once. They had covered four blocks and her quarry was still in sight.

He crossed Peachtree at the light, turned on Ellis Street and walked past the Ritz Carlton Hotel. At mid-block, he crossed the street and entered a parking lot. Sarah needed transportation if she was going to continue following him. Her training kicked in and she took in the scene, assessing the situation. It was a street-level parking lot with only one exit lane open. Three cars were waiting in line at the pay booth. She had a few minutes to find a ride but she did not have time to get her car.

Watching from the sidewalk she saw Hawkins pull what appeared to be a set of keys out of his pocket and point them towards a silver Mercedes. The car's horn gave a short beep and its lights blinked.

Sarah sprinted to the Ritz Carlton, past an elderly couple headed for a waiting cab. She cut them off and jumped in. The gentleman and his wife gave her disgusted looks and the bell captain started toward her. She gave the couple an apologetic look and held her wallet against the window of the cab, flashing her identification. The bell captain backed away.

"When you pull out of the drive turn back down Ellis, get in the right lane and wait along the curb, just above that parking lot. Be ready to follow the silver Mercedes," she told the driver.

The cabby glanced at the hotel and then looked over his right shoulder at Sarah. "This ain't no TV show lady and I'm not following anybody. If you want to catch him, get another ride."

Sarah gave a knowing smile, flashing her perfect white teeth for an instant. Sarah figured the cabby thought she was a scorned wife tailing an unfaithful husband. Then she switched to her practiced professional gaze, "FBI." She flashed her ID a second time. "This is official business; now get this thing in gear," she directed.

When the Mercedes pulled out of the parking lot the cab eased away from the curb.

"Don't get too close, keep one or two cars between us, but stay close enough to keep him in sight."

"Listen lady, I watch the movies too. I know how it's done," he claimed.

The cabby was right, he was doing just fine. Sarah looked at the information above the meter — Claude Jackson. Definitely not a clean freak. The inside of the cab was filthy. Sarah was glad she had a coat over her suit. She turned up her nose at the odor — sweat, cigarettes and God knows what else. She cracked the window to let in some fresh air.

They went down Ellis to Courtland Avenue — turned left and stayed on Courtland for a block then turned up International. Two blocks later they turned north on Peachtree and were still a couple of cars behind the Mercedes. "When you get an opening, ease up close enough for me to get the tag number, and then drop back."

"Yes, ma'am. What's this guy wanted for? Drugs?

Terrorism? Murder?"

"I could tell you, but then I'd have to kill you," Sarah chuckled, enjoying the look on the cabby's face.

Sarah leaned back and rubbed the three-inch scar below her left breast, another reminder of Hawkins.

THE FIFTH DAY DAWNED with a faint, pink glimmer creeping through the blinds when JJ heard Callie's first scream. A new day was beginning for the rest of the world. The normal world, where people felt safe, laughed, and got ready to go to work and school, having breakfast with their families. With those thoughts running through her mind, hot tears, not of fear but of rage, coursed down her cheeks. Something in JJ snapped. A rising fury overcame her and she vowed she would get even. One day, he would pay.

Her thoughts were interrupted when she realized something was different. Callie was screaming louder, and before each scream there was a whistling noise, a belt. He was using a belt this time rather than his hands. JJ jerked on her bindings, but the ropes still wouldn't give.

Later, when he came into the bedroom, JJ gasped. He was holding a thin leather strap, resembling a rider's crop. He undressed and moved towards her.

The crop whistled through the air before striking her, a prelude to the excruciating pain it inflicted, ravaging her flesh.

Afterward, when she showered, the water felt like fire as it hit the welts caused by the crop. She looked down and watched her blood wash down the drain. Hatred burned in her eyes as she glared at her tormentor through the shower door. He was cockier than usual and JJ suspected he was growing bored with them. It was only a matter of time. He couldn't let them go free. They could identify him — he had to kill them, and today might be their last.

Just maybe, the time had come — her break! He hadn't put his clothes back on after their session. He'd left the gun in the bedroom.

When she got out of the shower, JJ sat on the toilet. "I have to go again."

"Hurry and get it over with."

"Thank you." *He thinks he's broken me.*

He smiled and moved closer. "Take it in your mouth, babe."

"No way!" JJ's fist shot forward, hitting him square in the balls.

He screamed and fell back against the sink. JJ grabbed his penis and jerked hard, then punched again, with all the force she could muster.

"Ahhhhhhh!" Howling, he fell to the floor.

"See ya, babe!" JJ's bloody lips curled up into a smile for the first time in five days as she mocked his sinister laugh.

She leaped over him and her rubbery legs almost collapsed when she landed. Grabbing the door for support she blundered down the hallway, willing her legs to move faster. She turned to go for the gun but changed her mind. She didn't have the time, and besides, she had never even held a gun, much less fired one. JJ knew she was too weak to fight if he caught her. She had to get away before he recovered.

She ran toward the kitchen

"Hang on Callie, I'll bring help." She yelled over her shoulder.

Pure adrenaline fueled her, giving her legs strength. Reaching the kitchen, her bare feet nearly slipped out from under her on the slick linoleum floor. She grabbed the refrigerator to keep from falling, and then took the car keys off the hook.

Keys in her hand, she dashed through the kitchen and into the garage. She leaped in the Lincoln. With her hand shaking, she put the key in the ignition and turned it.

She pressed the door-locks and looked in the rearview

mirror. *The garage door...Screw it.* She put the Lincoln in reverse, floored the gas pedal and blasted through the door.

"That ought to make the place easy to find," she said aloud.

The Lincoln screeched out of the driveway and for the first time in five days, JJ felt safe. The afternoon sun was the most beautiful thing she'd ever seen. The heat coming through the windows felt good. Freedom! She looked down at herself, the bruises and welts, her naked body. Fear and determination replaced modesty. *At least I won't have any trouble convincing someone I need help.*

Honking the horn, she sped towards some tall buildings in the distance. "Where are the cops when you need them? Surely one will stop me for speeding."

She ran two red lights in a row. She began looking for a 7-eleven, a gas station, any place she could find help.

She wheeled around a corner and spotted a black-and-white stopped at a red light.

When she was less than fifty yards away, the light changed and the police cruiser began pulling across the intersection. "Oh no you don't, I need you!" JJ yelled.

She ran the light and slammed into the left rear fender of the cruiser.

"HE'S TURNING LADY. What now?" the cabby asked.

Sarah blinked pulling her mind back to the present. The Mercedes was turning into a parking garage of an office complex on Piedmont Road.

"Don't follow him into the garage. He might spot us. Pull up to the curb in front." The moment the cab stopped, she leaped out and raced to the front door of the building.

"What about my fare?" The cabby called.

"If you want to get paid, wait for me," she shouted over her shoulder, pushing through the door. *How am I going to find him now? I should've followed him into the garage. He could go to any floor.*

Entering the lobby, she quickly sized up the situation and realized fate was still looking out for her. The building had a designated elevator that served all the parking levels. Occupants either got off on another parking level or in the main lobby. A separate bank of elevators served the office complex itself. She reached in her tote and pulled out the Braves cap that she kept with her for rainy days. Cramming her hair under the cap, she pulled the bill low over her face. She took off her coat, reversed it and folded it over her arm. *He shouldn't recognize me from the bank.*

Hawkins got off the parking garage elevator and he walked to the bank of office elevators. By the time one arrived, there were seven people waiting. Sarah led the way and stood in the back against the wall. He got off on the seventh floor and she followed. He crossed the hall and entered the offices of Decker Software.

Sarah walked past the office and waited at the end of the hall for a couple of minutes before taking the elevator back down to the lobby. She withdrew cash from the ATM outside a coffee shop before going in and taking a seat, facing the elevators.

"Hey, lady!"

She looked up to see the cab driver standing in front of her.

"What the hell's going on? Where's my money? Are you trying to stiff me or something?"

"Here's fifty — wait for me. I'll be out in an hour. There's another fifty if you wait."

"I hope he's worth it."

"He is, believe me." The green flecks sparkled in her hazel eyes as Sarah chuckled; thinking the cabby probably still thought she was tailing her cheating husband. She watched him get a Coke and walk out the door.

Forty minutes later she decided Hawkins was in for the

day, and she needed to get to the office.

The cab was waiting out front. She climbed in, crinkled her nose, rolled down the window and leaned over the front seat. "You ever hear of air freshener?"

He shot her a dirty look in the rearview.

"I didn't think so. Take me to the Federal Building, downtown," she said.

She leaned back and closed her eyes, pleased with what she had accomplished. She had identified Hawkins, his car, and his office.

CHAPTER 4

SARAH GOT OFF THE ELEVATOR on the fifteenth floor walked to the agents' entrance to the Federal Bureau of Investigation and entered her access code. Stark white walls, gray desks, and bright fluorescent lights greeted her. Sarah was always amazed the government didn't do something to make their offices a little more inviting, but had decided this was Uncle Sam's way of telling its agents that they were more productive in the field.

Darcy was sitting at her desk in the center of the maze. The dark-haired, middle aged administrative assistant served as a secretary, receptionist and mother-hen to the five senior agents of the Atlanta office. She was four-foot-nine, one hundred and thirty-plus pounds of energy and efficiency. She managed the office with an iron fist, and no one wanted to be on Darcy's bad side.

"Hi Darcy, have I got any messages?"

"Good morning! No calls, but Scott wants to see you. The DA will be here Wednesday at one. She didn't seem to have a problem with rescheduling."

"Thanks. Have I got time to go by my office? Freshen up?"

"Honey, I believe I'd make time, if I were you. Unless that's some sort of a fashion statement." She smiled and wrinkled her nose at Sarah's headgear and wet sneakers. "I'll let him know you'll be there in five, no make that fifteen minutes."

Sarah yanked the cap off her head and shook her hair loose. "What? You never heard of team spirit. Won the Series in 1995, you know?"

Darcy's smile widened. She liked the feisty redhead. "You get by the bank?"

Sarah lowered her head. "No."

"Want me to take care of it?"

"Would you?"

"Leave me your check and a deposit slip. And Monday morning leave a dozen Krispy Kreme glazed and a dozen lemon-filled, right there." She pointed to an empty spot on her desk and winked.

"Will do," Sarah promised with a smile.

She walked through the maze of hallways and cubicles until she reached her office. The nameplate on the right of the door read: Sarah James, Special Agent, Corporate Investigations.

Unlocking her office, she walked in and hung the wet cap and coat on the back of her door and slipped off the wet sneakers, placing them in the corner to dry. Moving behind the desk she booted up her computer, and entered Hawkins' tag number as well as the names Gregory Hawkins, Gary Allen and Decker Software. She selected the searches she wanted conducted on each and hit the enter key.

She pulled the boots out of her tote, slipped them on and left her office. She stopped by the ladies room to brush her hair, touch up her makeup and add a little lipstick before going to see the boss.

Scott Justice was the agent in charge of the Southeast Operations of the Federal Bureau of Investigation. At thirty-three, he was the youngest AIC in the Bureau and many expected him to be moved up in the near future, which meant relocating to Langley, between Washington, D.C., and Richmond.

He was standing beside his desk putting a couple of thick binders on a bookshelf when Sarah reached his office. Scott had on his typical white shirt, striped tie and dark pants. Sarah didn't have to look to know that the matching suit coat hung behind the door.

The shirt was stretched tight across his back and shoulders, emphasizing his narrow waist. The sleeves strained as he put the binders on a shelf. Sarah stared for a moment, subconsciously admiring his physique, before knocking on the door frame.

Scott turned, "Come on in — sit down."

His hair is already mussed. He looks like a little boy who's been out in the yard playing. Wonder what he'd think if I brushed it in place? Yikes, behave yourself, Sarah!

Scott had a habit of running his hand through his brown hair when he was on the phone or concentrating on a report, causing his hair to be perpetually mussed. He ignored her steady gaze and got down to business.

"Your report on the Mason case was very thorough," Scott complimented her. "Anything new since last week?"

"A few things," she said, as she handed him a summary of her latest findings.

Scott scanned it. His left hand raked through his hair as he read the report. "Can we make all this stick?"

"Yes, I've already had preliminary discussions with the Federal Prosecutor and they want to take it to trial soon, starting with Michelle Smith, the financial officer. We think her boyfriend, the ex-cop, will turn on her, if things start getting rough."

"And the CEO? You still think she's not involved?"

"No. She has no reason to steal from her own company. The lady is worth a couple of hundred million — no motive," Sarah surmised.

"Is she as tough as they say?"

"Tougher. If we don't go after these two, she'll cut their balls off," Sarah assured him.

"Ouch! Let's save her the trouble. Set up the appointment with the DA over at Justice."

"Already set for Wednesday." Sarah didn't mention that she had canceled an appointment that morning.

"Let me know how it goes," Scott requested. "Anything I need to do?"

"No. I've got it under control for now. I think this wraps it up from our end. All that's left is testifying."

"Keep me advised and don't let it interfere with your case load."

They sat in silence for a moment. "That all Scott?"

"Yes, I guess so. Good work."

"Thanks." Sarah got up to leave.

Now Scott was staring. His eyes moved from her face, down her body to her legs. Not like he was checking her out. It was more of an appraisal, as if seeing her for the first time.

Sarah hesitated, surprisingly undaunted by his stare. In fact, she gave a slight wiggle of her hips as she turned toward the door, taking a deep breath, straightening her back to give him a better view of her figure.

"You've got on a skirt today."

She looked down turning back to face him. "Yes, I do, is it that unusual?"

She knew it was because she preferred pants. But she might reconsider, if a skirt drew that kind of attention from him.

Scott looked up and smiled, his dark eyes meeting hers. "Let's have dinner tonight to celebrate."

"Closing the case or my wearing a skirt?" she teased.

"The case."

"Okay, where are you taking me, McDonalds?" Scott was known around the office for being tightfisted with his money.

"Mickey D's? Well I admit it crossed my mind, but what the hell? You are dressed up today; skirt, boots, the whole nine yards. You name the restaurant. If it's too pricey, we can always go Dutch."

Sarah broke into one of her wide, eyes sparkling, white teeth flashing, heart-stopping smiles.

DID HE JUST ASK ME OUT? A date with the boss—a major no-no in the Bureau!

Scott Justice was one of the most dedicated FBI Agents she knew and a by-the-book sort of boss. At the office he was all business, friendly to a point, patient and understanding with his subordinates, but he kept his distance and never got involved in the personal lives of fellow agents. He didn't play favorites and expected employees to earn the right to be part of the FBI on a daily basis. The periodic social functions he set up included the entire staff. The only exceptions were one-on-ones to celebrate a promotion, a commendation or a job well done. In those instances, the agent's spouse or significant other attended.

A perfectionist, Scott was intense, quiet and professional. Only his brown eyes gave away his moods. When he was angry or intense, they deepened to a near black, and softened to a light shade of brown when he was laughing or smiling.

Away from work, he was relaxed and carefree. He loved to laugh and tell jokes. The combination of his killer smile and unforgettable eyes grabbed the attention of most women, and his rugged good looks kept their interest.

The females in the office jostled to be the one to take him his first cup of coffee each morning, hoping to solicit one of his rare at-work smiles. The only one that seemed unaffected by his looks and charm was Sarah — the key word being "seemed." She viewed him as a challenge because of his apparent lack of interest in her which she took as an affront to her femininity. Not that she wanted him hitting on her or that she ever intended to pursue him romantically, it was just that she had seen him eyeing other women and questioned why he never looked at her that way. Did he find her so unattractive? Not that she cared, of course.

She couldn't go out with her boss. It would never work and was definitely taboo in the Bureau. Besides, Sarah didn't need this. Hawkins had to take priority. She couldn't allow anything or anyone to divert her attention—that could be fatal.

They had been out twice. The first time had been to celebrate the conclusion of a ten-month long investigation Sarah had directed, resulting in the conviction of a high-flying corporate executive. The second was six months ago when Sarah was promoted to Director of Corporate Criminal Investigations for the region. She had enjoyed his company immensely on both occasions even though both were strictly business and ended before ten.

What am I thinking? This is strictly business, the Mason Case, and I'll be home by ten.

SCOTT HAD STARED at the same paragraph since Sarah left his office. Giving up, he turned in his chair, raked his hand through his hair and looked out the window at downtown Atlanta. In the distance he could see a hazy Stone Mountain.

Did I just ask Sarah James out? An agent, a subordinate! Am I out of my frigging mind? It's her fault. Why did she have to wear a damn skirt today?

He had been attracted to her since the day she arrived at the Atlanta office, two years ago. But internal affairs were prohibited. One or both of the participants were subject to immediate termination if the affair came to light, and that did not fit into his career plans. So, instead of pursuing Sarah, he had occupied himself with a series of short-term relationships, to keep his mind off Ms. James — most of the time.

Her image materialized in his mind...tall, athletic, long legs, strawberry blonde hair, sexy eyes and a pert nose with a small crook in the bridge. Scott wondered how she broke it — did he do it — the kidnapper?

As the agent in charge, Scott had been given access to Sarah's confidential file, making him aware of her abduction at seventeen. The file detailed what she had endured: the trial, the crooked DA and the suicide of her friend — events that would have been devastating to most people, but not to her. Sarah had handled it with strength and purpose — changed her identity, and put the past behind her. She had earned an accounting degree from Virginia and a law degree from Georgetown, finishing at the top of her class at both schools. After finishing Georgetown, Sarah joined Hazelton, Brock and Mobley, one of the top law firms in D.C. One of the senior partners in the firm, a retired U.S. senator, soon became her mentor. When she became disenchanted with the practice of law and decided she wanted to catch the crooks rather than defend them, he made a few calls.

Normally, her academic achievements and employment record would have qualified her for the Bureau, but Sarah's traumatic past kept her from being considered. That is, until the Senator took a personal interest and pushed her cause with the director. Since the senator had been instrumental in his appointment, the director respected his opinion and Sarah was immediately accepted. Sarah had proved herself worthy of the exception and was considered one of their top agents.

Scott had a deep admiration for her as a person and as a fellow agent. He pictured her again, standing in the doorway in that skirt, all legs. He shook his head, clearing it.

"What in blazes am I thinking? It's not a date. It's strictly business — the Mason Case. I'll have her home by nine-thirty," he muttered.

CHAPTER 5

SARAH JERKED AWAKE when something cold touched the back of her neck. *Maybe if I keep my eyes closed he'll go away.* She knew she was wrong when a rough tongue raked across her left cheek. The whining told her it was all over. Peeking between her lids, she saw two large brown eyes staring at her, pleading.

"Okay, Jax, I'm getting up. Is it too much to ask to sleep a little late on Saturday? Come on, get up here." She threw the covers back and the sixty-pound black and white Springer Spaniel jumped on the bed, slithered beside her and rested his head on her right arm. The soulful eyes bored into hers. The wet, cold nose burrowed into her throat. "Yikes!"

Sarah's mouth turned up into a loving smile. She rubbed the big, floppy ears with their curly hair looking freshly permed. "You just couldn't let mommy sleep, huh? I guess I owe ya, don't I pal? You did wait up for me last night."

Sarah didn't get home until after two and was still a little groggy from too much booze. She leaned on one elbow to look across Jax at the bedside clock. "Eight-fifty, no wonder you woke me up. You must be ready to pop!" She looked at his eyes. "Well, at least they're not floating. Let's get moving." Glancing out the window she saw that the weather had changed. The day was clear and sunny, perfect for a run.

Ten minutes later, in running shorts, an old Auburn tee-shirt given to her by a classmate at Georgetown, and her trusty New Balance shoes, Sarah was good to go. Jax was bouncing off the walls. Picking up his leash off the kitchen counter, she headed for the front door. As soon as she opened it, Jax sprang into the yard and hiked on the first bush in sight.

Pulling the door closed, Sarah turned to step off the porch and tripped right over the body reclining across the front step. Scott caught her and she tumbled into his lap.

For the first time since forever, Sarah didn't feel the fleeting tension or tightness in her chest at the sudden touch of a man. His arms tightened, pulling her snugly against his chest. "I thought we were going running but, hey, if you'd rather do this, it's fine with me."

Unexpected warmth rippled through her body, *Wow, there are worst places to land.* She leaned away from him and gave him a playful punch on the shoulder. "In your dreams! What are you doing lounging on my front porch, anyway?"

Jax came bounding over, trying to wedge between the two. Scott scratched the silky head. "Jealous, huh?"

Sarah rolled out of his lap. "He has nothing to be jealous of and what are you doing here?" She tried to look stern, but the green-gold flecks bouncing in her eyes nixed that.

"If you recall, after you cleaned out my savings at Veni-Vidi-Vici and drank the night away at Manuel's Tavern, you asked if I wanted to run with you this morning. At eight, I might add."

Sarah and Jax ran two to three miles every weekday morning and logged in six miles on Saturday, usually before seven. She had a fuzzy recollection of inviting Scott to join them this morning and delaying the start time until eight because of the late hour he brought her home. Her face turned the shade of her hair. "You've been here since eight?"

"Ten till, actually. It's a good thing I had a book in the car." He held up the latest William Bernhardt novel.

"Why didn't you knock, ring the bell, and wake me up?"

"Well. I started to, but I didn't get you home till almost two. I figured you needed your beauty sleep."

An insistent woof interrupted them as Jax raced around the yard stopping every few seconds, front paws splayed out with his rear high in the air.

"Come on, I think he wants to get this show on the road," Sarah laughed.

The trio started out at a slow pace, stretching and warming up, as they moved down the street. "I'm sorry; you should have banged on the door."

"It's okay. I'll forgive you if you take off that shirt."

"Take off my shirt? Have you lost your mind?" Sarah looked shocked.

"Anything would be better than that," he said, looking towards her chest.

"You think?" She responded while glancing down, then at him. She noticed his T-shirt, Alabama — his Alma Mater. Then she got it, Auburn-Alabama, the rivalry, and chuckled. "I didn't think you'd mind, you know, since Alabama doesn't play football anymore."

"Very funny!" His eyes brightened to a lighter shade of brown.

SPRINTING TO FINISH AHEAD OF SCOTT, Sarah was breathing hard as she neared home. Jax was waiting on the porch, having covered at least eight miles to their six, darting ahead, circling back and bounding into the woods bordering the trail. He was panting to cool down until Mom could get him some water. She was sitting beside him trying to get her breathing under control when Scott ambled in. "Glad you could make it. I was about to doze off, waiting for you."

"Sure you were. I wasn't that far behind."

"You weren't? Could have fooled us, huh Jax? I'm disappointed in you. I figured you'd be in better shape." Her eyes danced above a broad grin.

"You've got to be kidding! That run was a piece of cake. I was hanging back enjoying the view," Scott claimed.

"What view? The trail ran through cookie-cutter neighborhoods and a scenic three mile power line in the woods."

It was Scott's turn to smile. "Not that view." His eyes roved admiringly down her body, settling on her legs. A crooked grin appeared and his eyes turned a mischievous light brown. "That view."

"You expect me to buy that, huh?" We kicked his butt, didn't we Jax?" The dog lifted his head and grinned, his long tongue lolling out of his mouth. "Woof."

Scott and Sarah laughed.

"Come on in, I'll get us something to drink."

Sarah's house sat on a three-quarter acre lot just off Johnson Ferry Road. The first thing she did when she bought it two years ago was to put in an invisible fence, knowing she would soon have a dog. After all, in her mind, a dog makes a house a home.

Sarah's mom owned an interior design studio and had helped her daughter select furniture, flooring and colors, and — with her discounts — helped make Sarah's dollars go a little further.

The small entrance foyer had a black marble floor, giving way to hardwood flooring in the kitchen, dining room, breakfast nook and family room. The three bedrooms had off-white carpet. Soft pastels on all the walls, lots of windows and ten-foot ceilings made the house seem bigger than its twenty-one hundred square feet. The furniture was elegantly simple, comfortable and understated.

Sarah's favorite room was the small sun-porch leading

to the back yard. The wicker furniture, stereo and fanlight highlighted the black and white tile floor. She spent most evenings there reading with Jax curled up at her feet.

Scott followed her through to the kitchen. "This is nice. It has a comfortable, inviting feel."

"Thanks. My mom helped me decorate. I'll pass the compliment on to her." She turned her back and opened the refrigerator, not wanting him to see the pride she took in his reaction — surprised that she cared.

"I've got Diet Coke, PowerAde, sweet tea and Dannon water. I'm having water."

"A PowerAde would be great." He moved behind her. "Can I help?"

Turning she stood facing him. "No, thanks." Flustered at his closeness Sarah took a deep breath.

Acting on pure instinct, Scott took her in his arms and kissed her. Their lips met, just a light peck. Sarah dropped the two bottles, leaned into him and responded with a more passionate kiss. No tenseness, no rigid muscles, she relaxed, enjoying the moment. Pulling her head back, she looked him in the eyes. "Is this wise?"

"No. But it feels right."

"What about . . ."

He put his fingers to her lips. "Shhhh." He kissed her again, deeply and both moaned.

"Ruff."

A silky head wedged between them. Sarah stepped back and Jax stood on his hind legs putting his front paws on her stomach. Sarah and Scott laughed.

"Jack you get all her attention, can't you share?"

"Jax, J.A.X." She corrected him.

"Where did you get that name?"

"Remember when you sent me to St. Simons Island to watch over Morgan and Stella from Management Illusions because Michele Smith put a contract out on them?"

"Yes."

"Well Morgan's dad gave both of them Springer puppies while I was there. I saw them and fell in love with the breed. The pups came from a breeder in Jacksonville. I called, there were two left in the litter. I went to see them. As soon as I looked over the fence, this one came waddling up and stole my heart. I wanted an unusual name, something short. Jax is the acronym for the Jacksonville Airport."

"I like it. Sorry, Jax."

The spell was broken. He retrieved the two bottles and they moved out to the sun porch to relax. Half an hour later he got up. "I think I'll go."

She walked him to the door. Opening it, she turned into his embrace and enjoyed another kiss.

Scott pulled away. "If I circle the block and come right back can I get another one of those?"

"I don't think so, buster. We've only had one date."

"Two, if you count the run. What if I wait six hours and come back to take you to dinner?"

"Mexican and you're on."

CHAPTER 6

SARAH GOT OFF WORK at five-thirty Monday and drove her mid-gray government sedan straight to the office complex on Piedmont. Once there, she circled through the parking garage looking for the silver Mercedes with tag number GBA 111. She spotted it on the third floor. The sign on the wall indicated the spot was reserved for G. Allen, Decker Software.

She drove down to the exit level and parked in an open space to wait for him to leave. She had drunk half of her Diet Coke when the Mercedes headed through the exit gate. Fifty-five minutes and eleven miles later, after fighting the remnants of the Atlanta after-work traffic, he pulled into a Dunwoody neighborhood, three miles north of I-285. Sarah followed as they wound through the upscale neighborhood. The streets were lined with Dogwoods whose twiggy branches were heavy with buds that promised a dazzling display of pink and white blooms in a couple of months. Manicured lawns and shapely hedges surrounded the homes they passed. Allen slowed and turned into a drive on Troon Court. The brick, two-story sat on a large lot. Being in Dunwoody, Sarah figured it must be worth at least a small fortune in Atlanta terms.

"That monstrosity must have at least five bedrooms," she thought out loud. "I wonder if he has any guests who wish they were someplace else?"

She cruised past his house and parked at the curb two doors down. Knowing she couldn't stay in one spot for too long without attracting attention, she moved every fifteen to twenty minutes for the next two hours, always positioning herself so she could see the drive. After thirty minutes she checked her messages at home. The only call was from the pet sitter who would walk Jax. Scott hadn't called.

Sarah used the time to scan the preliminary results of the computer search on Allen's personal data. He'd been in Atlanta four months. The car was registered to Gary Bundy Allen. Gary Bundy Allen — talk about balls; picking a middle name for the most notorious serial rapist/murderer of the century. What significance would a profiler attach to that little gem?

IRS records indicated he claimed two hundred thousand in income last year, forty-four years old, single, and paid no child support or alimony. The other searches weren't back yet. One asked whether any females between the ages of sixteen and twenty-two had disappeared or been abducted in the past two years in or around Nashville; ditto from the Atlanta area for the past ten months.

She asked the Bureau system to give her data on any and all cases or incidents involving Gregory Alan Hawkins or Gary Bundy Allen and the court system. To include any and all warrants or arrests, and any pending or settled legal cases involving Hawkins in the cities where he had lived or where Hawkins Enterprises had offices. She wanted to know what he had been up to and to find out if the system had sold out any other women.

Her previous searches had been cursory reviews to determine his whereabouts and any prominent escapades in those locations. Now she wanted every violation — parking tickets, traffic citations, drunk driving — if he so much as jaywalked or spit on the sidewalk, Sarah wanted to know about it. Particularly any offenses involving women.

Once she had the information, Sarah would do an in-depth analysis of each crime and all victims to assimilate any similarities cross referencing the crimes and victims. She wanted a profile of Hawkins that would show his patterns of behavior and how or why he chose his victims — his likes and dislikes. It was time she used her training to achieve her ultimate objective — to take care of a bad guy — the bad guy. She had no compulsion about using the Bureau resources, after all that's what they were for, weren't they? When she had collected all the data and done her homework, she would make adjustments to her plan. Then it would be Greg Hawkins' time in the box. Her plan was for that box to be his final resting place, six feet under.

Sarah was well versed in the law, understood all the loopholes and would use it to her benefit. Her actions would be within the confines of the system. If all went according to plan, when this was over, there would be no suspicions and no charges. Her career with the FBI — her life — would continue without a ripple.

But then, there was the matter of Scott. Sarah's stomach did a few flip-flops as she remembered falling into his lap, the strength of his arms when he pulled her to his chest, the touch of his lips. Warm goose bumps tingled across her skin and she smiled, just thinking of him. This was the first time she had felt anything for a man since Hawkins entered her life. She wanted Scott Justice, to hold her, to make love to her. But, could she follow through on her desires? Would the past raise its ugly head and prevent her from being able to experience a satisfying sexual relationship?

Since Hawkins, she had tensed at the mere touch of a man and was repulsed when she allowed herself to be kissed, which didn't happen until her third year at the University of Virginia. Her classmates referred to her as the Ice Queen behind her back. Little did they realize just how accurate the nickname was, or the cause of her attitude toward men. The comments hurt when she overheard them, and Sarah eventually realized that if she was going to fit in, that she had to act more normal around the opposite sex. That meant dating, making out, or even...

It wasn't until her second year of law school that she forced herself to go all the way. A nice guy named Phil. He was one of the few that didn't give her the shivers when he touched her, held her hand or brushed up against her. She drank a couple of Margaritas to give her courage and loosen her up. Then she suggested they go to his place. It surprised the hell out of the guy when she launched herself at him. She felt nothing, and rushed home as soon as the act was completed. Alternating between retching, sobbing and cursing, she threw her clothes in the trash and submerged herself in a scalding shower, scrubbing her body raw to cleanse it. But she never felt clean. Soap and water could never wash away what Hawkins had done to her, the internal scars he had left. She would never feel comfortable with a man. Or so she thought, until Scott, this weekend. Falling in love didn't fit into her plan. No, she didn't have time to deal with it; she had to stay focused on Hawkins.

Sarah questioned the timing. Why now? Hawkins walks onto the scene and Scott strolls into her personal life, on the same day. Was it coincidence, fate, divine intervention? Sarah's mind reeled with a variety of possibilities as she sat in her car studying Hawkins' oh-so-proper neighborhood.

She couldn't get Scott out of her mind. Sarah missed him — his laughter, his touch, his scent. She had the feeling that he was more than a little interested. Now that they had both given into their mutual attraction, they would not be able to resist moving forward; even if the Bureau forbids such a relationship. Sarah had to stop it. She had to resist — at least until she'd dealt with Hawkins. She shook her head and groaned.

She had to put their relationship, or lack thereof, into perspective. Scott Justice was nothing more than an unforeseen complication. She had to end it.

She closed her eyes, remembering their kiss. The mere thought made her want more. Her mind jumped ahead, ignoring her will. Sarah Justice, the name ran through her mind, impinging her wavering resolve.

"Sarah Justice? You idiot! Get real, he hasn't even called. The jerk!" She screamed at herself in the rearview mirror of the car.

ON WEDNESDAY NIGHT, Sarah followed Hawkins to The Watering Hole in Midtown. They arrived during happy hour and the bar was packed. After blending in with the other females circulating through the room, Sarah surveyed her surroundings. She liked the atmosphere. The rooms were open and airy with high, beamed ceilings and skylights. Plants hung from thick rafters overhead, giving the place a modern, garden feel. Small tables were scattered around, but few people were sitting. Everyone seemed intent on circulating, accomplishing the mating ritual of one-night stands.

Men and women were intently assessing the opposite sex, in an effort to determine his or her chances of scoring. The male-female ratio was about equal, with ages ranging up to fifty or so.

The bar area was elevated three or four feet above the main floor and surrounded by a decorative railing. Four small tables nestled inside the railing gave their occupants a good view of the crowd.

Hawkins went directly to one of those tables and pulled out a chair. A waitress brought him a drink as soon as he sat down.

"Black Jack and water! Just what the doctor ordered. Thanks Janie." He sipped the amber liquid as he surveyed the crowd.

Hawkins is a regular, the waitress knows his poison, Sarah deducted.

Sarah ordered a Michelob Light and mingled, keeping her eyes on Hawkins. Three guys hit on her as she watched Hawkins. Sarah was polite but firm, no put downs, but she made it clear she was not interested, remembering why she avoided these type of bars. The pick-up lines, the swaggers boosted by alcohol, were all a turn off.

Hawkins sat at his table and assessed the women in the room like a connoisseur eyeing the wine selection at an expensive restaurant. His cold blue eyes scanned every woman within thirty yards. He seemed to take in every detail of a woman's appearance. Sarah tried to follow his eyes, looking for anything to indicate his preferences but to no avail. She would have to wait until he made his selection.

After finishing his drink, he stood and began circulating. He approached three women in twenty minutes, moving from one to the other, initiating conversations. The first one he approached rejected him with cool, polite disinterest. The other two welcomed his attention and accepted his offer of drinks. Sarah watched with repulsion as the second and third gave him their names and phone numbers. From their stares as he walked away, it was obvious to Sarah that the girls were not only interested but disappointed that he hadn't taken things further.

Sarah felt a knot form in her stomach, bile rising in her throat, thinking. Can't they see through the charm and good looks? Look deep girls, he's evil.

Sarah wanted to scream, to warn them, but she knew that wouldn't accomplish anything other than give herself away. If she spoke up he'd recognize her. Besides, she knew he would just find new prey. Sarah had to let nature take its course and stick with her plan.

Instead, she eyed each one carefully, looking for similarities, which were obvious; all three were medium height, had dark hair, good figures and full breasts. She wasn't close enough to get eye colors, but she'd do so before she left.

Hawkins returned to his table and stared at the one who had shot him down. Anger and rage dominated his expression. After a moment, he smiled and seemed to be stripping her with his eyes. The anger was replaced with lust. Then his expression changed again. Sarah was certain the intensity of his scrutiny would have upset the girl if she had noticed, but she didn't, apparently having written him off. Hawkins wasn't even on her radar screen. Sarah was sure that Hawkins realized the same thing and that was what brought on his rage. As he stared at the woman, his lips curled into the sneer that Sarah remembered so vividly. His eyes flashed and he jerked out of his chair when a man joined the girl and kissed her warmly. Instantaneously, he regained his composure and signaled for the waitress.

Sarah sidled close enough to overhear their conversation without being conspicuous.

"Hey Janie, see that dark-haired girl over by the window, the one in blue, with the bald guy. Do you know her?"

"Don't really know her, but her name is Theresa Paul," Janie said while smacking her gum. "She works for the big insurance company. You know the one down the street? She comes in almost every Wednesday for happy hour."

"That her husband?"

"Don't think she's married. She hung with another guy until a couple of weeks ago. You interested?" Smack, smack went the gum.

"Was, but not if she's taken. Don't want the hassle, too many fish in the sea" he said with a raise of his empty glass. "Bring me another one and a screwdriver for the lady I'm about to make queen for a night." He slipped Janie a twenty and moved back to the second candidate.

Unnoticed, Sarah moved to the table he had just vacated. Setting her tote on it, Sarah glanced around before draping a napkin over his empty glass. Careful not to smudge any prints, she slipped it into a plastic bag inside her tote.

Thirty minutes later, they left. She got in a Honda Civic and followed Hawkins home. Sarah followed her. At midnight it appeared she was staying the night so Sarah left. *This one's safe, her car's in the drive. He's too smart to use his house again. I hope — for her sake.*

SARAH DIDN'T FOLLOW Hawkins on Thursday, for fear of being spotted if she tailed him a fourth consecutive night.

On her way home from work Sarah picked up two rib-eye steaks and a six-pack of Michelob Light. When she got home, she put on a pair of old, soft jeans and a light sweater and took Jax for a walk. Striding down the street, she looked down at the dog.

"Sorry I haven't been around for the last few nights, but Mom's been busy. Besides, Lisa took good care of you, didn't she boy? You know what? I've got a treat for you when we get home."

Jax inhaled his rib eye when Sarah gave it to him. She took the other one and sat in front of the TV to watch The American President, her favorite movie. She was savoring the first bite of her steak when the phone rang.

"Whatcha doing?"

"Just pulled a couple of steaks off the grill, and I was sitting down to eat."

"Two? Do you need to go?" Scott sounded hurt.

"No, I can talk. Jax has already devoured his."

"You gave him a steak?"

"Sure, a rib-eye even. That's how I treat the men in my life. By the way who is this?" She smiled, picturing his expression — his fingers working overtime, raking through his hair.

"A hungry FBI agent wondering whether Jax left any scraps."

"You've got to be kidding. Are you back? Pick up a steak and come on over. We'll pop it on the grill. I've got cold beer."

"I'm around the corner. I'll be there in ten minutes."

"A little sure of yourself, huh?"

"No, hopeful. I've been thinking about you all week."

"Couldn't prove it by me; a phone call wouldn't have hurt," Sarah mumbled as she placed the phone in its cradle.

Five minutes later the doorbell rang. Sarah opened the door.

Scott stepped in and took Sarah in his arms and kissed her. In spite of the suddenness and intensity of his actions, Sarah's usual defense mechanisms didn't kick in. In fact, she returned his kiss with a passion she had never felt before.

She took half a step back. Their eyes locked.

"To hell with the Bureau, I can't stay away." Scott declared. He took Sarah in his arms, reclaiming the passion, kindling the flame of desire they both felt. Sarah didn't resist.

FOR FIVE WEEKS Sarah continued her surveillance of Hawkins. She learned the patterns of his life as Allen — his preferences in food, restaurants, bars, and women; the latter proving to be the most interesting and useful. As she watched him, she realized that she had trouble referring to him as Gary Allen. To her he would always be Greg Hawkins. So to keep her own mind straight, she stayed with Hawkins.

He left for work every morning between 6:15 and 6:30, arrived at his office by 8:00 and didn't leave the building during the day, except Tuesdays.

Every Tuesday during lunch, he went to the downtown branch office of the Bank of America, where Sarah had first bumped into him. On Friday's he stopped by the same bank before work. He always talked to the same teller, Lori, who looked to be in her early thirties. She had long, dark-brown hair, an hourglass figure and a sweet smile. Twice she accompanied him to lunch. He took her to dinner on three occasions. Sarah wondered if this was the love of his life. As a precaution, Sarah ran a trace on her. If the girl turned up missing, Sarah would know where to look.

Every Wednesday night Hawkins arrived at The Watering Hole by seven and his routine was always the same. Scope out the women, hit on two or three, zero in on one, pick her up and take her home. His charm, it seemed, never failed him. An attractive female, never the same one twice, spent Wednesday night at Hawkins' house. On Fridays he went to a different bar, more upscale, where the more affluent, sexually-active females congregated. His tastes never varied: good-looking, with dark hair and full breasts. Saturday nights appeared to be reserved for Lori.

By the end of the fifth week, Sarah began to wonder if Hawkins had changed. Had he put the aggressive behavior behind him? After all, he seemed to get all the action he wanted without it. Maybe he doesn't need to get his kicks that way anymore.

Then she remembered the Bureau courses on serial killers and rapists. They cool down, but never stop. They are intelligent, plotting and cautious. The rage burns internally, and periodically erupts like a volcano. For them, rape and murder are the release valve. And as time goes by, the time between episodes grows shorter. The information confirmed what Sarah already knew, Hawkins hadn't changed. He was in temporary remission.

In order to prevent the next episode and save some innocent woman's life, Sarah knew she had to identify what triggered his episodes. What event or circumstance caused Hawkins to lose control? The Bureau literature she had read on the topic led her to believe that it had to be related to something his victims did or didn't do.

Her money was on rejection. She believed Hawkins could not accept rejection. She recalled seeing his smooth façade slip away and become replaced by anger after a woman said "no" in a harsh manner. Observing him on the rare occasions this had happened recently, Sarah could tell that rage and violence was seething within him.

She knew a psychiatrist who might just help her understand Mr. Hawkins better. The more she understood, the better she could control him when the time came for their confrontation. Perhaps she could prevent a murder.

CHAPTER 7

SARAH'S PARENTS STILL LIVED in Concord. She talked to them several times a week, if not daily, but rarely visited. She would never feel comfortable in that community again. Instead, her parents drove to Atlanta about once a month to see their only child. Dr. Johnson was still protective of his little girl even though she was grown and an FBI agent. To him, she would always be his baby.

They had accepted her decision to change her name and to seek a different career path, without a word. They understood. Dr. Johnson encouraged her along the way, periodically telling her, "I just want you to be happy darling. My only advice is to always be proud of what you do and never compromise your morals or ethics. If you ever look in the mirror without feeling pride in the person looking back at you, revaluate. It may be time for a change."

That was her dad. He would always be there for her. He was her foundation and support. However, she was still surprised — shocked — when on her twenty-ninth birthday she learned he had set up a trust fund for her that had matured. It provided her with a sizable lump sum and an annual stipend, allowing her to make a down payment on a house and a new 350 Z. Her salary would never have allowed her to do either.

Her mom was just as important in her life. Anne Johnson was Sarah's confidant, spiritual advisor, and best friend. She was there, to help Sarah deal with the trauma and aftermath of the kidnapping. Her mom listened and quietly offered love, understanding, and advice. She was better than any therapist could have been.

During Sarah's college years, Anne had been there to help her daughter deal with her feelings towards men; the fears of a relationship, of rejection, the repulsion, and the nicknames. Mother knew all, and her love never wavered. She didn't have all the answers, but she listened and helped Sarah gain the insight she needed to grow, and to slowly put the past behind her. Sarah could discuss anything with her mother. Everything, that is, but her plans for Greg Hawkins. That, Sarah could share with no one.

Her folks had visited her last weekend and had met Scott at Sarah's favorite Mexican restaurant. Sarah's mom fell in love with him right away. Her dad conceded Scott was all right, telling her in private, "If you like him, it's fine with me, sweetheart."

Sarah and Scott had been seeing each other for more than six weeks. Whatever they did — dinners, movies, watching relevision at home — they always had a good time. And the dates always ended with a lot of passionate kissing, but no more.

At first Sarah feared he would try to take her to bed and wasn't sure how she would react. Now, she found herself wondering why the hell he hadn't. Did he think she was damaged goods?

She had talked to her mom about it, the night before her parents left to go home. Anne listened patiently, smiling occasionally, and silently thanking God for sending someone to bring her daughter out of her shell.

She was sympathetic, but firm, telling Sarah that maybe

it was time for her to take charge. "We often have to go after what we want. You've done it all your life, why stop now? Sarah James, you've never been afraid to take a risk. You changed your name, succeeded as a trial attorney and joined the FBI. If you want him, darling, go after him."

"You've got to be kidding? Go after him! Mother, that is just not me," Sarah claimed.

"Sarah, as you are so fond of saying, bullshit!" She smiled. "You're a woman. You've got all the equipment. Believe me, it will come natural. Women have been seducing men since the beginning of time. If you want Scott Justice, go get him!"

SARAH WAS AT HER DESK reviewing the responses she received from her inquiries into the Bureau system, including a chronological list of his offenses. Hawkins' past was right there in front of her, and she could not believe he was still walking the streets.

The reports confirmed Hawkins was evil. Any woman who came in contact with him was a candidate for the pain and suffering he enjoyed inflicting.

According to his records, Hawkins' first skirmish with the law occurred when he was in high school. He attacked a fellow student for talking to his girlfriend. The other boy had to be admitted to the hospital, Hawkins was suspended from school for a week and the juvenile authorities were contacted. It was the beginning of a criminal record that grew over the next few years. His vicious temper surfaced again and again, as he inflicted brutal beatings upon class-mates for minor transgressions. The attacks continued until his final year at Georgia Tech. One afternoon after class, he got angry over a foul during a pick-up basketball game. A fight ensued, and Hawkins beat the offender unmercifully. He then spent ten days in jail and narrowly escaped being kicked out of graduate school.

The next incident, and the first recorded one involving a female, occurred in Atlanta in 1969, not long after Hawkins received his graduate degree. He was working at the Hawkins Enterprises corporate headquarters. A fact that initially puzzled Sarah because the employment records presented at the trial in Concord, involving her and Callie, did not mention Atlanta or this incident. Those records stated that he began his career at Hawkins Enterprises office in Charlotte. After giving it some thought, Sarah felt she knew the answer. Hawkins Sr., had his son's employment record altered to prevent the incident from becoming an issue at trial.

The Bureau file included an affidavit from the woman, a twenty-nine-year-old administrative assistant in his department, that stated:

Within weeks of starting work at Hawkins Enterprises in Atlanta, Hawkins began making subtle passes at me. I initially ignored his sexual innuendos believing he would stop if I didn't encourage him. After all, I'm at least five years older than him and married. Surely, he should realize I wasn't interested and out of his reach. Besides, I was afraid to complain, who would believe me? He's the CEO's son.

After six weeks of rejection, he must have become frustrated and decided to take what he wanted. One evening while I was working overtime, I was returning to the deserted executive area from the copy room with an armload of papers, when Hawkins stepped out of the shadows and grabbed me. All my copies fell to the floor because he spun me around and forcibly kissed me.

He told me, 'Babe, you don't have to keep playing hard to get, I know you want me.'

I pulled away, slapped him and screamed. He reacted by backhanding me across the face and began tearing at my clothes. He was infuriated. I was stunned and stumbled back fighting, trying to protect myself. He hit me again. I fell against a desk and saw stars, and blood trickled out of the corner of my mouth. The jerk just smiled and began describing what he was about to do to me.

I continued to resist but I was fighting a losing battle; he was too strong, and crazy. He hit me again, and then he ripped my blouse open and shoved my bra up. Then he pushed me up on the desktop, and slid my skirt up. I was struggling to keep him from pulling my panties down when, thank the good lord, the cleaning crew arrived. Once he saw them, he stepped away and started cursing at them and ordering them to leave.

Since they diverted his attention, I rolled off the other side of the desk and fled. I held together my skirt and blouse and ran to the nearest office and locked myself in. I didn't know what else to do, so I called my husband. He works on another floor in the building. When he arrived, Hawkins attacked him. Hawkins broke his nose and fractured his jaw.

Then, this was really strange, Hawkins just calmed down and looked around at everything.

I tried to stop the blood gushing from my husband's nose, and Hawkins just stared at me.

I remember he said, 'If you know what's good for you, you'll pick up this prick, go home and keep your mouth shut. You make a stink and see what it gets you,' he chuckled. 'How long do you think you'll keep your job? I am Gregory Alan Hawkins, Jr., as in the CEO's son, bitch, and that carries a lot of weight around here. Who would believe you, anyway? For your information, buddy, this little bitch came on to me.'

Then he walked out the door.

Sarah continued skimming the case file.

In spite of Hawkins' threats, the couple reported the incident to the vice president of human resources and filed criminal charges. Hawkins was arrested. Daddy came to the rescue. All medical bills were paid. The woman received forty thousand dollars, resigned her job and was given exemplary references. In addition, she was kept on payroll at double salary for three years. The matter was dismissed. Greg was transferred to Charlotte.

Sarah gasped when she saw a photo of the young woman. *Oh my God, Callie. She could have been your sister.*

Six months later he abducted Sarah and Callie. After his father resolved that problem, Junior was transferred again. A pattern began to take shape. Hawkins got in trouble, Dad bought him out of the scrape, and Hawkins was transferred to another Hawkins location. Personnel files included reports of interoffice affairs, sexual harassment charges and charges of sexual abuse. It seemed that any woman who rejected his advances paid a price, and then Daddy paid her. In every instance, payoffs of irresistible dimensions persuaded the complainant to forget their accusations and walk away.

Hawkins' criminal records were worse. He got into trouble wherever he lived; in Tampa, there were two underage girls; in Boston, an attempted rape of a female who rejected him at a bar; Seattle, an abduction and rape. It went on and on — Dallas, Denver and Nashville— it was always the same, attraction, rejection, attack, arrest. It was always followed by bribes, job offers and powerful attorneys who got the charges dropped or dismissed.

CHAPTER 8

THE IMPLEMENTATION OF SARAH'S PLAN was in its early stages, so she still had time to forget or forgive what Hawkins had done to her and get on with her life. After all, she reasoned, eventually he'll meet his end with or without her involvement. A husband, boyfriend or a father will take the law into his own hands, or the judicial system will ignore Hawkins' father and punish him. But the question that hounded Sarah night and day was how long is eventually, and how many women will Hawkins destroy before he's stopped? No, she decided, waiting is not an option and forgiveness is impossible. Sarah would never forgive the bastard. She swore on Callie's grave she would stop him and Sarah was determined to follow through on her vow. Sarah made another promise, to herself. "He won't hurt another woman. Not on my shift."

Sarah was ready to put her plan in motion. She purchased the electronics equipment. The devices she'd acquired would allow her to place calls from any telephone number, to her home phone, and make it appear the call originated from a third location or number. Using the equipment, she could call her home and make it appear the calls were placed from

Hawkins' house. She could have requisitioned what was needed from the Bureau surveillance locker but decided that would be a mistake. If she had, and the devices were discovered, they could be traced back to her.

She initiated the first call to her house on Tuesday night, leaving a message, recorded in Hawkins voice, on her answering machine. The message was simple: consisting of silence, two words, more silence, then five words and then the call was disconnected. She'd add the last part of the message later. Another call was placed at two-thirty in the morning, same script, his voice. She'd place similar calls at odd hours over the next few weeks, randomly selected to coincide with times when she knew Hawkins would be home. The message was simple, harassing and threatening.

It had been easier for her to get the message she wanted, than she had anticipated. Once she understood what made Hawkins tick, it was simply a matter of pushing the right button. She went to The Watering Hole on a Wednesday night wearing a brunette wig, blue contact lenses, a short skirt, and an overflowing Wonder bra. Soon after he arrived, Sarah sent Hawkins a Jack Black and Water to get his attention. He graciously accepted the drink from the waitress, held it up in a mock salute and smiled at Sarah from across the room. She returned the smile and winked, gesturing for him to come over. He checked her out, decided he liked what he saw, and sauntered over. Reaching inside her tote, Sarah pushed the record button on the mini-recorder, when he was a few feet away.

Confident, he didn't waste any time, "Hi Babe, thanks for the drink. I'll buy the next round at my place." He reached out possessively, to take her arm. Sarah threw her drink in his face, and snarled, "I'm not one of your babes, asshole. Get out of my face."

Stunned he stared for a moment then yelled, "You bitch! I'll get you one day. Believe me, your ass is mine."

Satisfied, Sarah turned and stormed out of the bar.

Hawkins was standing at the front door of The Watering Hole staring, when Sarah's car roared out of the parking lot.

A couple of miles down the road she pulled into a strip mall and parked. She pulled off the wig, eased out of the wonder bra and removed the contacts. After brushing her hair and applying some lipstick, she freshened up her makeup. She took the recorder out of her tote, rewound the tape and then pushed the play button. Hawkins' voice resonated through the car.

SARAH WAS TAKING her mother's advice. Scott was picking her up in an hour and thought they were having an early dinner and then going to a movie. Sarah had other plans.

"If everything goes my way Mom, we'll never leave the house," she told her mom earlier in the day. After changing outfits three times, Sarah was satisfied. Smiling at her reflection in the mirror, she decided it was just right, sexy but not sleazy, comfortable without being too casual, and a little bit dressy.

She had settled on a knee-length white skirt with a side slit, no hose, a pale green, long-sleeve silk blouse that was almost transparent in the right light, and a silver choker and bracelet.

Pulling her hair back into a ponytail, she turned sideways to check out her profile. The blouse suggested more than it revealed. Her breasts were faintly outlined through the thin fabric.

The stage was set, soft music, dinner, candlelight and the "right look." Sarah had never dreamed she would deliberately set out to seduce a man. But she decided her mother was right. If anything was ever going to happen between her and Scott, she would have to take charge. Their kissing and fondling sessions had left her hungry, wanting, a feeling she had never experienced. Lying in bed after he left, she could think of nothing else. And the fact that Scott was the one who stopped before things got out of hand only heightened her desire. She checked the bedroom one final time, candles, covers turned down, ceiling fan humming on low, just the right ambiance. Sarah discovered she liked being the aggressor. The doorbell chimed.

When she opened the door, butterflies surged in her stomach. Sarah was anxious because something might not happen, rather than because it might. This was a new feeling. One she liked.

"Dinner was great! I loved the pasta. I'll help with the dishes. If we hurry, we can make the seven-twenty movie." Scott pushed back his chair and began gathering dishes.

Sarah stood. "Thanks but they can wait," she said, standing.

"I don't mind."

"I do," she said, while taking his hand and leading him into the den. "Dance with me, instead?" She walked over to the bookcase to turn on the CD player. As she moved, she made a point of stretching to give him a full view of her legs and kept the light behind her so he could see the outline of her breasts. The song was slow. All the songs were slow and romantic.

Evidently he liked the bait. Scott didn't hesitate taking her into his arms and pulled her in close. Sarah snuggled in his embrace, lightly grinding her body into his. Scott nuzzled her neck and nibbled on her ear. Feeling his warm breath on her neck, her own breathing quickened.

"What about the movie?" He whispered in her ear.

"Maybe the nine-thirty."

"Why do I get the feeling you're not interested in the movie?"

"I wouldn't know."

"What have you got on your mind? Are you seducing me?"

"What makes you think that?"

"I am a trained investigator you know, FBI."

"Uh huh." She blew in his ear before kissing it.

He tilted his head back, and his lips met hers. He kissed her hard at first, then gentler. His tongue danced around hers. Sarah melted into him, content to let him take charge.

"It seems you've forgotten the movie, Mr. Agent man."

"What makes you think that?"

"Oh, call it female intuition. After all, I'm a trained investigator, too."

Scott pulled back, afraid of scaring her off. He didn't want to rush things. "Are you sure Sarah? I can wait."

"Shut up, I can't."

She took his hand and led him to the bedroom.

They undressed each other and she slid onto the bed. When she saw him naked, standing over her, Sarah felt a sense of panic. A fine sheen of sweat broke out over her body as she tensed and grew rigid.

For the first time ever, Sarah was aggressive, wanting, needing. They didn't stop until they were both sated. At midnight, they fell asleep in each other's arms, totally spent.

THE BED ROCKED when Jax sprang on top of Sarah and Scott. Arms entwined, they didn't have time to react before sixty-five pounds of happy, eager dog landed on them, jarring them into wakefulness. Jax wedged between them, licking Sarah's face and whining.

"Is this how you wake up every morning?" Scott asked.

"Yes. Well, minus the man in my bed."

"I would hope so. I'd like to think I've broken new ground here. We missed the movie, you know?" Scott chuckled.

"You are a trained investigator aren't you — FBI even." She mumbled. "Take your dog out and wake me up in an hour." Sarah pulled a pillow over her head.

Jax wedged his head under the pillow until his cold nose pressed her cheek.

"Okay, come on." She rolled out of the bed and pulled a long T-shirt over her head. "I'll take him out, you wait here. I'll be back in a jiffy and we'll see if all that FBI training has given you endurance when it counts."

She grinned, leaned over and kissed him on the cheek. Fifteen minutes later she nuzzled against Scott.

"Lucy, is that you?"

"Lucy? Who the hell is Lucy?" Sarah punched him.

"I just wanted to be sure you're paying attention. My lovemaking skills tend to put the average woman into a daze." He laughed. "But there's nothing about you that is average, lady."

He turned towards her and lightly kissed her forehead, brushed his lips across her eyelids and then her mouth. "Where is that lovely T-shirt you had on a few minutes ago?" His lips moved from her mouth to her chin, and down her stomach.

"I CAN'T BELIEVE you kept me in bed all morning. It's after ten," Sarah said in a low throaty voice when she turned over and saw Scott standing in the doorway. If Sarah didn't know herself better she would swear she was purring like a contented cat as she stretched.

Scott had gotten up first and let the dog out again. After letting him back in, Scott poured juice and made toast before waking Sarah. She pulled on her T-shirt, followed him into the kitchen and sat across from him at the table in the breakfast nook. Jax curled up at her feet and began snoring lightly.

Later, freshly showered and bright-eyed, Sarah and Scott talked like children who had discovered the secret of life.

She had on jeans, an oversized Georgetown sweatshirt and sneakers. Scott wore the same slacks and flannel shirt from the night before and was shoeless.

"I can't believe we missed the movie and our morning run. It's your fault." She smiled seductively, her eyes twinkling with mischief.

"Me? I never stood a chance last night. Not from the second you opened the door.

Sarah smiled. "The day's still young, we could..." She jumped when the phone rang, fear flashing in her eyes as she answered. "Hello." She relaxed. "Oh. Hi, Mom, everything is great here. Scott stopped by to exercise with me and we're having toast and juice." Her eyes twinkled, a smile lighting up her face as she thought of the play on words. She looked at Scott. "No, we won't overdo it. Uh huh, I'll tell him."

"Mom says hi."

"Tell her hi for me."

"Mom, let me call you later."

"Stopped by? Why didn't you mention it was last night? And what kind of exercise routine her daughter has put me through," Scott said grinning like the famous cat.

"Sure." Her face turned a pretty shade of pink. "I'm going to tell my mom that we spent the last twenty hours in bed screwing?"

"I hope not." He chuckled. "Dr. Johnson would be down here with a shotgun if you did."

After a few moments, Scott's smile faded. "Why did you jump when the phone rang? You looked frightened."

"No, I didn't."

"Yes, you did. Sarah you were scared. Why?"

She sat in silence trying to decide if she should tell him. He waited. The ticking of the clock became audible and Jax's snoring suddenly seemed louder. Finally, she looked up, her gaze meeting his. Looking, she saw the tenderness and concern in his. Still she hesitated.

He blinked, cleared his throat.

"Sarah, I'm falling in love with you. Whatever it is, you can tell me."

Sarah's face brightened. "What did you say?"

"I said, whatever it is, you can tell me."

"Before that."

"I said I love you. I can't believe I blurted it out like that, not very romantic, huh?" He got up and walked around the table and stood behind her chair. Wrapping his arms around her, he kissed the top of her head. "Now, tell me, what's bothering you."

With her face down she spoke so softly he could barely understand the words.

"I've been getting some harassing phone calls. At first I ignored them, now they're scaring me."

"Been getting? Why haven't you reported them? The Bureau requires all agents to report any type of harassment."

"I didn't think they're related to the Bureau. At first they were just hang ups. Now he's leaving messages." She pushed her chair back and walked over to the phone mounted above the kitchen counter. Pushing the play button she stepped back.

Silence, then "Hi Babe…more silence…I'll get you." Then the mechanical voice of the recorder noted. "Friday, three p.m."

The muscles across Scott's back and in his arms and neck stretched taut. "How long have you been getting them?"

"A couple of weeks."

"And you haven't reported them? Why not?"

"Like I said, I didn't think they were related to the Bureau. I think it's just some pervert."

"The Bureau needs to be the judge of that."

He walked over to the phone and pressed the play button, and listened. "I'll get you, sounds like some angry perp carrying a grudge, not a pervert."

"I was afraid."

"Afraid. All the more reason to report it."

"No, not that kind of afraid. I was afraid I would stir up my past for nothing. If it's some pervert and I ignore him, he'll just get bored and stop calling."

"Your past?"

"You know what happened to me when I was seventeen, up in North Carolina. You must. As my AIC, I'm sure you have access to my file, and most of the details are in it, I'm sure."

"Yes, I did. No one else in the office knows, though," he quickly added.

"I thought you knew about it. Last night proved it to me. You were so gentle, so kind, concerned about my feelings. You saw how I tensed up. When I was on the bed and saw you standing over me, I had an instant flashback. I almost bolted. But you understood. You didn't rush me. You were so sweet, Scott. So tender and caring, you made it all right. You didn't say anything, but I knew you knew."

And now, again, he said nothing, just listened.

"Do you know that was the first time I've ever made love or been made love to in my life?"

Scott walked over to her and pulled her out of the chair.

"It's not going to be the last time. Not if you let me hang around. Yes, I knew. Why do you think I've taken it so slow? You've been driving me crazy but I had to be sure you were ready. When you broke out in that sweat last night, I almost panicked. If you hadn't calmed down, I would have just held you all night," he confessed.

He pulled her wrists to his mouth and kissed them. The faint scars from the bindings were still visible. "I'd like to kill the bastard that did this to you."

He kissed her and then pulled her shirt up to just below her breasts. He kneeled in front of her and kissed the scar below one of them. "Did he do this?"

Tears streamed down her cheeks.

"Yes. That last day…he…he beat me with a leather strap. That is a reminder. I thought of plastic surgery to erase it, but, the other scars…the ones inside…they'll always be with me."

He kissed the scar again before lowering her shirt. "Not if you let me help. Surgery can get rid of this one if you want, and I'll help you with the internal ones, if you'll let me."

She reached under her shirt and touched the scar. He placed his hand on top of hers. "Can you tell me about it?"

Sarah pulled her feet up onto the chair, locking her knees against her chest, pulling the sweatshirt over them, withdrawing into herself. She began talking, remembering that day, in a voice barely above a whisper. Scott had to strain to hear her, at first listening as a friend, then as a cop, a trained investigator, and finally as an angry lover.

She told him all the repulsive details, omitting nothing. She described the abduction, the time in the trunk, the beatings, the repeated sexual abuse, and her escape. She told him about her feelings during those five days; fear, helplessness, abandonment, anger, and finally determination. She seemed to relive those emotions as she talked. Scott could see them in her eyes and in the shadows fleeting across her face.

It was the first time she had ever confided in anyone, telling the whole story. When she finished, his eyes were misty.

"What happened after you crashed into the patrol car? You rammed a cruiser? Naked?"

"Everything became a blur. One look at my body and he knew what I'd been through. There had been an APB out on Callie and me for five days. A statewide search was in progress. He recognized me immediately, threw a blanket around me and radioed for backup. Callie was still there, in that place, tied to the bed. Hawkins had run, but they picked him up within hours."

"Tell me about the trial," Scott prodded. "Our file only contained a summary and frankly, it was a puzzle. The evidence was conclusive. The guy was guilty. How did he walk away?"

"The trial was a travesty, a horrible miscarriage of justice. Callie and I were the ones on trial, not Hawkins. I'm sure you've heard how defense attorneys attempt to disguise the truth by painting a tainted picture of the victims? Well, I experienced it first hand. This guy destroyed us."

"How? You two were just teenagers, innocent teenagers. Why did the prosecutor allow that to happen? The case was a no-brainer. A second-year law student could have handled the case."

"And that's exactly how the district attorney summarized it, right up until the day the trial began. Open and shut, he said over and over. Hell, all the evidence was conclusive. Hawkins took us to his home, in his car. They proved we had been in the trunk. DNA matched everywhere. Our blood, his sperm, and the physical evidence proved he raped us. Those beds told their own story. Pictures showed our bruises from the beatings. Callie was in much worse shape than I was. He must have really taken his rage out on her. I don't know how she survived it."

Sarah turned away, wiping her eyes on her sleeves, her back rigid, her chin thrust defiantly upward. Scott remained silent, waiting for her to regain her composure.

"The DA said he had everything he needed to put the guy away forever. He even pushed for a speedy trial date. He wanted a jury trial so he could get a stiffer sentence. 'Hawkins will be an old man before he gets out of prison,' he assured us. Just before the trial started, an attorney representing Hawkins' father approached Daddy and offered us fifty thousand dollars if we'd drop the charges. Daddy told him to go to hell."

"So what happened? How did he get off?

"A plea bargain, everything went wrong. First, the judge ruled against a jury trail. Then, the defense attorney was allowed to attack us. He vilified us. The DA let him get away with it without raising any objections. He allowed the defense to do and imply whatever they wanted. And what they wanted was to make it sound as though Callie and I chose Hawkins, that he was the victim of two promiscuous teenagers.

"He said, 'you like sex, don't you? You chose to stop and give directions, didn't you? You had seen him pass through that intersection before, hadn't you? A good-looking guy in a fancy car, who wouldn't notice? You had it all planned, didn't you? The two of you were waiting for Mr. Hawkins that morning weren't you? You don't date? You hang with a crowd, is that because you enjoy group sex? If you weren't having a good time, why did you wait five days to leave?'

"It went on and on. The attorney kept pounding away. He sneered at every answer we gave and then turned our words on us. Callie and I left court each day in tears."

"What was the DA doing all this time?"

"Listening. Oh, he'd object every now and then, never strenuously. He let the defense control the flow of the trial. He showed only a few of the pictures and never mentioned we each lost fifteen pounds in those five days. The only nourishment he gave us was a peanut butter and jelly sandwich and a glass of water each day."

"It's a wonder you survived or had the strength to escape," Scott remarked.

"That's not the half of it. The press was brutal. Hell, we were virgins when he took us, but that's not what the press implied."

"Are you serious? They were allowed to attend? A good prosecutor never allows that to happen."

"Now you're getting the picture. Yes, he allowed it and they printed it, in big bold headlines. Every lying, one sided word, the defense's version hit the papers. In the public's eye, Hawkins became the victim. Callie and I became a couple of teenage whores. The community, our friends, our neighbors began to believe it all. They looked at us differently. Our friends began avoiding us. They would actually turn and walk away if they saw us approaching.

"After the first week they talked behind our backs but loud enough for us to hear. At the end of the second week they said it to our faces. They called us whores — white trash and one even called us a couple of gold diggers.

"At the end of the third week, the DA approached Dad and told him it wasn't looking good."

"What did he say? How did he justify what was happening in the trial?"

"He didn't. He told us the defense was building an impressive case and the judge was being influenced. He even asked our parents if they were sure we were virgins before this happened. Suddenly the truth seemed irrelevant."

"What about the DNA? What about all of the other evidence you mentioned?"

"The defense was able to prevent most of it from being introduced which minimized our case substantially. As for the DNA, remember it was in the early nineties. DNA wasn't the factor it is now. It became obvious, evidence and truth weren't the issue, Callie and I were. Dad was livid! He wanted to strangle the prosecutor and do worse to the defense lawyer. He knew none of it was true but he could see that it was destroying me. So, when the DA said the defense approached him with the plea bargain, and he recommended it, Daddy reluctantly agreed."

"His love for you overrode justice. He wanted to protect you." Scott said with conviction. Sarah could see the pain and admiration in his eyes.

"Yes. Thank God, Daddy never doubted me, or I might have ended up like Callie."

"What do you mean?"

"Poor Callie, she never had a chance. She wasn't strong enough to handle it all, especially with no support. Her father began doubting her. After the first week, he forbid Callie's mother to attend the trial. He didn't want her to have to listen to what happened to us. So Callie had no one. How could he do that? How could any parent be so callous and insensitive?

He was a minister, for God's sake! And that was part of the problem. He was more concerned about public opinion, his congregation, his ministry, than he was his daughter's well being. He seemed to go with public opinion. During the last few days of the trial, Callie overheard her parents arguing. Her father was questioning our story, our innocence. Her mother was furious, yelling at him, defending Callie."

"He turned on his own daughter?"

"Yes, he stopped talking to Callie. It got to a point where he wouldn't even touch her, his own daughter. He jumped at the plea bargain to save face. His, not Callie's. It broke her heart.

"We were shocked when the judge sentenced Hawkins to only three years, and then suspended the sentence putting him on probation. The DA never told us he would get off that easy. Dad was outraged. He would never have accepted the plea if he had known the arrangement."

"He couldn't have known. What about Hawkins?"

"That was the real irony of it all. He was actually upset. He thought he should have gotten off. He screamed at his attorneys when he heard the sentence. Then, when he left the courtroom, he passed us and whispered to Callie and me that he wasn't through with us. He would see us again." Sarah bit her bottom lip to keep it from quivering.

"The night after the trial ended, Callie went home, climbed the stairs to her room, got into a hot bath and she slit both her wrists. I should have gone over to her house and talked to her. She was just next door."

Sobbing quietly, Sarah wrapped her arms around her knees, literally holding herself together. Scott placed his hands on her shoulders, gently, carefully as if she might break.

"Sarah, I'm so terribly sorry."

"And then, do you know what that bastard did? Hawkins called me at home the next day. He told me, 'I heard about your friend, killing herself. Isn't that a shame?' He laughed then said, 'I knew Callie was the weak one. You're different; stronger, but not strong enough. Not for our next session, and there will be another one, little girl. Callie got off easy, but not you. I'll take care of you. One day, we'll meet again."

"My dad overheard the conversation and called the DA."

"What did the DA say?"

Sarah's nostrils flared. "That there was nothing he could do about it. That we had agreed to the plea bargain. And after all it was just a phone call. How could we even be sure it was Hawkins? Did he identify himself?"

"Dad said he didn't have to identify himself. We knew it was Hawkins. Then he called the DA a few choice names and slammed the phone down. Daddy was so angry that he got a hunting rifle and left the house and went looking for Hawkins. He told my mom. 'If the courts won't punish him, I will. My little girl is not going to spend her life looking over her shoulder!"

Scott stroked her hair. "What happened?"

"The sheriff was a family friend. Mom called him and he caught up with Dad and took him into custody until he cooled down. Then he sent Dad home, without the rifle. The sheriff told Daddy he would return it later. After he sent Dad home, the sheriff paid Hawkins a visit and told him to be out of town by morning and not to come back. Word was that Hawkins had a couple of broken ribs when he left town, compliments of the sheriff."

Sarah reached for a box of Kleenex and blew her nose, wiped her eyes and continued.

"It was months before we realized we had been set up. Dad found out that Hawkins Enterprises owned the big newspaper that covered the story. That's why they printed the defense's version of the story. Then within the next year, the judge built a million-dollar home on the river. As for the DA, he accepted a cushy job as corporate council for Hawkins Enterprises. Their 10-K indicated he received a five-hundred-thousand-dollar recruitment bonus."

"And you think it was the system that sold you out?"

"There's no doubt in my mind! Callie and I never stood a chance."

"I would have felt the same way then, but surely you know better now, Sarah. It wasn't the system that sold you out. It was the players. The system is only as good as the people running it," Scott reminded her.

"You can blame whomever you choose, but bottom line is, justice did not prevail. After losing Callie, I had to get on with my life, find something to focus on, a goal."

"What was that?"

"Revenge, vengeance, payback, I want Hawkins to pay for his sins."

"Is that why you joined the Bureau?"

"I won't lie to you, Scott, yes, that's part of the reason. Before it happened, I wanted to be a pediatrician just like dad. It had been planned for years. I'd already been accepted to the right college. But Hawkins changed all that. What he did to us, what he said after the sentencing, and then that final phone call. It was no idle threat, Scott. He will come again, and when he does, I will be prepared. I wanted the best training possible, to defend myself, legally and physically. Georgetown gave me part of it and the Bureau gave me the rest."

"Sarah, I can't blame you for feeling the way you do. If he does come after you, you have every right to defend yourself. And I'll be right there with you. But you can't be a one-woman execution squad."

"Scott, you need to understand, he will come and when he does, I will defend myself. And this time, I will dispense the justice he deserves. I will be a jury of one."

"I'd do the same. But don't go looking for him, Sarah. And don't use the Bureau."

Scott continued, "Is that the only reason you joined the Bureau, to get revenge?"

"No. Well, what happened to me gave me the idea, the

purpose. But getting personal revenge, no, unless it's against people like that DA, the judge and of course Hawkins, people who violate others' rights. And those that manipulate the system for their own personal interests. I want to prevent that from happening to others. Those unsuspecting victims that believe in justice deserve to be treated fairly. Scott, my oath is as important to me as yours is to you. Believe me."

His expression told her he wanted to believe her. She could see it in his eyes.

"Scott, I joined the Bureau for all the right reasons. Sure, I'd like to right some past wrongs, personal injustices. But primarily I want to be sure the system doesn't fail. That people like Hawkins' father don't run over innocent victims. That the guilty pay for their crimes no matter how powerful or rich they are. To be sure the system doesn't get subverted, not for money, cushy jobs, or political favors."

"What about Hawkins? Where does that leave him?"

"I'm content to wait for him. Let him pick the timing. But have no doubt, Scott, when he does come, I will kill him. Because if I don't, he'll kill me."

"You really believe that, Sarah?"

"Scott, this guy thinks he's immune to justice. There is no telling how many women's lives he has destroyed, or will destroy. He's still out there, and he hasn't stopped. He won't stop. Why should he? As long as his father's alive, Hawkins is immune to justice, at least the legal kind. That means personal justice will have to do. And I take what he did to me and my friend very personal, I owe him."

"And if you're wrong and he never comes?"

"Then so be it. But that isn't going to happen, he'll come."

"Sarah. Maybe he has changed and has forgotten about you. Put the past behind him."

"Maybe, but I don't think so. The guy is sick, psychotic. He can't change. He's an animal. He has, and will, continue to hurt other women. One day he'll find me and then he'll keep his promise and come for me. Only, I won't be as easy this time."

"Sarah, I hope you're wrong. We have a future and I don't want this to come between us. Don't make me choose between you and what's right. If he comes we'll use the system to seek justice. It won't fail you again, I promise. I'll be there for you." He pulled her closer.

"A future, you think?"

"I'm sure of it," he promised.

"Me, too."

She kissed him. Sarah didn't tell him that she had kept track of Hawkins over the years and knew he was in Atlanta. Some things were better left unsaid.

"Scott, there is something else. It's probably nothing."

"What?" Scott stiffened when he heard her response.

"The phone calls I've been getting, I know it's Greg Hawkins. It's his voice. Hi babe is what he said every time he came into the room. I'll never forget it."

CHAPTER 9

STEP THREE OF SARAH'S PLAN had now become more complicated for her to put in motion. Her conflicting emotions were raging within her. It had been easy to get Scott involved. All she had to do was tell him about the phone calls. But her conscience was nagging at her, causing self-doubts, second thoughts about using him and the Bureau to execute her plan. She hadn't counted on falling in love with him.

Scott had reacted as if a mule had kicked him when she played back the messages for him. After he heard them, he had wasted no time in taking charge.

"If it is Hawkins, we'll nail him," he vowed.

Within minutes he had set up surveillance on Sarah's home and coordinated having her home phone monitored. A Bureau communications tech met Scott at Sarah's home to retrieve the tapes from her answering machine and take it to the lab to be analyzed. Scott had used his cell phone to make the arrangements so no one would suspect he was making the calls from her house.

That was several weeks ago. No actual threats had been made, no one was observed following Sarah and the calls stopped. The Bureau decided that the calls were random, probably from some kid playing a prank.

While her phone was being monitored, Scott couldn't call her on that phone. Instead, they used their cell phones for personal calls. Nights weren't a problem. Since that first night, they spent most together, typically at her place because of Jax. They ran together each morning, took showers together, ate together, and made love frequently. They couldn't get enough of each other.

Work was different. They knew they had to maintain their distance at the office, since interagency affairs were dealt with quickly and decisively. It helped that both spent a good deal of time in the field working different cases.

Falling in love had changed them both. Coworkers noticed the differences in their behavior, but no one had made the connection, yet. After all, Scott was a by-the-book leader and Sarah was the ice queen. Who would ever suspect they were lovers?

Scott actually smiled at the office, seemed to be happier. He began asking fellow agents how their families were doing, getting personal, unusual behavior. Behind his back, one bold male agent commented. "I don't know if he's in love, but I'll bet a dozen Krispy Kremes he's getting it regular."

Sarah seemed happier, more accessible, no longer the reserved person who withdrew into her shell. She seemed to have found an inner peace, and there was a definite glow about her. The female agents' grapevine was active with speculation. And like the men, the ladies attributed the change to sex.

Finally, one of her friends couldn't stand it any longer. At lunch she blurted out, "Okay Sarah, who is it?"

"Who is what?"

"You know exactly what I'm talking about. Who's the man in your life? The one that has put this permanent smile on your face."

"I don't know what you're talking about." In spite of herself, Sarah smiled.

"I knew it! I knew it! You look like the cat that swallowed the canary. Who is he? Is he good in bed? And how long has this been going on? When do I get to meet him?"

"My, gosh, is nothing sacred? I have to tell you about my sex life?"

"Well, duh, I think so, especially when it makes you glow like one of those lighthouses on the coast."

Sarah leaned across the table, glanced about in mock caution and gave a conspiratorial grin. "Scott, our boss, the AIC himself, and let me tell you he's great in bed!" She winked.

"Scott?"

"Yes, haven't you noticed all the attention he's been giving me?"

"Scott, our Scott Justice. He's your lover?" Her momentary shock gave way to disbelief. She smiled, shaking her head. "Sure," she laughed. "You and Scott Justice, get real!"

Just the reaction Sarah had counted on. She knew that sometimes the best way to quell rumors and speculation was to use the truth in such a blatant way that no one would possibly believe it. No one would ever link her and the AIC romantically. For her to tell her friend that it was Scott would definitely send her off track, for now. But her friend's reaction still frosted Sarah.

Sarah felt her and Scott's secret was safe for a while. However, towards the end of the second week she learned that there was one person in the office who wasn't fooled. Darcy. And when she put her two cents worth in, it sobered Sarah. The reality check made her think twice. It happened one afternoon just after Sarah had finished talking to Scott on the phone.

Darcy stuck her head in the door.

"Can we talk?"

"Sure Darcy, what's up?"

Darcy walked in the office and closed the door. "When Scott calls again, tell him I need to talk to him."

Sarah's eyes widened. Her mind raced to come up with

a reply. But before she could, Darcy charged on. "Listen sugar, as a friend, I'm happy for you. If anyone ever needed a man, it's you. And you two are a perfect couple, if. If you didn't work together and if he wasn't your boss. Sarah, you're smart enough to know that an affair with Scott could ruin both of your careers."

"What if it's not an affair? What if we're serious?"

"I'd say wonders never cease and offer my congratulations. Then, I would say that one of you should find another place to work, pronto."

Sarah felt like she had been kicked in the gut. Darcy was right. If she and Scott continued seeing each other, it could only spell disaster for their careers within the Bureau. But, Sarah had a hedge, one that only she was aware of, and one she didn't like to dwell on, but had to face. If she dealt with Hawkins as she intended and followed through with her plan, she would sabotage any future she had with Scott anyway.

"You've already thought about that, haven't you sugar? As a friend, I'm telling you to be careful. If you two are serious, do something before the Bureau finds out."

"Thanks for the advice. Darcy...don't..."

"Don't worry; I'm not going to say anything to anyone. And I don't think anyone here suspects a thing. But telling Becky it was Scott at lunch the other day wasn't the smartest thing you've ever done. You threw her off track temporarily but you planted a seed. She's mentioned it to some of the other agents already."

"What did they say?"

"No way, just like Becky." Darcy gave Sarah an indulgent smile, like a mom would give her five-year-old. "Well you have to admit, you two are a mismatch, at least outwardly. You seem to avoid men and he changes girlfriends as often as most men change underwear, and never ever dips his wick in company ink."

"Dips his what, where?" Sarah burst out, laughing at Darcy's colloquialism.

"You know what I mean. You're not that naïve, Sarah." Darcy looked Sarah in the eyes, "I don't want you to get hurt, but two or three months seems to be his limit with a woman. What then? He may have a guilty conscience afterwards and where does that leave you?"

"Okay. What if it's for real this time?"

"I hope it is, for both of you. I happen to think you two are perfect for each other. But if it is, we're right back at square one."

The other person who knew about them was Sarah's mother. After all, she was the one who told Sarah to go for it. Sarah had called her back to thank her for the advice. Her mother was delighted and asked for all the details. They talked almost daily and Mrs. Johnson was pleased at the changes in her daughter. Anne Johnson hoped it would work out for the two. If it didn't, she wasn't sure how Sarah would handle a breakup.

The more Sarah and her mom talked, the more Sarah opened up, gushing about Scott, their relationship, his tenderness and understanding and her new found freedom. Dr. and Mrs. Johnson were overjoyed that their daughter had a beau.

They weren't sure how serious the two were, but intended to find out. They invited the couple to Concord for a weekend, and surprisingly, Sarah accepted. It would be one of her rare visits to her hometown.

SINCE JOINING THE FBI, Sarah had earned the respect of the higher echelon of the Bureau by solving high profile cases involving tax fraud, financial manipulations to inflate stock values and embezzlement. Her tenacious attitude, uncanny ability to "read" people and her legal and financial knowledge had been instrumental in exposing culprits. With names like Enron and Adelphia in her case files, promotions had come faster than normal and she had surpassed agents decades her senior.

The Mason Manufacturing embezzlement and murder cases were the most recent of her successes. Sarah had been instrumental in uncovering the embezzlement scheme and identifying the mastermind orchestrating it. As the case progressed, she discovered the link between the killer and the culprit. Naturally, Sarah's testimony and the evidence she had gathered was key to the prosecution's case. So, for the past couple of weeks Sarah had either been attending or on call for the trial of Michelle Smith, the former senior financial officer of Mason Manufacturing.

Attending and testifying at trials was the part of her job Sarah enjoyed the least. Catching crooks was challenging and in a way, fun, but prosecuting them was boring. The court system was necessary to punish the crooks, but to Sarah, trials seemed to be a waste of her time. This trial was worst than most, it seemed to be dragging on, making little progress. Sarah had spent the past three days cooling her heels waiting to testify. This morning, she was even more impatient than usual because she and Scott were planning to leave town as soon as court recessed for the weekend.

This would be his first visit to her parent's home and her first visit in over a year. Sarah still harbored hard feelings for the town where she had grown up. Sure, it had been the site of her happy childhood. Yet the same community had listened to all the lies that came out at Hawkins' trial and judged the two girls guilty. Neighbors her family had known for years and considered friends had turned on Sarah and Callie, gossiping about the two teenagers. The lies and speculation had made the girls' lives miserable. Sarah and her parents had faced them all with resolve, with their heads held high.

Callie hadn't been as fortunate. Her father doubted her and as a result, had forbid Callie and her mother to even go out in public.

Sitting in the stuffy, poorly lit and poorly ventilated

courtroom, Sarah had trouble focusing on the proceedings, her mind wandered, regressing to the past and returning to the present. She continually glanced at her watch, willing the trial to end for the day; simultaneously looking forward to and dreading the trip to Concord. She couldn't help but smile as she wondered what her mom and dad had up their sleeves. Mom would probably have Sarah and Scott engaged, if not married, before the weekend was over and Sarah would be pregnant a week later. Will Daddy take Scott off for some man time? I can hear him now. "Son may I ask what your intentions are towards my daughter?"

"Objection, your honor!" The prosecutor's voice brought her out of her reverie. She forced herself to focus on the proceedings, looking at the prosecutor in wonder.

Why don't they call me? Don't they know I have other cases I need to be working on? Other corporate jerks to catch that are stealing from their companies or rigging the financials to mislead investors. Not that it does much good. As soon as I get the goods on them, some lazy, inept prosecutor like this one botches the case. What is going on anyway? Why is the prosecutor letting the defense tie him up in knots?

Michelle Smith had stolen more than half a million dollars from Mason Manufacturing. When the chief operating officer of the company began suspecting what she was up to, Michelle got an ex-cop, who she happened to be living with, to murder the guy. Her reign of terror didn't stop there. When she learned the COO had hired corporate consultants to look into her scam before his death, she put out contracts on them, too. The only reason the consultants were still alive was that the FBI had gotten involved. Now here they were, sitting in a hot courtroom, the first of two trials. The murder trial would follow the fraud case. Sarah knew if this case was blown, Michelle would definitely go down for murder.

Sarah loved the Bureau, her job and the sense of achievement she felt each time she closed a case. And down deep, she knew the system worked, most of the time.

"The system is only as good as the people running it." Scott's words echoed in her mind.

At one o'clock the judge recessed for the weekend.

"TELL ME ONE MORE TIME! What did my dad say?"

Friday evening, Sarah and Scott were having dinner at The Front Page News, a popular Atlanta restaurant. The prior weekend had been wonderful. Her parents had treated Scott like a member of the family. Sarah figured her mom was probably hearing wedding bells already.

Scott and Sarah had returned to Atlanta late Sunday night and he left town Monday morning. The week apart had passed so slowly that it seemed like a month to both of them. He got back Friday afternoon, put in a couple of hours at the office and dashed home to shower before picking Sarah up for dinner.

"I told you already. How many times do you need to hear it?"

"As many as it takes for you to tell the story the same way twice. Why not try the truth this time, okay?" She gave him her most intimidating glare. The one she reserved for interrogations.

"Are you accusing me of exaggerating, giving false testimony?"

"Oh no, not you!" She laughed. "Now tell me what he said, for real this time."

"All right. He took me out on the porch and offered me a beer. A cold Ultra. My favorite, I might add."

"Cut all the crap. You've made your point. Porch, your favorite beer, my dad likes you, okay. I've got all that. Now get to the facts."

"Are you telling this story, or am I?"

"Okay, go ahead. I can see you're enjoying this." She

could tell that Scott was having fun. Truth be known, Sarah was enjoying the charade too.

"As I was saying, we were on the porch, having a cool one. We made a little small talk, sports, the Bureau, man talk. I was getting real comfortable, then he changed the subject, ambushed me. 'Scott', he said. 'My little girl is special. She's all Anne and I have, her happiness is very important to us.'"

Scott's eyes twinkled, his mouth twitched. The story was growing with each retelling. "I said, 'Dr. Johnson, it's easy to see that you love Sarah and how much she loves you and her mother.' Your dad smiled. 'Thanks, Scott.' He even got a little misty eyed and then said. 'Then you can understand why we are concerned. Sarah is still very fragile. We don't want her hurt.' I reassured him, 'Dr. Johnson, believe me, I would never hurt Sarah. I know she's special.' Then he drops the bomb, 'Are you in love with Sarah? Scott, do you plan to marry my daughter?'"

Sarah gasped, her eyes wide in astonishment. "He, what? He didn't — what did you say?"

"I was stunned, Sarah. I mean right out of the blue like that. What could I say? I didn't know how to respond. Your dad just stared at me. You know how he does, that intense, don't-disappoint-me look. He didn't let up. He wasn't going to let me off the hook. I was speechless.

"Finally, after what seemed like an eternity, your dad says. 'Scott I know Sarah's kind of homely, tall, kind of flat-chested, but she has nice legs and a great ass. And there is a dowry, if that helps. We want grandchildren.'"

Sarah squealed. "Scott Justice! My dad didn't say that! He doesn't talk like that. Besides, he thinks I'm perfect." She glared at him. "Wait a minute. You've never complained." She looked down at her chest. "Small, huh? So that's what you think? Well, consider them off limits, as of this minute. At least until I get the truth."

"Okay! Okay! This is the truth, I promise. He said,

'Scott, are you going to marry my daughter?'"

"What did you say?"

"Sarah, I had to be honest. I told him, 'Not in this lifetime, Dr. Johnson. I don't go for bossy women.' I could tell he was upset and hurt. He thought he had the perfect son-in-law and you'd blown it. He glared at me and asked, 'What if I doubled the dowry?' I hesitated, and he asked, 'Oh, she's good enough to sleep with but she's not good enough to marry?'"

Sarah threw her napkin at him. "He doesn't know we're sleeping together."

"Sure he does. I think the fact that we slept in the same bedroom, one that had only one king bed, would be his first clue. Add to that clue, the fact you had a huge, satisfied look on your face both mornings and my guess is he knows."

Sarah sat back and stared, trying not to laugh. "You may be right, but keep in mind Dad isn't with the FBI. He's not a trained investigator like you." She shook her head and her eyes twinkled. "You're not going to tell me what you two talked about, are you?"

"No. It was man talk."

The waiter interrupted them, bringing their food.

They attacked their dinners with vigor. Scott devoured his salmon almost as soon as it was removed from the sack it had been baked in, while Sarah expertly wrestled a lobster from its shell. As they ate, she found herself relishing the companionable silence, the ease with which they'd settled into a comfortable relationship.

Later, over a shared tiramisu, Sarah was telling Scott about one of Jax's funny antics when she stopped in mid sentence and her face turned ashen. "It can't be!"

"What? What's wrong?"

"It's him! Greg Hawkins is at that table by the window. That guy sitting with the dark-haired woman in the black dress."

THE MAN SARAH GESTURED TOWARD got up and moved behind his companion's chair and began to slide it away from the table. Obviously finished with their dinner, they were ready to leave. He was medium height and build, wearing an expensive charcoal gray suit that fit him like a glove. His hair was dark with a smattering of gray. He carried himself with an air of confidence. That and his good looks attracted the attention of several women at nearby tables.

With his date walking ahead of him, his head turned slightly as he checked out the women he passed. He winked or nodded as his eyes lingered on one in particular, and an appreciative half-smile crossed his lips. Then his eyes met Sarah's and his expression changed, his gaze grew more intent. There didn't seem to be a message in them, lust perhaps, but nothing more. Then he stepped beside his companion, circled an arm around her waist and escorted her through the doorway.

Scott felt an immediate dislike for the man. His every move seemed staged, rehearsed, an elaborate little tableau, like an actor moving across a stage. The arrogance, the way he looked at the women, and particularly the stare he gave Sarah, irritated Scott. Most of all, Scott didn't like the fleeting look of terror and confusion that he saw in Sarah's eyes when the guy passed her. Scott excused himself to leave the table and walked across the room to speak to a waiter.

Sarah's thoughts were focused on Hawkins. Her body was rigid. Her lungs burned and her face flushed. She hadn't realized she was holding her breath until her lungs screamed for air. She was seized with a sudden chill and began to shiver. Angry, she shook her head to regain her focus and rubbed her arms for warmth.

"Are you all right? You're shaking," Scott said when he returned.

He took off his jacket and put it around her shoulders. The chill subsided as the warmth of his coat and his scent in its fabric enveloped her. She relaxed, knowing he was there.

"I'm okay. Seeing him like that, out of nowhere, so unexpected, was unsettling."

"He's not your man. I stopped the waiter and checked the charge slip. His name is Gary B. Allen."

"I don't care what the slip says. That's Greg Hawkins. I'd recognize him anywhere."

Scott didn't argue. Instead he paid the check. "Let's go into the lounge. I think you could use a drink. I know I could."

The lounge was low-key, with plush red carpeting, dimly lit chandeliers, and a pianist playing soft jazz, candles on the tables and pricey art on the walls. Sarah and Scott sat on a corner sofa with a small round table for two. A leggy blonde wearing a skimpy, white mesh outfit took their order. When she returned with their drinks, she made a point of leaning over giving Scott a full view of her ample cleavage.

"When your eyes refocus you can look this way," Sarah snickered.

"Now that is a set of knockers," Scott said with a little dramatic flair, to lighten the moment. He knew Sarah thought hers were too small, and even though he disagreed, he enjoyed teasing her.

"Smart ass, I hope you got an eyeful. Those are the only ones you're going to see for a while."

"That's your loss, darling. Hmm, does that mean I won't get the dowry? Your parents will be disappointed. Not only do I think I'm the son they always wanted, I may be their only hope."

"You're impossible. They were only pretending to…" She didn't finish her comment, as someone interrupted her.

"Hi. I saw you in the restaurant. Have we met before?" Greg Hawkins, a.k.a. Gary Allen was beside their table, looking directly at Sarah, ignoring Scott.

"No."

"You sure? I never forget a face." The cliché seemed ironic since he was staring at her legs, encased in dark stockings and crossed under the small table.

"I'm sure. Believe me, I never forget an asshole." Sarah turned away, repulsion evident on her face.

"Hey babe, there's no need to be a bitch. I'm not trying to pick you up or anything. You aren't that special." Hawkins tensed, seemed to be coiled, ready to strike. All that was missing were the warning rattles.

Scott stood up and got in Hawkins face. His voice was quiet, deadly, the missing rattle. "The lady said you're mistaken. Now move on."

"Screw you, buddy. See ya, bitch," Hawkins sneered.

In a single, lightening move, Scott grabbed Hawkins lapels and twisted the fabric until his knuckles ground into Hawkins' rib cage just above his solar plexus. "Apologize to the lady."

Only a tensing of Hawkins' jaw muscles and a sharp intake of breath revealed the pain Scott's knuckles inflicted. "Sorry, my mistake," He nodded to Sarah, looking neither scared nor apologetic.

Scott released him.

Hawkins straightened his coat and looked at Scott, memorizing and cataloging him, hatred and something else, madness perhaps, burning in his eyes. "This isn't the time or place, friend, but we will meet again." He gave Sarah a fleeting half-smile, "You too, babe." He turned and walked away.

THE FEAR AND PAIN kept Sarah from sleeping. Her body ached and with the morning light shining through the slits of the blinds, came an overwhelming sense of panic. Sarah knew what the day held for her.

"No, not again, please! Noo..." Callie's scream filled the morning silence.

Sarah jolted awake to a long, penetrating scream coupled with anguished barking. She sat up in her bed.

Tears streamed down her cheeks, she was shaking. She looked around the room, her bedroom. It was moments before she realized the scream had echoed from her own throat.

Covered in a fine sheen of sweat, tangled in the damp sheets, Sarah tried to orient herself. Frantic, Jax was circling the bed barking, ready to attack the unknown menace.

At last Sarah realized she was in her own bedroom. She was alone, just she and Jax — alone and safe — and free. Her wrists and feet were not bound. But the nightmares had returned. Shivering, she glanced at the bedside clock and said, "Nope, it's too early to get up." She curled into a fetal position and began taking deep, measured breaths, in an effort to quiet her racing pulse. Gradually, her pulse slowed and she felt a calm taking control, just as it had so many times in the past thirteen years.

Jax peered at her, his big brown eyes alert, concerned. "It's okay, boy. I had a bad dream." Jax seemed to understand, his body relaxed, and he climbed on the bed and snuggled Sarah. She began rubbing his silky ears, explaining the cause of the nightmare, as much to herself, as to the dog.

"Seeing him last night brought it all back. They always come back. My nightmares won't go away. Not until he goes away."

With the dog curled against her, she nestled her head into the pillow and closed her eyes. She fought sleep, afraid the nightmare would return, but in spite of her efforts, Jax's snoring lulled her to sleep.

The phone rang.

"Hello," she slurred.

"Sorry to wake you, I was worried about you. You okay?"

"I'm fine. Thanks. Why?"

"You were upset last night. I hated to leave you." Scott had been beeped around eleven.

"That's okay, duty called. I understand. An AIC has gotta do what an AIC has gotta do. Is it anything serious? Can you come over?"

"Sorry, but I can't. I've got to go to the office, and it's not good. That's why the locals called us. Go back to sleep and get some rest, I may need you."

"What's going on? What time is it?"

"It's a little after four. Are you sure you're okay?"

"Absolutely. Thanks for being concerned but really, I'm okay. It was just that seeing him last night. It brought everything back."

"Sarah, it wasn't him. The guy's name was Gary Allen. You're safe. I wish I'd picked up something to run some prints on, just to prove it to you."

"I wish you had too, to prove it to you. And as for being safe, I'm just fine. He's the one in danger, if he comes around here."

Scott didn't respond, instead he asked. "You sure you're okay?"

"I'm fine, now that I'm awake."

"Are you having those bad dreams again?"

"Yeah, coming face to face with a serial rapist can have that affect on a girl."

"Why didn't you call me?"

"There was nothing you could've done. I've got to handle it myself. Besides I didn't want to sound like a wussie."

He chuckled. "You are a wussie. Believe me, I know. A very nice wussie, I might add."

"Smart ass, I'm glad you think so…tell me about the call-in. I'm up now."

"Missing person, a female, she hasn't been heard from since Wednesday."

"That's less than three days. Isn't it a little early to be

classifying it as a missing person? Why is this one different? Missing persons aren't a rarity in Atlanta. Why call us?"

"Her family's a Who's Who in Atlanta. She's engaged to another well to do. And she works for one of Atlanta's power law firms."

"So the locals need quick response and us to blame if she isn't found?" She surmised.

"That about sums it up."

"What do we know? Got a description?"

"Not much. Got recent pictures though — Caucasian, twenty-seven, brown hair and attractive."

Sarah was immediately alert. "Dark hair, what about her body?"

"Good figure."

"Breasts?"

"She's looks to be well-endowed. Why?"

"I'll be dressed in fifteen minutes. I'll meet you at the office in thirty."

SARAH WAS SITTING in Scott's office at five, listening intently as he reviewed all the available details on the missing person. Jessica Syms, twenty-seven years old, brown hair, blue eyes, attractive and well-built. She is a legal assistant to a founding partner at one of Atlanta's leading law firms.

It all fits, it's him. Hawkins has a new victim. I've waited too long and it may cost another life, she thought.

"I've talked with the parents, fiancé, her employer and her best friend. Jessica was last seen leaving work at five-thirty Wednesday. She was supposed to be headed to Emory's Law Library to study for the bar exam. She takes it in two weeks. That's it. Everything we have learned so far. That and her roommate gave a detailed description of what Jessica was wearing when she left for work."

"She disappeared Wednesday. Why are we just hearing

about it?"

"We probably wouldn't be involved now except its high profile and the Atlanta papers will give her disappearance front-page coverage in the morning edition."

"What do we know about Jessica, the person?"

"She shares an apartment with another young woman, a pretty successful pharmaceutical rep. Her roommate said it wasn't unusual for Jessica to spend the night with her fiancé, so she wasn't worried when Jessica didn't come home Wednesday night. Her boss missed her Thursday and Friday. She rarely missed work, but she always called in if she was going to be out. She didn't call. The boss let it slide Thursday because he knew she was cramming for the exam. When she no-showed Friday, he called her apartment himself and left a message.

The roommate was of town Thursday and didn't pick up the message until late Friday. She called Jessica's office, parents and fiancé. No one had heard from her. The fiancé called Atlanta PD. They went through the routine for a day before pulling us in last night."

"You feel any holes in any of their stories?"

"It's hard to tell. Everybody's so worried and upset it's hard to get much out of them at this point. All want to be helpful but they're too emotional. If there's a hole, it's the roommate. She's upset and really concerned, but something just doesn't sit right. It'd be good to interview her again."

"You think she is involved somehow?"

"No. I don't think so. My gut tells me she's on the up and up. Just holding out some tidbit that would look bad, but she doesn't think is relevant."

"Why don't I talk with her? Maybe I can get her to open up."

"Good idea, but what about court?"

"You're the AIC, get me out of it. Give this priority. Anyway, this prosecutor is blowing the case. He seems to be counting on Smith going down on the murder rap."

"You accepting that?"

"No. It sends a bad message. The courts telling them that they can get away with a little financial razzle-dazzle as long as they don't kill anybody. I don't like it, but what can I do?"

"Speak up, talk to the guy. Tell him how you feel, diplomatically, like you just did. Do it when you go back. For now, I'll get you excused for a couple of days. Go see the roommate, as soon as possible. Here's her info." He handed Sarah a sheet of paper.

AFTER LEAVING THE OFFICE, Sarah went to the shooting range for an hour. Time on the range kept her skills finely honed and gave her self-assurance a boost.

An expert markswoman, Sarah had pulled her weapon six times in the line of duty and fired it twice, once to disable a perpetrator and once to deliver a kill shot to save a fellow agent. This morning she had been preparing for another kill shot, in the line of duty, of course. But on the black silhouette of every target, she envisioned the arrogant face of Greg Hawkins. Afterward, she felt the calmest she had since seeing him at the restaurant. The day of reckoning was near and she was ready.

She went back home to shower to get rid of the gunpowder smell and to dress for work. Sarah decided on a black Chico's pants suit, a Joan Vass camel tunic and comfortable black Stuart Weitzman flats. The weather had warmed up so she didn't need a coat. Sometimes she envied the local cops. They got to wear jeans, casual tops and comfortable running shoes. The Bureau didn't allow that. Dress professional was the motto with black and white or white and black as the unofficial dress code. Sarah's only transgression was changing into her New Balance sneakers on long days.

Sarah left her house at nine-thirty, and as soon as she

was on the road, she used her cell phone to call Anna Ricks at her office.

"Ms. Ricks, this is Sarah James with the FBI. I'm sure you're aware that the Atlanta Police Department has asked us to assist them in locating Jessica Syms?"

"Yes, I talked to Mr. Justice last night. Has something happened? Oh, God, Jessica's okay isn't she?"

"Yes, as far as we know, Ms. Syms is fine. I didn't mean to upset you. She has not been found yet, and we're assuming the best until we know different. It was late when you talked with Agent Justice last night and we thought it would be wise if I talked with you this morning, if you're available. My questions may be redundant but perhaps I can jog your memory and help you think of something that might assist us in locating Ms. Syms."

"I told Mr. Justice everything I know, but God yes, I'll be glad to talk to you. Where do you want me to meet you?"

"Thanks, but that isn't necessary. I'm in my car and I can be at your office in fifteen minutes."

Sarah spent the fifteen minutes mentally preparing for the meeting. She needed to be friendly and understanding, but firm. If Anna was holding out something, Sarah had to get it out of her.

Anna Ricks was an attractive woman. She had her dirty-blonde hair tied back in a ponytail, accenting her chiseled cheekbones. Her oval, green eyes misted over as soon as she shut her office door. She was petite and thin and wearing a navy blue pants suit that looked expensive.

She sat across from Sarah and crossed her legs, her right foot moving back and forth at a fast rhythm. Anna Ricks fit Sarah's mental image of a successful sales rep who called on physicians: high energy, bubbly and attractive. She was pretty enough to get doctors to meet with her, and she had the warm, outgoing personality that wins over the office personnel. She spoke well, was self-confident and smiled a lot.

"How can I help you Ms. James?"

"Sarah, please. Tell me about Ms. Syms. What kind of person is she? What are her habits? Where does she like to hang out, her favorite restaurant, bar, anything that will help me locate her?"

"I've already talked with Mr. Justice. I told him all that but if it will help, I'll be glad to go over it again."

"Please. You may have forgotten something. Sometimes it helps just to go over it again. Maybe something more will come up this time."

"Sure. Jessica is my best friend. I'll do anything to help."

"How long have you known her?"

"Since middle school."

"What kind of person is she?"

"Jessica is up-front, honest and loyal. What you see is what you get, so to speak. Everybody likes her."

"Everyone? Doesn't she have any enemies? Old boy-friends, jealous ex-girlfriends of guys she's dated, anyone who might have it in for her?"

"Yes, and none."

"How long have ya'll lived together?"

"We've lived together for nine years, four here in Atlanta and five at The University of Georgia in Athens."

"Then you know Jessica better than anyone else. What are her habits, her hobbies?"

"No hobbies. First, she was busy working and going to law school and now she spends her spare time working and studying for the bar exam."

"Her parents are well off. Why does she work?"

"That's Jessica. After she got out of college, she wanted to pay her own way. Her dad helps with her law school tu-ition, but she pays for the rest."

Anna rambled for forty minutes talking about her friend, answering all of Sarah's questions. It was obvious that she loved and respected Jessica Syms.

Sarah felt a moment of sadness, knowing Callie had

been that kind of friend.

"Anna, you've painted a picture of a person with absolutely no faults, but Jessica is human. Surely she had some bad habits. Tell me about them."

"There's really nothing to tell. Sure, we had some wild times, mostly at the University of Georgia. You know how it is at college. We were into guys, tried drugs but nothing serious, drank a little, and partied a lot. After we graduated we grew up. Bottom line, I wanted to build a career and she wanted a law degree. We had to take life a little more seriously. Yeah, we still party occasionally, but keep it under control."

"What about men?"

"We've both had our share, Jessica more than me. She's better looking. Now she's engaged, and I'm seeing somebody regularly."

"Does she sleep around?"

"NO! Not since college. Sure a few guys got her in the sack, but none since she met Jeff."

"How long has that been?"

"Since her first year of law school. Jeff was a year ahead of her. About four years now."

"So, she hasn't slept with anyone else in four years?"

"Right, at least not since they got serious, which was almost right away."

Anna's eyes flickered. A small pulse beat just beneath her jaw line. She twisted a large silver bangle on her right wrist. Sarah could tell that she was holding back. She'd seen the signs before.

"They have a fight recently?"

"No, why do you ask that?"

Sarah leaned toward the younger woman. Her voice was soft and very serious.

"Anna, what are you not telling me? Whatever it is, if it's worth holding out, it could be important. It could help me find her. She and Jeff have a fight?"

"No nothing like that."

"Has she been running around on him?"

"No, nothing like that. It's just…She …"

"Then what is it? Is she having second thoughts, doubts about the marriage?"

Sarah could see the small pulse racing now, and a delicate flush colored Anna's pale skin.

"Tell me Anna. Whatever it is, tell me. You aren't being disloyal. You're helping us find her. Maybe even saving Jessica's life."

Anna shuddered and covered her face with both hands." You don't mean…you don't think…"

"We aren't thinking anything yet. But my gut tells me that Jessica's in trouble. And I need to find her, pronto. Help me, please."

"Okay. Look. I don't want you getting the wrong idea about Jessica. She isn't, I mean, Jessica's not promiscuous. She's serious about being married. You know, the death till us part business, never knowing another man. You've got to believe that. She just wanted to make it with another man one more time, before she gets married. Jessica adores Jeff but she knows once she says, 'I do' its forever. She wanted a one night fling with no strings attached."

"A one night stand?"

Anna chuckled. "Yeah, 'Wham-bam-thank-you-sir,' was how she put it."

"She pick a time? A man?"

"Spur of the moment, last Wednesday night. She called me when she left work and told me that she was going to skip the library. She was laughing. She said, 'I'm horny! Come meet me.'

"I couldn't meet her. I had to leave town early the next morning. She understood. Told me not to wait up and if I heard any strange noises from her room, not to investigate, just in case she got lucky." Anna sniffled. "It'll kill Jeff if he finds out and will wreck the wedding. That's why I didn't say anything."

"It's all right, Anna. You're doing the right thing telling me. Now, where was she going? Did she have someone in mind or did she intend to pick somebody up? You think she was serious? Wednesday was the night?"

"Yes. She had that tone. The one she always got when she was about to do something wrong. The first time I heard it was when we snuck into an R-rated movie in the eighth grade." Anna's brow creased and Sarah imagined she was debating with herself about how much to say. Her concern for Jessica won out and she continued.

"There was a guy. She'd met him the week before when she and a couple of girls from her office stopped by the bar. She said she blew him off, but if he was there again, she'd have a go at him."

Anna tried for a smile. "Jessica told me, 'If he's there, I'll nail him. After all I'm wearing my lucky outfit.' She called it that because whenever she wore it good things happened." The hint of a smile quivered and faded as tears rolled down Anna's face.

"Did she tell you this guy's name?"

"No, I don't think she knew it. It was her first time at that bar and at the time she had no interest in the guy and didn't intend to go back."

"What's the name of the bar?"

"The Watering Hole in Midtown."

CHAPTER 10

LIEUTENANT ROY NELSON, Atlanta PD's lead detective on the Jessica Syms case, met Scott and Sarah at The Watering Hole at four that afternoon to assist them in interviewing the bar's employees.

"When I called to set this up, the owner told me that the afternoon and night shifts overlap from four to six-thirty. And since Saturday is his busiest day, he has entire staff on duty." Sarah told the other two, "Fate must be smiling on us for the first time since Jessica was reported missing. We can talk to everyone today."

"Did the owner give us the go ahead to talk to them?" Roy asked.

"Yes, I figured we could divvy them up. I can talk to the waitresses. Roy, you focus on the bartenders and buspeople. Scott can meet with the bouncers and the owner." Sarah suggested.

"Sounds like a plan." Roy and Scott answered in unison.

"Keep in mind that I promised the owner, no overtime and that we wouldn't keep anybody tied up any longer than necessary. I said we'd keep this low key and out of the papers."

"Any special instructions?" Sarah asked Scott.

"No, you guys know what we need. Verify the Syms girl was here Wednesday night. Who did she talk to? Did she hook up with anyone? If so, who was he? Did she leave with him?"

"Got it!" Roy and Sarah replied in unison.

"If we get anything substantial, all three of us will get together and discuss it. I'll see if the owner will let us use his office if we need it," Scott told them.

The three split up and moved to different areas of the bar to set up interview space. Typically, preliminary interviews were long, boring and nonproductive. But occasionally an investigation hit pay dirt on the first run. This needed to be one of those days.

Sarah had wanted to talk with the night crew first but had to meet with the early shift before they got off duty. She figured they wouldn't have anything for her since Jessica couldn't have gotten to The Watering Hole before seven, based on when she called Anna Ricks. But, FBI procedure required an investigator to leave no stone unturned, so everyone had to be interviewed with no overtime. It took Sarah over an hour and a half to get through the afternoon shift and her gut had been right, no one remembered Jessica.

Interviewing the night crew was proving to be equally unproductive until the third waitress walked over and sat down with Sarah in the quiet, somewhat secluded corner she was using for her interviews. The bottle blonde wore a short, denim skirt and matching shirt with the top four buttons undone. The black shoes she had on were definitely for comfort, not looks. Large silver earrings dangled from each ear. Sarah guessed the woman to be between twenty-five and thirty. She looked familiar.

The waitress's most striking feature was her name tag, JANIE, perched, as it was, atop a set of breasts that defied the laws of gravity.

Janie? Wait a minute, Janie. I remember her from my

first visit here. Janie seemed to know him. She took Hawkins a drink as soon as he sat down, knew his poison. There was something else, something, something important! Then it flashed into her mind — Hawkins asking, "Hey Janie, see that dark-haired woman over by the window, the one with the bald guy? Do you know her?" *She knows this guy. He's a regular. If he hit on Jessica, Janie saw it. I've just got to get her to tell me about it. This is the break I've been looking for.*

SARAH'S INSTINCTS kicked in. She had to establish opportunity. Did Jessica and Hawkins hook up Wednesday night? If so, did she leave The Watering Hole with him? Janie might just have the answers.

Sarah had to tread carefully. She couldn't reveal that she'd been following Hawkins and had done searches on him. Everything initiated from this interview had to come from Janie. It was vital that Sarah appear neutral in the investigation. She couldn't lead or coax the woman.

"My name is Sarah James." She showed Janie her identification, "Federal Bureau of Investigation." The badge, the FBI, the introduction never failed to grab a person's attention. John Q Citizen, a successful businessman, a hardened criminal or Susie Streetperson, they were always impressed and maybe slightly afraid or intimidated. Sarah felt a surge of pride each time it happened.

Janie was no exception. She looked like she had swallowed her gum.

"FBI! All three of you?"

"No, just Mr. Justice, the gentleman in the dark suit, and I are with the Bureau. The one in the sports coat is Lieutenant Nelson. He's an Atlanta homicide detective."

"What's going on? What's happened? Did somebody get killed?"

"We hope not. Actually, we're looking for someone. We

believe she was here Wednesday night."

Janie's eyes widened. "Here? You mean I might have served a murderer?"

"No. She hasn't killed anyone. She's missing."

"A lady hit man. Cool! What's she look like? Who'd she pop? The mayor, the governor?

"No, Janie. Listen to me. We hope no one has been killed. A lady is missing, and we've been asked to find her."

"Must be somebody important, huh? I bet the husband got rid of her for the insurance money."

"Janie, work with me, please. No one has been killed. No hit man, no lady killer, no insurance money. It's a missing person. You could help save her life though, if she is in trouble and you help me find her. Okay?"

"Okay. Whatcha want me to do?"

"Just answer a few questions. Now, the schedule indicates you worked Wednesday night. Correct?"

A nod.

"Nods won't do, Janie. You have to speak up. Okay?" Sarah gave her a stern look. "You worked Wednesday?"

Janie's back stiffened. "Yes."

Sarah handed her a recent picture of Jessica Syms. "Do you remember seeing this woman?"

She stared at the picture, smacking her gum and concentrating on the woman's face.

"I don't know. She's not a regular, I can tell you that. Wednesday is kind of a professional night. Lotta women like this come in Wednesday."

"What kind of women?"

"Professionals, they dress well, got an attitude, you know." Staring at the picture, Janie added, "She fits the mold, though. What does she do? What's she done? FBI, means it's bad, huh?"

"Janie, we've been through this. Trust me. She's done nothing, except disappear. She's missing. She's a lawyer, if that helps. Think hard, look again. She was probably in around seven. We don't think she was a regular, but she may have come in the week before."

"Maybe. Was she with anyone? A group? Buncha women? A guy? Gimme a clue? Help me here." She frowned and then laughed. "Guess that's why you're here? Huh?" Janie blew a bubble then popped it, opened her mouth and pulled the gum out with her fingertips, stretched it, keeping the end in her mouth before sucking it back in.

"Pardon?" Sarah asked, puzzled.

"You're looking for the clue. You want me to help you. Huh?"

"That's right. Now let's see if you can help us. We think she was by herself, at least when she came in. She might have left with someone, though." Sarah tapped at the picture in Janie's hand. "Any particular guy stick out? One that she would appeal to, I'm sure you know what I mean. Some guys seem to gravitate toward the same type women. Any you can think of that would like her type?"

"You're kidding, right? This girl's young, sexy and a lawyer. Every guy alive would be chasing this!" Then Janie brightened. "Wait a minute. There's this one guy. He comes in almost every Wednesday night, and I don't think he's ever left alone. To him this is just a meat market."

Sarah felt a surge of adrenaline. "Yes?"

"Yeah. She's his type, all right. He likes em good-looking. She fits his mold. She's got dark hair and she's a knockout." She wrinkled her nose and frowned, shaking her head, "Nah, maybe not."

Sarah's adrenaline slowed. "What do you mean Janie? Why not?"

"Can't say. It just doesn't fit, you know."

"Janie, let's try something that I've found helps people remember events. Bear with me, okay?"

"Okay. Whatcha want me to do?"

"Relax and close your eyes. Free your mind for a second. Think of something you like to do that really relaxes you."

Sarah waited a few seconds as Janie obediently closed her eyes. The gum stilled in her mouth.

"Now, think back to Wednesday night. Picture the woman in the photo. She's wearing a red suit with a long straight skirt, a double-breasted jacket with rounded lapels, a double strand of pearls, and black half boots? Got her?"

Janie's eyes were closed. She was concentrating, playing Sarah's mental game. Her expression changed. "Yeah, cool! I can see her. She's coming in the door. Walks over to my area, says hello. Now, I remember her from last week, the classy, big tipper."

"Last week? She was here last week?" Sarah tried to keep her voice from rising.

Janie was totally focused; eyes still closed, jaw moving again, chomping on her gum—giving it a real workout.

"Yeah, gave me a ten for a tip. She talked to me while her friends circulated. It was like she appreciated us working class. Nice person! She treated me like one too. She had a big diamond on her left hand. It didn't make sense. Why was she here?"

"What do you mean?"

"Women come in here to find somebody. On the prowl, you know, just like the men. If she was engaged, why was she prowling?"

"How do you know she was engaged?"

"I just told you, the ring with the big rock. Something else though." She squeezed her eyes tighter, concentrating. "Maybe it'll come to me."

"Was it something that happened or something she said? Wednesday or maybe last week, her first visit? Think, Janie."

"Yeah, that's it. That's why it didn't make sense."

"The ring?" Sarah was puzzled.

"No, her attitude. Last week she made it plain she was not looking for any action. Turned some guy down and then came to me to pay her tab so she could leave. She didn't even finish her first drink."

"Did she make a scene?"

"Oh, no, not this lady! From what I could see, she was nice about it, but firm. No interest. When she paid her tab, she explained it to me. Didn't need to, just did. Confided in me like I was a friend or something, she told me she was getting married soon. That's what's so strange."

"What?"

"She turned him down last week, then zeros in on him. She still had the rock on."

"Good, Janie. Now think about this guy, whoever he is. Picture him moving in the crowd, talking to different women. How did he approach the one in the red suit?"

"He didn't. I already told you, she went to him. Surprised me, since she shot him down the last time. That's why I checked out her left hand for the ring, you know."

"You sure she went after him?"

"Oh, yeah, without a doubt. He was interested, too, a good-looking broad like that. It only took a few minutes for him to be all over her. I've never seen him like that. They looked like a couple of dogs in heat."

"Did they leave together?"

"Yeah."

Sarah's blood was pumping, she leaned forward almost in Janie's face. "Do you know this guy's name?"

"Sure. Gary Allen."

Janie's description nailed him. Right down to the evil, cocky grin Sarah would never forget.

"NO. WE DON'T HAVE ENOUGH to justify a warrant, but he will be interviewed, and no to your next question, too. Sarah, you will not be there when we talk to Allen. You can't be objective." Scott's tone was emphatic.

Roy Nelson and Scott had commandeered the owner's

office at The Watering Hole to listen to Sarah and Janie run through their interview again. After that was done, Roy took Janie to police headquarters for a formal statement.

"You're convinced Gary Allen and Greg Hawkins are one and the same. That's prejudicial and will affect your judgment. Hell, it already has. We will not discuss this any further." Scott's eyes had darkened and his mouth was set in a grim line. "Are we clear?"

"Yes sir."

"If you recall, I had words with Allen the other night. I may let Roy handle the interview."

"Who are you kidding, Scott. That's not going to happen. You aren't about to hang out on the peripheral, sitting on your thumbs. You'll be center court for the interview."

"It is a cooperative effort between the Bureau and Atlanta PD, so yes, I'll be there."

"What about when she turns up dead? Are you going to involve me then? He will be the prime suspect, you know."

"We'll address that when, and if, the time comes."

"What do you think the chances are of her still being alive?"

"Slim. With all we've found out about this lady. If she was alive, someone would've heard from her by now."

"She's dead and Hawkins killed her. I know it, Scott."

"Don't start that again. This has nothing to do with Greg Hawkins. If, and I emphasize the 'if', Jessica Syms is dead, Gary Allen will be our prime suspect."

"Why won't you listen to me? Allen is Hawkins and Hawkins is Allen, and he has already murdered Jessica Syms. He doesn't want any survivors. Survivors become witnesses. You know why I'm so sure of it?"

"No, but I'm sure you are going to tell me."

"That time he called, after Callie...after Callie died. He told me she got off easy. I wouldn't be so lucky. He didn't like loose ends. Said he'd never leave a witness again. There were too many fish in the sea to hang on to one too long."

"Sarah, that's not relevant to this case. You're off base, obsessed with this thing, seeing Hawkins behind every tree. Drop it or you'll find yourself on leave until the Bureau shrink gives the okay for your return."

"Is that all?" She grumbled.

"Yes! "Hang on." Scott said. "I'll give you a ride to the office so you can pick up your car."

"That's all right, I'll take a cab."

"Agent James, wait outside." Scott picked up the phone, dismissing her.

Neither spoke during the ride to the office. At least not until Scott pulled behind Sarah's car to let her out, and said "I haven't slept in thirty-eight hours. I'm going home to get some sack time. Meet me at Roy's office tomorrow morning at nine."

Scott rolled down his window. "Sarah, go home and get some rest. Cool down, get this in perspective. I need you on this one."

CHAPTER 11

"SARAH JAMES," she answered the phone in a sleepy voice and glanced at the bedside clock. The display read 2:28 A.M.

Cell phone static initially filled her left ear then, "They found Jessica Syms. I'll pick you up in twenty minutes."

He didn't need to identify himself. Sarah could recognize Scott's voice anytime, anywhere, even half-asleep. She was immediately alert, ready for details. Law enforcement officers shared that trait with doctors. When called in the middle of the night, they were able to pull themselves out of a deep sleep to respond to an emergency. To seek the details necessary to save a life, or in this case, to verify the loss of one.

"Alive?"

"No," Scott answered.

"You want me to meet you?"

"Nah, I'm on the way."

Blue lights were strobing on half a dozen cruisers when Scott pulled into the Merchant's Walk parking lot. Merchant's Walk is an upscale shopping plaza on Johnson Ferry Road near Riverside Drive, not far from Sarah's home.

"Think Krispy Kreme has the hot sign flashing?" Sarah quipped.

"Don't you wish?" Scott smiled.

He flashed his ID at the officer directing traffic and was told to circle around to an alley behind a row of retail stores. He parked behind three unmarked cars with their dash-mounted lights flashing. The two headed toward a flurry of activity around a large Dumpster beside a grocery store loading dock. Bright lights had been set up around the perimeter to illuminate the scene. The cool night air and the artificial lighting created an eerie, surreal atmosphere. The hairs on Sarah's neck bristled as she reached the Dumpster. This was the only part of her job that she hated; the bodies.

There were at least fifteen people working the Dumpster. Two guys and one woman had on yellow jackets with Medical Examiner emblazoned across the back. Several were wearing black ones with Atlanta Homicide, while two other jackets were white with black letters spelling Coroner. The rest were royal blue with Atlanta PD in big letters. Scott and Sarah were no different. Both were wearing blue FBI jackets.

Roy spotted them and walked over. "Scott, Sarah." He nodded. "Stock clerk found the body a couple of hours ago. He was putting some boxes in the Dumpster when he noticed the odor. Looked down and saw a foot sticking out of a garbage bag."

"Garbage bag?" Sarah asked.

"Yeah, one of those big black lawn bags."

"He touch her?" Scott asked.

"No. He ran in and got his boss. Manager came out, saw the foot and called 911. The officers taking the call handled it routinely. Verified there was a body, called forensics and the Medical Examiner, who brought in the Coroner. They called me as soon as they identified her."

"That was quick," Sarah commented.

"Hell, every cop in the city has her picture."

"Where is the body?" Scott asked.

"She's over there." He pointed to the other side of the Dumpster.

"Mind if we take a look?" Scott asked.

"Go ahead."

The body was nude, lying on the plastic lawn bag, which had been slit down the middle, to allow the body to be examined. Sarah had the eerie feeling that Jessica's lifeless blue eyes were demanding her attention.

Sarah looked at the wrists and ankles. A raw ring circled each one just above the feet and wrists. Dried blood was encrusted on either side of the circles, a sure sign the girl had struggled with the bindings, tried to get free.

Sarah squatted down and looked a little closer, without touching the body. Sarah was in her analytical mode.

She was dead when he untied her. No blood flow.

The medical examiner who had been gathering various samples; tissue, blood and other body fluids, looked over at Sarah with an inquisitive, helpful look on her face. "Emily Benson." The jackets kept anyone from having to identify their agency, saved words.

"Sarah James." She nodded toward Scott. "Scott Justice, AIC." The three nodded at one another. "Looks like she was bound?" Sarah asked, taking the lead.

"Yes. There's rope fiber imbedded in her wrist and ankles. This girl put up a hell of a struggle after she was tied up. The rope dug into her flesh, almost to the bone."

"Why after? Why not before?" Sarah asked.

Since she had taken the lead, Scott let her keep it. Content to allow Sarah to ask questions until she ran out, then he'd cover anything she missed. That way Emily wouldn't feel double-teamed.

"Don't think she was able to resist. Can't be definitive at this point, but I think she was drugged. Rohypnol, maybe?"

"The date rape drug?"

"Yes. Slip it to the victim in a drink and within twenty minutes the victim experiences a slowing of psychomotor performance, muscle relaxation, decreased blood pressure and in some instances, amnesia. She's in a euphoric daze, doesn't have the physical presence to resist and may forget any event that took place while she was under the effects of the drug."

"When will you know?"

"The autopsy will tell us."

"How long has she been dead?"

"Thirty-six to forty-eight hours."

"Cause?"

"Strangulation. It appears her larynx is crushed. The autopsy will confirm it."

Sarah scanned the body. "What caused all the bruising?"

"Somebody beat her, used something firm but with a soft shell around it, three to five inches wide from the looks of these bruises. Not a fist, there's no internal bruising. What you see is surface bruising only."

"He?"

"Yes. She was sexually abused."

"Raped, any semen?"

"Rape is a given. Otherwise, why feed her Rohypnol and tie her up? Semen we won't know until we get her to the morgue."

"What are those cuts on her inner thighs and in the center of her chest?" Small nicks or puncture wounds were visible in all three places. The one on her chest was centered between her breasts.

"Your guess is as good as mine, but as far as what caused them, I won't know until I get her in the morgue, but my guess is a knife. Right now I can't figure any significance. Maybe something will come to light when I examine them closer."

Sarah knew their purpose. They were superficial and they were knife wounds. She could almost feel the point of the knife pricking her skin as it turned and sliced up to remove her gym shorts and running bra thirteen years ago. A shiver ran up her spine as she turned away. She kept the information to herself for now.

"Thanks Emily. Send me a copy of your report," Scott said. He slipped one of his cards in her jacket pocket.

"Atlanta PD won't mind?"

"Why would they? It's your case."

"No, we're just assisting."

"I was told you guys are taking over." Emily glanced in Roy's direction then back at Scott.

"Well, let's see what else this lady can tell us." Emily bent over the body and went back to work.

Sarah and Scott turned and walked away. Emily called over her shoulder. "Agent James!"

"Yes?"

"Catch this one! He's brutal and my guess is he's not done."

"GIVE ME A MINUTE. I need to talk with Roy." Scott took off at a fast pace leaving Sarah standing alone, deep in thought. She felt she had missed something — something obvious, but what? It was right there, but she missed it.

An Asian man in a royal blue jacket walked past Sarah. A bell rang in her mind. She tried the same exercise she used with Janie, closed her eyes and pictured the body, analyzing every detail. Something clicked. Softly, in the back of her mind, the little voice whispered. She opened her eyes, smiled and turned around, returning to the body.

"Emily."

The ME jumped at the sound of Sarah's voice.

"Sorry, didn't mean to startle you."

"That's okay."

"Could the guy have beaten her open-handed, hard slaps, real hard and methodical?"

"Methodical?" the examiner asked.

"Yes. It looks as if he purposely avoided bruising her breasts, pubic region and her face."

"Areas he wanted to enjoy?"

"That's my guess," Sarah said.

"That is as good an explanation as any, but slapping? I don't know. I've never seen that before, at least not to this extent, but it fits. Is that significant?"

"Possibly. I attended a lecture recently by Dr. Henry Lee, a forensic pathologist. He indicated, depending on circumstances such as time of death in relation to a beating, that blood could form under the skin, leaving perfect prints of the perpetrator."

"Yes. I've read about successes Dr. Lee has had in solving some cases based on such prints."

"Could that work here? Provide us with a set of hand-prints, fingerprints?"

Emily looked at the bruises again. She lightly poked a couple. "Yes, that's a possibility. I'll contact Dr. Lee and get some guidance." She smiled. "You don't miss much do you, Ms. James."

"No, she doesn't."

It was Sarah's turn to jump. She hadn't heard Scott walk up behind her.

"You don't either, Dr. Benson." Scott grinned. "I owe you one. It is our case now. Call me when you have something."

SARAH AND SCOTT left the crime scene at a little after eight. The morning sun was breaking through the clouds, shining through their car's rear window, as Scott drove to the Syms home where Jessica's parents, fiancé and Anna Ricks were waiting for news. Scott requested Roy attend and the two agreed Sarah would be their spokesperson.

It was the first time Sarah had to tell a family that a loved one had been murdered. And it was more difficult than she imagined, especially when they insisted on being told the details of their daughter's death. The mother cried uncontrollably and the father openly sobbed. Anna and the fiancé wept while trying to console Jessica's parents.

"Did she suffer?" Mrs. Syms asked repeatedly.

Sarah had never faced a worse task. At least at the crime scene, she had been able to detach herself emotionally, switching to a professional, analytical mode. But here in the Syms elegant living room, face-to-face with distraught loved ones, no such retreat was possible.

At least she was allowed to omit telling the fiancé that Jessica had gone to the club looking for sex, in essence, causing her own death by picking the wrong man. Telling the grieving man would have served no purpose.

Before leaving their home, Scott and Roy assured the family that Jessica's killer would be brought to justice.

Walking down the Syms' drive to their cars, Scott and Roy decided they would question Gary Allen immediately.

Overhearing the decision, Sarah asked. "Are we going to call first?"

"No, and there is no "we." Roy and I will handle this. You go home and get some rest. Take my car. Roy can give me a lift over to your place to pick it up, later."

Jax met Sarah at the door when she got home. She knelt down and rubbed his back, scratched his ears and gave him a hug. The big fella always greeted her with a bark, some whining and a lot of stubby tail wagging. It didn't matter if she'd been gone for five minutes or five days, Jax met her at the door with the same sense of excitement.

Still scratching his ears, she thought aloud. "You are always happy. Never sulk, never get mad at me and always put me first, don't you, boy? Not like our friend, huh? Oh, well, so be it. I would have had to break it off soon anyway. It was fun while it lasted."

A few tears leaked out of the corners of her eyes. Jax whined and licked her cheeks.

Jax rolled over on his back with his legs straight up in the air so Sarah could rub his belly. "Besides, this will make it a little easier for me to deal with Hawkins. It won't be as complicated with Scott out of the picture.

"Hawkins has killed again, I can feel it. I knew there would be another victim if I waited too long. It's my fault, Jax, I should have acted sooner. Jessica was a pretty girl with a bright future. He left her body in a frigging Dumpster. Threw her away like a piece of trash."

Sarah was crying uncontrollably, an all consuming rage building inside her.

"Jax, I could feel her reaching out to me. Telling me it was Hawkins and to stop him. I intend to do just that. He will pay, I'll see to it. He won't hurt another woman."

After taking Jax for a walk, Sarah hopped in the bed, too exhausted to undress. She was asleep in seconds, knowing the nightmares wouldn't bother her this morning — she was too tired.

THE STIFLING COURTROOM was empty except for Sarah, the judge, his staff, the defense team and the prosecution. Usually spectators rotated in and out to observe the proceedings, but today they were no-shows. Sarah didn't blame them — in fact, she would like to skip out herself. For two and a half days, she sat waiting to be called to the stand. This was Sarah's fifth week on call without testifying.

The defense team, consisting of the defendant, Michelle Smith, the former chief financial officer of Mason Manufacturing, and a battery of high-powered attorneys, sat at a table in front of the railing separating the participants from the spectators. On their right sat the opposition, the chief prosecutor and his assistants, representatives of the U.S. Attorney's office. Beside them were rows of boxes full of evidence. During one of the more boring afternoons, Sarah had counted them, three rows, twenty boxes long and five boxes deep, over three hundred boxes of files. She wondered who indexed them and how the attorneys would ever locate a document needed to be introduced as evidence or used to support a testimony. As much fun as she was having counting boxes, Sarah was bored.

The only thing that kept her awake was the defense attorney's booming voice. On the other side of the coin, the prosecutor spoke in a low monotone that Sarah swore put the judge to sleep a few times.

The highlight of proceedings occurred when Marlene Mason, the principal owner and cofounder of the company in question, attended to monitor progress. The dark-haired, pale-skinned beauty always dressed the part of an upscale professional. Her Jimmy Choo heels clicked on the marble floor as she glided along with the graceful stride of a runway model. The entire proceedings seemed to come to a halt each time she entered or exited. When she arrived earlier, the judge stopped in mid-sentence, his eyes glued to each swing of her hips.

Sarah could see Marlene fidgeting and glancing at her watch. It was obvious she was getting antsy.

Not that Sarah felt differently. She was tired of sitting and waiting, watching the prosecutor blow an airtight case.

Jessica's funeral started at two and she planned to be there. No, she had to be there. Besides she'd had all she could take of this farce.

The judge must have felt the same way because he brought her out of her semiconscious boredom with a bang of his gavel. "Court is now recessed for lunch. We will resume at one,"

"Thank God! I'm out of here," Sarah mumbled as she stepped out into the aisle and moved toward the exit. With a change of heart, she stopped, turned around and made her way to the federal prosecutor.

He looked up from the briefcase he was filling with documents and gave Sarah a disdainful look.

"Have you actually bothered to review any of those documents?"

"I beg your pardon?"

"I asked if you have bothered to even scan those documents or are you content to just shuffle them in and out of your briefcase."

"What is that supposed to mean?" His voice shook in anger, exhibiting emotion for the first time since the trial began.

"It means that it doesn't sound like it. It also means I hope you aren't assigned as the prosecutor for the murder charge."

"Why is that, Ms. James?"

"Because, if you are, the deceased will be convicted and Michelle will walk away. Are you blowing this case on purpose?"

"What?"

"One of three things is happening here; you've been bought, you're incompetent or you're just plain lazy — or all three. You tell me!"

The short, stubby prosecutor sucked in so much air that Sarah thought a button would pop off the pinstriped vest under his suit coat. She was ready to lean right or left to dodge it.

His eyes bulged in anger and his face turned scarlet. He sputtered, and said almost incoherently, "No one has ever dared speak to me like that!"

"Then it's long overdue," Sarah said, making eye contact. "This is our chance to send a message to corporate executives. To tell them that the system is looking over their shoulder and if they cross the line, they will pay for their sins. Instead you're telling them, don't worry about it, the system doesn't care."

"How dare you question my integrity! Who are you to question how I handle this case? I don't care for your attitude."

"And I don't care for your piss-poor preparation and your lackadaisical performance."

The fifty-something, thirty-year veteran of the federal

prosecutor's office reached out as if he were about to grab Sarah, then stopped.

Regaining his self-control, he responded in a deep threatening tone, enunciating each word succinctly, as if talking to an errant child, "You have stepped across the line, young lady, and I will be calling your superior. I hope you've enjoyed working in the federal system."

"When you get him, tell him I'm skipping this afternoon's session." Sarah turned and walked away, head held high, her back straight. She had only taken a few steps when she heard heels clicking on the marble floor just behind her and felt a tap on her shoulder.

"Sarah! Just a moment, please."

Sarah turned and looked into Marlene Mason's eyes, the confident, self-assured eyes of a woman worth several hundred million dollars.

"I heard what you told that incompetent blowhard. Thank you."

The prosecutor was eavesdropping on their conversation. "Thanks. Unfortunately, I'm afraid I didn't accomplish anything."

"More than you think. I've sat through this mockery of a trial for weeks and I'm coming unglued. That bitch stole half a million dollars from my company, and he's letting the defense make it sound like it was my fault."

Sarah nodded.

Marlene smiled, "Don't worry about his threat. I have a feeling he doesn't have a lot of pull, besides, that buffoon better start worrying about his own job. I'm going to make a few calls, myself.

"If you're interested, I'd like to talk with you about coming to work for me. Mason Enterprises could use you. I like tough ladies with integrity and attitude — we're a rare breed."

"Thank you. I like what I'm doing for now, but I'll keep the offer in mind."

"Do that." Marlene glanced over her shoulder at the prosecutor then back at Sarah. "I should have done something myself. Now that you got the ball rolling, I intend to. He will be off this case by morning. You can take my word for it."

CHAPTER 12

THE WHITE-COLUMNED CHURCH sat on a hill at the intersection of Peachtree Road and West Wesley. Splendid stained glass windows depicting the life of Christ added to the spiritual environment that invited all of God's children to come inside and worship the Father.

The solemn beauty of the church captivated Sarah as she walked toward it in a long-sleeved, ankle-length, black dress. Overcome, she silently repeated the Lord's Prayer and then quoted the twenty-third Psalm, which seemed apropos for her task.

As she joined others walking along the sidewalk, Sarah overhead expressions of sympathy for the family and anguish over Jessica's brutal murder. It was unusual for an FBI agent to attend the funeral of a victim in an active case, but Sarah could not stay away.

Of everyone attending the service, Sarah was sure she was the only one who truly knew how Jessica suffered.

She entered the sanctuary and found a seat at the end of one of the mahogany pews. Once inside, she studied the stained glass windows surrounding the choir loft. With tears trickling from the corners of her eyes, she focused on the glass mural of Jesus reaching out — to her.

"If not for the grace of God, he would have done the same to me. Thank you for sparing me, Lord. Help me to understand why. What purpose do you have for me? Vengeance is mine! Lord, please forgive me," Sarah's silent prayer echoed in her mind.

Regaining her composure, Sarah joined the procession of mourners walking to the front of the church. When her turn came, she looked into the casket at Jessica's once-pretty face, now still and paled in death. She felt Jessica's presence, her spirit and sensed Callie was there, too. They were asking for closure. Their spirits were telling Sarah they would not be at peace until she dealt with their murderer, Greg Hawkins.

AFTER THE FUNERAL, Sarah didn't join the procession going to the cemetery, instead she called the office.

'Darcy, I need to meet with Scott. Does he have any time this afternoon?"

"He's free after four-thirty."

"Put me down for five."

Scott looked tired. His face was drawn and pale, and his eyes, usually alive and sparkling, were dull and glazed over from a lack of sleep. Kidnappings, especially those that resulted in murder always took a heavy toll on agents. They took it personally, feeling a sense of failure. Scott Justice was no exception. Sarah knew that he would not rest until he identified and caught the man responsible for Jessica's murder.

As she weighed her words, waiting to begin, she looked around his office, noticing for the first time that the only personal touches were a small cactus sitting on the credenza and a Bose Wave Radio beside a nondescript lamp on a small table. Framed prints of Atlanta landmarks hung on the walls: Stone Mountain, Kennesaw Battlefield, Downtown and Turner Field. The bookcases were filled with Bureau manuals, legal texts and other work related materials. She guessed the reason she had never noticed this before was the fact that the décor was right in character for his office persona. The radio clock read 4:49 P.M., she was a little early. Sarah was trying to decide how to begin when Scott spoke, "You went to Jessica's funeral?"

"Yes." She wondered if the prosecutor had called. "How did you know?"

"You're dressed for a funeral and have a somber look on your face. Do you think that was wise? It's still an open case," he reminded her.

"Probably not, but it was something I needed to do."

"What about the trial?"

"I skipped this afternoon," Sarah responded.

"Skipped? Why? Who said it was okay for you to duck out on your responsibilities?"

"No one. Me. Jessica's funeral was more important."

"So you just gave the court the finger?" Scott's eyes looked like two pieces of coal.

Her vendetta against Hawkins, her vow, was creating a wedge between Scott and her. Sarah realized it would probably get worse. She could make things right between them if she tried. All she had to do was stop. Let Hawkins self-destruct. It would be the prudent thing to do.

Suddenly the air seemed still, frigid. Sarah was having trouble breathing. She had to choose. Which was more important, sacred—Scott and her oath to the Bureau or her vow to Callie, and now Jessica. She wanted to believe the system would work and would stop Hawkins but Jessica's death was too fresh in her mind. And Sarah would not, could not attend another funeral. She knew there would be others if she didn't stop him. Her heart felt laden in her chest. Sarah decided she had to stick to the plan and do whatever she had to, to end it.

"How is the investigation into Jessica's murder going?" She asked.

"You know I can't discuss that with you."

"Sure you can. I may not be officially on the case, but I'm still part of the team, aren't I?" She made eye contact, challenging him. "I was at the scene when the body was found, at your request, right? And I did conduct the interview that got the first real lead, didn't I?"

"Yes, to all of the above. But you have become so obsessed with this idea that Hawkins is Allen and Allen is Hawkins that you have lost your objectivity. Isn't that why you had to go to the funeral?"

"Yes," she admitted.

"Then you cannot be a part of this investigation and I cannot, no, will not, include you in any briefings on it."

"So, I'm no longer part of the team?

"Not the Jessica Syms investigative team. No."

Silence was one of Scott's most effective tools. His silence was more intimidating than the harshest of words because most people were unable to cope with it. Rather than sitting in the quiet, they would rattle on, saying more than they intended. Sarah needed this meeting to appear to follow that pattern, so she let the silence drag on for minutes before breaking it.

"I need to tell you some things. When I'm through, I hope you'll understand. If you don't, I'll resign," she rattled off.

Scott sat up straighter, his eyes darkened. "What, exactly, have you done, Agent James?"

Sarah told him about her outburst in the courtroom, re-iterating her conversation with the federal prosecutor, word for word. And then her conversation with Marlene Mason.

"That explains an e-mail I received about an hour ago. A new prosecutor has been assigned to the case and Edwards is on leave."

"So, Marlene had made good on her prediction. Just

goes to prove that money and power can still manipulate the system, huh? And if one has enough of both, he or she can control it."

"You mean like Hawkins' father does? This is different. Obviously, Ms. Mason does have clout and she's using it to the good of the system."

"This time, you mean. To get what she needs now. Don't get me wrong, I like Marlene, at least what I know of her. And, I certainly respect her, but the next time she uses her influence, it may not be for the good of anything, other than Marlene Mason."

"I don't see how you can be so cynical of a woman you say you like and respect. This time you ought to be thankful for Mason's clout. You owe her. While she was destroying Edwards, she made you out to be a hero for uncovering the scam and pointing out the errors in the way the case is being handled. Even so, I don't like the way you handled the situation. Agents do not mouth off to Federal Prosecutors, understood?"

"Even if they're wrong?"

"Sarah! Let it drop. My plate's full right now. I've got a murder to solve."

"There is something else."

He waited for her to go on.

There was a brief hesitation before Sarah began talking. "One morning a couple of months ago, I literally bumped into Hawkins coming out of the Bank of America across the street. I recognized him immediately."

"And?" Scott's voice was quiet, steely. His eyes as dark as Sarah had ever seen them.

"I've been tailing him off and on ever since. I found out where he worked, where he lived and that he's using the name Gary Allen. Got prints and they matched."

"How?"

"Easy to get them, easier to use the Bureau system to make the identification."

"What?" The word and his tone jabbed at her, deadly, like a poison dart.

You think I'm some over-imaginative female without any brains, no guts? You think I've lost sight of my training, my common sense? Good for you, Scott Justice. That's exactly what I want you to think. I can't believe that I thought I loved you or you loved me.

"I used the system to run name, background and criminal searches and the lab ran some prints. It's all here." She held up a thick file that had been sitting in her lap.

"You did that without authorization? Without telling me what you were up to. Why didn't you mention this when we talked the other day? Damn, Sarah I trusted you! You promised me that you wouldn't go off on a vendetta. You are not the Lone Ranger!"

"Would you have given me authorization?"

"We'll never know will we? But I always listen to my subordinates."

Sarah's head snapped up. "Scott, you know what he did to me. I have to do this. You've got to understand."

"Yes, I do. And I can't pretend to understand what you've been through or how you've lived with it. But, Sarah you excluded me, personally, when you chose to withhold this from me — that hurts...but here, now, I've got to assess what you've done from the Bureau perspective. You've violated my trust as your AIC and used Bureau resources for personal reasons without approval — violations that could result in suspension or possible termination. Are you so blinded by revenge that you can't see that? Allen is not who you think he is, accept it."

"But he is! Scott I'm telling you Allen is Hawkins and he is a serial rapist, a vicious murderer and he's here, on our beat — our jurisdiction. He has to be stopped."

"Sarah, listen to what you're saying, think about what you've done. You could have put our entire case in jeopardy. You're losing all perspective. You're becoming a vigilante!

I'm not even sure you have any business being in the Bureau."

Sarah was shocked at that statement. Then anger took control. "Bullshit! My field record speaks for itself. I'm one of the best agents you've got. And you know it."

"You were, up until now. You've abused the Bureau trust, my trust."

"No, I haven't! I've taken initiative, something agents are trained to do. Scott, the man vowed to kill me. When I saw him, there was no way I was going to sit around and wait for him to come after me. The Bureau taught me to act, not to react, if I want to stay alive."

"Sarah, Gary Allen is not Hawkins. How many times do I have to tell you that?"

Sarah set a thick file on Scott's desk. "Allen is Hawkins. If you were half as good an agent as you think you are, or if you gave a tinker about me, personally, or as your subordinate, you would have checked it out."

The file on Scott's desk was momentarily forgotten. "Are you questioning my professional judgment?"

"Yes." Sarah lowered her head. "I see it doesn't bother you that I'm questioning whether you care about Sarah James or not. All you're worried about is your precious reputation."

Scott slammed his fist on the desk. "Get out of my office before I do something I may regret."

"No, let's finish it, now."

"Are you trying to force me to ask for your resignation?"

Sarah stood up and held a sealed envelope containing her resignation, in her hand. "Why wait? At least take a look at the file. I ran prints from a glass that Gary Allen left on a table. Check the dates and times. Go through my notes. See when Hawkins disappeared and Allen materialized. The where and when is the key. Follow both of their careers and exploits, the women they've abused and damaged. Look at Callie's picture. Compare it to Jessica's and to his first victim, a lady from Atlanta. It all links back to her. That's when it all started. There's even a profile from the Bureau psychiatrist, outlining an Anger-Retaliator Rapist. It's Hawkins to a T. Read it and you'll see why I reacted so fast when you described Jessica Syms to me."

"You did this, even contacted the Bureau Psychiatrist, unauthorized?"

"Is that all you can think about — that I did it without your precious approval?" Her voice shook, her eyes blazed. "Well. You're damn right. If I hadn't, it would not have gotten done. Think about it, you would never have approved anything. Hell, you still don't believe Allen's the guy who caused my best friend to kill herself." She stared at him, her eyes daring him to respond. "He killed Jessica Syms." She pointed to the file. "Read that!"

He picked up the file, holding it out between them, like something distasteful. "This proves my point, Sarah."

"You know what? Screw the Bureau, and screw you!" She laid the envelope on top of the file, made eye contact with Scott, "Thirty days or immediate, it's your choice."

Sarah stormed out of the office, slamming his door so hard that one of the cool, impersonal prints of Atlanta fell off his wall, a thin, diagonal crack now reaching from corner to corner.

THE BLACK 350 Z rumbled north on Peachtree Dunwoody Road. Alan Jackson and Jimmy Buffet were singing their new hit on the car's stereo, something about it being five o'clock somewhere and Margaritaville.

Sarah planned to cut across Hammond Drive to Ashford Dunwoody into Hawkins' neighborhood just after dark.

The twilight added to the beauty of the suburban neighborhoods she passed. Bradford pears that would have blossoms as thick as snow in a few weeks lined the Dunwoody streets. Soon, brightly colored spring flowers blooming around homes would compliment the azalea and dogwood blossoms in the yards. Sarah pictured the colors of spring and could almost smell the fragrance of flowers and freshly cut grass. And she imagined the squeals of children playing in their yards while their dogs barked, joining in the fun.

The day had gone pretty much as planned, although she certainly hadn't intended to unload on the prosecutor. In retrospect, she realized that the anticipation of Jessica's funeral and the meeting with Scott had frayed her nerves, triggering her rash behavior. All in all, she felt losing it with the DA had served a purpose. He was gone and perhaps his replacement would see to it Smith got punished, sending a message to corporate crooks around the country.

Everything seemed to be falling into place. First the chance encounter with Hawkins at the restaurant and now the blow up with the prosecutor. Neither could have gone better if she'd planned them. And best of all, Hawkins still hadn't recognized her. He hadn't linked Sarah James to JJ Johnson. The scene at the restaurant was because she looked familiar. He probably spotted her while she was shadowing him and had a sense of recognition at the restaurant.

Sarah knew that when Scott put it all together, the restaurant scene, the threatening phone calls and the info in the file, he would realize Hawkins was after her, stalking her and she was in real danger.

Then he would understand she had been right in tailing the guy, running the record search, and putting out the alert. He'd tear up her resignation, ignoring the broken rules. If not, perhaps he'd discipline her by ordering her to take a week or so off without pay. Which wouldn't be all bad, she could use the time...to finish up her plan.

He definitely wouldn't understand about tonight. She was breaking the law and he could never find out.

Sarah turned into Hawkins' subdivision and cleared her mind so she could concentrate on the task at hand. After scouting through the neighborhood to be certain that neither Atlanta's finest nor the Bureau were staking out Hawkins' home, Sarah pulled into the driveway of a vacant house, a block away from his. After parking between hedges that provided privacy from the neighbors, she pulled the small gym bag with her extra clothes in it off the back seat. Turning sideways in her seat, she stretched her long legs across the console onto the passenger side.

"Damn these tight quarters. I should have stopped somewhere to change." She slipped her dress up around her waist, kicked off her heels and then slid her black panties down her legs and over her feet. She quickly put on a fresh pair of panties and twisting and squirming in the small front seat, pulled a pair of black jeans up her legs and over her thighs and hips. She pulled up the zipper and buttoned them. Then she pulled the dress over her head and took off her black bra.

Headlights blinded her when they beamed through the windshield. She slid down in the seat to keep the lights from reflecting off her bare upper body.

After the car passed, she sat back up and slipped a dark sweatshirt over her head and retrieved her fanny pack from the backseat. She unzipped it and checked to be sure that she hadn't forgotten anything. Inside was her Glock-22, two clips of .40 S&W ammunition, lock-picks, latex gloves and a mini cassette recorder. The gun was a precaution, just in case Hawkins came home early. She stuffed the bra and panties she had just taken off into the fanny pack and zipped it closed.

Stepping out of the car, she buckled on the fanny pack, reached back into the car and retrieved her Braves cap and put it on. Lastly, she slipped on a dark rain jacket. She checked her watch. He ought to be at The Watering Hole by now.

It was tonight or never because after Scott reviewed the file, both she and Hawkins would be under surveillance. To catch him, and to protect her. Planting the evidence and doing a little reconnaissance were key elements to her plan. Tonight she was crossing the line.

SHE BEGAN WALKING down the street at a fast pace. She wanted people to think she was just a lady out for some after-dinner exercise. The weeks of scouting the area had paid dividends. Not only did she know Hawkins' schedule but she also knew his neighborhood and his neighbors' habits. For instance, his backyard neighbor did not get home until after nine Mondays and Wednesdays, and that Hawkins had a six-foot privacy hedge surrounding his backyard. And she located a vacant house near Hawkins.

On her second trip around the block, she walked up the driveway of Hawkins' neighbor and continued through the yard. Once in the back, she wedged through a small gap in the hedge into Hawkins' yard. She crouched behind the nearest shrub for several minutes.

Silently, staying low she crept across the brick patio to the back door. Checking her watch as she put on the latex gloves, Sarah had an hour and ten minutes to get in, out and back on the street before the neighbors returned. Pulling the picks out of the fanny pack, she had the door unlocked in seconds.

Staying low, she moved inside and listened. All was quiet — no moaning or groaning. Apparently Hawkins and his Wednesday night conquest weren't home yet. She had three minutes to get to the control panel and deactivate the alarm. The security company had a sign in the front yard. With their name, it had been simple enough to tap into their system from the office and retrieve his code and panel locations. The closest panel was on the kitchen wall by the door leading into the garage. There were two others, one by the front door and another just inside the master bedroom.

She hurried to the one in the kitchen, punched in the

code and a long beep sounded, noting — code accepted, alarm deactivated.

Sarah took the penlight from her pack and began scouting the house. Even in the poor light she could tell it was beautiful.

A crystal chandelier hung from a high ceiling in the foyer. The entry had a polished tile floor, a circular staircase leading to the second floor with a landing overlooking the entry. The foyer was decorated with a five-foot oriental vase and a colorful impressionist painting. "Yang" was the signature barely legible in the lower right corner. Sarah wished she could turn on the chandelier to get a better view.

She scouted the rest of the house. Downstairs, she found the kitchen, family room, dining room, a breakfast area off the kitchen, an office and the master bedroom. Upstairs were three more bedrooms, an exercise room with a big screen TV, a stereo, a treadmill, a Precor elliptical trainer, a small whirlpool and a sauna. She checked her watch again. She was down to fifty-five minutes.

She picked up the phone in the office and dialed her phone number, let it ring and hung up when the answering machine picked up. Then she went through the desk looking for anything significant; names, addresses, phone numbers, and rental documents for homes or houses in the area, any kind of clue as to where he had killed Jessica Syms. She found nothing.

Picking up the phone again, she hit redial and waited. When the message ended with a beep, she held the receiver next to the fanny pack and pushed the play button on the recorder inside and played the entire message for the first time. Hawkins voice said, "Hi Babe. You bitch! I'll get you one day. Believe me, your ass is mine!" Sarah was upping the ante.

In the master bedroom she checked every drawer, under the bed, in the closets and even searched the bathroom. Nothing. She moved upstairs. She found nothing of interest in any of the bedrooms. The exercise room was the only area left. She had decided not to bother with the rest of the main floor because the rooms were too public.

The only area to check in the exercise room was a small closet next to the door leading into the sauna. Inside, she found towels, terry cloth robes, and condoms.

There was nothing of value, no clues, in the closet. She wasn't sure what she was looking for, but whatever it was, either it wasn't there or she missed it. There were no hidden panels in the sauna. Discouraged, she decided to go downstairs and plant the evidence. Shining the beam of light around the room one more time before giving up, she spotted something. There were two small panel doors by the whirlpool. She crouched down and removed the first door and discovered valves and controls for the whirlpool. After putting that door back in place she opened the second.

An area the same size as the other, about two feet square, contained five shoe boxes. She slid the closest one out and opened the lid. Inside was an array of panties and bras. Lying on top were a red lace bra and matching panties. The souvenirs that profilers say serial rapists often collect.

Sarah opened another box. It also contained more panties and bras. She picked up a pair of panties. "Ooohh, No!" She dropped them as if they were on fire. Sarah began to shiver as she forced herself to pick them up again. Looking closely she could she see that the panties were cut up the front from each leg to the waistband?

These were cut off, not taken off. A long-suppressed memory rose, unbidden, into her mind. She remembered Hawkins using the curved blade of a knife to slice through her running shorts. She reached down and lightly rubbed the inside of her thigh, through her jeans, where he had pricked her skin with the point of the blade.

She willed herself to relax, to calm down. She couldn't lose control, not now. Sarah picked up a bra and saw that it was still fastened in the back, but was cut open between the cups. She inspected the other panties and bras in the two boxes. All had been cut off their owners. A numbing thought entered her mind.

She checked her watch. She didn't have time to look in any more of the boxes but she couldn't stop herself. She had to know if he had kept them. Her hands shook as she pulled the other boxes out. She felt lightheaded. Her hands were shaking. Sweat beaded on her upper lip as she looked through the contents of each until she got to the bottom of the last box.

"Oh. My. God!" Sarah gagged. Bile rose up into her throat. She had to fight being sick.

Inside were two pairs of running shorts and two jogging bras. All sliced open to remove them from their owners, Callie and JJ.

Sarah felt the fanny pack to be sure the Glock was still inside. "I'm going to shoot the bastard the minute he walks through the door," she whispered.

She sat back on her haunches and put her head between her knees and willed herself not to cry. When she finally stopped shaking, and her stomach settled, Sarah put everything back into the shoeboxes and carefully returned them to the secret compartment, arranging them just as she had found them and then replaced the panel door.

Of course, she couldn't report what she had discovered in an illegal search. But, there will be a legal search, and these will be discovered. She guaranteed it.

Sarah tapped the fanny pack, knowing the evidence would be out of place with his souvenirs, but where? After recalling what she had seen in the house she mentally picked the spot, stood up, and went back downstairs to the master bedroom. She remembered looking through a row of shoeboxes in his closet.

She opened the shoebox containing cuff links, cummerbunds and suspenders wrapped in tissue paper. She lifted the contents out. Then Sarah took her black bra and panties out of her fanny pack and put them in the empty box. DNA analysis would confirm they were hers. She placed the original contents, still wrapped in tissue paper back in the box, adding the extra set of lock picks she had in her fanny pack. She had used that set to pick the back door of her house and had purposely scratched the surface of the area around the key slots of the doorknob and the dead bolt. Again to set Hawkins up for a fall — how else could he get her underwear, if not from a break-in? Now she needed a pair of his shoes. She picked up a pair of broken-in Rockports, tucked them under her arm and carefully rearranged the remaining shoes to fill the space.

Sarah retraced her steps to the back door, noticing the clock in the den, 8:49. She was behind schedule. She opened the back door.

"Throw it to me, Johnny." A child's voice called from the other side of the hedge.

"Catch!" Another yelled.

Sarah froze. The neighbors were home early.

Just then she saw a football come sailing over the hedge. "I'll get it. Mr. Allen won't mind." A small head poked through the same gap in the hedge that Sarah had used. The head swiveled, looking for the ball.

"There it is." The little body leaped through the hedge and raced toward the ball.

Sarah pulled the door closed and dropped to the floor before he could see her. She couldn't afford to wait for the neighbors to go to bed. Hawkins might come home first. She crawled on her belly to the front door, stood up and activated the alarm. Then she walked out, locking the door behind her.

SARAH WENT STRAIGHT HOME, played the message and smiled. *Perfect! Now, I've got to finish up.*

After taking off her shoes, she slid a plastic baggie over each foot and then put on the shoes she had taken from Hawkins' closet. Going out her back door, she walked around the yard, making sure to step in the topsoil beneath a window, and returned to the back door.

She went inside and walked around the house as if she were searching for the master bedroom. Satisfied, she entered the bedroom and went directly to her dresser and opened and closed several drawers. She purposely left the one containing her lingerie slightly open, the edge of a bra causing it not to close. Then she walked into her closet, squatted down in front of the laundry basket and rearranged the clothes inside. Finished, she turned and retraced her steps to the back door. She sat on the threshold and took off Hawkins' Rockports and placed them in a plastic grocery bag that she'd left by the door. She took the bag out to her garage and placed it on the backseat of her old Suburban, in plain sight, beside three similar bags filled with groceries. She had purchased the groceries that afternoon for her trip the next day, and purposely left them in the Suburban. She removed a couple of grocery items from the other bags and placed them on top of the shoes. Leaving the bags on the seat, in plain sight, would discourage anyone from looking through them. She'd dispose of Hawkins' shoes in the morning before leaving town.

She went back into the house, used scissors to cut the latex gloves into small shreds and flushed them down the toilet. Then she removed the tape from her cassette recorder, cut it up and flushed it, also. She returned the recorder to the desk in her makeshift office.

She took Jax outside and sat on her front steps. Pulling her cell phone out of her pouch she dialed the number. The Bureau operator answered on the second ring. "This is Agent Sarah James. I know the phone monitors were removed a few weeks ago, but I have had another call, a different message, and may have had a break in. Yes, that will be my next call. Thank you."

She dialed Scott's home number. There was no answer. Next, she tried his cell. "This is Sarah, I just reported another call. It's a new message. And I think I've had a break-in."

"I'm on my way. Why didn't you call me first?"

"Just following procedure, sir!"

Scott hung up without a word.

Scott arrived seconds ahead of the crime-tech van and the first police cruiser. Sarah and Jax were waiting on the front porch.

"What happened?" Scott took control.

"I got home about seven, changed clothes and took Jax out for a walk. We were gone about an hour and when I got back the message light on the phone was blinking. While I was listening, I noticed some black dirt just inside my back door. It definitely wasn't there when I left. I looked through the house but didn't notice anything different at first. Then on a second walk through I saw black dirt in my bedroom."

"Anything missing, out of place?"

"I didn't check. I didn't want to disturb anything before I called, and you and our guys were on the scene."

"Good. Did you spot anything?"

She hesitated as if she was thinking. "Well, it's dumb, but there is one thing."

"What?"

"In my closet, the one off the master bath, my dirty clothes basket, there is something different."

"Yes?"

"When I got home, I changed clothes. Dropped every-thing I wore today in the basket. The black dress was on top. I don't like my panties and bras to be on top." She shrugged and rolled her eyes. "You know, sitting out, exposed."

"So?"

"The dress is on the floor beside the basket now."

"Maybe you missed the basket?"

"Maybe, but I don't think so. I'm always careful to cover

my lingerie."

Scott shrugged. Then he sent the lab crew into the house to go to work and asked Sarah to wait outside. Before he went in he looked at Jax. "You sure he didn't track in the dirt?"

"No, I don't think so." She responded.

The five crime techs were thorough, checking through every nook and cranny of the house and outside every door and window. They finished in two hours and gave Scott a preliminary report before they left. "The message is new. The call is still too short to trace but we'll try. I'll compare the current voiceprints to the prior messages to check for a match."

One of the female techs spoke up. "Someone entered through the back door. He or she used picks to open both locks. My guess is that it was an amateur. There were faint scratches around the key slots of both locks. There isn't any rust or dirt around or in the scratches so it was recent, probably tonight."

The third tech took over. "We found a footprint in the soil outside the window looking into the den. The same soil was inside the door and in several spots around the house. It grew fainter until we got to the clothesbasket in the master closet. I think he squatted down to look in it."

"You keep saying he?" Sarah pointed out.

"That's my guess. The print under the window was at least a size ten. My guess it's a Rockport man's shoe."

"Rockport?"

"Yes, the treads." He smiled. "And the impression spelled it out. Their logo is on the bottom of the shoe."

The lead tech took his turn.

"Good work, Ms. James. I don't know that I would have noticed the dirt inside the door. And you made our job easier by staying outside until we got here."

"Thanks. I wouldn't have seen the dirt either, if it hadn't been for the message. It put me on alert."

The female tech nodded then looked over at Scott. "That all, Mr. Justice?"

"Yes. How soon can you have a final report?"

"Agents take priority — first thing in the morning."

After the crime techs had departed, Scott asked Sarah to look through the house again, to see if anything was missing. He sat at the table in the breakfast nook and drank coffee while she did so. He was on his second cup when she screamed.

"Scott!"

He raced to the bedroom. Sarah was kneeling in the closet. "My panties and bra, the black ones I wore today, they're not here. He took them!"

Scott pulled Sarah up by her shoulders, turned her around and took her in his arms. She clutched to him as if he was a life preserver and she was adrift in the ocean. Neither one moved for several minutes. She wondered if the safe hug would turn into an embrace. Would his hands slip down and pull her in tighter? Would he kiss her? God, she hoped so.

He answered her unspoken questions by letting go and stepping back. "Make a description of the items, color, manufacturer, any specifics to help identify them. Is anything else missing?"

"No. I don't have a lot of valuables. No silver or anything like that."

"Anything else catch your eye, look out of place?"

She walked over to her dresser and pointed at two small drawers. "These are open. I think they were closed when I left."

"You sure? When was the last time you opened them?"

"Tonight when I changed. That's what's suspicious. I only got panties out." She pointed at the drawer on the left. "I didn't go into that one." She pointed to the other, the edge of a bra strap sticking out.

"You sure?" Scott asked.

"Yes. I didn't need to open it, I'm not wearing one,"

Sarah replied.

"Really? I didn't notice." He smiled.

The corners of Sarah's mouth eased into a bright, half smile. "Really. And I'm not about to prove it to you." Sarah's eyes twinkled and her mouth formed an impish, half grin.

Scott hesitated, stepped away, turned and started out of the room, "We need to talk." When he got to the kitchen he opened the refrigerator and got two Diet Cokes out, sat one on the counter for Sarah, and leaned against the wall, holding the other.

Sarah sat on a stool facing him. "Okay, let's talk."

"We've done all we can here tonight. Sarah, from what I've seen, I honestly don't think you're in danger."

She tilted her head, said nothing, surprise evident in her eyes, and waited for him to continue. "So, I'm going home to get some rest. You need to clean up this mess and then do the same. "

"Okay. I'm not in danger? All of this means nothing? Is that what you're saying?"

"Basically, yes. I don't think this break-in is related to any of our cases. I believe your gut instinct was right when you initially reported the calls. We've got a pervert that's infatuated with you. No one is stalking you."

Sarah bristled, her eyes narrowed as she eased off the stool.

"Oh, really? You don't think I'm being stalked. And your professional assessment is that the calls are just some kid's sick joke. Well, I disagree. But, in the event I'm wrong, I apologize for wasting your time and putting the crime techs to all the unnecessary work. Please tell them that for me. Since all this is nothing, you might as well leave, boss."

"Sarah, I didn't say it was nothing. I'm just saying it's possible that you're overreacting."

"So, it's common for a woman to get threatening phone calls and to have someone break into her house and steal her panties and bra? Ones she just took off. Scott, one of us needs to look up stalking in the manual." She paused, staring defiantly into Scott's deep brown eyes.

"Agent James, I've about had it with your attitude. I know you're concerned, I am too, so believe me, this break-in and the phone calls will not be treated lightly. I told you what I suspect will be the end result of our investigation. Until we prove it, this will be given priority. You are an agent, after all, one of us. Now, cool down, before you say something we'll both regret."

His voice softened. "I repeat, you didn't waste anybody's time. Sarah, I think it's a good idea if you take some time off, starting now."

"Am I being suspended?

"No."

"How long are we talking about?"

"Plan on reporting back to work a week from Monday. The envelope you gave me this afternoon, which I assume is your resignation from the Bureau, will be waiting on you, unopened, when you get back. If you want me to open it then, so be it."

"May I ask why I'm taking the week off?"

"You need some time to reevaluate this obsession you have about Hawkins being Allen."

"Do I have any choice?"

"No."

Considering the topic closed. Scott took his notebook out of his pocket. "Now, let me give you something to think about while you're gone. If you have your head screwed on right, when you get back, I want you on the Syms case."

She nodded, saying nothing.

"Giving you the benefit of a doubt, I'm going to share what we have so far. Run it through that mental computer of yours and see what you can come up with, okay?"

Sarah nodded a second time, trying to keep the surprise out of her eyes.

"We talked to several of Jessica's coworkers. All of them

confirmed what we already knew. Jessica was intelligent, professional and career minded. She didn't fool around and she loved her fiancé. He was the only thing she put ahead of her job.

"Then we talked to the two women that took her to The Watering Hole. They're sure that Jessica left the bar alone on the night she disappeared, and planned to go straight home. Several guys hit on her that night, but none scored and in fact, none of the conversations lasted more than a minute or two. I showed them Allen's picture, nothing. They couldn't say if he was or was not one of her want-to-be suitors that night.

"Were either of the women aware that she planned to return last Wednesday?" Sarah asked.

"No. Only Anna knew that. Now, back to the first visit. Anna Ricks confirmed Jessica was home by eight-thirty."

"Talking about the two Wednesdays gets confusing, doesn't it?" Sarah added.

"Yes, but we are trying to see if one relates to the other. If she met whoever murdered her on the first visit."

Sarah leaned forward. She didn't want to miss a word.

"Roy and I met Allen for lunch yesterday. When we introduced ourselves, he immediately recognized me from the scene at the restaurant. He brought it up, and apologized for his behavior, that night. I thought he was sincere."

Scott held up his palms. "Hold it, I know, before you say it. It might have been legit or could have been because I'm an FBI agent, who knows. Anyway, he said he thought he recognized you from one of his client's offices and wanted to say hello. Since he couldn't recall your name, he used the old standby approach, haven't we met? Or, don't I know you? He didn't remember which. Your response shocked him and he reacted accordingly. Considering the circumstances, I can't say that I blame him."

Sarah wanted to speak up, but held her tongue.

"He said there was no excuse for his behavior and asked

me to express his apologies to the lady. I assured him that the matter was forgotten. I didn't volunteer your name or that you were an agent. Roy didn't know who he was talking about and didn't ask me about it then or later. He probably will though."

"What will you tell him?"

"Tell him the specifics of the incident and say it was just a date, no one special."

"Then I asked Allen about his background; profession, how long he'd been in Atlanta, where he moved from, his education and marital status. You already know all that or think you do. So, I won't cover it now.

Scott looked at his notebook. "Here, I'll let you read my notes from the interview."

Mr. Allen, have you ever been arrested or convicted of a crime?

No, I've never been convicted of any crime. I've had a few scrapes with the law, but nothing that stuck. Greedy women were always involved, scorned and looking for money.

Does that mean that you're wealthy?

Let's just say, I've invested wisely and manage to live well. I've got a house in Dunwoody, drive a Mercedes, and wear Armani suits. The chicks see that and want some of it. They put out in hopes I'll marry them. When they realize that I'm not the marrying type, they cry wolf to the cops, thinking I'll offer them some cash to go away.

(Lt. Nelson asked) So you paid them off? How many are we talking about?

I haven't given any of them a dime. As to how many women we're talking about, that's confidential. That is all I'm going to say on the subject, unless you have a specific purpose for needing that information.

(Justice asked) You didn't answer my question.

Have you ever been arrested?

Yes I did, I said I'm not discussing it without my attorney. Suffice it to say, I've never been convicted of a crime. I'm sure the FBI has access to my records. If you want it badly enough you can get it.

When Sarah finished the first page of notes, Scott added, "We didn't press the issue. He was right. We can get his records out of the database, and that takes care of the general questions. From there, we asked about The Watering Hole and Jessica Syms."

Sarah skipped reading the questions to focus on Allen's answers.

Yes, I'm a regular at The Watering Hole. I go there for the women and I seldom leave alone. I picked it because it has a higher-class clientele than most places. The women are professional, classy, and mostly single.

No, I don't remember a Jessica Syms.

(I showed him her picture and he immediately recognized her.)

Oh yes, I remember her. Who wouldn't? She's a knockout. One hot chick!

No, I only met her that once. Last Wednesday night. She followed me home.

I didn't have to say anything. She came on to me.

She was looking to get laid, and who was I to argue. No man would turn that down. We left the bar within fifteen minutes of her saying hello, if that tells you anything.

Oh yes, we had sex; made it a couple of times before calling it a night.

She left around midnight.

I have no idea where she went after leaving my place.

No, I don't think I'll ever see her again. When she left, she told me that she was engaged and us getting together was a one time thing.

No, I didn't think it was odd. I'm a good looking guy. She wanted a last fling, who better?

She's dead, murdered? No, I didn't know. How would I? I didn't even know her last name until you told me.

Yes, I'm sure Wednesday night was the first time we had ever met.

Your witness is wrong. I did not talk to that woman the week before.

That doesn't make sense. Why would the woman tell me no one week and then jump my bones the next?

Sarah looked up, "Did you believe him?"

"No, he'd met her before that night, we know that, and he wasn't surprised she'd been murdered. I think he's lying about that to keep from being involved. But, that doesn't mean he's the killer."

"So where are you?" She asked.

"Suspicious? He was too prepared, but I don't think he's our guy."

"How can you say that, Scott? He was the last person seen with her. He admits that she went home with her. And no one has seen her since," Sarah demanded.

"No one saw her after Allen that we know of, Sarah!"

"Bullshit. He's our guy and you know it."

"No, I don't," Scott replied.

"I can't believe what I'm hearing. Just let me read the rest of his answers," Sarah said.

Yes, I remember seeing the article about a woman's body being found but I didn't read it. I don't like reading about murders. I guess, I think that if I don't read about them, they don't exist, naïve, huh?

No, I didn't know she was engaged until she was ready to leave, but it wouldn't have mattered. She was horny, and I'm not one to deny a beautiful woman. What can I say?

Yes, I noticed the engagement ring but I didn't ask her about it. I didn't want to mess up a good thing. Her reasons weren't any of my business. One night stands are my forte. Sometimes women tell me their problems, or the reason they are on the prowl, but I don't really listen because I don't care. Jessica was one of those that didn't.

"That's it." Scott took his notebook back and closed it. "Other than a gut feeling that he was lying about knowing she was dead, I found nothing to justify taking him down."

"Does Roy agree?" Sarah asked.

"Yes and no. Allen is not priority with him, but he wants to take a closer look. He thought the apology was bullshit and didn't believe Allen's story about not remembering Syms from the first Wednesday."

"Good for Roy! You don't really believe Allen's story, do you, Scott?"

"He answered all of our questions without hesitation, and with the exception of his refusal to elaborate on his scrapes with the law, he seemed forthright. A little arrogant but there's nothing illegal about that. I don't like him or his attitude toward women but I don't like a lot of people. I can't arrest any of them for that. At this juncture, Gary Allen is low on my list of suspects in the Jessica Syms murder."

"Suspects?" Sarah questioned. "You have a list of one."

Her stomach was churning. Hawkins was slick. No doubt about it. The man was guilty. He was a serial rapist and murderer. She knew where they could find the proof. But since she saw his souvenirs while breaking and entering, she couldn't mention them. And based on the interview and Scott's current knowledge of Gary Allen, she couldn't argue. After all, Allen had been cooperative and had said all the right things. Besides, she was confident that when Scott took the time to read the file she had given him yesterday, he would see it her way.

"Has Jessica's car and the clothes she was wearing when she disappeared been found?

"No. All the Dumpsters in the shopping center have been searched, and nothing. Atlanta PD has an APB out on the car. I'll let you know if we get anything new."

"Thanks," Sarah responded.

"I think I'll take off. While you're gone, relax. We'll call you, if we need you."

Scott left a few minutes later. No kiss, no hug, no soft spoken words — just see you in a week. After cleaning up the mess the techs had left behind, Sarah ran water for a bath. Soaking in the hot tub, crying and feeling sorry for herself, she thought:

I guess I'm just one of his agents again. I thought we had a future? How could I have been so stupid? I guess I was just another conquest. Darcy warned me, damn her! Who am I kidding? I caused this—brought it on myself. No, Hawkins is to blame. Why didn't he get himself killed during the past thirteen years? Save me the trouble! Oh well, I knew I couldn't get him and have Scott too.

She called Scott before going to bed. "Scott, promise me that you'll look at the file I gave you yesterday?"

"Okay, I'll read it, but, listen to me, Sarah. Hawkins is not Allen. And, we've found nothing to indicate Allen is a killer."

CHAPTER 13

JAX WAS SITTING in the passenger seat of the nine-year-old Suburban with his head hanging out of the window. Sarah reached over to scratch his back. Her hazel eyes danced as she laughed at the sight of his curly brown ears flapping in the breeze.

Jax turned his head and gazed at her with loving eyes as if he was asking, "Where are we going, Mom?"

"We're going to the coast, boy. St. Simons. You love romping on the beach there, remember?"

He smiled his long-tongued, doggy smile, then turned and leaned his head out the window again.

She would rather have driven the 350 Z, but Sarah never took Jax on trips in it. The used Suburban was a gift from her dad four years ago when he bought a new car, and up until recently, it was her only mode of transportation. She hung on to it when she bought the 350 Z, so she'd have a car to haul Jax around in. Even though it had over a hundred thousand miles on it, it was still 'truckin' along and perfect for them.

They were traveling east on I-16, just beyond the Dublin exit. Savannah was couple of hours ahead. I-16 from Macon to Savannah was a long, boring drive. Over the one-hundred fifty-six-mile stretch, there are only three or four exits offering gas, lodging or food. Otherwise, it was an interstate lined with pine trees, monotony, and state troopers.

Sarah left home at five, before the sun was up, so she could swing through Hawkins' neighborhood while it was still dark. Thursday was trash day, and residents rolled their garbage cans to the curb early. After making certain his house wasn't being watched, she pulled alongside Hawkins' trash can and dropped the plastic bag containing his Rockport shoes in it. Sarah was counting on her cohorts being smart enough to find out that today was trash day and check Hawkins' garbage can. If so, the shoes with topsoil from her yard embedded in their soles would be proof that the man broke into her house. Threatening phone calls, breaking and entering and the scene at the restaurant — all were actions of a stalker. Add to stalking, his history with JJ and the fact that he was the last person seen with Jessica Syms, and you have a stalker with murder on his mind. Sarah's plan was coming together.

Sarah was ten miles west of Savannah when she decided to call the office.

Sarah knew she'd brought this on herself, but that didn't stop the empty ache in her heart. *Damn, I don't want to lose Scott!*

"Hi Darcy, it's me."

"Sarah, where are you? Why don't you answer your phone?" Darcy's words tumbled out as soon as she recognized Sarah's voice.

"On the road. I've had my cell turned off, no reception. Why, what's going on?"

"I've never seen Scott this upset. He's pacing like a caged tiger. He walks past your office, peeks in and then storms over here, wanting to know if you've called."

"Maybe he just misses me?"

"Like the plague. If I were you, I would lay low today."

"I will, today, tomorrow and all next week. He put me on leave and told me not to call."

"He must have forgotten. Let me get him. Good luck!"

"Sarah, where are you? Why haven't you called?" he yelled.

"What are you so upset about? You told me not to come in and not to call. In fact, I believe your exact words were, 'We'll call you if you're needed.'"

"That was before I read this bombshell you gave me yesterday. Why didn't you get this to me sooner?"

"I just finished it. I could have given it to you in pieces, but you would have told me to stop, and I wouldn't have blamed you. It didn't all come together until recently."

"Where are you?"

"Savannah."

"What are you doing there?" Scott asked.

"Going to lunch," Sarah answered.

"You drove to Savannah to go to lunch?" Dismay was evident in his voice.

"Of course not, I'm on leave for eleven days and the only male in my life wanted to go to the beach. So I decided to take him to St. Simons. I thought I'd stop at Mrs. Wilkes' Boarding House in Savannah for lunch."

"Where are you staying?"

"I've rented a cottage on the island."

"Give Darcy the information after we're through, in case we need to reach you."

"Does this mean I'm out of the doghouse?"

"No, it means I'm a lot more concerned about your safety than I was yesterday. How long are you staying?"

"Until next Sunday. Unless something breaks and you need me to come back before then."

"Keep in touch and tell Jax hello."

It took Sarah a few minutes to navigate around the squares and find a shady place to park the Suburban. Lowering the windows a few inches, she patted the silky head. "Okay Jax, you be a good boy, and I'll bring you a people bag from the restaurant." Glancing over her shoulder at his accusing eyes, she steeled herself and hurried along the sidewalk.

Mrs. Wilkes' was on the bottom level of an old Georgian home. Sarah was in the back of a waiting line running down the sidewalk for a half-block. The smell of fresh-baked bread, fried chicken and peach cobbler floating in the breeze had her mouth watering as she waited. She was getting hungrier by the minute. Finally, after a lifetime of starvation, Sarah was escorted to a round table with ten other guests. Pitchers of iced tea, bowls of mashed potatoes, peas, green beans, creamed corn, and collard greens were placed on the table with turkey, roast beef, and fried chicken. A plate of cornbread and biscuits sat in the center.

"Pass the chicken. Are there any peas left? Isn't the corn good? Wow, these biscuits melt in your mouth. Peach cobbler with homemade ice cream," echoed around the room while hungry patrons crowded around twelve tables ate lunch. Waitresses hovered around each table refilling bowls, plates and pitchers as soon as they were emptied. When Sarah pushed herself away from the table, she felt like she had gained ten pounds.

The paper napkin-wrapped roast beef disappeared in two gulps as Jax slurped his long, rough tongue around her fingers, getting the last drips of gravy. They started out on a leisurely stroll, but Savannah's charm and beauty overwhelmed her, and the short walk stretched to four hours of sightseeing. Nine squares and a city park spread through the historic district.

She showed Jax a sign noting the birthplace of six generations of Uga, the mascot of the University of Georgia Bulldogs. After touring the city on foot and paw for hours, Sarah and Jax were both exhausted.

About an hour later Sarah turned off US 17 onto the F.J. Torras Causeway that connects the mainland, Brunswick to

St. Simons Island. Roughly halfway between Jacksonville and Savannah, the small historic Georgia Island is noted for its relaxed atmosphere, good food, and great golf.

Sarah checked into the cottage, unloaded her bags and took Jax out to take care of personal business. Then she took a long hot shower, slipped on her Victoria's Secret nightshirt and curled up in a chair on the cottage's small back patio with Jax at her feet. Sipping a cold beer, serenaded by the sounds of the birds, the rolling waves of the Atlantic Ocean and the rhythm of Jax snoring, Sarah began to relax.

She leaned her head back and closed her eyes. She could almost feel the sway of the ocean as the fragrance of the salt marsh filled her lungs. At peace for the first time in weeks, she drifted off to sleep. Hours later, the barking of her Springer penetrated the night sounds. Easing her eyes open, she could see Jax, faintly visible in moonlight, charging out of the marsh, hot on the trail of a rabbit. Sarah's bare feet glided across the spongy St Augustine grass. "Jax! Get in here before you wake up the whole world."

Yawning, she tumbled into bed, unconcerned with Jax's sandy paws, and fell into a sound sleep.

SHE TOOK JAX for an early morning run Friday. The crisp morning air and the sounds of the ocean seemed to energize her as she glided along the beach and flat island roads, covering almost nine miles. They passed one historic marker after another: Bloody Marsh, Retreat Plantation, the old Tabby house, and Gascoigne Bluff, where the USS Constitution docked while waiting for Georgia timber to be felled for its main mast. But by far, the most fascinating sights to Sarah were the "faces" carved into Live Oaks. Sarah thought they looked sad and wondered what meaning they held; what story did the faces tell. She hoped she could find the answers to her questions before she left the island.

That night she had dinner at Mullet Bay in the village. With its tin roof and wide covered porch lined with tables for diners, and plants hanging from the ceiling, like a place in Key West. Rather than wait for a table, Sarah sat at the bar.

When the bartender sat a light draft in front of her, she asked. "I noticed three oak trees around the island that had faces carved in them. What is the story behind them?"

The bartender shrugged. An older gentleman on Sarah's right spoke up. "Actually there are five that I know of. Yep! Local folklore calls them the tree spirits. Legend has it that the families of sailors lost at sea commissioned a local wood carver to chisel likenesses of their loved one in a tree in their yard. They chose Live Oaks because they knew the tree would be around for hundreds of years. By so doing, the family believed their loved one's spirit would return home and remain there as long as the tree thrived."

Sarah recalled the faces set in the trunks of huge old oaks, set among its drooping limbs and low hanging Spanish moss. "Why are they so sad?"

"The tree spirit reflects the sadness of the sailor because he was unable to return home and his regret that his family had to go on without him. Many believe the tree spirits are still among us and come out to warn us, or lend a hand, when a hurricane threatens our village."

Sarah stayed at the bar so she could listen to the old man's stories. Finally at eleven, she excused herself to go home. "Thank you for a great evening."

"You're welcome young lady, come again." Sarah was amazed at how friendly and warm the residents were.

She took Jax for a walk on the beach as soon as she got home. They walked along the beach to get back to the cottage. The moon was riding high in the sky, glistening on the waves as they rolled in to shore, causing Sarah to feel melancholy. She missed Scott.

She and Jax entered through the front door of the cottage and walked straight through to the kitchen. She planned to go out on the patio and sip a beer while enjoying the night air and the ocean breeze. As she approached the patio doors, Sarah noticed her cooler sitting on the patio and she didn't remember leaving it out there.

Sliding open the patio door she stepped out and was grabbed from behind and pulled into a sitting position. Shocked, she jerked free and drew her right leg back to deliver a kick.

"You're making a habit of this. You must enjoy falling into my lap."

His thick arms circled her waist from behind and pulled her back down. Scott kissed the nape of her neck.

The kiss, the arms, the cologne and the lap were familiar and welcome. Warmth flooded her body. She relaxed, leaned back and let herself melt into him. Sarah turned slightly to see his face.

"And you are making a habit of lounging on my porch, uninvited." He pressed his lips against hers, cutting off her words. His hand slipped under her blouse. When he touched one of her breasts, her breath caught in her throat.

"You could always ask me to leave, or call security," His said in a gravelly voice.

"I could, but you're here already. You might as well stay." She gave him a deep, hungry kiss, wanting more.

"Might as well. Aren't you warm in all those clothes?"

"Now, that you mention it. I am kind of hot all of a sudden. Let's go inside."

Leading the way, Sarah thought about the night of the break-in, when he left her house, with no kiss, no hug, and no offer of comfort. She had thought they were through. That she'd pushed him too far. But here he was. All thinking stopped when they entered the bedroom. He slipped her blouse over her head and eased her onto the bed.

Later they sat on the patio and enjoyed the ocean breeze. The three-quarter-moon cast just enough light to highlight the water as it crashed to shore splashing over a sea wall made of large stones. High tide always brought the ocean to the wall while low tide allowed for stretches of pristine beach. The homes facing the water were dark. Residents and tourists were asked to keep their lights off after dark to allow the sea turtles to come ashore to lay eggs. The lights disoriented the large turtles and many times caused them to go elsewhere to nest.

Scott handed Sarah a beer. She glanced in the cooler and then at Scott. "I hope you plan to replenish my stock."

"Not really, I'll just consider it payment for services rendered." His eyes were the color of a Starbucks light mocha.

"Oh, you think I ought to pay you. I believe you've got it backward. You're supposed to be paying me. Not with money, mind you, but with pretty trinkets, diamonds — a bracelet, earrings, or a ring. Instead, here you are, sitting on my patio in your boxers, sloshing down my beer, uninvited, I might add. By the way, where are you staying tonight?" The gold flecks danced in her eyes.

"Since I'm now too weak to travel, thanks to you, I guess I'll have to stay here. If you promise that you won't take advantage of me in my weakened state." His mouth formed into the half-grin that Sarah found irresistible.

"Oh, all right you can stay over. And, if you sleep on the sofa, you won't have to worry about me bothering you." Sarah joked, as she started into the cottage.

"You keep this up and you may never get that ring you mentioned, the diamond one."

Sarah stopped in the doorway and turned to face him, her body silhouetted in the moonlight. "What did you just say?"

CHAPTER 14

SCOTT GRABBED THE PHONE before it could wake Sarah. Finished with the conversation, he shook her. "That was Roy. They found Jessica's car."

"Where? When?"

"This morning, at a strip mall parking lot, not far from Phipps Plaza."

"Any clues?"

"Not yet, they just found it. Her clothes were in it and they've already sent them to the lab. The car is on its way to the shop. Hopefully, they'll find something, prints, stains, fibers. We need a break. I've got to get back."

Sarah sat up and leaned on one elbow. The sheet slipped below her breasts as she stretched one of her long legs out on top it.

"Now? It's already noon. Can't you wait until tomorrow? It'll take at least a day for the lab to process everything. There's nothing for you to do, till they're through."

His eyes raked her body with a long, hot look. He reached out and lightly touched her exposed thigh. "You're right, there's not much I can do there today."

They were having a quiet dinner at a little restaurant

down the street from the cottage when Scott surprised Sarah by telling her, "Sarah, we're meant for each other. I love you and I want you to be my wife. Will you marry me?"

Sarah was stunned, happy, in love and speechless. Scott didn't notice. He had to finish what he wanted to say.

"As soon as you get back, and I get your father's permission, I want us to find a ring. Then we'll make it official. Okay?"

Sarah hooted. A broad, snorting laugh, "Ask Daddy's permission, you're kidding right?"

"I've never been more serious about anything in my life. I only plan to do this once and I want to do it right."

"Yeah, but asking my father for my hand in marriage. That's old fashioned, sweet but outdated, besides its not like I'm a blushing virgin, you know."

Her laugh changed to a quivering half-smile. "After all, you know my history, what happened to me. Some people would consider me damaged goods."

Scott reached across the table and took her hands and held them tight. "Don't ever say that again! You are perfect. I love you and I want you to be my wife. The past is just that. You suffered a terrible ordeal when you were a teenager. It would have ruined a lot of women, but not you. It made you stronger. I thank God that he put you in my path. Will you marry me, Miss Sarah James?"

"Oh yes…yes! I love you Scott."

"Good. And I love every square inch of you. Now that's settled, all I have to do is talk to the good doctor and get his okay for me to marry his only daughter."

Scott left the island late Saturday night to drive back to Atlanta. He wanted to be at the office early Sunday morning to review any evidence discovered in Jessica's car.

Sarah decided to remain for the rest of the week, as planned. For the next few days she and Jax roamed the beach and jogged the island paths, Sarah couldn't believe that she'd found love. That someone like Scott wanted to marry her, knowing her past.

During their walks, she poured out all her joy and excitement into the dog's silky ears. "Can you believe it? Mommy is getting married! You like Scott, don't you pal? Guess we'll have to go and find me a gown. What do you think about that Jax?"

Jax approved of anything that made Sarah happy, that put excitement and joy in her voice. He sprang into the air and woofed his delight.

During the long, quiet nights, with only the ocean in her ears, Sarah tormented herself with the decision that she couldn't put off much longer. She had to choose: betray Scott's trust and love, or forsake her vow to Callie and Jessica?

Which vow was more important, the one to the living or the dead? Could she live with herself if she betrayed either? What if Hawkins killed again? She had until Saturday to decide. When she got back to Atlanta and picked out a ring, it would be too late. What should she follow, her heart or her soul?

Tuesday around midnight, her phone rang. "Do I get to give you away?" Sarah's father asked.

"Of course! Scott called?"

"Yes, and I gave him my permission. Your mom gave hers, too. We're so happy, honey. Congratulations! Here, your mom wants to talk to you. I love you!" Sarah and her mother talked for two hours. They decided on a June wedding on St. Simons.

Sarah wouldn't consider getting married in her hometown. She had never forgiven the community for the way they had treated her and Callie. Her parents had considered leaving, but her father couldn't desert his practice; the children he had treated since birth, but his relationships with his friends and neighbors were never the same. He often regretted his decision to remain, but as the years passed, it became harder to relocate, and eventually it was no longer an option.

Sarah's mother was excited about planning a wedding, but it was only a couple of months away, and St. Simons was a five-hour drive for them both, so she suggested Sarah look for a local wedding planner. Sarah was a step ahead of her mom.

"I've already found someone. She's a dynamite lady, a nurse, who has a wedding planning business on the side. The events coordinator at the King and Prince hotel recommended her. She told me the lady was tenacious, organized and thoughtful. I met her and she's perfect."

"Good, sign her up. Dad says money is no object!" Sarah heard her dad groan.

Sarah called Scott as soon as she hung up with her parents.

"Sarah! What's wrong? It's two-thirty in the morning." He asked in a sleepy voice.

"I thought you were going to wait until I got back to call dad, so we could do it together."

"Then I wouldn't have been calling him, we would. Besides, I couldn't wait. He said okay. He is okay with it, isn't he?"

"Yes, but you might not be. Mom and I set the date for the first weekend in June. Here!"

"Great! Now all we have to do is get you to call my mom and ask her permission. That's only fair. I called your dad."

CHAPTER 15

DARCY INTERRUPED Scott's Thursday morning staff meeting. "Richard from the Crime Lab is on line two. He says he has something you will want to hear."

"Scott, the dirt on the shoes recovered from Gary Allen's trash matches the dirt under Sarah's window. It's ninety percent conclusive. It could be argued the soil could have come from adjoining yards. It would be a weak argument but a good defense lawyer could make a lot out of it."

"So we can't really use it unless we get something else?"

"I guess, but it should justify a warrant."

"Normally, yes, but, this one is different. His family has all kinds of connections and if we move too soon it could have a lot of political ramifications. Will the dress or the car add anything?"

"The dress is definitely Jessica's. Fibers found on the body matches the dress and the hairs found on the dress are hers."

"What about her panties, any semen?"

"They never found her panties or bra."

"Damn, Roy didn't tell me that. What about the car?"

"We found blood and secretions in the trunk. She was in it."

"How, she was in a plastic bag and the medical examiner says she was dead when he put her in it."

"My guess is that she was locked in the trunk when he kidnapped her. Probably rolled around in there and got cut somehow. There weren't any signs of her struggling to get out, so we figure she was drugged when she was put in the trunk. That's all we've go for now, but I'll keep you posted."

Scott called Atlanta PD. "Roy, I think it's time we paid Gary Allen another visit."

They arrived at Decker Computer Services at eleven-thirty. Scott wanted to interrupt Allen's workday, to break into his routine, and catch him off guard, if possible. It was the stereotypical computer company environment, staff mostly under thirty, casual dress, jeans and open collar shirts, modern furniture, bright lighting and colorful prints on the walls. Scott and Roy flashed their IDs and the receptionist immediately called Mr. Allen, who materialized moments later in a doorway to their right. He said nothing, but motioned for the two to follow him.

When they were seated in Allen's office with the door closed, he asked. "Couldn't this have been done after hours? Did you have to barge in here like G-Men or something? I'm an officer of this company. Do you know how this looks?"

"Mr. Allen, I am a G-Man, even though the term is somewhat outdated. I apologize for any inconvenience or embarrassment we may be causing, but we were in the area, needed to talk to you, and decided to drop by."

"You could have called. Let's make this quick. What do you want?"

"Where were you last Wednesday night?"

"At home, why?"

"You didn't make your weekly trip to The Watering Hole?"

"No. I didn't feel like going."

"Any particular reason?" Scott asked.

"I guess there is no harm in admitting that I was a little shook up over the questioning concerning that woman's death. I felt it best if I stayed away from the Hole for a few weeks."

"If you weren't involved, why would you avoid the place?"

"It's not every day the FBI and a homicide detective from Atlanta's finest pay me a visit and question me about a woman I screwed, whose only connection to me was apparently that we met at The Watering Hole. I didn't want to go back there until you identified the killer. If someone else disappeared, and I happened to be there that evening, you would be right back questioning me. I want to avoid that."

"Should we suspect you, Mr. Allen?" Roy asked. "Is someone else going to disappear, Mr. Allen?"

"Whoa here, I'm trying to cooperate, so don't jump to any wild conclusions, gentlemen. I was just speculating. I mean let's face it, you obviously have nothing to go on, no leads, so what's to keep whoever is behind this girls disappearance and murder from doing it again?"

"We aren't exactly clueless Mr. Allen, that's why we're here. I believe you know more about Ms. Syms' murder than you're telling us," Scott stated.

"I've heard enough. I don't like this line of questioning, or your inferences, gentlemen. I will cooperate, but only with my attorney present."

"Are we talking about your attorney or your father's attorney, Mr. Hawkins?" Scott asked.

Hawkins' face paled. His eyes grew wide with surprise and perhaps, a flickering of fear?

"I called you by your real name. It is Gregory Alan Hawkins, Jr., isn't it? And your father has made a habit of hiring attorneys to get you out of scrapes with the law, hasn't he? To be sure nothing sticks. I believe that is how you phrased it the first time we spoke."

Anger flared in Hawkins' eyes and he clinched and unclenched his fist. The two had pushed him to the edge. "I have nothing more to say to you. Leave my office. Now!"

Scott relaxed against the chrome and leather chair, crossed an ankle over his knee and exchanged a quick glance with Roy, then asked softly. "Where were you last Wednesday night? You weren't busy breaking into the home of one of my agent's were you? Is that the reason you weren't at The Watering Hole?" He pulled a small notebook out of his inside pocket and studiously thumbed through several pages. "Let's see, she's missing a pair of panties and a bra, ones that she had worn that day. Is that how you get your jollies, sniffing women's underwear?" Scott prodded.

"You're one sick bastard, you know it?" Roy accused.

Hawkins shot out of his chair and it careened into the wall behind him. Leaning across his desk he yelled. "Get the fuck out of here, now!"

Neither Scott nor Detective Nelson moved. Roy smiled.

"We got you pegged, sicko. Did you think you could escape your past by changing your name? Didn't you think we could put two and two together and make the connection? You killed Jessica Syms and I'll prove it and tie you to a few others while I'm at it. Mr. Hawkins, Allen, Teflon Man, or whatever your name may be next week. You're ass is mine." Scott stated. Roy was smiling at Hawkins, nodding his head in agreement.

Hawkins' eyes were bulging. His face contorted in rage as he struggled to control himself. "You two can't prove shit! I'm telling you, one more time, get out of my office!"

Both lawmen stood up. "I think we made him mad Roy."

"Yes, I think you're right, and it appears he doesn't think too highly of the Bureau," Roy chuckled.

"That's his mistake. But you know Roy, I don't think he likes you."

"Do I look like I care, Scott? Maybe we'll grow on him

if we hang around. Is it all right if we follow you around for a while?"

Hawkins sprang around his desk, his hands balled into fists and his eyes bulging in anger. Scott and Roy were ready to react, violence for violence, no quarters given. But Hawkins surprised them, by slinging the office door open.

"Get out!"

In less than a heartbeat Scott was on him, close, crowding him, challenging him to take a swing. "How long do you think Daddy will keep bailing you out? Hell, he's already made you change your name. You're an embarrassment. He doesn't want anyone to know you two are related. What will he say when we tell him that you killed that girl?" Scott knew Hawkins was ready to explode.

"You want to take a shot at me don't you? Go ahead." Scott challenged.

Roy stepped into the doorway. "He won't do that, Scott. You're not tied down. He's gutless, unless he's got a drugged out woman tied to a bed." Then he stepped through the door. Before he followed, Scott got in Hawkins' face. "Stay away from my agent or I'll take it personal and you won't like that!" His words rumbled from deep inside his chest, the menace unmistakable.

ROY'S CELL PHONE BEEPED as they stepped off the elevator in the lobby. "Yeah." He listened for several minutes, asked a few questions. "He's with me. I'll tell him. Be right there."

He put the phone in the holster on his hip and turned to Scott.

"We got another body."

Scott followed him to the scene. A Dumpster behind a grocery store in an upscale strip mall a couple of miles from the one where Jessica had been found. Techs were stooped over the nude body lying on a black plastic garbage bag that had been slit open to expose the girl. Bruises were visible similar to the ones on Jessica's body. Scott recognized the medical examiner from the previous crime scene.

"Emily."

She looked up. "We've got to stop meeting like this, Agent Justice." The ME gave him a thin smile.

Scott squatted down beside Emily, next to the body, while Roy lounged against a police van, content to look on and listen.

"What have we got?"

"She looks to be between twenty-five and thirty, same physical description as the other victim. Body temperature indicates that she's been dead twelve to eighteen hours. I'll know for sure when we get her back to the lab. Bruises are the same as on the Syms woman. Made by a wide, firm object and cushioned somehow. My best guess is that Agent James is right. The guy's using his bare hands. Same pattern as before — rib cage, thighs, legs, buttocks, and back, strategically placed to avoid the face, pubic region and breasts. She has rope burns on her wrists and ankles. Vaginal and rectal tears caused by excessive force, no semen...same as Syms."

"Cause of death?"

"Strangulation. Same as Syms." Emily pointed to dark bruises around the girl's throat.

"Are there any differences?"

She looked over the body for several seconds, conducting a visual exam. Scott guessed her mental computer was searching the hard drive for comparative details. She pointed to the inside of the girl's thighs. "Those scratches, they're actually cuts. See them? The other one had puncture wounds in almost the same spots but they didn't have the trails or thin cut lines like this. I'll have to look at the autopsy photos to be sure. These cuts are deeper at the lower edge and seem to be more superficial as they move up her thigh. He's getting sloppy or trying to make it more painful for his victims."

The cuts were about an inch and a half long and were located in the same area on both thighs. "I think they were made by a knife. He evidently stuck her and then turned the blade upward. It's almost like he was cutting something away from her skin."

"Could it have been her panties, maybe?" Scott asked.

Emily studied the cuts and their location without touching them. "Yes, could be, if she was wearing a bikini. But why do it this way?"

"Because he's a sick sumbitch," Roy stated. "Any sign of her clothes?"

One of Roy's uniforms, who had been listening, answered the question. "Yes, they were neatly folded on the back seat of her car which was parked in the lot out front."

"Did she put up a fight?" Scott asked.

"Not until after she was tied down. Then she struggled like a wildcat to get free. Look at her wrists and ankles. My guess is that he used the Rohypnol again. The toxicology screen will confirm it. That's all I can tell you for now. Except that he's not through. I told Sarah that, now I'm telling you two."

Scott stood up and walked away. He took out his cell phone and punched an auto dial number.

"Beach Bums Anonymous, Sarah here."

"Wash off the suntan oil. I need you back at work."

SARAH DROVE STRAIGHT THROUGH to Atlanta, stopping once for gas. She dropped Jax off at her house, changed clothes and went to the office. Wearing jeans, a knit top under a sweater and comfortable pair of Merrells, she joined five other agents and four Atlanta PD detectives at 8:30 in the fifteenth-floor conference room. After making the introductions, Scott got down to business.

"Ladies and gentlemen, we have a serial killer on our

hands. There have been two murders. Normally, we wouldn't move this quickly with the classification but the similarities are too strong to be coincidental."

He paused to look around the room making eye contact with each person then continued, explaining the matching characteristics of the two cases. "The victims were drugged prior to being abducted, held captive and abused physically and sexually, prior to being strangled. Toxicology screens confirm Rohypnol as the drug of choice. Both women were single, in their mid-twenties, dark hair, blue eyes, good figures, and between five-five and five-seven, and weighing between one-fifteen and one-thirty.

"Physical abuse was the same, similar patterned bruising avoiding sexual regions, and thin cuts on the inner thighs and the center of the chest. It appears our perp prefers to cut his victims' underclothes off."

He paused again to give the group time to absorb the information. "Both bodies were found in Dumpsters, stuffed in black plastic bags, and left in such a way as to assure discovery. One had a foot sticking out and the other had a hand outside the bag. The holes in the bags were cut, not torn. No DNA from the perpetrator."

A chunky cop in the back of the room asked, "Profilers got anything for us?"

"Male, probably single and between the ages of thirty and forty, educated, and white. He is organized and a planner, probably an engineer, accountant or a computer guru. They say leaving the bodies in trash bags is indicative of the low value he places on females. Also, he has some deep-seated anger at women who fit a certain description. They can't explain how he selects his specific victims."

"They select him," Sarah commented.

"What do you mean?" One of the agents asked.

"They reject him or better him at work, something like that. It pisses him off. My bet is that this guy can't accept rejection."

"You mean he does this to a woman because she does a better job at work or shoots him down, so he kills her?"

"The work issue is a stretch, my money's on rejection. If a woman that he's really interested in rejects his advances, it makes him so angry that she becomes his next target. It may not be bad enough to justify kidnap and rape, for some it may just warrant verbal abuse or some other form of retaliation. But if he feels belittled... she's as good as dead," Sarah answered.

Scott nodded. "Sarah may have a point. Her logic fits with why our psychologists think he disposes of the bodies the way he does. Leaving them in a Dumpster in a highly visible location not only shows his contempt for females, but also demonstrates his disdain for law enforcement. He is telling us we can't catch him."

"Or if we do, we can't convict him," Sarah added.

Scott gave her a stern look.

"What do you mean?" Roy asked.

"He's keeping everything so clean. We know he is sexually abusing these women, yet we haven't found any semen, hair or skin traces that can lead us to him. The medical examiner thinks he bathes them before bagging them."

"Without any specific evidence, he probably thinks he's smarter than we are, and he can beat the rap even if we catch him."

"Then we need to shoot the sumbitch and be done with it," Roy quipped.

Scott continued. "The short time span between the two murders does not indicate a specific pattern at this point. Suffice it to say that if we do have a serial rapist-killer on our hands, he will attack again."

"Unless we catch him," Sarah added.

"Right, in case you haven't figured it our already, the people in this room comprise the multi-agency task force that will catch this killer. PAM, Prevent Another Murder, is the acronym for the group. I'm assuming overall leadership.

Lieutenant Nelson will coordinate Atlanta PD efforts while Agent James will coordinate the Bureau resources.

"Atlanta PD will monitor missing persons reports for potential victims and canvas the areas where the bodies were found, looking for clues and witnesses. Someone has to have seen this guy delivering the bodies to the Dumpsters and leaving the scene. Interviews of suspects, families of victims and witnesses will be a joint effort to be assigned as we proceed. Agent James will work with the profiler and the ME to pull together whatever they find and to make sense out of it. Look for patterns, signs and anything else that might give us a better feel for this guy."

One of the detectives asked if there were any suspects.

"Yes. Agent James initially brought him to my attention. At first I had my doubts, but he is now the primary suspect."

Sarah was shocked, first at being included in the task force, second at being given significant responsibility and lastly by the fact Scott was covering her ass. He was going to use her research on Hawkins and give her credit.

"Unfortunately, we have to walk on eggshells with this guy. His father is wealthy and has friends in very high places. Lieutenant Nelson and I interviewed him this morning, and I've already had a call from the deputy director who received a call from the director, who was called by the attorney general. I was told to back off. Once I explained what we had on the guy, which at this time is nothing but suspicions and a pattern, I was told to proceed with caution and to go by the book. So at this point, we can get no warrants and have to keep our distance."

"I got a similar call from the commissioner who heard from the mayor and the governor," Roy added. He distributed photos of Hawkins to each PAM member.

"Who is he?" An agent asked.

"Gary Bundy Allen, a.k.a. Gregory Alan Hawkins, Jr."

"What?" Several people responded.

174   JIM DAHER

"This information is not to leave this room. As you can see, his history goes back almost twenty years. His first abduction was two teenagers in North Carolina."

Sarah squirmed in her seat, uncomfortable for the first time. Fortunately, victims' names had been omitted from the rap sheet. She knew she didn't belong in the meeting and questioned Scott's judgment.

The only other female in the room, an Atlanta homicide detective, whistled. "How in the hell is this guy still on the streets?"

"Good question. Daddy is Hawkins Enterprises and his money and influence, plus some unscrupulous attorneys come to the rescue every time the son gets into trouble," Scott answered.

"How? With these offenses?" A cop to Roy's right asked.

"Payoffs, lucrative job offers, threats, and connections! Power and money talk so loudly that even judges and district attorneys listen," Sarah answered.

"What's different this time?" The cop asked.

"PAM! We will dot every I and cross every T and federal prosecutors will be in charge of the case. He won't get off," Scott responded.

Roy spoke up. "Here's some additional data Agent James retrieved. She requested searches everywhere this creep has lived. She asked for missing persons as well as those that eventually turned up murdered. There are six spread over several states. They all match the MO, bodies found in Dumpsters, in garbage bags with an arm or a leg exposed, the females' physical descriptions, cause of death and clothing recovered — never any undergarments."

Sarah had not seen this data. The searches had been delayed, which was common for interagency and multi-jurisdictional searches. She realized Scott must have pulled the data and then shared it with Roy. Six more women had been tortured while she was getting ready.

The female detective bristled, "The lieutenant is right. This pervert doesn't need to be arrested, he needs to be shot; the first one in the balls and the second right between his eyes." She glanced toward Sarah.

Scott ignored the comment and the look in Sarah's eyes.

"I guess that's it for now. Lieutenant Nelson will get with his staff to make assignments and I'll get my people moving. Sarah, will you wait over?"

After the others had left the room, Scott closed the door. "Are you going to be okay? Can you handle this, professionally?" He paused to let the question sink in. "We both know that you shouldn't be anywhere near this case. But your insight into this guy is too valuable. So, I'm ignoring your behavior and disregard for Bureau regulations over the past few months. After all, it got us the suspect. Can I trust you?" His eyes drilled into Sarah's, trying to read her thoughts.

"I won't let you down. Why are you doing this, Scott?"

"You deserve to be part of the team that nails this guy. You know him better than anybody. Get in his head, Sarah. Tell me what he's thinking. What will he do next?"

"I can handle that, thanks."

"Sarah, you have to promise me you won't play vigilante when the time comes. I want him behind bars, not murdered. Remember, we're a team. Our goal is to gather the evidence to arrest this guy and get him convicted."

"Scott, I promise you, whatever happens, it will be by the book."

CHAPTER 16

IN THE WEEK SINCE its formation, PAM had accomplished little. They had gathered lots of circumstantial evidence but not enough to justify warrants, much less an arrest. Scott and Roy were frustrated, both knowing if Hawkins was not in custody soon, he would kill again. The "hands off" dictum on the father and son had their hands tied. The most powerful law enforcement agency in the land, coupled with the full force of the Atlanta Homicide Division, was reduced to waiting for the next victim. They prayed someone would report her missing before she wound up strangled, bagged and dumped.

Canvassing the areas where the bodies were found had turned up nothing. No one had seen or heard anything. Additional interviews of The Watering Hole's employees provided nothing new. Yes, Hawkins had been seen leaving with Jessica Syms and he had admitted that, but there was no evidence linking him to her death. Victim two had been in The Watering Hole on a Wednesday night, the last time she had been seen alive, but Hawkins had not been there that night. Without anything concrete, there was no way to justify the warrants to search Hawkins' house or car. In fact, they weren't even supposed to question him again without additional justification.

"I want to get into that house. According to the Bureau shrink, all serial killers keep trinkets, records, pictures, some kind of reminders of their victims, their successes," Scott told the other two.

Scott, Roy and Sarah were meeting Thursday afternoon over coffee and Krispy Kremes in his office.

"Souvenirs?" Sarah asked, glad they were finally on target.

"Yeah, I figure the missing panties and bras from his victims have to be hidden someplace. The psych boys say if he follows the pattern, his souvenirs are close, so he can look at them, remember the victims."

"We need to get in that house. The question is, how! Can we get a warrant?" She asked.

Both looked to Scott. "You got any ideas, Roy?" Scott asked.

Roy shook his head no, but Sarah sensed he was holding back; that he was hesitating to say what was on his mind.

Sarah knew that as head of Homicide, Roy was used to leading and not following. His subordinates respected him and said he was a man of action. Sarah surmised that he had to be frustrated. Knowing Scott was in charge, Roy felt that his hands were tied. Scott, on the other hand was equally frustrated and ready to take a few risks. Earlier, in private, he told Sarah he was ready to make something happen. But he needed to be sure Roy signed off on whatever was decided.

"Roy, what are you not saying? Spit it out. You're among friends," Sarah prodded.

Roy didn't disappoint her. "Yeah, I got something to say, screw the brass, let's go for it. We all know if another body turns up, the shit is going to hit the fan and the big boys won't remember their dictum. We need to make this guy sweat, pressure him."

"What have you got in mind?" Sarah asked.

"Find some way to tie him to the second victim and use that to get a warrant. If that doesn't work then lie to get a search and seizure for his house." Roy looked at Sarah. "If he is not taking them home after snatching them, then where are they? He's holding the women, torturing and raping them someplace, where? You got us this far. How do we find the spot?" Roy prodded.

"I haven't the foggiest. We need a break. Maybe we'll get lucky in the next twenty-four hours."

One of Sarah's techniques when facing a dead end was to change the subject to free up her mind, so she decided to get personal. She had checked and knew Roy had been an Army ranger and a jumper before joining Atlanta PD. After joining the police force, he attended and graduated from Kennesaw State University. But his personal life was a mystery. Grabbing another glazed, she pushed the box of Krispy Kreme donuts to him.

"Roy, we've been working together for a couple of months now and I just realized that I know nothing about you except your troops respect you. You married, got kids?"

He smiled for the first time in hours. "Don't usually mix family and the job, but yeah, been married eighteen years and we have fifteen-year-old twins, boy and a girl. Want to see a picture?" He reached for his wallet.

Sarah studied the picture. "Cute kids, she's a knockout. Must have gotten their looks from their mom."

"Her looks, my brains, both are honor students."

Sarah rolled her eyes and all three laughed.

Looking at the picture Scott asked, "Hey, I read about a receiver for Parkview High, that him?"

"Yeah," Roy beamed. "That's my boy. A hell of a ball player, gonna be all-state next year. He plays and she cheers."

"You okay with us taking over this investigation? Most cops would be pissed," Sarah asked.

The three laughed.

Darcy knocked and then came into the room. "Sorry, but I heard laughter and thought it'd be okay to interrupt. Sarah, you got a call from Janie at The Watering Hole. Says it's important. She's at work, call her."

"Thanks, Darcy." Sarah looked at the other two. "Guys, Janie is a good source. If it's okay, I'd like to go see her in person?" Both nodded. "Darcy, call her back and tell her I'll be there in thirty minutes."

There were only two or three customers and they were sitting at the bar. The waitresses were straightening up, wiping down and setting up the tables after the lunch push. The bartenders were restocking the bar and filling the coolers with beer. Janie waved the minute she saw Sarah and pointed to a table in the corner. She got them both a coke and sat down. Janie's jaw was working double time, softening up a new wad of gum.

"Thanks for coming over, Sugar."

"Sure thing, Janie. You said it was important.What's up?" She asked.

"Well, I've been thinking this thing over, ever since that Atlanta cop came in here last week, asking about the girl that got murdered — the second one."

"Yes." An electric tingle moved up Sarah's spine. It was a feeling she got when a case was about to turn. A premonition that something was about to break.

Janie chomped on the gum like a horse chewing on an apple. Then she blew a bubble and popped it.

"I wanted to talk to you instead of those other cops, because, you know, you bring out the best in me. Using that trick you taught me the last time we met, where I closed my eyes and thought real hard. Well. I did it again after the cop left and at first I thought it wasn't anything important. Then a little while ago, something new came up and I did your thinking thing again. It worked, that's why I called you."

She actually had her eyes closed while she talked as if she was creating a mental image of something. She pinched the gum in her mouth and pulled it out about six inches then sucked it back into her mouth and began chewing again.

Sarah waited, anxious but patient. That little voice that was never wrong was silently shouting. This is it Sarah, the break we've been waiting for.

Janie's eyes popped open. "Yes, I'm right. I recognized the girl's picture but told the cop Gary Allen wasn't here that night, and he wasn't. But then I got to thinking about something you said the first time we talked. What you said after that girl, Jessica, was killed. You know, about Gary not liking to be shot down."

"Yes."

"Well. The week before he tried to put the make on another girl and she shot him down. But he wouldn't take no for an answer. Pickings were slow that night so he went back to try again. She was brutal, told him off big time, and raised her voice so everyone could hear. Man was he upset! Asked me who she was and then left a few minutes later."

"What did you tell him?" Sarah asked.

"The truth, I didn't know her," Janie responded.

"Did he follow her out?"

"No. She was still here when he left."

"Could he have waited for her?"

"I guess he could have. I'm not even sure when she left. I just know he stormed out. I've never seen him that upset." She smacked the gum some more and stretched it outside her mouth again and then sucked it back in. "Except this one time when some broad threw a drink in his face. Whew, he was pissed that night."

Janie chewed some more, popped another bubble. "I hope I helped and that I didn't waste your time. You want a beer, on me?" She took a deep breath and rotated her shoulders, her huge breasts almost jumped out of the tank top.

"Thanks, but no, I'm on duty. I appreciate all your help. You are going to be key in helping me break this case open."

Janie beamed. Sarah started to get up. Then remembered

something Janie had said.

"Janie. When you first started, you said something new came up and made you start thinking. What was it?"

"Oh yeah. I almost forgot. The real reason I called you — there's another woman that shot Gary boy down. She works at the insurance company down the street. She's a vice president or something, good-looking if you like the type, which he obviously does. Cause he never gave up on her. Every so often he makes his move again, takes another shot. She was always nice but firm, no interest. Well, she was here last night. Gary tried to pick her up again, and she shot him down, again, but this time she must have said something cute because several people around them laughed. He turned red, looked pissed. Anyway, a little while ago, at lunch, I over-head some girls from her office say she wasn't at work today. Might be nothing, but I thought I'd mention it to you."

"What's her name?"

"Theresa Paul."

"You did good Janie. Thanks!"

Sarah got some more information on Theresa Paul from Janie: the company where she worked, how often she came into The Watering Hole and the names of any friends that came in with her. Janie described the girls that had been in at lunch and one that had been with Theresa the night before.

Sarah thanked Janie again, hurried out, and headed for the insurance building down the street. The name rang a bell in Sarah's subconscious...*Theresa Paul...Theresa Paul... why is that name so familiar?*

ANN DODD, THE DIRECTOR of Human Resources was reluctant to talk with Sarah even if she was an FBI Agent. Having the FBI in her office, checking up on one of her employees made the woman nervous. Sarah had to get her over the jitters and talking. Normally, she would take her time and build a comfort level with someone she was interviewing but today she didn't have the time — Theresa's life was at stake.

"I hope there is nothing wrong, but I want to be sure Theresa is okay. I'm probably wasting my time and yours, but I need to find out why she's out today. There is a possibility she could be in trouble, so it's essential that I find out all I can about her, now."

"It must be serious to get the FBI involved? She's only missed one day. What has she done — robbed a bank, killed somebody — blackmail?"

"Theresa hasn't done anything. As I said, Theresa could be in trouble. I hope not, but we're checking out all females in this area who are missing work and not calling in. It could be nothing, or Theresa could be in jeopardy. If she is in trouble, anything you can tell me could save her life. Now, tell me about Theresa the person, Theresa the employee, and who are her friends here at work?"

"Disappearance! Has she been kidnapped? Oh no, not like that other woman!"

"Please calm down Ms. Dodd, we're merely doing routine follow-ups at this point."

The woman pulled a folder out of a file cabinet beside her desk.

The company was one of the largest insurance carriers in the southeast and Theresa Paul was the youngest of five Vice Presidents. The HR director described Theresa as a career driven professional, extremely competent who seldom missed a day of work and when she did, she always called.

Sarah got Theresa's home phone number — the answering machine kicked in on the fifth ring. Sarah identified herself and asked that her call be returned ASAP. She got copies of Theresa's personal information, home address, phone number and family contacts from her personnel file. With that done, she got the names of Theresa's friends at work.

"I'd like to see Theresa's office. Maybe something there

will tell me where she could be today. I'll talk with her secretary while I'm there. I won't be long. Then I'd like to meet the women you mentioned. Have you got a small conference room I could use?"

Sarah added, "Also, would you call Theresa's parents and see if they have heard from her? Don't alarm them. Just tell them that you have an important message and need to reach her."

Sarah met with Theresa's secretary and talked to the four women that were Theresa's at-work friends. They painted a picture of a highly motivated, well-educated, twenty-six year old professional who had not had a serious relationship since her marriage failed four years ago. She had married a fellow grad student while working on her MBA. A year after she had begun work at the insurance company her husband was transferred to Texas. They both realized they made a mistake. Since they had not accumulated enough possessions to fight over, the divorce had been amicable. After the divorce, Theresa had dedicated herself to her job and had moved up to vice president quickly.

Her closest friend, Paula, told Sarah, "Theresa just isn't interested in a serious relationship. She dates and occasionally she'll sleep with a man she enjoys being with, but she's not about to make any sort of commitment."

Paula had been with Theresa on Wednesday night. She recognized Hawkins' picture. "Oh, yeah, he tried to hit on Theresa that night. Theresa was in a bad mood because of something at work. When she's like that, she goes out of her way to be nice to people, trying to be sure she doesn't let work problems effect others. So she wasn't ugly to him, but told him no. She politely asked him to leave her alone. When he returned half an hour later, Theresa let it all hang out. She told him, 'Read my lips, I am not interested. If possible, let the brain in your head process my message and quit thinking with the head on the end your pencil dick.' Everyone within earshot got a good laugh out of that," Paula chuckled, remembering.

"How long after that did Theresa leave?"

"Twenty or thirty minutes, I guess. She had driven her own car."

"Did this guy come back around?"

"No. He disappeared after she humiliated him."

"Did anything unusual happen between the incident and when Theresa left?"

"Not really." Paula thought a minute. "Well, one thing. It's probably nothing but somebody sent us a drink. It's not unusual for one of us to get a drink, but never all of us from one guy."

"One guy, who was he?"

"I don't know for sure. The waitress said that he said to tell us he was a secret admirer. So we figured it was the guy that Theresa blew off."

"Do you remember the name of the waitress, or what she looked like?"

"I don't remember the waitress's name but she had bleached blond hair and boobs the size of Stone Mountain. Oh, yeah, she had a wad of gum in her mouth."

Sarah asked to use the phone. She called Janie and found out that Hawkins had sent the drinks just before he left. He had ordered them at the bar and then took them to Janie. He gave her five bucks just to deliver them.

After hanging up she asked Paula. "How long after you got the drinks did Theresa leave?"

"About ten or fifteen minutes, she said she felt tired all of a sudden. She didn't even finish her drink. She said it tasted strange."

"Were all of you drinking the same thing?"

"No. I had a beer, the others were drinking screwdrivers and Theresa had a scotch and water."

"Have you got a recent picture of Theresa?"

Paula showed Sarah a picture of her and Theresa and she immediately remembered where she had heard the name.

Can I take this with me? I'll get it back to you."

"WE'VE GOT VICTIM NUMBER THREE!" Sarah told
Scott as soon as he answered the phone.
"What do you mean? Nothing has been reported."
"Janie, the waitress gave me the lead. Lady's name is
Theresa Paul. She is twenty-six, divorced, a VP at an in-
surance agency. Judging from the picture I've got, she is
medium height, about one-twenty, good figure and medium
length dark hair. She fits the profile perfectly. The reason we
haven't heard anything is because she disappeared last night.
She was last seen at The Watering Hole. She had a run-in
with our Hawkins. He tried to pick her up, she humiliated
him in front of a crowd, and now she's missing."
"How soon can you be here?"
"Thirty minutes."
"I'll call Roy."
Sarah had one stop to make. The offices of Decker
Software just happened to be on her way. "Screw procedure,
the mayor, the governor and the horses they rode in on. I'm
confronting the psycho."
Sarah flipped her ID at the receptionist. "I'd like to see
Mr. Allen please."
"Mr. Allen called in sick today and said he would be out
tomorrow, too." The receptionist hesitated. "Just a minute
please." She picked up her phone, talked briefly and looked
at Sarah.
"Could you take the time to talk with Mr. Decker, the
president of the company?"
"Of course."
A small, frail-looking man in his mid-forties entered the
lobby and introduced himself and asked Sarah if she could
come to his office. Once they were seated he asked, "What's
going on?" He looked at her card. "Agent James, why is the

FBI interested in Gary Allen? Has he done something I need to be aware of? Has he done something that could have a bad reflection on my company?"

"This is merely a routine inquiry, and I can assure you it has nothing to do with your company. I'm sorry, but I'm unable to give you any information at this time, but I'd really appreciate it if you would answer a few questions."

His answers were positive and forthcoming. "He's a good employee, knows his job and does it well. Frankly, I was shocked to learn the FBI had questioned him."

Sarah quizzed him about where Allen might be if he wasn't at home. Mr. Decker had no idea. He wasn't aware of any other local residences Allen owned and assumed that since he was ill, he would be at home.

"He had an apartment for a few months when he first moved to Atlanta but he gave that up when he bought his home. We aren't big enough to have temporary quarters but we did arrange for the apartment so I know he gave it up."

Sarah assured him that their investigation was not related to Decker Software and thanked him for his time. She started out of his office and then had another thought and returned.

"Mr. Decker, could I have a copy of Mr. Allen's attendance record for the past six months?"

All members of PAM were in the conference room when Sarah arrived. She gave them the information she had on Theresa Paul. "Not only is she missing, but Hawkins called in sick and indicated that he would be out tomorrow, too. Coincidence? The HR director called while I was on the way here and Theresa's parents have not heard from her. I got Allen's attendance records for the past six months. Let's see if he was out when Jessica was missing." Sarah told the group.

One of the Detectives left the room to check it out and returned within minutes. "She was missing for four days. He missed work those same days."

Roy immediately dispatched a couple of officers to Theresa's condo, authorizing them to enter her residence to see if they could find anything that might indicate her whereabouts. In addition, officers were sent to stakeout Hawkins' place. The group had decided that it was too confusing to keep using both names so they would stick to his birth name, Greg Hawkins. The same judge who authorized entry into Theresa's condo denied entry into the suspect's home unless there was probable cause.

Twenty minutes later, Roy got a call from the officer coordinating the search and surveillance. "We found nothing in the girl's condo and all is quiet at Hawkins' place. We don't think he's home."

After Roy told the group what had been reported. Sarah said, "We have to come up with something or the ME will be examining another body. I figure we've got forty-eight hours, max, to find her. If he's not home then he's got a second residence in the metro area. That's where we'll find the girl."

The task force decided to conduct searches of the metro Atlanta property tax files to determine if there were any properties owned by either Allen or Hawkins. An APB was put out on his car with specific instructions not to apprehend him but to locate and tail him. A query into the state's vehicle registration system was initiated to see if he owned any other vehicles. An APB was put out on Theresa Paul's car. Having done everything they could think of, the group was about to break up when Sarah made two suggestions. "Why don't we dispatch some officers to go over to The Watering Hole to interview the employees? See if we can identify any other females he has left with in the past? Then go see them, find out if he took them anywhere other than his home, another house, a motel, hotel, anything."

"It's got to be a residence. I don't see how he could keep a hostage at a motel for more than one night," Roy responded.

"I agree. But we can't leave any stone unturned, which

leads me to my next suggestion. Let's go interview Hawkins' father," Sarah suggested.

"He is off limits," Scott grumbled.

"I know that, but now's the time to act. I agree with what Roy said earlier, screw the brass, Theresa Paul's life is on the line. We have to talk to the dad. I'll do it on my own time, if you want. That way, if it backfires, I can accept full responsibility. Come on guys! We don't want to be called to another Dumpster to identify a corpse; another one of his victims. Knowing we sat on our hands doing nothing while she was being brutalized and strangled."

"It's your case, your decision," Roy stated.

"Let's see if he's there." Scott interrupted.

"I've already checked. He's there until three." Sarah smiled. "Are you coming, Roy?"

"Someone has to stay, to head up the investigation after you two get fired," he joked.

SARAH AND SCOTT had to go through three receptionists before they were allowed entry to the executive floor of Hawkins Enterprises. The lobby had patterned teakwood floors and expensive furniture. Issues of Money, Fortune and the Wall Street Journal were spread around the room. Paintings of New York, London, Paris and other international cities graced the walls. Thick, plush carpeting and heavy drapes muted the conversations of the well-dressed staff. Dimmed lighting seemed designed to set a reverential tone, as if in honor of the powerful executives housed beyond the oak doors. A prim, hawk-faced, dark haired woman behind the desk greeted them as soon as they stepped off the elevator.

In a cool, cultured murmur she greeted them, "Good Afternoon. I realize that you are here to see Mr. Hawkins, but I'm afraid he will not be available this afternoon. If you care to schedule an appointment for another day, I can do that for you."

"That isn't possible. I'm sure all your checkpoints told you that we are with the FBI." Scott showed her his credentials. "Tell Mr. Hawkins we need to see him right away."

The woman picked up her phone and punched a button. She lowered her head and spoke in a low voice so Scott couldn't overhear her.

"Someone will be with you in a moment."

"I thought I made myself clear. We are not here to see someone. No one other than Gregory Alan Hawkins, Sr. will do," Scott politely informed her.

"I'm afraid that is not possible for you to see Mr. Hawkins," A deep voice announced.

Scott looked to his right, directly at a well-dressed man in his late fifties. Tall, gray headed, beyond heavy, the man wore glasses with rounded lenses. He held himself erectly, his posture suggesting a military officer or a self-important executive. Scott recognized the look in his eyes, the way he moved — the practiced arrogance. "Afternoon, counselor."

"I beg your pardon?" the man asked.

"You are an attorney, right? My guess is that you're the company's in-house legal advisor, one of Mr. Hawkins' gophers? Well, tell Mr. Hawkins that the FBI needs to talk to him," Scott ordered.

Sarah had been instructed to allow Scott to do the talking. She was there as an observer only and had been content to sit on one the chairs off to the side and watch Scott handle the situation. And he told me to behave, Sarah mused, but Scott needs to know who this imbecile is.

She stood up and was beside Scott in three long legged strides. "Ah, Mr. Harris, back in the fold, I see. Scott, this is Mister Julian Harris, formerly Esquire. He was a Chief Prosecutor in North Carolina before joining Hawkins Enterprises for a short time. Then he joined the law firm that just happened to be Hawkins Enterprises' corporate counsel.

Interestingly enough, he left the DA office not long after blowing a big case that let Mr. Hawkins' son off the hook for kidnapping and rape." Sarah stared into Harris's eyes, daring him to dispute her. "He stayed with the law firm for about nine years until some, um, shall we say, improprieties surfaced and he was disbarred. So it is inappropriate to call him counselor."

Harris's upper lip quivered, his eyes narrowed, flickered almost imperceptibly before he responded. "That is slander, young lady. Just who the hell are you?" The hatred in his eyes told Sarah that he knew exactly who she was. Not that he realized that she was JJ Johnson, his memory wasn't that good. Besides he had written that teenager off the minute he sold her down the creek. No, he remembered her as Sarah James, the Georgetown Law graduate. The new-hire at Hazelton, Brock and Mobley, the law firm he joined after he left Hawkins Enterprises. She was the promising young lawyer who discovered his improprieties, mail fraud involving billing discrepancies, and selling out clients by divulging attorney-client privileged information to competing corporations for personal gain. He wasn't likely to forget that wretched young woman who turned her discoveries over to the justice department, the SEC and the American Bar Association.

After Sarah's role in Harris's demise became known, she was treated like a pariah within the firm. When the dust settled, she had only one remaining ally in the firm, a retired senator who headed up several major congressional committees during his political career and was now a senior partner in the firm. The senator admired her chutzpah and sense of integrity and gradually became her mentor. Eventually, she took him into her confidence and told him about her past — including her reason for seeking out and destroying Julian Harris. Only one detail did she omit, her vendetta against Gregory Alan Hawkins, Jr.

She was never sure why she told him the story. Perhaps,

she had been seeking the senator's approval or his forgiveness for what she had done to Harris. After she finished, the Senator told her he understood. He didn't say whether he approved or disapproved of her actions, just that he understood. He gave her some advice to carry through life.

"Sarah, think before you act and act before you speak. Never seek anyone's approval for your actions or attempt to justify yourself to anyone. Either course of action will be regarded as a weakness and used against you, maybe not right away, but eventually. At the end of each day you only need one person's approval, your own. At the end of your life that's another matter. For that, there is only one judge. Live your life knowing that and you will be okay."

Sarah became disillusioned with the practice of law and told him so, saying she would rather enforce the law than interpret it. He suggested she consider applying to the FBI. After soul searching and researching the Bureau, Sarah agreed. The senator contacted the director of the Bureau who he helped get appointed and intervened.

"You! You bitch, how dare you..."

Scott interrupted Harris. "You will not speak to Agent James in that manner. Now go tell Mr. Hawkins that we want to talk with him. Now! I will not tell you a third time! If I have to, I will come back with a warrant and place him under arrest. The charge will be accessory to murder and you can add obstruction of justice to your resume."

Minutes later the receptionist's intercom buzzed.

"Mr. Hawkins will see you now." She led them to a small conference room with a walnut table circled by eight leather chairs. A chandelier hung over the center of the table and a sideboard sat against the end wall with decorative porcelain sitting on it. The walls were covered with framed documents from public offerings, Letters of Intent to purchase companies and pictures of an older version of Greg Hawkins shaking hands with former U.S. presidents.

GREGORY ALAN HAWKINS, SR. entered the room in a flurry. He was an inch or so taller than his son, slightly leaner, and was just as good looking. He had the same blue eyes but without that glimmer of evil that his son's contained. His dark power suit fit perfectly. Sarah wasn't sure what an Italian-made suit looked like but guessed this must be a fine example.

He sat at the head of the table, offering no introduction and expecting none. There was no small talk. Hawkins's face might have been carved in granite, cold, contemptuous and angry. He looked at each of them slowly, using his silence and his eyes as weapons.

"Don't ever come into my office and attempt to intimidate or threaten me again. You better have a damn good reason for doing it today."

Scott took his time responding. His words were deliberate. "Let me assure you, Mr. Hawkins, we would not be here if it wasn't a matter of life and death. Intimidation won't cut any ice today. If you want to make some calls now, go ahead, pull out all the stops. But, when it's all said and done, we will talk. It can be here, at my office or police headquarters. Atlanta Homicide can have a warrant delivered within the hour. You've got your attorney, excuse me, legal advisor present so we can head over to Bureau now to save time if you want. It's your call. How do you want to play this, sir?"

That's my fiancé. Give him hell Scott.

"I don't care for your attitude young man. What do you want?"

Sarah didn't like the man even though this was the first time she had ever met papa Hawkins or even been in the same room with him. She knew he would be on the phone the minute they left. She decided to respond so Scott wouldn't suffer any repercussions alone.

She pulled a file folder out of her briefcase, braced her shoulders and spoke up for the first time. "We have a very good reason for being here, Mr. Hawkins. Actually we have a number of them. Unfortunately, there are two new ones in the last three weeks. We are here today to prevent a third. We are talking about multiple murders here. Is that a good enough reason?"

"I presume you will be able to explain how this pertains to me?"

"Certainly, that's the easy part, Mr. Hawkins. Your namesake is our prime suspect in a series of murders and a kidnapping. In the past thirteen years these are the women we suspect your son has abused and possibly murdered. What all of these ladies have in common is that they told your son 'no.' The names in bold type were murdered. The two photos are of two women found here in Atlanta. All the victims were abducted and raped. Some were murdered."

She slid a typewritten sheet across the table followed by photos of Jessica Syms and the other victim lying on the black garbage bags. The Dumpsters where they had been found were in the background.

He glanced at the list and turned to the photos, his eyes locking on the picture of Jessica. He maintained rigid control over his face and body, but his eyes gave him away.

"She does kind of reach out to you, doesn't she? It's as if she is demanding that we stop him before he harms another woman. You may know her parents. Mr. Syms is well known in Atlanta. Did you know Jessica Syms?"

"I know Frank and Martha. I've met Jessica, a delightful young lady. I went to her funeral." His eyes had been downcast. Now he looked up and locked eyes with Scott. "Are you accusing my son of these atrocities? Jessica, and all those others? You think my son's responsible?"

"Yes," Scott answered.

"I don't believe it! If you're so sure its Greg, why hasn't he been arrested?"

"All we have at present is circumstantial evidence tying him to the women and, of course, his history," Scott responded. "Unfortunately, it's not enough to pick him up, yet."

"I am appalled. You interrupt my business day to accuse my son of these atrocious acts and have no proof. What kind of imbeciles is the FBI hiring these days?"

"Now I resent your tone. If you want to trade insults, let's go downtown. Lieutenant Nelson in Homicide can referee," Scott snarled.

Sarah touched his shoulder, urging him to remain seated. Knowing they had to reach Mr. Hawkins, now, if they were going to save Theresa. "Mr. Hawkins, I know your son is responsible for these murders and I will prove it. I think you know it, too. He needs to be stopped. Please help us."

Sarah looked at another photo, and then ever so slowly, slid it across the table to him. "This is Theresa Paul. She had a run-in with your son Wednesday night. Told him no when he tried to pick her up, insulted him in front of others, embarrassed him — she hasn't been seen since. We believe he has her, somewhere. Help us find her before its too late."

Rigid, Hawkins sat, glaring at Scott, then at Sarah and the picture of Theresa, his eyes moving from one to the other. Sarah saw the ever so subtle shift in his features. The initial anger gave way to what? His face visibly sagged and in his eyes, acceptance. He knew. But how could a man acknowledge that his son was capable of such acts?

Sarah knew she had to get his cooperation if she was going to save Theresa. Perhaps honesty and understanding would do it. "How long will you let this go on, sir? How much longer will you back him? How many more times will you bail him out of trouble? And more importantly, how many more women have to suffer?"

He looked back at the photos of the victims. His gaze settled on Theresa Paul. Sarah's voice softened. She bent in toward the man, trying to find a way to reach him, thinking of her own father, what he had suffered, of Jessica Syms' father, his anguish. She willed herself to see the same maternal love in this man.

"I know you love your son. But these women had parents who loved them, too. You said you went to Jessica's funeral. Do you remember the look on Mr. Syms face that day, the anguish, the horror, the helplessness, the loss? Will you attend this woman's funeral if we don't find her in time?"

Her eyes misted over as she poured her soul into the task at hand.

"Think about the ones who escaped. The victims who dropped the charges against your son or whose cases went nowhere because of job offers or money that changed hands. If you had attended those trials or talked to the women he brutalized, I don't think you would ever have intervened. Not if you had heard what he did to them. You're not that kind of person. I can see it in your eyes. Imagine what those girls are living with, not a day goes by the horror doesn't haunt each one of the survivors. They may never have a normal relationship with a man again. But at least they lived. They didn't end up like Jessica Syms. Her father, your friend, will never hold his daughter again."

She laid her hands on either side of Theresa's picture, palms up, as if in entreaty. "Help us find him and save this girl. Let her father hold her again."

Hawkins breath rattled as he stared. Then he appeared to be trying to pull himself together. "I just don't believe my son is capable of this."

He raised his head and looked at Scott, avoiding Sarah's eyes, "Sure, he's made a few mistakes, maybe been a little forceful with some women who misunderstood or misjudged him."

He knew the truth, he had to. But of course he didn't want to believe it. He was a father with a natural instinct to protect his son.

"Sir, I can assure you that he has gone beyond just being forceful. Think about the two teenagers in North Carolina.

One of them chose to commit suicide rather than live with what he did to her. He is sick, he needs help. But I'll be honest with you, Mr. Hawkins. I don't care about your son. I think he is beyond help. He is the lowest form of criminal, a serial rapist and murderer. How many more times will he have to change his identity?"

Hawkins looked up. Sarah's words had struck him like knife wounds. True or not, he could not bear hearing his child described as a killer. No parent would. But he said nothing. His eyes were dull and pain glazed.

Sarah kept talking. "I know you want to help your son, but I am interested in helping Theresa Paul. I don't want to go see another body stuffed into a garbage bag and thrown out with the trash. Don't make us have to invite another father to the morgue to identify his daughter's body. Help us find her—alive."

Hawkins sat gazing into the distance, saying nothing. Finally he looked up.

"What would Becky say?"

"Becky?"

"His mother. She died when he was a small child." He turned and looked, admiringly, at a picture of a pretty young woman holding hands with a young Greg, Sr. "I've done my best. I can't turn on him."

Sarah was startled when she followed his eyes. The woman's features were familiar. *She fits our victim's profile.*

"Mr. Hawkins, think about it. Help us. Your wife must have been a fine person. Would she want another woman hurt? I don't think so. I believe she'd be doing all she could to help. Please think about it. Let me come back in an hour. I'd like to give you more time, but Theresa doesn't have it. Tell us where he might be, where he may be holding Theresa. Think about how frightened she must be."

As she began to describe the scenario, Sarah fought to stop her limbs from shaking, fought to keep herself from reliving her own nightmare.

She leaned across the table into Hawkins face. "Right now, Theresa is tied to a bed somewhere, waiting for him to come back and beat and rape her, again. That is what he does, he punishes his victims, humiliates them by raping and abusing them, over and over. She doesn't know when he will be back but knows he will, and the next time could be her last. Think of the pain and fear and humiliation she is feeling. The dread and horror her parents are enduring. Right now, they are somewhere, their home or maybe their church, praying that their daughter will not meet the same fate as Jessica Syms. Help Theresa. Help her parent's prayers to be answered."

He looked up. His eyes were clouded, blind, like an injured animal. Sarah could see him struggling to decide — to do what was right or protect his son. "I just don't know. I have to think. I'll call you."

"Make it soon, please. We want to save her." Sarah left Theresa's picture on the conference room table.

CHAPTER 17

"AGENT JAMES, what do you want to know?"

"Mr. Hawkins?"

It had been less than thirty minutes since Sarah and Scott left Hawkins Enterprises. His voice, subdued, had regained some of its authority, "Yes. I want to help that girl. If Greg has her, I want him stopped. But, you need to understand I don't believe my son has committed these deplorable acts and I am cooperating to prove it."

"Thank you. I understand. Do you know if Greg has a second residence under a different name, or can you think of a place he has access to where he could be holding her. Do you have a condo, a home, anything within an hour's drive of Atlanta?"

"No. All of my properties are in resort areas in other states. And as far as I know, Greg doesn't own any properties other than his home in Dunwoody."

"Can you suggest anywhere he could be? Has he called you in the last few days?"

"No."

"If he calls you or if you think of something that will help us find him, please get in touch with me or Agent Justice.

You have our cell numbers. Thank you for your help."

"I'm afraid I haven't been able to shed any light on your inquiry, but if you think of something else you need to ask, call. I'll tell my secretary to put you through."

She repeated the conversation to Scott.

"You think he was being honest?" Scott immediately asked.

"Yes. If he wasn't going to cooperate he wouldn't have called."

The record searches had turned up nothing so far and there was no activity at Hawkins' house and no results from the APB. Time was running out for Theresa Paul and they were out of options.

"I feel like I'm walking around in a trance. I know there is something we're missing, that I'm missing, but I can't put my finger on it. It's lost in the fog shrouding my mind," Sarah grumbled.

"Yeah, me too, if we don't get some rest soon, we'll be worthless when something breaks. I need a bath, some shuteye and fresh clothes."

There had only been time for an occasional fifteen or twenty minute catnap during the past two and a half days, not nearly enough rest for the intensity of the life or death situation they were dealing with. Nor had they had time to shower or change clothes since the ordeal began.

"Let's go to your place, clean up and get some rest. The office can call if anything develops," Scott suggested.

After walking Jax, Sarah climbed into the shower. She was leaning forward with her forehead against the wall, letting the warm water run over her shoulders and back. Just as she was beginning to relax she felt a rush of cold air then heard the shower door close. Sarah groaned as she felt Scott reach around her and cup her breasts in his hands.

He moved in closer, positioning himself up against her. Sarah eased. Slowly she turned and kissed him deeply. He moved her against the wall and entered her.

At four in the morning she got out of bed and went to her computer. Fifteen minutes later she ran into the bedroom. "Get up! We've got to go."

"What?" Scott was instantly alert.

"Something Hawkins' boss Decker said when I talked with him kept gnawing at me. The light dawned a little while ago. A lot of big companies own condos or townhouses around their corporate offices for visitors and transferees to stay in on a temporary basis. I did a computer search and Hawkins Enterprises has three, two in the Lenox area and one by the Galleria. The Galleria is not far from here. We can check it out while Roy's people check out the others."

Sarah was already in her jeans and running shoes and was pulling a sweater over her head.

Scott pulled a clean pair of Levis and a long-sleeved knit shirt from a drawer. He had been keeping clothes at Sarah's house for a few weeks. He handed Sarah his keys as they headed out the door. "I'll call Roy, you drive."

They decided against calling Hawkins Sr. to see if any of his staff were using the units or to ask his permission to enter them. If his son was in one of them, Daddy might get paternal and warn him. And, if he said no, it could delay them twelve to twenty-four hours getting a court order. They had to move tonight.

Before calling Roy, Scott requested search warrants for the three locations. When he reached Roy they agreed if they determined probable cause at any or all of the locations, they would go in, with or without warrants. Atlanta PD units were dispatched immediately.

Sarah and Scott were the first to arrive at the Galleria condominium complex, a gated community. They entered the universal code used to allow emergency vehicles immediate access to a complex. Inside, they slowly circled through the complex looking for the unit.

"There it is over there, the second building on the right."

Sarah parked in a space at an adjacent unit. They split up

and Scott went around back while Sarah peeked in the front windows. They met back at the car a few minutes later.

"I didn't see anything unusual," Scott noted.

"Me either. But there is a light on upstairs in the rear corner. I saw it from the side there. It may be a bedroom, there's no way to know without going in. Let's do it." She started for the door.

"We don't have probable cause. Let me check to see if the other units have anything."

Scott pulled out his cell phone.

Sarah sprinted to the front door, kneeled down and took a set of lock picks from her fanny pack. She had the door opened in seconds and stepped inside staying low and against a wall to be sure she didn't create a silhouette against outside lights shining through the windows.

Immediately her instincts snapped to full alert. Training and experience took over. Her breathing was controlled and steady. She felt good, alive and ready for action. Her gut told her they had found his lair but not whether they were in time.

Scott didn't realize she was gone until he looked up and saw the open door. He ended his call, leaped out of the car and followed her inside.

Staying low, Sarah crept forward, her penlight close to the floor to guide her. The house was quiet. The Kevlar vest suddenly felt heavy and sweat began to collect under it. As her eyes adjusted to the light inside the condo she recognized shapes: a sofa, some chairs, a coffee table, and several lamps, a large den or great room. There was a doorway directly in front of her, across the room leading into what she assumed to be the kitchen. To her left were some stairs leading to the second floor. She could smell stale food; pizza, burgers? Somebody is here, or has been. Her senses were keen, smell, sight, hearing and feel.

She had taken only a few steps when the alarm sounded. She jumped then momentarily froze, then inched forward.

She instinctively knew Scott was behind her. She looked over her shoulder and nodded.

"FBI!" Scott shouted.

A loud crash startled them both and they hit the floor. Scott crawled up beside her.

"I think it came from upstairs. Be careful. There may be some executive and his family staying here. We don't want to harm innocent people."

"FBI," she shouted. The alarm was deafening.

They heard footsteps. A figure ran down the stairs and into the kitchen. The back door slammed. They remained where they were for another few seconds before Scott leaped up. "I'll go after him. You find Theresa."

"Be careful!" she shouted to his retreating figure.

Scott took off and Sarah moved to the hallway. She heard Scott pounding through the kitchen.

"This is the FBI! Theresa — Theresa Paul! FBI!" She shouted.

Sarah reached into the first room on the left and decided to risk flipping on the light. Glued to the wall, listening, tuning out the alarm, Sarah imagined she could hear her watch ticking, but nothing else. Sweat trickled down her face. Her sweater was soaked under the vest.

She lunged into the room staying low, an empty bed. She repeated the procedure for the bathroom adjacent to the bedroom, still nothing. She retraced her steps and moved to the stairs and started up.

She eased upward, stopping on each step to listen. When she reached the top, her legs were burning and her eyes had to readjust to the darkness. She found a wall switch and flicked on the upstairs lights.

"FBI, Theresa, Theresa Paul! FBI!"

There was no response. Then she heard or thought she heard a faint whimpering. She stood motionless, listening, trying to identify the sounds, something new, a creaking, was it someone moving on a bed or a chair. No, it was definitely a bed. Sarah moved down the hall and stopped outside the door on her right. Staying against the wall she reached inside and flipped the light switch — waited and listened. Silence, nothing was moving, so Sarah stepped into the room in a shooter's crouch, with her pistol held in a double grip and swung it around the room. She saw a rumpled bed, probably where the runner was sleeping.

She slowly moved to the bathroom and followed the same entry procedure. The bathroom was empty. Some clothes were lying in the corner. She walked over and sorted through them, keeping her eyes on the doorway. She held them up, one by one. There was a tan skirt, a dark blue blouse and a bra and panties — both cut open.

Sarah felt sure she was alone in the house, except for a frightened woman tied to a bed. Theresa. Oh, God, let me be in time," she silently prayed.

She called out again, "FBI, Theresa Paul, FBI, I'm here to help you. You're safe!"

Keeping her weapon in the ready position, she moved quickly down the hallway to the other bedroom. She stopped at the doorway, reached inside and flipped the wall switch. The light came on and she spun into the room.

A pair of wild, frightened eyes stared at her. Theresa Paul was thrashing on the bed trying to jerk free of the bindings. "Anybody else in here?"

The girl shook her head no. Tears were running down her cheeks. Sarah wanted to run over and free her but her training stifled the urge. She turned and looked down the hallway one more time checking her back. She stepped back into the room and closed the door, locking it. She moved to the bedside table, laid her gun on the table, and untied Theresa's wrists.

"It's all right. You're safe. He won't ever harm you again."

The girl pulled the tape off her mouth. "Oh, God, I was so scared!"

Sarah untied her ankles.

"Can you sit up? Take it easy, no need to rush."

Instinctively Sarah knew where to find clean sheets. She took one out of the drawer and wrapped it around the weeping girl. "I don't want you to clean up yet. I'll get your clothes in a minute and you can put them on. We need to call an ambulance." Theresa nodded.

"Do you have any life threatening injuries that need immediate attention?"

The girl shook her head, no.

"I need to check. I promise I won't hurt you. But I need to be sure you don't need immediate attention. She reached for the sheet. "Okay?" Theresa nodded, but held the sheet like a lifeline. Sarah gently loosened her fingers. "I understand Theresa. Believe me, I do. I won't be but a minute."

Sarah slowly opened the sheet. The girl's body was darkly bruised. Thin cuts ran between her breasts and inside each thigh. The marks and cuts were similar to the two bodies retrieved from the Dumpsters. Looking at Theresa's body, Sarah was reminded of the teenager that broke away from Hawkins. We are the lucky ones. We're still alive. Her eyes flooded with tears and her throat was so tight that she couldn't speak. She turned away to regain control.

"Sarah! Where are you? You okay?" Scott called from downstairs.

Wiping her eyes with the back of her hand she turned to Theresa. "Stay here, I'll get your clothes." Sarah opened the door and moved down the hall.

"She's safe…we got here in time!"

Scott stopped at the landing at the top of the stairs. "Thank God! Good work."

"Hawkins?"

"No luck. By the time I got around front, a pair of taillights was headed through the gates. I re-conned the area to be sure he wasn't around. He got away, must have had an escape plan. Finding him will be the easy part. We just need an ID from her." He nodded towards the bedroom. "How is she?"

"Scared, battered and bruised, and she looks dehydrated. Give me a few minutes with her." Sarah had retrieved Theresa's clothes and was taking them to her.

"Careful. I don't want to jeopardize an evidence chain!"

"Letting her dress isn't a problem," Sarah responded sharply. "Medical personnel and the rape team can still get whatever samples they need. Letting her dress will give her a little dignity on the trip to the hospital."

Scott nodded.

Sarah glanced toward the bathroom. "Her panties and bra are in there. They're the beginning of the chain. Take a look before they're bagged and tagged, you'll see what I mean."

"I'll get the alarm shut off and call for an ambulance."

"Ask the rape team to be waiting for us at the hospital. I don't want her to have to wait on them. She's been through enough already."

He nodded again and headed toward the bathroom with his cell phone pressed to his ear.

Dressing seemed to have a calming effect on Theresa. She clung to Sarah and began to talk, seemed to need to purge herself of the horror she had endured. Sarah told her to save her strength. They would take a formal statement later, but Theresa insisted. She had to get it out.

SARAH GUIDED THERESA downstairs to the kitchen and eased her into a chair at the small breakfast table in the corner. Scott joined them as soon as he finished his calls. After taking a sip of the water Sarah had given her, Theresa began talking.

"Wednesday night I met Paula and Lisa, my friends from work, at The Watering Hole. We go there once or twice a month. I never stay long and only have a couple of drinks before leaving, alone. To me the place is nothing but a meat market and most of the guys there are losers. Paula and Lisa don't agree, but to each her own. I go because I like to hang out with them, plus, it's close to the office and the DJ plays good music. I didn't plan on Wednesday night being any different.

"We got there about six-fifteen and had just gotten our first round of drinks when he, Gary Allen, came over and hit on me. It wasn't the first time he had hit on me, so I knew his name. At that time, he seemed nice enough, but he was a little too slick for my taste. Even if that wasn't true, it wouldn't have mattered. I don't go out with guys I meet at bars. You just never know what you're getting into.

"Anyway, the three or four times Gary approached me, I tried to be polite and tell him I'm flattered, but not interested. He accepted that and moved on. That's what happened Wednesday night, the first time."

Scott handed her a Kleenex, she wiped her eyes and continued.

"Maybe a half an hour later, Gary came back. This was a first. He'd never tried twice in one night. This time he had an attitude. He was cocky, arrogant and even seemed a little put out. Told me it was my last chance. I was already frustrated with Paula. I'd had a bad day at work and I guess I took it out on him. Besides, who did this asshole think he was anyway, God's gift to women? So, I decided to end it right then, get him to leave me alone, once and for all. Being kind didn't get through, so I tried to hit him where it hurt, his ego. I remember I said something like, 'Are you learning impaired? I'm not interested and I never will be. Read my lips, brainiac. No! And process that with the brain in your head and not the one on the end of your pencil dick. Goodbye.' I said it louder than I intended and several people around us laughed. When he heard them, he turned beet red and got very angry. I thought he was going to hit me. Instead he gave me a threatening look, nodded and moved on.

"At first I was a little frightened, and then decided that was silly. I mean what could he do? Never talk to me again. That's what I wanted. I have to admit, I felt a little guilty for humiliating him in front of people, but he brought it on himself. He should have taken no for an answer. I thought I was finally rid of him.

"The encounter with him had ruined the evening so I was ready to leave. I finished my drink and started toward the door. The waitress stopped me and said that she had a round of drinks for me and my friends. I assumed they were from Gary, as an apology. The girls came over and we weren't going to accept them, but Lisa looked around the room and said he was nowhere in sight. So, we decided to accept the drinks. But mine didn't taste right. It even looked kind of odd, had a purple tint to it. I took a couple of sips and then left it on an empty table. I started feeling tired and nauseated. When I told the others that I wasn't feeling well and was calling it a night, Paula offered to take me home. I told her no, that I'd be okay after getting a little fresh air to clear my head. If only I'd let her take me home.

"When I first got outside, I did feel better but as I walked across the parking lot, I began to feel dizzy. My body felt heavy, and I felt like I was moving in slow motion. I could hardly pick up my feet. It was like my body wasn't listening to my mind. I barely made it to my car. When I did, it took all my energy just to push the key remote to unlock the doors. I had never felt like that before. I didn't have the strength to open the door. So I just leaned against my car with my forehead on the cool surface of the roof. I was wide-awake. My mind was working, but not my body. I fumbled with my purse to get my cell phone, to call 9-1-1.

"Then someone tapped me on the shoulder. I managed to slowly turn my head to see who it was. When I was able to focus, I was looking into Gary's blue eyes. They looked cold and distant. I remember feeling an initial chill when I looked into them. I didn't know where he came from and I hadn't heard him come up behind me. It was as if he materialized out of nowhere. He seemed to be looking right through me. And he was smiling, as if he knew some joke that I didn't. It was odd. I felt like I should run, get away, but my brain couldn't get my body moving.

"He asked me if I was okay. His voice sounded strange and whatever he said after that I couldn't understand. His words were so slurred that I couldn't connect them into sentences or thoughts. I sensed that something was wrong, but I couldn't react. He took my keys out of my hand and walked me around to the passenger side of my car. He opened the door and helped me get in. I remember asking him if he would go get one of my friends. He closed the door without a word.

"I didn't realize that he'd cranked the car and started driving until I looked out the window. Street signs, trees and other cars were just a blur. Looking out the window made me light-headed. I remember leaning my head back and closing my eyes. I was so tired that I didn't even ask where he was taking me. I must have passed out.

"I have no idea how long I was asleep, but when I opened my eyes I was cold and disoriented. I didn't know where I was. Nothing was familiar. I tried to sit up and I couldn't. My arms and legs felt paralyzed. That was when I panicked becuase I knew something was bad wrong. I tilted my head up and looked around. My arms and legs were tied to the bed. Then I realized why I was cold, all I had on were my bra and panties. I closed my eyes, willing it to be a nightmare and screamed.

"Someone laughed. I turned my head and looked in the direction the laugh had come from, and that bastard from the bar, Gary Allen, was standing beside the bed, without any clothes on. He slapped me across the face and told me to shut up. He said that we were out in the country and no one could hear me. I screamed again and he hit me in the ribs. It hurt like hell! I thought he broke my ribs. I couldn't take a breath without pain shooting through my right side. I began to cry and he started laughing. He stopped abruptly, leaned over me and stared directly into my eyes with a blank, cold look in his eyes, and told me, 'You need to learn some manners, bitch' in this slow, deliberate voice. Then he began hitting me, slapping me really hard, with his open palms."

Theresa started crying again. The memory seemed to bring the pain and terror back. She began to shake. Sarah got out of her chair, moved around the table, and put her arms around her.

"Are you sure you want to do this now? We can wait, you know, until you feel stronger."

"No, I've got to tell you about it. What...what he did to me! You understand. I can see it in your eyes."

"Okay, go ahead. Tell us," Scott whispered.

"He kept hitting me. I screamed for help. And every time I did, he'd slap harder and move to a different part of my body. He was laughing hysterically. The more I cried, the louder he laughed. He was enjoying it. Finally my throat was so hoarse that I couldn't yell or cry anymore. The pain was unbearable. I stopped fighting. I quit. I gave up. He stopped hitting me, but he wasn't through.

"He stared into my eyes again and in that same deliberate voice asked me if I wanted to apologize for my behavior at the bar. Maybe beg for his pencil dick. I panicked. He was getting even for what I said at the bar. He was crazy. I could see it in his eyes.

"So, I did, I apologized and begged him for it; anything to get him to stop hurting me. He laughed. Then he pulled a knife out of a drawer and held it in front of my eyes. I thought he was going to kill me. Initially, I was scared. Then I thought, 'Thank God, it's over.' But I was wrong, it was only the beginning.

"He cut my bra off and then my panties, one leg at the time. He must have cut me because I could feel something running down the inside of my thighs. I was so scared I couldn't think. He climbed on the bed and straddled me, and bent over and bit my nipples, hard. Then he...everything was a blur, until he rolled off me, dressed and left the room. I don't know how long he was on me or how long he was gone. Time no longer had any meaning to me.

"When he returned, he beat me again and then climbed on me. While he was on top of me, I realized this was it. This was what was in store for me from then on. When he was finally done with me, he wouldn't let me go. He couldn't. He had to kill me."

Theresa sobbed and put her head in her hands. "I was so scared!"

"That's enough for now." Scott said in a hushed voice. "You can tell us the rest, later."

Theresa didn't seem to hear him. Or if she did, she ignored his words. "I wasn't going to keep on enduring the torture and I didn't want to continue humiliating myself by begging, by being his source of pleasure. I decided, no more pleading.

"I began taunting him. I told him I would never apologize to a pathetic loser like him. The only way he could get a woman was to drug her and kidnap her, that I'd had better fucks in high school, anything to get him mad enough to kill me.

"I almost succeeded. When he finished he sat up, straddling my chest. His eyes were menacing. I knew I had won. He grabbed my throat and began squeezing. I gave in, didn't struggle. I began choking on my own spittle. Blackness filled my mind. My last thought before I passed out was, 'I won.'

"But I didn't. I woke up and he was sitting in a chair beside the bed, staring at me. He began laughing the second our eyes met. You fooled me, I almost killed you. That's what you wanted, wasn't it? You wanted the easy way out. Well, that is not going to happen. No, you'll suffer. I'm going to keep you around for a long time, much longer than the others. Then I'll untie one arm and let you kill yourself."

Before Theresa could finish, the paramedics arrived. As they loaded her on a stretcher, Theresa clung to Sarah and begged her to go with her to the hospital. "He's still out there. What if he comes back? Please stay with me. Don't let him get me," she cried, on the verge of hysterics.

The EMT gave Theresa a light sedative so she'd rest on the way to the hospital. Sarah held her hand, whispering. "You're right, I do understand. More than you will ever know. You see I was his first victim, my best friend Callie and I. I lost her." Tears streamed down Sarah's cheeks as she confided to the sleeping figure.

"Callie couldn't live with what he had done to her. She took her own life. We suffered the beatings, the rapes and the humiliation, too. I'm so happy I was able to save you. That I got there in time."

The physicians and rape team spent several hours examining Theresa. She was a trooper through it all, never complaining or refusing to do anything they asked. She was happy to be alive and wanted her attacker caught.

When the physicians gave their approval for Theresa to be interviewed, Scott, Roy and Sarah crowded into the small cubicle with her. Theresa recounted what had happened to her, repeating much of what she had told Scott and Sarah earlier and filling in additional details when questioned. She ended her tale with the voice in the dark, Sarah's voice, yelling, 'FBI, we're here to help!' I couldn't believe it, the FBI. I was safe. I heard Gary running down the steps. Then a man's voice, saying, I'll go after Hawkins, you find Theresa. Then you called out, Sarah James, FBI! Theresa Paul we're here to help you. I remember thinking, who is Hawkins? By the way, who is Hawkins?"

At the conclusion of the interview, Theresa was shown a series of photos and asked to pick out the man that had abducted and abused her. She positively identified Gary Allen, a.k.a. Gregory Hawkins.

"That's him. There is not a shadow of a doubt. I'd know him anywhere. He is the one, the bastard that did this to me. I know he planned to kill me and would have if Sarah hadn't gotten there when she did. I owe you my life." Clutching Sarah's hands Theresa sobbed, "I'll never forget those words that came out of the darkness, Theresa, Theresa Paul, FBI! I'm here to help you! Sarah James, FBI!"

"How can I ever thank you? You can't possibly know what it was like for me." Theresa's eyes brimmed over with tears.

"I was just the agent that got to you first. You have Atlanta PD and the FBI to thank." Sarah gestured toward Roy and Scott. "Believe me Theresa, it was a team effort."

After several minutes Roy broke the silence that ensued. "Are you positive that this is the man?" He held a picture of Greg Hawkins.

"Yes! Catch him! Catch him before he hurts another woman. I want mine to be the testimony that puts him behind bars."

"You can count on it," Scott vowed.

Sarah was secretly relieved, knowing that she wouldn't have to kill him. He would be tied to all the murders, caught and punished. To him, life in prison would be worse than death. She felt good for the first time in years. She had been instrumental in getting the bastard, keeping her vow to Callie and Jessica, without violating her oath to the Bureau. Now, Sarah could marry Scott with a clear conscious.

CHAPTER 18

AS SOON AS HE CLEARED the gates of the condo complex and was sure he was not being followed, Hawkins slowed down and drove within the speed limit. He was angry and confused.

How did this happen? How did they find me so soon? Another day and Miss Theresa Paul would have been history. Disposed of like the garbage she is. Why did I wait? She wasn't even that good, the snide little whore. I should have killed her when she begged me to, taunting me.

Being methodical, he had a plan. He just had to get himself together and start thinking straight. He turned up the radio in the red Accord and told himself how lucky he was. *This is just a minor setback. All I have to do is put my plan in motion.*

As always, he was prepared. He had a new identity. A safe place to hide, with money and clothes stashed there. He could stay there as long as he needed, but his plan, if the cops got too close, was to be out of Atlanta within twenty-four hours. He had purchased a home in New Orleans using his new identity months ago, just in case something went wrong. He had a new home, bank accounts and even an idea for a new job there. He would start a new life. Gary Allen would simply disappear without a trace, just as Greg Hawkins had done. His future was secure. He took a deep breath and began to relax. He felt better, rational, back in control

He took I-285 east and got off on Johnson Ferry Road. He knew exactly where he wanted to leave Theresa's Accord. He circled the block to be sure the house wasn't being watched, no cops and no FBI.

He pulled into the driveway. Before getting out, he checked the package sitting on the back seat. The envelope with the note in it was still on top. He laughed out loud. *This will blow the little bitch's mind! Does she think I'm stupid, that I wouldn't recognize her? Hello, JJ. This is your wake-up call.*

He got out and locked the car. Started down the drive and stopped. He heard the dog barking. *I ought to kill that damn dog, just to spite her. After all, she cost me my dad.* He turned around and started toward the house, then stopped. *Nope, it's not worth it.* Hawkins turned and retraced his steps, down the drive and headed for the little strip mall a mile away.

He got in the black van and drove away. The van had been there for two weeks. He had moved it around the parking lot every few days to keep it from being noticed. He hated having to change his plans. It would have been the coup de grace to leave the girls' body in her own car, parked in an FBI Agent's driveway. He chuckled at the message that would send the feeble Feds. The fools!

ROHYPNOL IN LIQUID and tablet form, fingerprints, bloodstains, bed sheets with secretions and vaginal stains, hair, and other forms of DNA were found in the bedrooms and bathrooms of the condo where Theresa had been held captive. Print matches for Hawkins and the three Atlanta victims had been verified and Scott, Roy and Sarah were confident conclusive DNA matches for Hawkins and the victims would be forthcoming, also. Warrants had been issued for Gary Allen, a.k.a. Gregory Hawkins' arrest and to search his house. An APB, was out on Hawkins and Atlanta PD and the FBI would jointly conduct the search.

"We saved her, Scott. Theresa is okay." Sarah voiced her feelings for the first time, now that they were alone in his car.

"No, Sarah you saved her."

Turning onto Hawkins' street they saw flashing lights surrounding his home. Atlanta PD had the street barricaded. Scott and Sarah passed through three checkpoints before being allowed in the house. Crime scene techs were in every room, looking for trace evidence, fibers, hair, and prints to determine if any of the victims had been in the house or that their DNA had piggybacked in on Hawkins' shoes or clothes. Simultaneously, Roy's detectives and Scott's agents were searching for tangible items to tie him to the crimes.

Sarah was working with the detectives on the first floor while Scott's team concentrated on the second floor. The first floor search was proving fruitless, when Scott called. "Up here!"

Three shoeboxes were sitting on the floor next to a small opening leading under a whirlpool spa. Roy and Sarah watched Scott open the first box. Gloved, he carefully removed panties and bras from the box and handed them to a tech to be photographed, bagged and tagged. Roy knelt beside Scott who held up a pair for him to see.

"Are they all cut open like that?" Roy asked.

"Yes, the bras are cut open too." Scott answered.

Roy picked up the bag marked "Box 1-Item 2." Matching bras and panties were bagged together and labeled in the sequence of their removal from box one, two or three. "1-2" was a pair of red lace panties and a matching bra.

"Wasn't Syms wearing red when she disappeared?" Roy asked.

"Yes," Sarah answered. "So, it's only reasonable that

those were hers. Wait a minute. Scott, was there a set on top of the red ones?"

"Yes, a matching white set."

Those weren't there, before, Sarah thought in surprise. "Do we have a victim unaccounted for?" She asked the other two.

"No, remember the second, most recent, victim's clothes were white, a skirt and sweater." Roy answered. "Found them in her car."

"That's right." Sarah watched in silence as each box was emptied. Even though she was prepared for the last items in the third box, she gasped when Scott lifted them out.

Scott looked at her over his shoulder and guessed immediately what he had found, Sarah's running shorts and exercise bra. No one else in the room grasped the significance.

Sarah turned away and went downstairs.

Regaining control, Sarah found the detectives searching the downstairs rooms. "Some shoeboxes upstairs were loaded with evidence, panties and bras. We think they're from the victims. Check out any shoeboxes or bags down here, never know what you might find."

Minutes later a detective called out, "Found some shoeboxes in the closet in here." Sarah followed his voice to the master bedroom. The last box he opened held formal wear accessories, cummerbunds, cuff links and bow ties. All wrapped in tissue paper.

"Look under the paper." Roy ordered.

The detective found a set of lock picks. *No black bra or panties! What the...Where are they?* Sarah thought as she stared on in disbelief.

"Bag 'em for the lab, tell them to check for matches to the doorknob from Agent James' back door. I'll bet they tie into the break-in at her home."

Suddenly Sarah felt uneasy.

"You find anything else of value down here?" Scott asked when he joined them.

The detective in charge of the downstairs search told him about the picks.

"Call Templeton and tell him to go over the Galleria condo again, looking for panels hidden in walls. We might have missed something," Scott directed one of his men. Hal Templeton was the Agent assigned to coordinate surveillance and search activities at the condo where Theresa had been held.

Sarah and Scott left Hawkins' house shortly after two on Friday afternoon. Atlanta PD would secure it. They stopped by Hawkins Sr.'s office to advise him of their findings at the company owned condo. He was not aware that his son had been using it or that he even knew of its existence. He was visibly shaken when he heard what had happened there, but he was relieved to learn that Theresa Paul had been found alive.

Scott made a plea to the father. "Mr. Hawkins, I don't know how else to say this but your son is a murderer. He no longer deserves your protection. Please contact me immediately if he gets in touch with you."

Mr. Hawkins agreed. "He will always be my son, but he's become an animal. I will do all I can to assist you in apprehending him. You have my word."

The evidence gathered at the condo and at the house would be enough to convict Hawkins of the murders of the two Atlanta women and to link him to numerous murders in other cities over the past fourteen years. Sarah was certain that he would not escape punishment, and she hoped he would be tried in a state with the death penalty.

But first Hawkins had to be apprehended. The wait would be excruciating, but in the end, he would be caught and dealt with. He had nowhere to hide. The wire services had the story and by morning he would be front-page news. Mr. Syms was offering a one hundred thousand dollar reward to anyone assisting the authorities in the capture of their daughter's murderer. Hawkins would be in custody before the weekend was over.

At the office, Scott and Sarah completed the paperwork covering their activities over the past twenty-four hours. Their entry into the condo was dicey, but Scott covered Sarah's butt by justifying probable cause. His report gave her full credit for solving the cases and saving Theresa Paul's life. After an hour and a half, the words and sentences began running together and Sarah could barely read what she had written. Just after six she asked Scott to take her home.

Friday night was pizza night, so when they were close to her house, Sarah called and ordered delivery. She was tired, sore and mentally exhausted, she wanted to eat, soak in a hot tub, and get some sleep.

"Don't tell me the pizza guy got here before us?" She wondered aloud when she saw a car sitting in her driveway.

"I'm glad he waited," Scott replied.

"Why doesn't he have his lights on, the sign on the top?" She asked as the sensor lights at the corners of her house came on, illuminating the red Accord. Sarah made the connection first. "Scott! That's Theresa's car?" Sarah reached for her gun as he hit his brakes.

"Call dispatch," he ordered.

Sarah made the call. Both heard the response. The tag number matched. Theresa's car was parked in Sarah's driveway. She requested back up.

"Let's check it out. You take the passenger side." Scott pulled his weapon and eased out of the car.

Staying low, they cautiously approached the Accord. Once they reached it Scott banged on the door. "FBI. Open up." He ordered.

When there was no response and no movement inside the car, they peered through the windows.

"Empty. I'll go around back. You watch the front. Don't go in until we have backup. He sprinted off and Sarah got in position, using the open door as a shield and focused on the front of the house. She could hear sirens approaching.

Thirty minutes later, after thoroughly searching the house and finding it empty except for Jax, they were standing on the front porch talking with Roy who responded to the call.

"Why did he leave the car here?" Roy asked.

"Maybe he realizes Sarah is responsible for his being identified?" Scott suggested.

"How does he know where she lives?" Before they could respond, a lab tech called from inside the car. "There's a package on the back seat addressed to Agent James." The three moved to the car. "Bring it out here," Roy ordered.

Wearing gloves, and being careful not to smudge any prints, the tech took it off the backseat and sat it on the hood of the car. An envelope with Sarah's name on it was taped to the top of the box.

"See if there is a note in the envelope."

The tech used a razor knife to remove the envelope and open it. He pulled out a single sheet of paper and looked up at his boss.

"Read it."

JJ

Didn't you think I would recognize you? After all, you were my first. The only one I let get away, a mistake. One I plan to correct. I like the black lace, thanks. I bet you look sexy in them. However, I prefer to obtain these my way, so I'm returning them, for now.

See you, soon!

The note wasn't signed. No one suspected a bomb in the package, so Scott told the tech to "open it."

How the…Sarah caught her breath when the tech held up her black lace panties and matching bra. Her panties and bra, the ones she'd left at Hawkins house. "Is one of you going to explain this?" Roy looked at Scott and Sarah.

Sarah felt her face flaming. Now, either she or Scott

would have to inform Roy of her link to Greg Hawkins.

"Let's go inside and I'll tell you," Scott answered. He motioned for Sarah to wait on the porch as he and Roy walked to the house.

Watching them disappear inside, Sarah thought, "Killing Hawkins is the only way to end this. I won't endure another trial. He's got to die, even if I lose Scott. At least he'll have his career." Straightening her shoulders and lifting her chin, she went inside to join them, despite Scott's silent command.

SARAH LISTENED AS SCOTT told Roy about her past. Why she had changed her name and her life. The overview gave him a glimpse of the person she had been and who she had become, the impact the former Senator had on her life and how and why he had interceded with the Bureau. To Roy's credit, he didn't make any judgments or question her involvement in the current investigation. He silently eyed Sarah as he listened to the story. Stone faced, he showed no emotion.

Scott told him about the harassing phone calls and reminded Roy of the break-in a few weeks ago and what had been taken. The panties and bra in the box were one in the same, proving Hawkins was the burglar. He also indicated that with the proper warrants in place, he suspected Hawkins' phone records would verify he made the calls.

"So this is the first time you realized he knew who you were?" Roy looked at Sarah.

"Yes. Until now, I figured he thought I was an FBI agent who was getting too close. I thought the break-in was a result of my interviewing a bar waitress who put us on his trail. I never dreamed Hawkins would connect me to that teenager in North Carolina. Hell, that was fourteen years ago."

"Why did you think he stole your underwear?"

"Easy. He's sick. He collects women's underwear."

"Not any woman's, just his victims. Have you thought about that?"

"No, I didn't think he'd made the connection or that he even knew JJ existed. And we won't know if he was responsible for the break-in until the lab checks out the lock picks we found at Hawkins' house," She answered.

Roy nodded. "Well, we know now. He knows you're the teenager from North Carolina. Maybe that explains the break-in. He wanted to go through your things to verify his suspicions. But, that doesn't explain the underwear."

"Why do you think he returned them?" Scott asked her.

"That's simple. The note said it all. I'm no longer the agent tracking him. I'm JJ, a mistake that needs correcting." She paused looking from one man to the other.

"Theresa is in danger, too. He can't leave her to identify him," she told the other two.

"What difference does it make now? He's already been identified and we found enough evidence in his house and that condo to tie him to at least eight murders," Roy stated.

"He doesn't know that. In his mind, only an eyewitness can nail him. Without one, he believes he can get off," Sarah responded.

"If the past is any indication, then he's right," Scott commented.

"He obviously thinks we're pretty stupid. He's announcing his intentions to kill an FBI agent. He's challenging us to stop him," Roy stated.

Sarah's inner voice was screaming.

Sarah and Scott didn't get to bed until after midnight, so it only seemed reasonable that they sleep past noon on Saturday. Up, dressed and relaxed, Scott found Sarah in the kitchen reading the newspaper.

"Woman, get off your duff and get the keys to the 350 Z. We're going shopping. It's time we picked out a ring. I want everyone to know you're off the market."

"Wait a minute, off the market? Is that what you think

being engaged means? No, no, you're off limits, not me!" Sarah's smile could have lit up a coliseum.

"Very funny!" He swatted her on the butt. "Now get it in gear before I change my mind."

"Not likely, buster, just give me a minute." Sarah went to the bathroom to touch up her makeup. Retuning to the kitchen she asked Scott, "Should we leave? You know, what if...?"

Scott knew Sarah was thinking, what if something broke on the case? "There's nothing we can do, there's an All Points Bulletin out on Hawkins, and he'll be on the front page of every paper in the southeast by morning. It's out of our hands for now. So, we might as well spend our Saturday, what's left of it, doing something useful, so move it!"

"Yes sir. Enjoy today. It may be the last time you get to give orders away from the office," She saluted. "I hope you have a lot of money. I want a rock. If I'm off the market, I want the men to be able to see my ring from across the street." She grabbed her keys.

Sarah found the ring at the third store they visited. It was pricey, too expensive for an agent's budget, but Scott insisted. Sarah cried when he slipped it on her finger.

Roy called later that afternoon and suggested Scott get Sarah out of town for a few days. Both men were confident Hawkins would be in custody by Monday, but neither wanted to risk Sarah's safety until then. She was at risk as long as Hawkins was at large. The message from the psycho had been all too plain; he intended to kill Sarah James.

Scott and Sarah decided to go back to St. Simons for a few days. Scott didn't really want to leave town. He wanted to be in on the capture, but he knew Sarah wouldn't go without him. Besides, the more he thought about it, he wasn't about to let her go alone. What if Hawkins followed her? No, he wouldn't risk that. After all, the sick bastard had broken into her house and stolen her underwear. She wouldn't be going anywhere alone until Hawkins was in custody.

CHAPTER 19

I BET THEY ARE SCOURING Atlanta looking for me. The Cops and the Feds are such idiots. If I put that homicide detective and lover boy, Mr. Agent-in-Charge, in a paper bag with directions, they'd suffocate before finding their way out. As long as they underestimate me, I can do anything I want. I would have loved to see their faces when they spotted the car in the agent's drive, pure genius.

Two can play her game. Only I'm changing the rules. She is in over her head. Damn, I wish I could've have seen her face when she spotted the girl's car in her driveway. Or, when she opened the package and pulled out her own underwear. That must have been priceless. She thought she was so clever breaking-in and planting them in my closet. Was she out of her mind, trying to set up the master?

The motion-activated camera in his bedroom had picked up her every move. He laughed when he saw the tape. *How fitting! I use it to film my sex sessions, now my first victim gets caught trying to outsmart me!*

Lying on the bed in his motel room, Hawkins could hear cars and sixteen wheelers roaring up and down I-75, which was a stone's throw away. Macon was an hour south of

Atlanta and the interstate was the major corridor to Florida from there.

When the Feds found out he'd spent his first night there, they would assume he was headed south and look for him in the sunshine state. By the time they realized he wasn't there, if they ever did, he would be settled in New Orleans. The Big Easy, the perfect environment for anyone with exotic tastes!

He would wait a while, until things cooled down, and then take a long, pleasurable weekend to return to Atlanta to deal with JJ and the other bitch. When they were out of the way, there would be no one to testify against him and his dad's attorneys could get him off.

The sun was shining when he walked down the street to the Steak and Shake. It was a fine Saturday afternoon. Hawkins believed the day was an omen for his bright future. Sure he had to be careful while he was in Georgia but as long as he steered clear of Atlanta he would be safe. The authorities would be so busy protecting JJ and Theresa they wouldn't think to look elsewhere.

So he'd give up his job and home. Big deal, he'd get others. And he'd be happier in New Orleans. It'd be easy enough to find a job there, not that he needed to work. Everything was turning out rosy. That FBI agent had done him a favor.

The only negative was his father. He was really angry, but Greg knew he could take care of that in due time. He planned to handle the loose ends before contacting his dad. The two women needed to be out of the picture first.

In no time, he'd have pops believing his son was the innocent victim of a self-serving FBI agent. And when he pointed out that the agent had been JJ, carrying a grudge, all hell would break loose. Funny how such an astute businessman could be so gullible where his precious son was concerned.

Steak and Shake was full. The only seat available

without a wait was a stool at the counter. Not wanting to waste his time, Hawkins took that one.

"Double cheeseburger, fries and a chocolate shake." He gave the waitress his best smile.

He made small talk with her while he ate his burger and fries. By the time he was ready to leave, she had agreed to have dinner with him. He hadn't planned on staying another night but what the heck. He was in no hurry and could use some diversion. What better than an attractive female in the sack! He smiled when he saw the slogan over on the wall, "Take home a sack full."

I plan to. He checked out her ass.

And she could serve more than one purpose. He would tell her about his plans to go to Florida, Tampa maybe. If the cops interviewed her, she could tell them his plans. Brilliant.

He would use Gary Allen's VISA to pay for the room and dinner. When the cops checked his charges they would find he'd stayed in Macon. He arranged for the waitress to meet him in the lobby and would make sure the desk clerk saw them together. That way he would steer the cops in her direction when they questioned him.

He got to the lobby a few minutes early and struck up a conversation with the clerk, making a point of commenting on how friendly Macon was and asking about a restaurant that would impress his date, dropping her name and that she worked at the Steak and Shake. When she picked him up, he pointed out a new BMW in the lot with a Florida license.

"That's my car. I need to get it washed. Thanks for driving. I've got a long drive to Tampa."

The evening went better than expected. The meal was good, his date was fun and best of all — she was better looking out of her clothes than in them, and she was outstanding in bed.

Sunday turned out to be not such a great day. It started out well, but went to crap in a glance. Hawkins was up first and offered to go to the Dunkin Donuts down the street and get them something to eat. Whistling, he walked past the office and the paper racks out front. Glimpsing at the Atlanta paper, he froze. Stunned!

Across the top of the paper the headline shouted, "Have You Seen This Man?"

His picture, one he recognized from his father's study, filled a quarter of the front page, underscored by the subtitle, "Serial Killer-Rapist on the Loose!"

The blood froze in his veins as the realization hit him. Minutes ago, he had thought it would be days before they tracked him to Macon. Now it could be minutes. At least the waitress thought his destination was Tampa. He had to leave without making her suspicious. She would see the papers soon enough. Hopefully, she had such a good time that she would refuse to believe the guy in the paper could be him.

He risked going to the donut shop and then returned to the room. She was walking out of the bathroom, freshly showered, with a towel wrapped around her. She opened it up to display her body. "Interested?" She smiled.

This was one of the rare times that sex wasn't Greg's first priority, but he had to keep her from becoming suspicious. He got that tingle in his groin as he looked her over. Sunlight was streaming through the windows focused on her like a spotlight. "Damn, you look great this morning, I can't think of a better way to start the day!" He took the towel from her and dropped it on the floor and kissed her while backing her onto the bed.

An hour and a half later, he was on the road, rethinking his plans. He had turned on the television after the girl left and Gary Bundy Allen, a.k.a. Gregory Alan Hawkins, Jr. was the lead story on every station. Someone had put up a hundred thousand dollar reward for information leading to his capture. He never expected this. He couldn't be seen in public. He couldn't go to a hotel, a restaurant, a gas station. He could be recognized anywhere. He had to find a hole and climb in it.

Once he thought about it, there was a bright spot.

The reward would work in his favor. Greed will have people seeing him behind every tree. The cops will get thousands of leads and they'll have to check out every one of them. That is until they get frustrated with all the dead ends. Then they'll get lax and he could slip through the cracks.

All he had to do was lay low until the press died down. In the meantime, he'd hide right under their noses. That way, he wouldn't spoil the setup in New Orleans.

Hawkins' mood changed and he began singing with the radio. The tune happened to be "Rainy Night in Georgia," sung by Lou Rawls.

AT 11:16 ON SUNDAY MORNING, Sarah was walking to the restroom at a gas station on the corner of Riverside Drive and Arkwright Road in Macon. Scott was filling up the Suburban. Neither noticed the black van with Louisiana plates pull out of the motel across the street and proceed to North I-75. But Jax did. He woke up at that precise moment, stuck his head out the window and barked a warning to Scott and Sarah. Of the three, he was the only one to sense danger. He leaped through the open window and hit the ground at a dead run, pursuing his prey. Hawkins turned through the light and got on the entrance ramp without looking back.

"Jax!" Scott and Sarah yelled.

He barely missed getting hit by a car before realizing he had lost the black van. Proud that he had chased off the threat, he trotted back to Sarah.

"What were you thinking?" Sarah scolded the dog. "You could have been killed." She attached a leash to his collar.

"You were supposed to be watching him!" She yelled at Scott.

"I was watching him. The dog just suddenly went nuts."

"He's never done that before, never! I don't know what got into him." She shook her head and put him back in the car. "I'd like to know what he saw. He sensed something." She visually scanned the area. "He was on the attack."

Opening the door on the driver's side, the sunlight flashed into Sarah's eyes, off the "rock" on her finger. Goose bumps ran up her spine as the sunlight enhanced the brilliance of the marquee diamond centered in the setting.

Oh, my gosh! Oh, my gosh! I'm engaged. Leaving the door standing open, she circled around the car and gave Scott a deep kiss. "I love my ring! And, I'm sorry I yelled at you."

"I'm glad, apology accepted."

Jax jumped out of the car and wedged between the two and whined. Sarah pulled out of Scott's reach, knelt down and took Jax's head in her hands. "I love my dog, too." She stroked his curly ears and he adored the attention, his stubby tail was wagging.

"That's enough. He wasn't even with us when we got the ring." Scott chuckled and opened the back door. Jax jumped into the Suburban and Sarah grabbed Scott again as soon as the door was closed.

You keep this up and we'll have to go over to there." He nodded toward the motel across the street. "Maybe they rent by the hour?"

"We'll need more than an hour, believe me!" She hugged him.

He looked at her adoringly. "Definitely, let's get on the road. The sooner we get going, the sooner we'll get there."

Sarah and Scott spent the next few days enjoying St. Simons — eating great food, running or bicycling around the island every morning and taking long walks on the beach at night. Scott fell in love with the island, the people and the relaxed atmosphere, agreeing that it was the perfect location for their wedding. Even Jax seemed to be enjoying himself and Scott was growing on him. The dog even allowed the interloper to feed him treats.

Wednesday afternoon Sarah walked into the condo after spending most of the day on the beach. Her pale green bikini was a showstopper and Scott whistled when he saw her.

"Whoa! That's new! You look great, and here I spent the day on the golf course."

"It was your choice, golf over the beach, or whatever."

"If I had seen you in that teeny-bikini first, it would've been whatever!" Scott was all but drooling.

She grazed his lips with hers. "Too late, lover. How was your golf game?"

"I didn't play that well, but I had fun. The course was in great shape and I met a nice guy, a retired Veterinarian that loves life, golf and his wife. He sprayed shots all over the course and still shot a seventy-nine."

"How did his wife come up?"

"He talked about her constantly."

"And I'm sure you told him all about your fiancée?"

"Of course, especially how sexy she looks in a bikini!"

While Sarah was showering, Scott called Roy for an update on the manhunt. Roy told him that more than five hundred leads had been received and only one was valid. Hawkins had been spotted in Macon but had slipped through their net, currently his whereabouts was unknown.

"What did Roy say?" Sarah asked as she walked out of the bathroom toweling her hair.

"Jax is smarter than we think." The Springer lifted his head at the mention of his name. If dogs could talk, Sarah was sure he would agree with Scott.

"We knew that, what clued Roy in?"

"Me. You remember how upset the mutt got at that gas station in Macon Sunday morning?"

"You mean when he charged out into the street?"

"Yes. That happened somewhere around midday, right? Do you remember the motel across the street?"

"Yes. So?"

"Hawkins checked out of that same motel at eleven-forty. He could easily have pulled out of the lot while I was pumping gas. Jax must have sensed he was a threat. You said he knew something was wrong."

"He did!" Her eyes widened. "You think Hawkins was following us? Is he here?"

"No, and Roy doesn't think so, either."

"Hawkins spent Friday and Saturday nights in Macon. So he was there before we drove through. It was a coincidence."

Sarah shuddered. "I hope you're right."

"Roy and I think he was just laying low. Probably didn't know how far along we were on the investigation, or that an APB was out on him. He had company Saturday night. A woman he picked up at a nearby restaurant stayed the night. Macon cops have already talked to her. She said the guy told her that he was on his way to Tampa. He pointed out a white BMW with a Florida tag, said it was his. It wasn't his. The car was pulled over in Florida. The owner stayed at the motel Saturday night and had never heard of Hawkins. We believe it's a ruse to get us to waste time looking in Florida, but we alerted The Tampa Bureau just in case.

"Where is he? Your best guess?"

"Atlanta."

"Atlanta?"

THE SUN ROSE OVER the Atlantic when Scott rolled over to find an empty spot in bed where Sarah should have been. In the thin morning light he could see her silhouette in a chair on the patio. Slipping on a pair of shorts, he joined her. Neither spoke as they watched the huge orange ball rising from the ocean far away on the horizon. Shrimp boats were trawling close to the coastline. Seagulls and dolphins followed the boats, vying for the fish churned up by the nets dragging behind the shrimp boats. The two lovers held hands, enjoying the sights and sounds of the early morning, bathed in the briny scent of the ocean.

When the sun had fully cleared the ocean, Scott spoke for the first time since rising.

"Are you okay?"

"Yes. But, I don't like the waiting. It scares me, never knowing when he's going to turn up, or where."

"I'm not going to let him harm you."

Sarah turned to face Scott. She had been dreading this moment for weeks. No, she wasn't frightened of Hawkins. Well, she was, but what scared her at this moment was what she needed to tell Scott.

He deserved the truth, the whole truth, all her illicit actions, breaking into Hawkins home, planting evidence, staging the break-in at hers and why. She would leave out none of the details. Tell him that she was setting Hawkins up in order to justify killing, no murdering him. About her vow to Callie and the silent promise she had made to a woman lying in a coffin. She needed to be honest with the man she wanted to marry. Her right hand closed over the ring on her left, knowing she may have to give it back.

She played the scenario in her mind, rehearsed the words. "I know I've abused your trust and the Bureau. Can you forgive me?"

He would take her in his arms and tell her she was forgiven. Then he would slide the ring back on her finger. But, she knew it wouldn't, couldn't happen that way. As her lover, he might forgive her but as her AIC, never. She would have to leave the Bureau. Her actions had compromised their case against Hawkins. Because of her, Hawkins could get off. And Scott could lose his career. And she would have broken her vow to Callie and Jessica. She would almost certainly lose the man who had taught her to love, the man who had made her whole.

She couldn't risk it. She couldn't tell him! If it were my future alone that's at stake, I could handle it. But, it's not that simple. Head down, body tense, she decided. *I can't tell him.*

Night after night, in the dark, lonely hours, she had debated with herself, finally reaching the only conclusion she could. That she had to live with the deception. She would have to bear the deceit, partly because of her vow to Callie and Jessica, but even more for the unsuspecting women Hawkins hadn't gotten to, yet, but would if he was allowed to remain free. Sarah was thinking about the potential victims who would not have to suffer at the psycho's hands, if he were put away. Those women would never be drugged, abducted, abused, murdered and finally stuffed into black plastic bags, to be thrown away like garbage.

If she kept quiet, Hawkins would be caught, convicted and punished. Who knows, perhaps he would resist arrest and receive the ultimate punishment, saving the courts a lot of trouble. She and Scott could get married, have kids and live happily ever after, and Callie and Jessica could finally rest in peace.

She drew a deep, shuddering breath and after Scott repeated his question. "Are you okay?"

She answered quietly. "Yes, I am. I'm happier than I've ever been. You've made me feel worthwhile for the first time since that morning fourteen years ago when I thought Hawkins had destroyed my life. After that, I never dreamed I could have a normal relationship with a man. You've changed that; you changed me. You have made me whole. Let me know that I'm clean. But I know he's still out there, on the periphery of my mind. It's not enough that he's haunted me all these years, now he's playing games with me. Letting me know it's not over. And it won't be over until one of us is dead. Or he's behind bars, forever. I hate to admit it, but I am scared. He recognized me and I didn't think that was possible. You and I both know that Theresa and I will not be safe until he is behind bars. No, Scott, I want the bastard dead."

Scott looked out into the rose flooded sky. "I can't

imagine what you are feeling. How you must hate and despise Hawkins. How much you must want to be the one to punish him. But you can't, you have to trust the system, trust me. Hawkins will get what's coming to him.

"He will never harm you again. He'll have to go through me to get to you and that is not going to happen. You're safe and so is Theresa. Consider me your guardian angel, and Roy's got his people watching over Theresa."

HAWKINS HADN'T BEEN OUTSIDE since arriving at his south Atlanta safe house on Sunday. He had rented the small house using a fake name, months ago, just for this purpose. A place to hide if needed. Atlanta had been his only alternative when he fled Macon. He considered going to New Orleans but discarded the idea quickly. It was too risky. He'd have to stop several times for gas. If he paid with cash, he would have to go inside the station and risk being recognized. If he used his credit cards, which were in Gary Allen's name, the charge slips would lead the authorities straight to New Orleans and that would compromise the new life he had planned for himself.

No, Atlanta was his only option, but being there did have one advantage. He could take care of a couple of loose ends sooner than he had originally planned. He could dispose of the two witnesses as soon as the heat died down. That red-headed bitch had haunted him long enough. Now, she had ruined him with his dad, sidetracked his career, and made his life miserable. She would pay, but not before she suffered. Hawkins smiled, thinking of what he had planned for Miss JJ, the FBI whore.

His hatred for her had grown into a raging fury since he talked to his dad. Hawkins had called him from Macon. His father had never been so angry. The bitch had been to see him, convinced him he was guilty. His dad actually told him to turn himself in to the police. That he would not help him anymore. He had to pay for his sins.

My own father called me a psycho. The bitch has ruined my life. Now I'll get even, she'll pay. I have a plan. I always have a plan. And they can't stop me because I'm always one step ahead of them.

As soon as he had figured out that the FBI agent was JJ from North Carolina, he began watching her. He even planned to check out a house down the street from her home. He had seen the 'For-Rent' sign when he was leaving her driveway, after dropping off Theresa's car.

JJ, you're a creature of habit and your predictability will be your downfall. That makes it easy for me, almost too easy. I may even kill that guy that's been hanging around you. Make you watch him die! Why not? You took away my dad, Miss FBI!

Methodically, he plotted his revenge. He knew her schedule, when she was vulnerable, when she wasn't and how he was going to take her. All he had to do now was decide the day, the time and the place. Actually, she'd do that for him. He'd take advantage of her routine, just like before. When he was through with her, she'd regret the day she ran. There would be no escape this time.

He paced around the house. Checked the old car in the garage, the one he would use to pick her up. Using it would keep the van available for his ultimate get-away. He went into the kitchen. The stash of Rohypnol was in the cabinet. In the bedroom, the knife was in the drawer of the bedside table and the handcuffs were attached to the four bedposts, each set with one cuff open, waiting for her. He fluffed the bed. Her deathbed! He laughed.

Looking at it, he made a decision. *I won't kill the boyfriend. When I'm out of here, I'll let him know where to find her. An anonymous tip, so he can find his whore. Then he'll know what it's like to be alone, abandoned.*

SCOTT, SARAH AND JAX returned home on Saturday. St. Simons was great, but they were glad to be home. Jax had his yard, Sarah had a wedding to plan and Scott had a serial killer to catch, and two key witnesses to protect, one of whom was soon to be his wife.

The trial of the corporate executive resumed the following Monday and Sarah spent her days at the courthouse. During the five weeks of the trial, Sarah soon fell into a routine. An early morning run with Scott and Jax, skip breakfast, shower and dress, then drive downtown arriving at the courthouse no later than nine. She ate a quick lunch during the midday recess and left as soon as court adjourned each afternoon, usually between four and five. She drove straight to the Bureau shooting range where she empted clip after clip of ammunition into targets, each bearing the imaginary face of Greg Hawkins. Marksmanship and deception being her goals, she practiced a variety of moves; slipping her weapon from the back of her waistband, retrieving it from a hidden ankle holster or drawing it from a holster on either hip or strapped across her shoulder. Drawing the weapon in one fluid motion and firing it with accuracy was paramount in her mind. She became quite adept at both. She had to, her life depended on it.

By seven-thirty each evening she was home preparing dinner for two. After eating and cleaning up the dishes, they walked the dog, watched television, talked and read. The only drawback to the routine was her loss of privacy. Sarah was never alone. Scott, another agent or courthouse security watched over her, twenty-four-seven. A female officer even accompanied her to the courthouse restroom.

The new prosecutor assigned to the fraud case by the Justice Department built an airtight case and was out for scalps. The Management Illusions team of Morgan Macy and Stella David gave brilliant testimonies that left no doubt that Michelle Smith, the former CFO, was guilty of embezzlement and fraud, and the precise manner in which she had committed the crimes.

Having established the defendant's guilt in the embezzlement and fraud schemes, the prosecutor didn't let up. He wanted first-degree murder charges added to her offenses. Surprising the defense team, he called Michelle's live-in lover to the stand. The former police officer admitted to committing the murder at Michelle's request, sealing her fate. A civil charge of murder was added to her crimes.

Sarah called Scott as soon as court adjourned, "Pablo's at seven, dinner is on me."

"You sound happy, trial over?"

"Yes, she was found guilty on all counts! The judge will sentence her tomorrow." To Sarah, the guilty verdicts more than justified her actions in getting the former prosecutor replaced. Justice had won!

"So, you're pleased with the outcome?" Scott asked while divvying up a platter of fajitas.

"Oh, yes. She's history in the outside world. Mercy is not part of this Judge's vocabulary. On top of that, the woman still has a felony murder trial to face. Today's conviction was only for embezzlement, fraud, and the civil charge of murder. I think the judge may award a cash settlement to the murder victim's family."

"Is there cash left in her account?"

"Just over a million dollars."

"You think the murder conviction is a sure thing?"

"After the boyfriend's testimony, it's in the bag. And the Prosecutor is pushing for a speedy trial. He'll get it, too."

"Was Stella there today?" Scott asked.

Sarah and Stella had become friends during the course of the trial and had lunch together several times a week. Sarah found the auburn haired Australian intelligent, witty, and sincere. Traits they had in common were that both were tall and had crushes on their bosses. The difference was that Sarah had landed hers, and Stella was still waiting for Morgan to make his move. "Yes, I'm going to get us together for dinner next weekend. Your job will be to get Morgan there."

"Are you playing matchmaker?"

"No! Just helping move things along, thank you."

"So you're still convinced she and Morgan have the hots for each other?"

"Definitely. It's funny really, watching them. I call it the ritual mating-dance of two professionals working together."

"Like the two of us, huh?"

Sarah smiled and nodded, her eyes sparkling. Then her expression changed and her stare grew intent. *New subject, the one we've been avoiding.*

"You haven't mentioned Hawkins this week. What's happening?" Sarah asked.

"We're totally frustrated. It's been four weeks and we don't have a clue. Thousands of leads are flooding the system. All the media attention has everyone after the reward. We've expended hundreds of man-hours following-up, with nothing to show for it."

"Nothing?"

"Nope. We have no idea where Hawkins might be. The only thing we think we know is that he is not in Florida. I'm worried that he's already assumed a new identity and relocated."

"If that's happened, it'll take another body to lead us to him."

"Don't even think that, Sarah."

Sarah leaned forward, her voice a whisper. "How long can you justify providing protection for Theresa and me?"

Scott's eyes narrowed, darkened, he dreaded the answer. "Another week or so, Roy and I are getting pressure about the man-hours."

"Lift mine and keep Theresa's as long as you can. Use our people to watch over her after Roy has to pull his."

At the end of the fifth week it was decided that Hawkins was no longer in Atlanta and Sarah's protection was discontinued. Theresa's continued for two additional weeks. At the end of that period both were free to move about as they pleased, use the bathroom or do anything else they desired, alone. Sarah called Theresa the first evening that she was alone. "How're you doing?"

"I'm glad to have my freedom, but, I'm scared, Sarah. I know I have to get on with my life, but how? I'm afraid to stay home and I'm afraid to leave. I sleep in the bathtub with a gun beside me. I'm afraid he's coming back. No, I know he's coming back. I'm afraid to go to my parents because I don't want to put them in danger. This guy is nuts, he'd kill them to get to me."

"You can't let him get to you like that Theresa. You're letting him win, dominate you. What does your therapist say?"

"Nothing that helps, she's reassuring but all the logic in the world doesn't mean squat. You know why?"

"Why."

"She wasn't the one tied to that bed, getting beaten and raped. Even you can't understand that!"

If you only knew. "You can get through this, Theresa. Just be careful. Don't take any chances. I guarantee you that Scott and Lieutenant Nelson wouldn't have pulled your protection if they thought you were in danger. Nothing is going to happen to you. I promise."

"I wish I could believe that, Sarah. I want to."

"Believe it. Believe me!"

"Sarah, I...I don't think I could have survived this without you." She gave a bitter little laugh. "I mean that literally, if you hadn't come along when you did!"

"I've told you before, it was a team effort. I just happened to be the one to get to you first. We're still here for you, remember that Theresa."

"I'm trying."

"Call me if you need to talk, twenty-four seven, okay?"

"Okay. Let me know if you hear anything! If they find him! God, I hope he resists and they kill him. Kill him Sarah, if you're there, shoot him dead. Please!"

"I can't promise that, but I will let you know when he's in custody."

"Or dead!"

"Or dead," Sarah reponded.

"Promise?" Theresa asked.

"Promise!" Sarah admitted, if only to herself, that she wanted Hawkins dead too.

That she, too, was frightened. But she had Scott, and she was trained to take care of herself. Poor Theresa had no one, and she was on her own, with no way to defend herself. She had told Theresa all the right things but...nagging at the back of her mind was that little voice, the one that was never wrong. It was telling her he could be anywhere. And he is coming!

HAWKINS WATCHED A RERUN of "Mrs. Doubtfire" last night and was now in the middle of Tootsie when inspiration struck. *All the big stars have done it at one time or another. Why can't I?*

Although he usually ventured out only after dark to avoid neighbors, he decided to risk a Saturday, mid-afternoon visit to Wal-Mart. *Every hick and his brother will be there. Who'll notice one more?*

He had reluctantly given up his sleek, fashionable style for plaid shirts and faded, baggy jeans acquired at a thrift shop. Work boots, a John Deere baseball cap and jean jackets with messages such as, "Everybody has to believe in something...I believe I'll have another beer!' completed his look. His hair was now long and shaggy and its color altered dramatically, thanks to Clairol hair coloring.

Pushing a shopping cart through Wal-Mart was a new experience for Hawkins. *So this is how the other ninety percent lives?* He felt safe mingling with the crowd. It wasn't long before he made an astute observation. *They're from all walks of life, and some of the chicks are hot! This might be a good place to score some action.*

He picked out three women's outfits that he thought would fit, undergarments and a pair of fairly unisex shoes. He stopped a disinterested salesgirl and asked where he could find the wigs. "I want to get one for my mama. She's done had that there chemo stuff and feels bad about her hair."

"Nah, we don't carry wigs. Best bet would be Sally's Beauty Supply down the street, next to Payless Shoes. Good luck to your ma."

He thought better of using Sally's down the street. Instead, he found a wig shop several miles away.

At Tiffany's Hair and Nail Delight he repeated his routine about the sick mother, improvising and adding inspired details such as, "How 'bout if I get some different colored ones and maybe different styles? Ya think it'd give ma a lift?"

With three wigs of various hues he left the shop and headed home, where he put on an oversized girdle stuffed with padding to make his butt and hips look larger and a 38-D bra with foam in the cups. Then he tried on the clothes—a simple blue dress, a black pants suit and a denim blouse with a pair of ladies jeans. The different colored wigs would alter his appearance with each outfit. He decided not to worry about makeup of any kind, being clean-shaven would have to suffice.

He began monitoring Theresa and Sarah every few days, driving past their homes to see if "unmarked" cars were parked nearby. Then he began following them to work, memorizing their routes. He sat in the café in the lobby of the insurance building or the cafeteria of the courthouse at lunchtime. Between five and six, he would sit at a bus stop outside the courthouse or the insurance building. Mondays and Thursdays were Theresa days, Tuesdays and Fridays he devoted to Sarah.

Then he got a lucky break. The couple that owned the house two doors down and across the street from Sarah responded to his inquiry. Wearing his disguise, he rented it for two months, paying in advance. He planed to spend only a few nights a week there. That way he could keep an eye on JJ without attracting attention. He bought a used car to drive back and forth. One he could just abandon when the time came.

He knew there was some risk involved but figured it to be minimal. *The cops are looking for strangers in her neighborhood, and the two lovebirds don't see anything but each other. No one's worried about the old woman down the street.*

Eventually his patience paid off. Sarah was no longer being shadowed. Shortly thereafter, Theresa was fair game as well. He stayed away from both of them for another week.

On Tuesday, the anxiety and excitement began building, the familiar thrill rising in his veins. He hadn't realized how much he had missed his women. He hadn't been with one since the waitress in Macon, and you could hardly count her. His last real sexual adventure had ended with Theresa's rescue.

I've got to do something soon, either one of you or someone new. No, don't fret ladies it will be one of you and soon, girls, soon. Just a few last-minute preparations and I'll be ready to entertain. And I have such special plans for you both, special plans for special bitches.

He had to move swiftly to insure success, and since this would be his greatest accomplishment to date, everything must be perfect. Fortunately for him, the police had grown lax, not only with their protection of the two but in other areas as well. He would never be guilty of that kind of stupidity, never get that careless. He had never been more alert, more precise and careful; totally aware of his surroundings, traffic patterns, neighbor's routines, and the weather, anything that could affect his activities or his plan. He knew exactly where he would go with the first one.

Sitting at the kitchen table in the safe house, a bottle and glass at hand, he smiled. He reviewed timing and prepared notes, finalizing his plans. A tingle of excitement coursed up his spine as he perfected the plan. The biggest joke was not that he would snatch her again, but where it would happen. *How apropos, the fools continue to underestimate me.*

He poured himself another drink and laughed out loud. Had there been anyone to hear, the listener might have shuddered, thinking the laugh edged into madness.

CHAPTER 20

THERESA LEFT WORK at five-thirty on Thursday. Her life was slowly getting back to normal. At work, people had stopped tiptoeing around her and the looks of pity were replaced with admiration. Her therapist had begun making progress. Theresa was feeling good about herself and she no longer blamed herself for what had happened. Theresa understood that she had done nothing wrong. And most of all, her frequent conversations with Sarah James boosted her self confidence.

Although they were still worried, her parents no longer called every day or treated her like a piece of fragile crystal. She kept them informed of her whereabouts, but they no longer questioned her every movement. She knew that things would never be totally normal again. She would always have a fear of men and may never have or want a relationship with one. But at least she didn't have a panic attack every time one spoke to her. She was no longer jumping at shadows and had even slept three full nights in the past week, in her bed.

She was going to her parents for dinner. And it had been her choice. She wanted to see them, to talk to them. She was not going to hide out any longer. For Theresa, life was better, maybe not great, or even good, but better. That was a step in the right direction.

She backed out of her parking space. All of a sudden an older woman was standing behind her car. *Where did she come from?*

Before she could hit the brakes, Theresa felt a bump or heard a thud, she wasn't sure which, and then in her side mirror, saw the woman fall. Oh my God! I hit her. Theresa leaped out of the car and ran to the woman who was lying beside the rear bumper. She knelt beside the heavy woman in the blue dress. "Oh God! Are you all right? I'm so sorry."

The woman turned her head toward Theresa and smiled. What? Is that a trace of a five-o'clock shadow? Who? Those eyes!

His fist came from nowhere, connecting with the left side of her jaw and knocking Theresa on her back. The second punch knocked her unconscious.

THERESA WANTED TO RUB her jaw but her arm was immobile. Her legs wouldn't move either. Panic closed over her like a suffocating blanket.

She opened her eyes and stared at a familiar ceiling. The same fan with the broken light fixture, with one of the five bulbs burned out and the same ugly putrid blue walls. How can this be happening?

She screamed as loudly as the pain in her jaw would allow.

The backhand across her face silenced her. There was pressure on her thighs. He was straddling her. "Hi, babe! Have I ever told you what a beautiful body you have? You're all healed up. The last time we were together you were bruised. I like you better this way."

He bent over and tongued her belly button. Then he

reached across her and took the knife out of the drawer. He ran a finger lightly along the blade. "Nice and sharp, you know the routine. Don't move now, I'd hate to cut you."

He slipped the blade inside one leg of her panties. Theresa tensed as the point pricked her skin, then he guided it up the inside of her thigh, slowly across the crotch of her panties, stopping at the center, cold steel against her most vulnerable spot. The blade hesitated a moment. Terrified, she didn't flinch, didn't move a muscle. Then she heard the silk ripping.

He did the same with the other leg and he peeled away her panties. He pulled the garment away from her and trailed it across his face, inhaling deeply. "Ah, the sweet, sweet nectar of love!"

In one quick motion he sliced through her bra and she felt the cool air on her breasts. He began licking and sucking them. He bit one of her nipples, hard. Theresa screamed in terror and pain and suddenly felt nauseous and began thrashing trying to throw him off. Her arms and legs felt like they were being torn out of the sockets, but the pain didn't stop her. She kept bucking, trying to throw him off.

"You bastard, get off me! Get off me!"

"Yee-ha! Ride 'em cowboy", he yelled, reaching back and slapping her legs. Exhausted, at last, she stopped. He continued riding and slapping — the rodeo star on his bucking bronco. Tired of the game, he stopped, waiting.

Theresa was hysterical. "Why? Why?" she screamed between sobs. Hawkins merely smiled.

When he was finished he rolled off the bed, stood beside it, looked down at Theresa and laughed. He left the room, closing the door behind him. Alone, she prayed. Not to be found, not to be released, but to die. She lost track of time, of place. Once she thought she had died, died and gone to hell, to be punished for some unimaginable sin.

When she heard the door open, she knew she was still in the hell on earth. But the look in his eyes told her that her prayers were going to be answered. She only hoped it would be soon.

"Isn't it nice of the cops to let us have a homecoming? Do you recognize the place? The stupid cops released it as a crime scene weeks ago. It was just sitting here. I had a key and figured what the hell?"

Hawkins undressed, "Did you notice? I'm no longer practicing safe sex, no condom. But don't worry. You won't get pregnant."

When he was done, he moved up, straddled her chest and wrapped his hands around her throat. "Don't worry. JJ will be joining you soon."

JJ? Who's JJ?, was Theresa's last thought.

CHAPTER 21

SARAH AND SCOTT were snuggled under a blanket on the sofa watching a DVD movie. She pushed the stop button on the remote when the phone rang.

"Hi, Sarah, is Scott there?"

She handed him the phone. "It's Roy Nelson."

The strain in Roy's voice told her something was very wrong. Scott listened, asked a few questions and told Roy he'd meet him at headquarters.

"What is it?"

"Theresa Paul is missing. She was supposed to be at her parents by six for dinner."

Sarah glanced at the clock on the DVD player. "That was less than three hours ago."

"It doesn't matter. Her parents are in a panic. Since the abduction, she continually touches base with them, calls to tell them where she is, where she's going, when she will get there, and when she plans to leave, and if she is more than thirty minutes late, she calls.

Tonight she was having dinner with them and called before she left her office. She said she was going straight to their home and would be there in forty-five minutes."

"What time was that?"

"Five-thirty, they checked with a coworker and verified she left around that time. Theresa hasn't called. She's not answering her cell phone and she's not at home. Roy has already sent a car to check. Her parents are frantic and are raising hell with him."

Scott began punching numbers into the phone.

Sarah's instincts told her that Hawkins had her. He had Theresa. She was as good as dead, if she was still alive. Sarah could almost feel Theresa's fear and despair. Sarah felt like someone had kicked her in the stomach. She couldn't breathe. She began to shake. A veil of cold sweat bathed her body. She was angry and scared. But she knew how terrified Theresa had to be, if she was still alive.

Sarah stepped out on the patio. Maybe she could breathe out in the open, get some fresh air. She took deep breaths as tears began to stream down her cheeks and she began to shake uncontrollably. Jax moved beside her, sensing that something was wrong. He pushed against her leg and whined, licked her hand hanging by her side. Sarah got down on one knee, pulled him close and rubbed his head.

"It's going to be okay, boy." I can't lose control. *Pull your self together, Sarah. If I panic, he wins.*

She looked over her shoulder. Scott was putting on his shoes. I can't let him see me like this. She wiped her eyes with the back of her hand.

"Call when you know something."

"Call, you have to be kidding? You're going with me. I'm not about to leave you here alone with that maniac on the loose. Besides, you helped find him once, now I need you to do it again, before it's too late." He strapped on his shoulder holster. "Hurry and get dressed."

"Scott, it's already too late."

When they reached Roy's precinct, he was in his office with Mr. and Mrs. Paul. Sarah could only imagine what was being said. The grief and despair the parents must be feeling.

She knew words could not comfort them. There was nothing Roy could say. He had let them down, let Theresa down, and misjudged a killer. What could he say?

She waited while Scott went in to share the blame. It was thirty minutes before the Paul's allowed one of Roy's men to take them home.

After they left, Sarah joined Scott and Roy. Both were shaken, their faces paled from the deserved tongue lashing from the irate parents. The task force would be convening soon and they needed a game plan before the others arrived.

Two calls came within minutes of each other. The Police Commissioner and the Deputy Director of the Bureau were outraged, asking. "How had this happened? Why wasn't the man behind bars? How could the FBI and Atlanta PD have a serial rapist/killer in metro Atlanta and not catch him? Why had the protective custody been dropped? How were they going to find her? Who the hell was in charge?"

Both had the same parting comment. "Find this guy. I don't want another killing, find her! If you don't, the press is going to eat our lunch."

Roy ran his hand through his hair, wiped his eyes with a thumb and forefinger and looked grimly at the task force. "Twenty years on the force and I've never felt so helpless. Never have I been confronted with parents like the Paul's. Parents who have every right to take my head off, instead they plead with me, for us to find their daughter. People help me. We've got to find this girl. Scott?"

"I'm at a loss. I don't know where to turn. We've got to find this girl. If we don't, she's dead." He had the attention of everyone in the room. The silence was deafening. Scott could hear the vent blowing behind him. The crackling of the fluorescent lights seemed to echo around the room. No one spoke, eyes were downcast, sickened by the turn of events.

"Sarah how long do you think we have?"

"Hours, at best."

"Any suggestions, people?" Scott asked. They had no idea,

no clues, not the slightest idea as to how to find Theresa.

Sarah had been quiet, thinking. *Come on Sarah. Think like that bastard. What would the psycho do? Where would he take her? Where are you Theresa, where is he holding you? Speak to me Theresa, please.*

"We know he thinks we're idiots and he not only wants to prove it; he wants to rub our noses in it. Right?" She asked the group.

"So?" Scott tilted his head quizzically.

"Where is the last place we would look for him?"

Several answers emerged from the group: his house, his father's house, Theresa's home and a host of others. "My people have already checked all of those. They're clean." Roy stated in a loud confident voice.

"That's because those are the first places we'd look and he knows that. Where is the last place we'd look?" Sarah addressed the question as much to herself as to the group.

"Sarah, if you've got an idea, spit it out. This is no time for games." Scott ordered in a desperate tone she had never heard before.

"What about the Galleria Condo he took Theresa to last time."

"You've got to be kidding. No one's that dumb," Roy growled.

"That's the point, Lieutenant. He's not dumb! Just the opposite. Hawkins is brilliant, especially when it comes to outguessing us." Sarah stopped talking when the door opened and a desk sergeant brought in several boxes of pizza.

"Pizza's here."

"Who ordered this?" the lieutenant asked, as the boxes were set around the table.

The only answer he received was, "Never look a gift horse in the mouth," from an officer opening one of the boxes. Hands began grabbing slices from the box before he finished his comment. Someone else asked, "What about something to drink?"

A female cop opened a second box. "What the…?" The agent beside her looked. "Is that a bra?"

Sarah moved around the table. Lying on top of the pizza was a pair of women's panties and a bra, both cut open. On the inside of the lid of the box was a note.

> *JJ,*
>
> *Whoever said history repeats itself was right. Which one of you decided a criminal never returns to the scene of his crime? Was it one of Atlanta's finest or one of the FBI's elite? Not only are you stupid, but now you're too late! Poor Theresa! She thought you were going to come charging to the rescue, again.*
>
> *She cried for you JJ. You let her down. You're next and no one will to be able to stop me.*
>
> *I like the black lace. Keep wearing it, for me!*
>
> *See you soon,*
> *Your First and Last*

Roy leaped out of his chair and stormed out of the room, hollering, "Get that delivery guy. Dispatch cars to…" He gave them the address of the condo where they found Theresa a few weeks ago.

The deliver guy couldn't be found. The Desk Sergeant said it was some high school kid. Probably Hawkins gave him a few bucks to carry the pizzas into the precinct. The kid probably didn't have a clue that one of the boxes had more than pizza in it.

SARAH AND SCOTT arrived at the scene shortly after one in the morning, minutes behind Roy.

Theresa's body was handcuffed to the same bed, in the same bedroom, in the same condo that Hawkins had taken her to the first time he abducted her. Scott and Roy were embarrassed and humiliated, furious over being duped by the killer. They had not only failed to predict his moves but their failure had cost another life. The officers, agents and technicians all felt a sense of loss, embarrassment and anger, because this death should have been prevented.

All members of the task force, the Coroner, the Medical Examiner and all agents under Scott's command were dispatched to the crime scene, along with a host of police officers. Atlanta PD immediately blocked off the area.

Scott called his people together in the parking lot. He motioned to a rumpled agent, a man about five-ten with limp brown hair and a body that was beginning to lose its edge and give in to middle age.

"Eddie, you're in charge. I want every person in the complex interviewed. Find out what they saw, who they saw, what they heard, if any strange vehicles were in the lot today, anything that will help. You know the drill."

"It's one-thirty in the morning, boss. Everybody's asleep."

"Theresa Paul's not asleep. She's dead and it's our fault. Wake them up, Eddie," Scott growled at the veteran agent.

When Sarah walked into the condo, the first thing she saw was the back of a jacket with "ME" emblazoned on it. She recognized Emily Benson's wiry frame moving up the steps.

"Glad you're here, Emily."

The ME glanced over her shoulder. "Sarah. I just got here. I haven't seen the body yet. It will be a while before I can tell you anything."

Sarah nodded. Standing on the bottom step, she slowly took in the surroundings, recalling the layout of the condo. Then she closed her eyes and concentrated, calling on all her senses; memory, hearing, sight, and smell. The Condo smelled of death. It had been closed off for weeks and the air was stale. The death odor filled Sarah's nostrils.

Her ears tuned into first one sound and then another.

The AC blowing, hinges squeaking as crime scene techs opened their lab kits, muffled voices, and her heart beat racing, pumping blood to her weary body. She heard Roy on the front stoop barking out orders to his people. "Question every resident in surrounding complexes. If the lights and activities haven't got 'em up, you do it." He outlined the same questions Scott's people had been instructed to ask.

Sarah shut out the sounds and thought about Theresa. The terror she must have felt when she realized Hawkins had her, again. She had to have screamed. Somebody had to have heard her? Why didn't they call 9-1-1?

Sarah dreaded going upstairs, knowing the body was up there. *I'll bet he took her to the same room.* To postpone the inevitable, she slowly moved from room to room, every sense alert, eyes focused, missing nothing. Looking for anything that might point her toward Hawkins or to tell her what had happened there. Fingerprint dust covered every surface, in every room. She realized it had to be from before.

"Watch for prints in the dust." She told one of the women. The tape from the previous crime scene was still in place across most of the doorways. It was hanging down one side of the frame on the kitchen and bathroom doors. "He used those rooms. Maybe he was careless this time and left us something," she commented.

She stretched the tour out as long as she could, spotting nothing that really helped. It was time. She had to go upstairs. Sarah started up the steps on stiff, unsteady legs. Her chest began to tighten again. Her lips quivered and her eyes misted over as she put her foot on the bottom step.

Her body seemed to be warning her, holding her back. She didn't want to see Theresa like this. After all, Sarah had promised her she'd be okay. Sarah shook her head, willing the thoughts to go away, instead she thought, "I have a job to do. Maybe if I'd done it better the first time..." She took several deep breaths and continued up the steps.

At the top the death smell was stronger. Sarah never

quite understood that. Theresa hadn't been dead long enough to begin decomposing. There couldn't be an odor, maybe it was death itself she smelled, not the dead. *Is it some instinct that cops have the ability to smell death? Something we're born with?*

She looked in the other rooms first. Nothing seemed disturbed. Satisfied, she went to the bedroom, the one where she knew she'd find Theresa. She stopped in the doorway. *Get in the game, Sarah. You're acting like scared little JJ. Sarah, you're an FBI agent, act like one. Do your job, catch this psycho. What's his next move? Think. Anticipate, your life depends on it.*

Sarah regained control of her emotions and stepped into the room. She felt confident, in charge and was ready to do whatever was necessary to find Theresa's killer. *I'm right behind you, Hawkins. Look for me, worry. I'm the shadow from the past and the omen of your future. I will win this game of wits. I'm smarter, tougher and will do whatever it takes.*

Sarah's premonition had been right. Theresa was lying on the same bed as before. Only this time, she was dead. Her arms and legs were pulled out straight, her body shamefully, hideously exposed. Her eyes opened wide, staring at the ceiling. Blank to the casual observer, but not to Sarah. Sarah thought she saw relief in Theresa's dead eyes and understood. Her pain and fear is over. Theresa had known she was about to die and was grateful. She was free of her tormentor.

Theresa, we screwed up and you paid for it. I'm sorry. Hawkins had outsmarted them all, Atlanta's finest and the FBI, the elite of the elite. Sarah stood quietly, folded her hands and took one deep breath, summoning her analytical, investigative mode. She looked carefully, objectively at the body, trying to visualize what was different. Little by little it came to her.

He used handcuffs this time, instead of rope. Theresa's

clothes are strewn on the floor not neatly folded and placed in a chair like before. There are no bruises on her body, but her face is bruised. He wasn't in total control.

"He lost control," she thought aloud.

"Why do you say that?" Scott asked from the hallway.

"He was in a hurry, rushed. He knew we'd find him if he took too long. The signs are obvious, look at the room, at her." She pointed out her observations, and then added, "He wanted to be rid of her, to dispose of a witness, but he also wanted to send us a message. Me a message."

"Messages?"

"Yes. It's all linked; the pizza box, the panties, the bra, and this crime scene. He's telling us that we're stupid. We weren't smart enough to save Theresa and we won't be able to save me either.

"The message on the pizza box told us she was already dead, and that he is coming for me. He's saying that I can run, but I can't hide. Atlanta PD and the Bureau can't stop him."

"Then he's in for a surprise. He's through. He's killed his last woman. That's my message to him. You said he's sending you one?"

"Yes, he made it obvious he didn't enjoy doing Theresa and he blames me, and he will make me pay for that. I will be his ultimate pleasure. His signature kill."

"That's not going to happen!" Roy said from the doorway. "He's going to have to go through me and the entire Atlanta Police Force to get to you, and I bet he might be in the way, too." Roy looked over at Scott, who nodded.

"That's what we said about this." Sarah nodded toward the body cuffed to the bed. She looked steadily at Scott. She was amazingly calm.

Emily and the techs in the bedroom had overheard their conversation and were watching them. Roy caught them looking and responded to their unspoken questions. "We fucked up, it won't happen again," Roy spoke emphatically, striding into the room. He turned to the Medical Examiner.

"Emily, what have you got?"

"Preliminary only, nothing can be confirmed until we get the body downtown."

"Understood!"

"Body temperature tells me that she has been dead less than three hours. There are some key differences with this one. He used force instead of drugs to take her. See the severe bruising on her face." She pointed. "I think her jaw is broken and her left cheekbone may be cracked. A blow like that had to have knocked her out. Once he got her here he used handcuffs instead of rope. Probably afraid she'd wake up." She turned her attention to the body. "And this time there are no bruises on her body." She focused her attention lower. "He sexually abused her again but didn't use a condom this time. I think he was either rushed, careless or taunting you."

"Taunting?" Roy asked.

"Giving you what you need to prove his guilt, but at the same time challenging you to apprehend him. That's just my guess, but it goes along with what Sarah was saying."

"Doesn't he know the DNA matches are enough to convict him?"

"Not if we don't catch him," Sarah answered.

"Then he's the one making mistakes now. We will get him and that'll convict him," Scott growled.

"Anything else, you can tell us?" inquired Roy.

"Not scientifically, but in my opinion he's angry and he is escalating. Sarah's right. He did this to do it, not to enjoy it."

While she was analyzing the scene and listening to Scott, Roy and Emily, Sarah felt a strange sensation. Almost like an out of body sense of objectivity, a calm that allowed her to effectively do her job. Now looking at the body, listening to Emily, that calm vanished and was being devoured by a cold all-consuming rage. She no longer wanted justice, to merely punish Hawkins, not just to get even. She wanted to destroy him.

The bastard had killed again and he would continue to kill again and again and again. If they scared him off and he ran, he'd put Sarah off until later. He'd resort to killing others in the interim. That was unacceptable. She had to stop him. She had to figure out his next move and counter it. Was she next? Or would he toy with them by killing other unsuspecting women until he was ready to come for her. Sarah knew a way to force his hand. One he would never suspect. That would be her edge.

CHAPTER 22

HAWKINS EASED THE BLACK VAN into the garage and closed the door with the remote before getting out of the vehicle.

How do they do it? This bra is killing me.

He'd worn the disguise since taking care of Theresa, the first of his two "loose ends." He knew the manhunt would intensify when they found the girl's body, and explode when they discovered her car.

They must be going crazy. All those stupid cops and Feds looking for me, without a clue, what a rush!

He left Atlanta immediately after sending the pizzas to the cops and had driven nine hours to get to New Orleans, stopping only for gas.

Walking into the kitchen of his new home, Hawkins yanked off the wig and stripped off the padded bra and dress before he even flipped on a light. He was tired and stiff but still high. He wished he could tell the world how smoothly his plans were going. How he had outsmarted the cops and the Feds.

Maybe I will, he thought. *I'll write my memoir. Include pictures of Miss FBI. Before and after shots! Then after I'm settled here, safely hidden away, I'll send it all to the press. No, no why give the story away? I'll get a book deal. Swear the publishers to anonymity. I'll make millions and won't need daddy's money anymore. I bet they'll make a movie about me, some stud like Crowe or Pitt will portray me on the big screen.*

Killing that snooty whore in the company condo was ingenious, a brilliant tactical move. It ranks right up there with the idea of dressing as a woman or renting the house across from JJ. The cops never look for the obvious. They never expected me to go back to the crime scene.

It was all too easy. The girl fell for the scam. She thought she had hit an old lady. Never gave it a second thought, jumped out of the car and left the engine running! All I had to do was clip her twice, put her in her own trunk and drive off. She didn't wake up until I had her undressed and cuffed to the bed.

And when she came to, the look on her face was price-less. It was pitiful really. The way she screamed for Miss FBI. What a joke! Miss JJ is next and no one can stop me. She is as good as dead.

Wish I could have taken a little more time to enjoy Miss Snooty. But one can't have everything. Oh, well, that's okay. I'll take my time with JJ. Now, there is one hard body that I'm going to take the time to enjoy."

It had gone so well that Hawkins had been smiling for hours. He had parked his van in a lot on Ponce de Leon Avenue across from Police HQ and taken a taxi to the insurance company a few miles away. He waited on Theresa in the parking deck and then faked the accident when she was backing out. He took the broad to the condo in her own car. After he finished with her, he left her body there. Using her car, he picked up the pizzas and drove back to the police station. He parked the car on the curb, out front, in plain view. Then he paid a kid to take the pizzas to the Desk Sergeant saying they were for Agent Justice.

He hoped JJ and her lover and that Lieutenant were there when the pizzas were delivered. The looks on their faces when they found the girl's panties inside and the message had to have been priceless. And wait until the car was discovered out front.

I wonder how long it would take the cops and the FBI to find it. What a stroke of genius! Sometimes I even surprise myself. How do I keep out-foxing them? The supreme insults; Leaving the car right under their noses, telling them where to find the body and finally, the pizza delivery with the girl's underwear and the message for hot little JJ. It just keeps getting better and better!

Hawkins was now in New Orleans. He'd come for several reasons. He had to get out of Atlanta and he needed to assume his new identity. Using his new name, bank accounts and credit cards he would begin a new life.

He'd wait a couple of weeks before returning to Atlanta to deal with JJ. He'd use his disguise to fool the cops. No one ever suspected an old lady of doing anything wrong. He'd stay in the big city long enough to dispose of JJ and then return to New Orleans permanently. But, for now he had to review every detail of his plan. It had to be foolproof if he was going to succeed. Toying with the cops was almost as much fun as humbling those women who treated him like dirt, looking down on him. Everyone kept underestimating him, not that he minded.

He showered and rested for a few hours before dressing. It felt good to get back into fine men's clothing. Dressing in drag had been just that, a drag. And he really hated the blue-collar crap he'd worn when he wasn't dressing like a woman. But his disguises had been necessary, and it worked. One could never be too careful, even when dealing with a bunch of imbeciles. Methodical planning, unerring attention to detail, relentless precision and a cool head would guarantee success in snatching JJ.

Sitting at the kitchen table, he began by reviewing his

notes on her schedule. The trial made it easier to keep up with her weekday activities. She was always in court and if it kept her occupied for a few more weeks, he would be ready. The plan would be perfected, but of course, he would have an alternate plan drafted and ready. A night visit to her home, perhaps.

As soon as he had realized that the female FBI agent was his "JJ" from North Carolina, he had begun following her. Making careful notes on her activities; daytime, evenings, weekdays and weekends, he had it all covered. While the trial made it easy, that slimy lover of hers moving in had complicated things. Then he realized the advantage, the lover made her more predictable.

He had spent the time he wasn't watching her researching federal agents. He learned that unlike cops, they always carried their weapons, even off duty and at leisure. TV shows featuring female Marshals and FBI agents showed where they carried them. It became obvious that women's clothing created unique problems for concealing weapons. Shoulder harnesses were a no-no, probably because they bulged under form fitting tops or jackets or maybe they were uncomfortable strapped across a woman's breasts. If they wore them on their hips, a loose fitting jacket was worn, a dead giveaway. It appeared the preferred locations were in the waistband of their skirt or jeans, in their purses or a fanny pack and sometimes in an ankle holster which required a certain type of pants, another giveaway.

All of this helped because stripping Agent James of her gun would be his first order of business when he made his move. To do that he would need to have the element of surprise on his side, a diversion that would allow him to catch her off guard.

CHAPTER 23

MICHELLE SMITH'S MURDER TRIAL was in its second week and Sarah had been there all eight days waiting to testify. Fortunately, the prosecutor was aggressive, competent, thorough, and Sarah enjoyed watching him tie the defense lawyers in knots. He had won a conviction and a stiff sentence after assuming control of the fraud trial and was seeking a "Murder One" verdict in this one. Sarah felt it was a shoo-in. The Prosecutor was that good.

Sitting there, Sarah's mind often drifted, thinking through the details of her upcoming wedding. She and Scott had considered delaying the ceremony until after Hawkins was captured and behind bars but they had decided that the man had upset Sarah's life enough. He wouldn't dictate their wedding date.

They wanted a quiet ceremony with only family present; a small, simple, fun wedding. One that Sarah and her mother would enjoy planning. Often in the middle of some detail, she would stop and think of how her life had changed. It hadn't been that long ago that she had thought she would spend the rest of her life alone, afraid of intimacy with any man and now she had Scott, a man who had taught her how to love and be loved.

Other times, she looked beyond the wedding, contemplating her future. Headquarters would never allow her to remain under Scott's jurisdiction and to change that would mean relocation, which was out of the question. She had to make a career decision. Did she want to practice law or enforce it?

Scott's solution was simple. "Let's get pregnant! Hell, we'll be married in a couple of weeks! Who'll know it happened a little early?"

She knew a baby wasn't the answer, not yet. She wanted a career. She just didn't know where. She loved the Bureau, but after they were married, that was out. She and Scott had talked about her transferring to the Marshall's Service, Alcohol Tobacco and Firearms, or Homeland Security. But every possible government position would question her past, Hawkins. Scott didn't think it would be an issue. After all, she had been seventeen and Sarah was the victim. Besides, any stigma the event carried would be offset by Sarah's record with the Bureau.

Sarah had even considered leaving the government and opening up a private firm, but she couldn't picture herself as a Private Investigator. Scott had laughed when she mentioned it. "I can see you following a cheating spouse with a camera to catch him or her in action. Suzie Spade, PI." She punched him, but had to laugh at the picture that formed in her mind.

She met her old friend the Senator for lunch one day to seek his advice. He gave his opinions and offered to help anywhere he could. He agreed with Scott that Sarah's past was just that, her past, and would not be an issue.

She had kissed his cheek when they finished lunch. "Thank you so much, Senator Don. If only you weren't happily married."

The tall, lean, elderly gentleman's face reddened. "Don't you flirt with me, young lady! My Maggie will have both our hides," his gravelly voice and twinkling eyes full of humor.

So far nothing was resolved. It couldn't be until Hawkins was taken care of and she was sure she had a future, one free of nightmares and fear. She didn't want to spend her life looking over her shoulder or wake up each morning afraid to open her eyes for fear that he might be there.

Each day after court, Sarah went to the shooting range to practice the various stances, using both her Glock and the 9mm Sig-Sauer she used as a backup weapon, practicing her moves and grips in order to improve her speed and accuracy. She approached each practice session as if her life depended on the outcome. In this too, she realized practice makes perfect.

Sarah was becoming more and more convinced that she would have to personally deal with Hawkins. Who better to serve as judge and executioner, with Callie, Jessica and Theresa as his jury? After seeing Theresa's body cuffed to that bed, Sarah had relished the thought of dispensing justice, no matter the costs.

Between irate officials and a caustic media, Scott and Roy were, as Scott put it, "Ass-deep in alligators." That gave Sarah another reason to enjoy court duty. It kept her away from the media. An anonymous tip had alerted the press and they had arrived at the condo within minutes of the police discovering Theresa's body. The story blared in the headlines for days. The entire city was in an uproar over the incompetence of the police and the FBI. Women throughout the city were terrified. Restaurant and bar sales plummeted. Single females were afraid to go out, so there was little to attract men to bars. Declining revenues and frightened female employees made the business community nervous which pressured the Mayor who passed it on to the Police Commissioner and right on down the ladder. And every day the press screamed for results. When there was none to report, the press dug in their spurs demanding results.

Scott and Roy were under enormous pressure. Not only

had they let Hawkins snatch Theresa and kill her, but the killer had gotten away and vanished without a clue. The FBI and Atlanta PD looked like incompetent fools.

Then, five days after Theresa's murder, just as things were cooling off, the car was found, not by police work, but quite by accident. The number of parking tickets on the windshield told how long it had been parked in front of the police station.

The car had sat there, unnoticed, while every cop in the city was looking for it. An alert city wrecker driver recognized the tag number as he was hooking it up to his truck. The media overheard his call to homicide and the event made headlines. "If You Want to Commit a Crime Do It at Headquarters," "Car Found Under Cops' Noses," "Wrecker Driver Only Alert Cop in City," were some of the captions.

To make matters even worse, one alert photographer got a picture of Roy standing by Theresa's car, watching it being hooked up to the city wrecker, scratching his butt, "At Least We Know What This Lieutenant Was Doing." That one was priceless. Sarah was sure that Lieutenant Roy Nelson was the only person in Atlanta that failed to find any humor in the caption.

"Hell, my kids want to change their name," he bitched to Scott the day after the picture and story appeared.

Hawkins had completely eluded the statewide dragnet. No one had a clue as to his whereabouts. Sarah's protection was tightened. She had shadows wherever she went because everyone agreed that she was the killer's next target. The main questions were when and where Hawkins would strike again? Was Sarah James his next target? And how long could they afford to keep the manpower assigned to guard her?

On the second Wednesday after Theresa's murder, Sarah was asked to skip the morning session of the trial to attend the daily meeting of the task force. The Task Force reviewed everything that was being done and tried to come up with ideas on what to do next. She listened to the discussion and as it wound down, asked, "How do we know I'm his next victim? What if another woman turns up in a Dumpster?"

Everyone had been thinking the same thing. It was a valid question, one that could not be answered. Sarah was taking advantage of the situation. She knew that if they decided she was not in danger, her protection would be lifted. And it had to be lifted or at least relaxed, if she wanted to draw Hawkins out of hiding.

It was obvious that the Task Force had no idea as to how to prevent another murder from occurring, Sarah's or someone else's. Hawkins was calling the shots. He was in control. If he decided to taunt them with another victim, he could do so unhampered.

There were too many bars in Atlanta to cover. The force didn't have enough undercover cops and that was the only way they could catch him. They discussed watching those in Midtown and only on Wednesday nights but even that required too much manpower, a mission impossible.

"I hate to suggest this, but why don't we decrease the manpower assigned to me and reassign the resources to watching the bars?" Sarah asked.

One officer responded. "What about The Watering Hole. Maybe he's going to return to that scene. He's done it twice, why not again? We could put some people there."

"God forbid. If that happens we are all through. Okay, we'll have someone there every hour the place is open from now until we catch him," Roy snarled. "Are you sure, Sarah? Scott?"

Scott reluctantly agreed, and Sarah's protection was cut in half. Driving home, Sarah thought about Hawkins' next move. She was sure she knew what it would be and she was getting tired of waiting.

Now that I'm going to have a little freedom, maybe it's time I brought him out into the open; bait him — tease him a little.

CHAPTER 24

THE FOLLOWING WEEKEND, the black van returned to South Atlanta. Hawkins found his safe house still secure. The cops hadn't discovered it, not that Hawkins thought they would. Back in drag, he spent the next few days checking up on his quarry. JJ was still in court every day and spending her evenings with her boyfriend.

Hawkins was sitting in the rental down the street watching Sarah's house through his binoculars. The two had just come back from their evening run and were hugging and kissing on her front porch. And that stupid dog was prancing around barking. Don't they have any decency? Next thing you know they will be screwing in front of the neighbors. Well, one thing you can count on honey, we'll do our thing in private.

No one paid attention to the chubby, ugly woman, no matter where she went. In the van, on the street, in front of Police Headquarters, or even sitting in the back of the courtroom staring at the prissy FBI agent. One afternoon he watched her stride into the courtroom after lunch.

I'm glad you got away. You've developed into quite a woman. I'm going to enjoy you even more the second time around. I'll bet your boyfriend has taught you a few tricks. I'll have to thank the prick before I kill him.

As Hawkins watched her, he convinced himself that she wanted him. Why else would she be taunting him, wearing black all the time? At night, she paraded in front of her windows in a black negligee or black panties and bra. During the day, she wore skirts or pants and tight sweaters or silky blouses, always black. He had been facetious when he wrote the note on the pizza box. But now he realized JJ was very sexy in black.

He grew excited each time he watched her. He could hardly contain himself and he began fantasizing about Sarah, something he had never done before, with any woman. He picked up women for casual sex, moved on, and forgot them.

Except for the ones he reserved for special "sessions," the women who thought they were too good for him, who needed to be taught manners. He never forgot them. He had the exciting memories and a collection of frilly souvenirs. He'd never been obsessed with any woman, except for his mother. She was the only woman who had ever abandoned him. His own mother had rejected him, left him for another life.

Sure dad says she died of cancer. But I know better. She dumped me, didn't want me. He is just trying to protect me with his lies. She'll come back one day and she'll be sorry. It will be too late. I'll reject her, tell her to get lost.

He looked at the worn photo in his wallet, a pretty dark haired girl in her twenties, with big china blue eyes, her arm draped around his dad. The way they were looking at each other, it was easy to see they were in love. "You loved him. Why didn't you love me, Mom?" He said before kissing the photo and returning it to his wallet.

His thoughts returned to Sarah. You won't leave me? Will you, JJ? You did once, but you won't again. You won't get the chance, not this time.

He picked up a picture of Sarah. She was walking down the courthouse steps. "So sexy. I have to have you, my JJ. You may be that agent's girl now, but soon you'll be mine." He kissed her image and sat the picture on the table. His obsession for Sarah had him frenzied, hot, and hardly able to contain his desire, fantasizing about her all the time. He couldn't free himself of the thoughts. "Soon, soon we'll be together, JJ."

SARAH SENSED HAWKINS PRESENCE; instinctually felt he was watching her. She hadn't actually seen him, but she just knew he was there, hiding in the shadows. It was a survival instinct that street cops and field agents developed to stay alive, and Sarah's was on full alert. She could feel his eyes, could almost smell him, the way an animal senses danger. That same instinct warned her to be cautious, alert at all times.

Cautious, yes. Foolish, no. She couldn't allow him to pick the time. She had to draw him out into the open, throw him off balance. She had to let him think he was safe, un-noticed, observing her every move. She had to use her skills to set a trap and her looks to lure him into it. Control was Hawkins game, but this time she had to be in charge. If she was going to survive, she had to be in control.

He had evaded the surveillance team watching over her. They hadn't noticed anything unusual. For that matter, nei-ther had she. Just that tiny voice inside her head kept telling her he was out there.

Yes! He's smart, but I'm smarter. I've got to draw him out. And I have one weapon he can't resist. I know exactly how to do it. He may not have realized it but subconsciously he meant what he said in the note. He wants me in black. His mental image of me is in black, sexy black lace. I'll give it to him.

Sarah made a trip to Victoria's Secret, where she purchased negligees, panties, bras, garters and stockings; seductive, sexy and intriguing, all black.

Each night she bathed, dressed for the show and walked past her windows, modeling, parading. She had never done anything like this before. Self-conscious at first, she soon began to relax, to enjoy being sexy and provocative.

Hawkins wasn't the only one being affected by Sarah's new look. Scott was definitely infatuated with his fiancée's new outfits and she loved it. She had never thought she could be so wanton, enjoy being sensuous so much. After her show in front of the windows, she strutted in front of Scott. He couldn't keep his hands off her. They seemed to go to bed earlier each night.

"Do you feel like we're being watched?" She asked Scott Thursday morning in the kitchen.

"Watched?" His voice cracked and he moved closer to her, worry creasing his forehead. "Have you spotted him?"

"No. It's just a feeling, that he's watching me. I'm sure of it. Last night, before we went to bed, I just had a feeling, a sensation, that he was out there."

"Your instincts have never been wrong. I'll check with the team. See what they've spotted. Bobby Jackson is still on duty." He grabbed his cell phone. "Bobby, everything okay? Anybody around that you haven't seen in the neighborhood before, walking past the house, watching Sarah when she comes and goes? Okay, thanks."

"They haven't seen him or anything out of the ordinary. Maybe you're just jumpy. I know I am. And you're under so much stress. Michele Smith's case is ready to go to the jury. We've got all the media attention on Hawkins. That's causing the politicians to put pressure on us to catch the guy. And you've got a wedding to plan. There's a lot going on, it's enough to put anybody on edge."

He pressed his face to her neck, kissed her and rubbed her back, comforting her. "We could postpone the wedding you know, take that load off for a while." Sarah knew he was teasing.

She jerked her head off his shoulder and looked into his eyes. His pupils were large, the irises a light brown, dancing.

"We could, you're right. Or we could move it up, a small ceremony this weekend." Now Sarah's eyes were twinkling and a huge smile spread across her face.

Scott laughed. "Nope! Won't work, that would put too much pressure on your mom. I think it'd be easier on her if we waited a couple of months."

"Uh-uh, you jerk! I'm not letting you off the hook. The wedding date stands."

He kissed the end of her nose. "I don't want off the hook. I love you too much."

Hawkins put his binoculars down in disgust.

They make me sick. I've got to get ready for court.

THAT AFTERNOON, in the courtroom, Sarah spotted Hawkins for the first time. The shoes did it. The old-fashioned conventional, no-frill white Keds that Wal-Mart sold for less than twenty bucks. Sarah noticed them because no woman wore them with street clothes. The shoes were brand new, blinding white canvas, and large. Not many women had feet that big and if they did, they sure as hell didn't wear white shoes. The following day she saw them again, but on a woman with different color hair.

Sarah's training was paying off. Look for the little things, observe without being observed. The lady didn't realize Sarah had pegged her. Sarah's instincts had been right, Hawkins was watching her and the fact that he was in the open meant her plan was working. Hawkins was becoming obsessed. Sarah didn't alert her guards.

I want to turn up the heat a little. If he wants to play peeping Tom, I'll make it worth his while.

Hawkins showed up the next three days disguised in three different outfits and wigs, different styles and colors, but the same Keds day after day. When Sarah walked past him, he looked down to avoid making make eye contact. Sarah's plan was working, Hawkins was getting careless.

On Wednesday, Sarah decided it was time to bring it to a head. She wasn't due in court until after the noon recess. A grand entrance was in order. One to excite Mr. Hawkins or Miss Vivian or whatever Hawkins was calling himself now, into making a mistake. Sarah dressed in black; a tight sweater, short skirt, sheer black pantyhose and black leather shoes with short heels. When Sarah entered the courtroom, she swayed past Hawkins and settled in an aisle seat a couple of rows in front of him. Using her compact mirror, Sarah applied lipstick while checking out the woman behind her. It was Hawkins. The eyes gave him away. Blue like a clear mountain stream, but cold. The color cinched it, but the look in Hawkins eyes was startling; lust, hatred and confusion filled them.

I'm getting to him. He's losing it. I believe the bastard wants me right now. Hawkins loves the black. Sarah's mouth twitched into a half smile. Her eyes danced with mischief. *Let's push a couple of buttons.*

Sarah stuck one of her long legs out into the aisle to straighten her stocking. She traced a hand along her leg to the edge of her skirt. As she bent over her outstretched leg, she risked glancing back at Hawkins. He was captivated, almost drooling. He caught Sarah looking and averted his eyes and got up to leave. He was jogging for the door at the back of the courtroom.

She got up and headed for the side exit. Her long stride carried her out of the room and around the corner in seconds. Hawkins was leaving the building. Sarah flew to the closest exit and rushed down the courthouse steps. She sprinted around the corner of the building and moved behind a UPS truck parked at the curb.

There. There he is. Hawkins was running. He went straight to a black van in a parking lot across the street and hopped in. The van jumped the curb and squealed off down the street.

Sarah stepped into the street and watched the van. She jotted down the Louisiana tag number.

I SCREWED UP. I knew I should have stayed away today. But I had to see her. That scanty black outfit she wore last night. The more he saw of his JJ the more he wanted to see. He couldn't get enough of her. He couldn't get her out of his mind. The black lingerie was taking its toll on him. He was obsessed with the lithe FBI Agent.

I think she spotted me. But if she did, why didn't she call in the Cavalry? Her bodyguards were just outside the court-room. I saw them when I went in and they were there when I left. What kind of game is she playing? Is she protecting me? Does she want me? Realize I'm better than him? Can't be that! She didn't see me.

He mentally processed the events of the past weeks and could think of nothing to indicate that she was on to him. She was too involved with that FBI jerk to notice anything going on around her. Neither she nor her boyfriend seemed to be thinking straight. He sneered.

They're disgusting. All they think about is screwing! That's why she parades around in front of the windows in those black outfits, oblivious to the outside world. She's nothing but a slut. He did it, that bastard. He's ruined my JJ. Damn him!

Hawkins slammed his fists on the steering wheel. Then his sneer changed into a smile. *They're too busy in the sack to catch on and the cops have their heads up their asses. They don't even know I'm watching. They're making this easy! Hell, they haven't even checked out the woman renting the house down the street from her. They must think I'm a birdwatcher or something.*

By the time he pulled into the garage of the safe house in South Atlanta he had convinced himself that even though JJ had spotted the woman watching her, she didn't connect her to him. But he was still rational enough to realize that the scene in the courtroom was a close call, one that couldn't be repeated. He couldn't keep following her, getting so close, but he had to see her. He had to have her. That only left him one alternative. He had to move up his timetable and he had to think up a new disguise.

That bitch. I want her now. I want JJ in my bed. She's mine and the sooner she knows it, the better! I was her first and I'll be her last.

He changed clothes. His designer jeans and polo shirt made him feel better, back in control. He fixed a Jack Black and water and sat down to review his notes.

"I've thought of everything. My plan is foolproof." He laughed, the sounds bouncing off the walls and echoing. "Apropos, since I'm dealing with fools." He leaned his head back and dozed, JJ's image slipped into his dreams.

JJ walked into the room. Her long legs encased in fine silk stockings, held up by a black garter belt. A sheer, black silk top barely concealed her pert breasts. Her nipples were hard, begging to be touched. "Please forgive me. All I ever wanted was you," she whispered before kneeling at his feet.

He smiled and another scene leaped into his mind.

JJ was striding into the courtroom in a short black skirt and a tight black sweater. Her hips swayed provocatively inside the tight skirt, her breasts moved ever so slightly with each step. It was the sexiest sight he had ever seen. He could hear her heels clicking on the marble floor and smell her perfume as she walked past him. She stopped, looked back over the crowd, and smiled when she recognized him. She slid gracefully into the seat beside him and placed her hand on his crotch.

Hawkins jerked awake. He reached for JJ. She wasn't

there. He reached for the painful bulge in his trousers. She was doing this to him, tormenting him, even when she wasn't near. He cursed and slammed his head against the back of the recliner. "You bitch, look what have you done to me. Damn you! You'll pay! And it will be soon!" He screamed to the empty room.

He got up and went to the bedroom. He sat on the edge of the bed. Holding the knife, he pictured himself slicing through her underwear. JJ cuffed to the bed, naked and exposed, vulnerable and helpless. Just like all the others. He began to grow aroused again as he imagined dangling the black lacy underwear in his hands, burying his face in the silk.

"SCOTT, IT WAS HAWKINS. He was in the courtroom, dressed as a woman. I know it was him."

"How did you spot him?"

"The shoes. Those ugly white sneakers, no woman would be caught dead in them outside their home. Believe me!"

"You're positive it was Hawkins?"

"Yes. He got in a black van with Louisiana plates. I got the tag number. Scott, why didn't the surveillance team spot this woman in the courtroom day after day?" Sarah asked.

"They can't explain it. Don't think I haven't asked them that question, more than once, today. Several agents are walking around with half an ass tonight."

Knowing there was no need belaboring that point, Sarah asked. "Anything on the Louisiana plates, yet?"

"Yeah, the vehicle is registered to a Chase Gary. He resides in a little town on the outskirts of New Orleans. He's been there about a year."

That fits. Chase Gary, Gary Allen — it's him, Scott. It's Hawkins."

"That's a stretch honey. What are we going to do, investigate everybody that has Alan, Gary or Greg for a name?"

"I thought you said you trusted my instincts?"

"I do. That's why I've got the New Orleans AIC following up on this Chase Gary. He'll get back to me as soon as he's got something."

Thursday morning he was in the kitchen drinking a glass of juice and taking his daily regime of vitamins when his cell chirped. "Scott Justice."

"Scott, Ted Kinson, sorry for the early hour, but I think I've got something you'll be interested in."

"No problem, Ted. What you got?" Scott glanced at the clock on the microwave. The small digital numbers flashed 5:43 AM.

Scott carried his glass of juice to the bathroom where Sarah was putting the finishing touches on her hair. "Ted Kinson, the New Orleans AIC just called. We hit pay dirt there. Some neighbors positively identified Chase Gary as Greg Hawkins. Ted is in the process of obtaining a warrant to enter the residence. You were right. That was Hawkins."

"When are we going to New Orleans?"

"I'm going down there as soon as I can get to the airport. You need to stay here, it's safer. After you spotted him, the odds are ten to one that he high-tailed it to New Orleans. If luck's with us, he'll be in custody by the end of the day."

"I want to go with you. Be there when you go in."

"Can't happen and you know it."

The Bureau jet landed in New Orleans four hours later. Three dark blue SUVs were waiting at the private jetport. Ted Kinson, the Louisiana AIC, jumped out of the middle one and greeted Scott as soon as he stepped off the plane. Although Ted had been with the Bureau eight years longer than Scott, they made AIC at the same time and attended AIC training together. They talked on the phone often, discussing cases, procedures and Bureau politics.

Thick-shouldered and muscular, Ted moved with the grace of a big cat. His gray hair rustled in the warm breeze. He pumped Scott's hand with a firm grip.

"How the hell are you?"

"Not too good, worse if I don't catch this guy soon."

"Maybe we can dig you out."

"I sure hope so. Who's going in?"

"Assault team, forensics, lab, anybody and everybody that can help apprehend him if he's there or identify anything he's touched, bled on, showered in or pissed in, if he's not. You know the drill. If your man's been in that house, we'll know it."

"What about the van?"

"There's an APB out on it. I've got him listed as armed and dangerous and to approach with caution. With a little luck, we'll have him in custody by nightfall."

"If you do, I'll nominate you for Director!"

They drove into one of the numerous golf communities on the outskirts of New Orleans. Scott saw streets named Pebble Beach, Marion, Troon and Pinehurst. He was anxious and hot. The SUV's air conditioner was fighting a losing battle with the Louisiana heat and humidity. Scott's shirt was already sticking to his back.

After several turns, they pulled into the drive of a large, white colonial home. Agents in dark blue windbreakers with FBI printed on their backs poured out of SUVs, vans and cars. All exits and the perimeter of the yard were covered before AIC Kinson knocked on the front door.

"FBI! Open the door! We have a warrant to search the premises."

No one answered. He repeated the procedure two more times, and then turned to two men holding a small battering ram. "Force it!"

The battering ram splintered the door and it swung open. A covey of agents rushed inside, fanning out to search the interior.

"First floor empty," an agent called out minutes later.

"Second floor vacant," a second announced.

"Garage, too." yelled another agent.

"I knew it was too good to be true." Scott followed Ted through the house.

Two hours later they got an initial report from the head of the forensics crew. "Prints confirm Hawkins has been here. Items in the refrigerator and some stale bread suggest he hasn't been here in at least a week. We confirmed that by the dryness in the shower and tub and the ring in the toilet bowl. We found a second set of fingerprints, in the kitchen, master bedroom and master bath. They're not as prominent throughout the house as the first, probably a one time visitor. Two colors of hair were in the sink and shower of the master bathroom."

"Are they natural or a wig? He likes disguises."

"Natural. The darker is short. From the photo, I presumed that to be your man's. The other is long, red, and female."

A redhead—that's a change! Why? Why is he with a red-head? Fixating on redhead. What changed him? The answer came quickly. Sarah. Scott felt a chill at the thought.

"You might want to run a match on those prints and then try to locate the woman. Females don't have a habit of walking away from love sessions with this guy," Scott suggested.

"Do it," Ted told one of his men.

"Chief, take a look at this." A young agent brought over a file folder. "I found this in the drawer over there." Ted opened it on a table in the breakfast area. Scott looked over his shoulder. The photo on top was of a young woman with strawberry blonde hair, wearing jeans and a Georgetown sweatshirt. She was leaving the front door of a house with a liver-and-white dog by her side. A second photo showed the same woman walking down the steps of a courthouse. She was wearing a black business suit and carrying a briefcase. A third showed her in a black negligee. The image was hazy and appeared to have been taken through a window but in spite of the poor quality, her beauty was obvious.

The young agent whistled. "She's a looker."

"I'll say," Ted agreed. "Wonder if she knows she's posing?"

Scott stared at the pictures in disbelief while restraining the urge to grab the photos and shove them back into the envelope. He felt they were invading Sarah's privacy. No, Hawkins had taken the pictures, exposing her to their stares. Then the fear set in as he realized. *He's stalking Sarah!*

"This can't be."

"What?" Ted asked, puzzled. "Do you know her?"

"She's an agent in Atlanta. We have her under protective surveillance. Apparently we're not doing a very good a job. He's taking the pictures right under our noses."

"An agent? Under surveillance?"

"Yes. We're afraid she might be Hawkins' next target."

"From what I see here, the pictures and schedules, that's affirmative. And if this is any indication of your ability to protect her, she's in trouble. You've got holes in your coverage big enough to drive a truck through. And you better plug them quick if you want this girl to survive. Because if he's not here, my bet is, he's in Atlanta. And this lady is in real danger, because he's close."

Scott's face drained of color. He continued to stare at the photos of Sarah.

Ted looked at his friend with concern. "Scott, you said she's one of your agents. Is there more to thise? Scott, is this personal?

"She's my fiancée." He stepped away and took his cell phone out of his pocket. "Give me a minute.

"Sarah, Hawkins has been here. No, we didn't catch him. An APB is out on him. If he is in New Orleans, he'll be in custody soon. If not, he's there in Atlanta. Be careful, and don't go anywhere without the guards. Sleep with one of them if you have to, a female. I'm serious Sarah, don't take any chances. He has been watching your every move. Without a doubt, he's been close. Take my word for it...Okay, are you sitting down? It's bad. We found pictures of you, details of your daily schedules, and notes describing what he has planned for you...I know, calm down. I'm calling Roy as soon as we hang up and increasing the number of people watching you...Probably in the morning, I want to stay here and see the lab results and if the APB nabs him."

Disconnecting that call, he placed a second to Roy and gave him the same information.

"Roy, put some extra guys on Sarah. Don't let Hawkins near her." He explained what they had found, omitting nothing.

Ted and the agent were still reviewing the contents of the folder when Scott finished his calls.

"He's got some pretty meticulous notes here on her activities; day by day, hour by hour. Take a look."

Scott scanned the information. *Sarah's in real trouble, he's close, too close.*

Finished he looked up at Ted, who repeated. "She's in real trouble, Scott." He tapped one of the photos. "This is his next victim."

Scott nodded, staring at one photo in particular, the one of her wearing the black negligee. His mind began churning, thinking of changes in Sarah's behavior in the past week or so. He pictured her walking around the house in those sensuous new outfits before bed each night.

Always black! What is she up to? The pieces clicked into place. Suddenly he knew and he didn't like it.

TED FOUND OUT NO unidentified female bodies had been discovered in the New Orleans area in the past ten days, leading him and Scott to believe the redhead was still alive. Ted would run the prints they had found in the Condo through the system to identify and locate the woman. Then he'd have her interviewed to find out what she knew about Hawkins.

By mid-afternoon, it was obvious to Scott that Ted Kinson had the situation under control. An APB was out on the van and the house was under constant surveillance.

"Ted, you've got this in hand. If Hawkins is here, you'll get him. I need to get back to Atlanta."

"I agree, because if he's not here, he's there and your agent needs looking after."

"Yeah, she's in more danger than I suspected." Scott picked up the stack of photos. "If he slipped through our people to take these, what's stopping him from taking her? I've got to figure out how he did it and then make some changes."

Ted nodded. "Listen, I'm sorry about the comment about her looks."

"That's okay. You were just telling the truth. I'm sorry I let the other slip, about our personal relationship. It's recent...And right now, I'm just trying to keep her alive. We'll deal with the Bureau when Hawkins is behind bars."

"Don't worry about it. No one will ever hear about it from this office."

"Thanks."

"Hey man, just go take care of her. I'll keep you up to date on what's going on here."

The two-hour flight to Atlanta gave Scott time to review and add to his file on Hawkins. To predict the killer's next move, Scott had to understand the killer. Know how his mind worked. Complicating it was the wild card in the puzzle, Sarah. Her recent behavior had a purpose. Scott knew that. She wanted to drive Hawkins into a sexual frenzy by being sexy. Black outfits for work and black lace for play. She had to be driving Hawkins nuts. She wanted Hawkins to want her so badly that he unwillingly deviated from his plan, lost control. She's succeeding, too. The pictures, the schedules, the notes, all prove it. The guy's becoming obsessed with Sarah. And, he is getting sloppy; hanging around the court-room, letting her spot him.

Sarah, how can you play games with this psycho? Don't you know if he wins, it will cost you your life? How can you pull a stunt like this without telling me? His mind churned with warring emotions. He was worried, angry and scared. Angry with Sarah for risking her life so foolishly, worried that if she got into trouble he might not be able to save her. Afraid he might lose her. As he sat on the jet staring out at the clouds, he was sure of only one fact: He and his lovely bride-to-be were going to have a serious discussion tonight and all the black lace in the world was not going to get her off the hook. Not this time.

The more Scott thought about it, the angrier he got. She was deliberately trying to incite Hawkins, to get him to act on his emotions. To get him to deviate from whatever plan he had to abduct her. Scott continually checked his watch. The flight seemed to be taking forever. He called her cell, no answer. He dialed again. "Answer the phone, Sarah. Where are you? Answer the phone."

As the jet knifed through the clouds at eight thousand feet, he thought of Sarah; her smell, her touch, the purring sound she made when they were making love, her laugh, her smile.

He called the surveillance team and found out she was okay. She was still in court.

At least she is out of harms way—until I get home. As soon as the plane touched down he headed straight to her place.

Since she didn't expect Scott until the next morning, she was surprised to see his car parked in the garage. She was relieved that he was home. She wouldn't have to spend the night alone. Her heart skipped a beat. *I wonder if it's going to be like this every time he's been out of town. This is silly, I just saw him this morning.*

He was sitting in the den, no TV, no music. Sarah's welcoming smile vanished when she saw the look on his face. *Oh no. He's got that, agent in charge look, not the, come sit in my lap, look.*

"Is this the way it's going to be, Sarah?" He asked in a low, steady voice.

He is really upset. "What? How is what going to be?" Sarah asked.

"You must really think I'm dumb. All those sexy outfits you've been modeling every night. I'm so gullible that I thought you were doing it for me. But, that wasn't the case, was it? You've been teasing Hawkins, setting a trap for a stalker, a psychotic serial killer, haven't you?"

She stood open-mouthed, eyes wide, caught completely off guard, speechless for once.

"Don't you have one of your ready answers, some witty reply?"

She remained motionless, not sure what to say.

"How could you do this without talking to me? You're gambling with your life, our future. Don't you realize that?"

"Are you going to give me a chance to explain?"

Scott didn't seem to hear her. He was on a roll. "I thought you bought those outfits for us, knowing black turns me on. Well you fooled me. Especially when you strolled around the house in your black, take me to bed outfits before coming to me. I figured you were dealing with old issues, trying to get your emotions in check. That part of you was still ashamed of your desires, because of him, and the other part enjoyed making love to me. I felt so sorry for you, but knew there was nothing I could do to help. You had to work it out for yourself. I was so proud that you cared so much for me that you were willing to fight those demons, to overcome your inner feelings, to please us both."

If you only knew how right you are.

Scott kept talking, not giving Sarah time to respond. "It was an act. You wanted to be sure Hawkins saw you. You were using yourself as bait to catch Hawkins. Was sex with me an afterthought?"

Slowly anger replaced the guilt over the deceit, the

feeling that she had betrayed Scott. Tears welled up in her eyes, Sarah's back stiffened and she got right in his face, her hands clenched, resting on her hips. "If you think that, the door is right over there." Her right arm was straight, parallel to the floor, finger pointing.

Scott was stunned, silent for the first time since Sarah had come home. Now, she was on a roll. "And as far as Hawkins is concerned. Yes, I was taunting him! I'm tired of his calling all the shots, of all the waiting. I want him to come out of hiding. For fourteen years now, I've lived in terror, afraid of him, scared that I'd wake up one morning and those cold, blue eyes would be staring down at me and I would hear those words, 'Nice body' again! I'm the only person alive who can imagine what Theresa Paul went through, twice. Tied to a bed, waiting, knowing what was coming next. Believe me, I've thought of nothing else since we found her body. Did you see the look in her eyes?"

He nodded.

"She was happy, Scott. Theresa knew she was about to die and was happy. She was relieved that it was about to be over. She wouldn't have to suffer anymore. He wouldn't hurt her ever again. Scott, I knew that feeling. I wanted it to be over. Those first days, I prayed he'd kill me. Then somehow I changed. I was determined that I would endure it. I would live long enough to see him pay. But let me tell you, if I knew he was about to kill me, I would have felt the same way Theresa did. I would have had that same look in my eyes. Because, he was in control, he was the only one that could end it."

Sarah was shaking, silently sobbing as she talked.

"Do you know what that does to a person? Even now, years later, there are some mornings I wake up scared, afraid to try to move, because I might be bound to a bed, or to open my eyes for fear he will be there. Sometimes I lay there for minutes, frozen until I touch you or feel Jax beside me."

Scott reached for her, but Sarah backed away. Her words

ate into his very soul. No, he couldn't imagine it, not any of what she'd gone through or what she was feeling, knowing Hawkins was out there, stalking her.

But, one thing he did know. She was wrong to handle it the way she was, she didn't need to do it alone. "No, honey I can't imagine what either of you felt when he had you, when you got free or what you are going through now. But you can't do it alone! No, you shouldn't do it alone. I'm here. We will do it together. Let me help you. Trust me, Sarah. Talk to me; let me in. Tell me your plan. Don't you know how much I love you? How could you put yourself in so much danger without bringing me into the loop?"

"Would you have let me if I had?"

"I don't know. No! I wouldn't want to risk losing you."

"That's why, Scott. I can't afford not to risk it. I will not play his game any longer. I can't keep sitting around, waiting for him to come for me. What if he makes his move on our wedding day? That would be a good time, wouldn't it?"

"You could have told me what you were doing. No, you should have told me what you had in mind, that you were putting your neck on the line. It should have been our decision, not just yours."

"I'm telling you now. I'm taking control. I want him to want me so badly that he can't stand it, can't think of anything else. That way, we'll trap him."

"Okay, just bring me in on it?"

"Okay. From now on I'll keep you involved. Can you tell me what you found today in New Orleans?"

"He has been there, plans to move there. There were fingerprints, hair samples, sperm samples on sheets. He has a new identity, car, home. I was really scared by what we found there. He's no longer rational."

Scott pulled the file out of his briefcase and showed her the items, one-by-one. "He's got schedules of your daily activities, hour-by-hour, pictures of you leaving the house, walking Jax, at work, at the courthouse, in the yard and at night just before bed."

"How could he get close enough to do all this?"

"I don't know. But I intend to find out."

Sarah remembered the other day in court. "Disguises, that's how he's getting away with it. He's wearing disguises."

"He has to be," Scott mused. Scott had calmed down, accepting Sarah's explanation.

She decided to press for more detail on how he reached his conclusions about her behavior. After all, Hawkins may very well follow the same logic and if he figured out what she was doing, she'd lose her edge. "What gave me away?" She asked. "How did you know that I was playing with him?

"Actually nothing you did. It was more like the pieces of a puzzle coming together."

"Such as?"

"Several things. A woman visited his house in New Orleans, a redhead, and from what the lab got off the bed sheets, she did more than say hello. As far as we know, until now, he's favored dark-haired women, with one exception; you. And, I think we agree that was because you were with Callie who was his real target. I wondered what made him switch. Then I looked through the pictures of you again, you had on black in every one, but the nighttime photos were the key. It dawned on me, you changed him. You wanted him to see you like that, sexy, ready for bed. You were trying to get him aroused. You wanted him to start fantasizing about you."

"And?"

"Then I remembered the message on the pizza box, the comment about liking you in black. Initially, I wondered when he had seen you in black. My next thought was that he was referring to the black panties and bra he stole from you. He wanted to see you in them. Then when I looked through the pictures again, all the black lace, the night photos, it hit me. You were seducing him."

She acquiesced with a nod of her head.

"How did you know he was out there?" Scott asked.

"There was no way I could have known for sure. But, like I've been telling you, I could just feel him watching me. The same way I sensed, way back then, that he was standing in the doorway, staring at me. I didn't know for sure until the other day after court when I spotted him and the van."

He nodded. "Now that you've got him, you may regret your little game. Have you thought of that, honey?"

"Yes. But pulling him out of hiding is worth the risk. Where is he, Scott? You think he's still in New Orleans?"

"My guess is no, he's here in Atlanta. But if he is in New Orleans, Kinson will nab him."

"They won't. I think you're right. He's here, in Atlanta. And he's close. He's watching me again. I can feel his eyes devouring me. He'll make his move in the next few days. He can't resist it. He can't wait much longer."

"Well, you've succeeded."

"Yes. This time, I'm in control."

"Don't you mean we're in control? I hope so, because our future and your life depend on your plan working."

"Yes, we're in this together. And, I do know what I'm risking. That's why I can't go on like this. We'll never be happy as long as he's free. I need your help. He's smart, you've got to watch my back, my front, keep him from catching me off guard."

His eyes took on a dark hue. "What's done is done. I'm not losing you now." He reached for her. "I don't agree with the way you've handled this and I don't like being excluded from your plan, but you've brought it to a head and together we'll catch him, and put him behind bars where he belongs."

Not the plan, Scott.

They discussed what they thought Hawkins would do next. They needed to predict Hawkins' next move, to know how, when and where he would try to kidnap Sarah. Scott thought it would be around the house, because Hawkins wouldn't be stupid enough to try anything around the courthouse or the Bureau.

Sarah disagreed. "No, I think it will be in a parking lot or when I'm walking Jax. But there is no way to predict what Hawkins will do. We'll just have to stay loose and be ready. If he manages to surprise us, I'm history."

"Don't say that, don't even think it. It's not going to happen." Scott pulled her close and nuzzled her ear. "We'll get him. We've got the element of surprise this time. JJ's in control."

"You've never called me that before? It sounds strange. Why now?"

"To make a point, that's who he thinks he's dealing with, little seventeen year old JJ, not Sarah James, FBI Agent. That's our advantage. That's why we'll catch him. And when he's in custody, he'll stay there. The system will see that he gets his due, Sarah. DNA specifically ties him to Jessica and Theresa's murders and he will go down for both."

You're right. Hawkins will go down. Straight to hell, where he belongs.

BEFORE HE ARRIVED HOME Thursday evening, Scott scheduled a task force meeting for six o'clock Friday morning.

The meeting began promptly at six. Scott's eyes were pools of dark chocolate and his mouth was a tight line of anger. "Congratulations, ladies and gentlemen. You've allowed our fugitive to make total fools out of Atlanta Homicide and the Bureau. Hawkins has managed to infiltrate our surveillance, take photos of Sarah and establish her daily routine on a precise timetable."

Then he paused for emphasis. "There is no doubt in my mind that he intends for her to be his next victim. We've been asleep at the wheel. And as a result we've put the life of a member of this task force in jeopardy. You have my apology, Miss James."

His gaze moved from person to person, willing them to feel the shame of failing one of their own.

"How did he take pictures of Sarah without being noticed?" Scott slammed the photos on the table one by one: at court, at her home, at the Bureau! "Where were you guys?"

Sarah's face was bright red as she saw the others staring at the pictures. In her mind, all eyes were focused on the ones of her in black lace. *Damn you Scott. You didn't have to show those. You could've just talked about them. Get your eyes full guys. Look close Scott, you'll never get the opportunity again.*

No one said a word. The room was silent except for Scott's deep breaths as he tried to regain control. He failed and threw a folder on the table.

"Here is Sarah's schedule over the past three weeks. Memorize it. You can be sure he has. Hawkins put all this together for a reason, to kill Agent Sarah James, and I'm worried. Thank God, that he didn't want her yet, because this crew certainly couldn't have stopped him."

No one argued the point. Eddie and Roy's faces were crimson. Scott's eyes looked like two chunks of coal, his face was drained of color and his body was rigid. "Figure it out! Figure him out. What's his next move? Catch this guy, yesterday!"

He focused on the photos spread across the table, then looked up at Sarah, making eye contact. He could tell that she was embarrassed, angry that he had shown the group the photos. Scott ignored her. "How was he able to take those, to monitor her goings and comings? We have to answer those questions if we are going to save her. Here's what I do know. Hawkins has been in New Orleans. He has a new identity, home and vehicle. Once he's finished here, killed Sarah, that's where he plans to run."

He passed out copies of Hawkins new driver's license. "Ted Kinson, the New Orleans AIC found this in a safe in the house, along with bank books, credit cards and a passport. We've already frozen all of Hawkins' bank accounts. So he's got no running money. Ted's got the usual nets set up and if he's there, they'll arrest him. But that's not going to happen. He's here, in Atlanta, watching Sarah, getting ready to make his move."

Scott made eye contact with Roy and Eddie. "What ever is going wrong, get it corrected! Catch Hawkins, before he gets Sarah."

He let silence make his point before continuing. "Have you two got anything?"

"Yes, and it could be our first real break," Roy answered. "We got a lead yesterday that seems viable. A cashier at Target in Jonesboro reported waiting on Hawkins. I've got two officers picking up the store's surveillance tapes, as we speak, and another set of officers going out to interview the employee."

The atmosphere in the conference room changed in an instant. Faces brightened and downcast eyes looked up. One of the team members looked from Sarah to Scott. "I don't know how this guy did it, but I promise you," he looked at Sarah, his eyes apologetic and determined. "He won't get close to you again, no more pictures."

Sarah squirmed in her seat. Feeling exposed, embarrassed, with the photos lying on the table for all to see. Having no choice but to ignore them, Sarah put modesty aside and focused on the task at hand. "Thanks, I hope you're right, because the way things have been going, I feel completely vulnerable."

"I think it's for real, Sarah," Roy responded.

"Until we know, we've got to take some action. Let's assume it's not viable. Sarah, you seem to know this guy better than anyone. What is his next move?" Scott asked.

"Well, we know that I'm his next target." Her glance

moved from face to face making eye contact. "And, from all this," she pointed at the schedules and photographs on the table. "It's obvious he's become obsessed with me and he's taking unnecessary risks. He's losing control. I think he is going to try to take me soon, in the next couple of days.

"How, when and where he'll do it is the question we've got to answer. I think his statement "History will repeat itself" gives us the answer. He's telling us that he intends to abduct me in the same manner as he did Theresa, when I'm alone, using force and in a public area. And, he plans to use my vehicle to transport me to his final destination.

"He's issuing this group a challenge; 'Try and stop me'. He wants the Bureau and the Force to look stupid, losing one of their own. If he succeeds, the press will have a field day.

"Of course, I won't care, will I? I hope they're brutal." She tried to lighten it up a bit, at her own expense. "And they give Roy and Scott hell. Maybe get some nighttime photos of you two in your boxers scratching your privates." Everyone laughed, even Roy and Scott.

"Not going to happen," Roy stated emphatically. "I've grown kind of fond of you and it's obvious he is." He nodded at Scott, "We both plan to keep you around for a long time."

When the meeting broke up, Sarah followed Scott to his office. Hot on his heels, she slammed the door the minute they were inside. "I can't believe you showed them those pictures. I was practically nude. What were you thinking? Do you know how that made me feel?"

Scott turned and leaned into her face. Their noses were inches apart. Two sets of eyes blazing.

"Agent James, don't you ever come into this office using that tone of voice with me. You posed for them, didn't you? Willingly, I might add. You want to be a centerfold, expect exposure. They're evidence in an ongoing investigation. You're the next target of a serial killer. The task force needed to see them. To realize how close he has gotten to you. If they are going to protect you, to catch him, they have to know how smart he is. And how infatuated he is with you and why. Yes, I showed them and if it would help catch Hawkins, I'd circulate them to the local papers. You played the game, accept the consequences."

COURT RECESSED AT TWO O'CLOCK for the weekend and Sarah spent the rest of the afternoon at the range. Afterwards, still trailed by her shadows, she stopped at the mall, then went by Kroger to shop for dinner, went home and began cooking. She calmed down, realizing Scott was right about the photos. He didn't really have to show them to make his point or could have been a little more discreet about which ones he had displayed, but to be fair, they had an impact on the case and the task force needed to see them. If the roles were reversed, she would have used the pictures. They let their guard down and they had to realize how close Hawkins had gotten to her. She was confident no one on the team would let it happen again. And Scott had a right to be upset with her for not including him in her plan. In his shoes, she would have felt the same, but that didn't change the fact that it was her life on the line. She had a right to decide how to handle the situation, and she did what needed to be done.

Dinner was waiting when Scott got home. Three T-Bones marinated in Dale's sauce, garlic mashed potatoes and Caesar salad. Dessert was a homemade lemon icebox pie with a cool whip topping, made from a recipe given to her by her wedding planner.

She could tell he was in a better mood the moment he walked through the door and asked, "Three steaks?"

"The big one is for Jax."

"Jax?"

"Yes. He doesn't get any potatoes, salad or pie."

"Oh, to come back as your dog," he playfully swatted her on the butt.

"Well, you could, but I think you would be disappointed, or at least I hope you would be."

"Why? He has it made."

"Oh, he has it made, all right, but he has to settle for doggie treats when he's a good boy. You, on the other hand, my man, get to enjoy treats of a slightly more intimate nature when you're a good boy, if you get my drift."

He gave her a bear hug. "I've been good all day."

"Down, boy!" She patted Scott on the head like she would Jax, "Maybe later." Sarah was still amazed at herself, at the change that Scott had brought about in her. In a few short months she had been transformed from the "Ice Queen" who was afraid of sex, who thought she would never be interested in being with a man, into a woman who enjoyed pleasing her man.

After dinner, the three took a walk along the power line. Jax was able to be off his leash and was free to spring through the underbrush. Scott found himself becoming more attached to the dog every day. He looked forward to the dog's tail wagging greetings.

After returning home and taking a quick bath, she emerged wearing the black "Such a Flirt" lingerie outfit she had purchased at Victoria's Secret that afternoon. She walked through the house passing in front of several windows before going into the den.

Hawkins gasped, he had promised himself he would stay away but he couldn't, and now he knew why. He was drawn to the house in anticipation of just such a sight and he was not disappointed. Even the brief glimpse of JJ passing by the window set his heart racing. He envisioned himself inside, waiting in the bedroom for his JJ. He put down the binoculars, checked the disguise he planned to wear the next day and went to bed.

Scott's breath caught in his chest when he looked up from the television and saw Sarah in the Victorian corset, its garters supporting sheer silk stockings. Underneath, the lacy

Brazilian bikini panties left little to the imagination. Black. Everything was black against her silky skin. Her copper curls tousled in inviting disarray around her face. Suddenly he felt warm, all over.

The remote clattered on the floor and Scott stared, his mouth open.

Sarah stood, just out of his reach, hands on hips and feet slightly apart, posing seductively. Scott was speechless. She was the most beautiful sight he had ever seen and the look in his eyes made Sarah glow.

He reached for her. Sarah slowly, tantalizingly moved into his embrace, knowing this could be the last time they would be together.

CHAPTER 25

SARAH JUMPED WHEN Jax's cold nose touched her bare spine. She partially opened her right eye to check the time displayed on the bedside radio: 5:35 AM.

"Jax, I swear your kidneys must be hooked up to an alarm. Don't they know its Saturday? I can sleep later on weekends."

He whined to be sure he had her attention and then rested his head on the edge of the bed, his big brown eyes pleading.

"Okay, Okay." Sarah rolled out of bed, and went to the back door to let Jax out. Scott looked up when she came back into the bedroom. "Not again. Please, woman."

Without saying a word she slid under the covers and was almost asleep when the radio alarm sounded, signaling that it was six. She got out of bed, slipped on a T-shirt and padded to the bathroom.

"Let's run at Stone Mountain again this morning," Sarah suggested while brushing her teeth. They had gone there the past three Saturdays and she enjoyed running there because the park's scenery turned exercise into an adventure.

Stone Mountain is a massive dome of granite rising 825

feet into the sky. The three hundred million-year-old mountain is five miles in circumference and covers 583 acres. Three Confederate equestrian figures — General Robert E. Lee, General "Stonewall" Jackson and President Jefferson Davis are carved into the north face of the mountain. The Park's eight-mile running trail weaves through the park, circling the mountain and coursing in and out of wooded areas, with views of the golf course, lakes and various playing fields. Park visitors rollerblade, jog, play softball, football, throw Frisbees or merely laze around on blankets, enjoying the weather.

It was the perfect setting for Sarah and Scott's long Saturday morning runs. Today, however, was unique as both would be out for more than exercise. Scott was seeking a fugitive and Sarah wanted justice, the ultimate revenge. If all went well, today, Hawkins would meet his destiny and Sarah would fulfill hers. In her heart, Sarah knew that either she or Hawkins would be dead before the day was over.

"Think he'll be there today?" Scott asked.

"Yes."

"He'll try something in the middle of a crowded park?"

"Yes. And I'm counting on today being the day."

"Then let's do it! It's time we ended this, I'll arrange back-up on the way."

Sarah emerged from the bathroom in her black shorts and tank top. She pulled an FBI T-shirt out of a drawer and headed for the door. "Ready?"

He looked up from the shoe he was tying. "In a second. How do you think this will go down?"

Sarah leaned against the door jam and thought through her predicted scenario for the hundredth time.

"He'll make his move in or near a parking lot, before or after the run. Probably after, so we'll be tired and off guard. I don't think he'll try during the run, that'd be too risky with two of us. Plus, he'd have to either force or carry me to a car, even more risky, unless, he attacks us when we pass by one of the parking areas close to the trail. Remember, he needs to disable us quickly, get me in a car, and get away. He will not want a crowd and he can't carry me far without being noticed. So, whatever he does, it has to be close to a car, either ours or his."

"Does he think I'm going to just stand and watch while he loads you in the trunk of his car?"

"No, he's got to have a way of dealing with you in mind, some way to neutralize you. If he's as hyped as I think he is, he's outraged that you've been in bed with me, while he has had to settle for pictures and going home alone. Scott, I think he wants you dead."

"Humph...He's going to find out that I'm not that easy to kill. Why today, during our run?"

"Because that's how he got me before. Callie and I were out for a run. Remember his message, 'History Repeats Itself.' Today, because he can't wait any longer, his obsession with me won't let him."

"Why at Stone Mountain? Why not here, while we're running in the neighborhood?"

"He probably thinks we're too well guarded here. At Stone Mountain he's got a bigger area. It'll be harder for our guys to watch over us."

"Well, he's in for a surprise." Scott put an extra clip in the fanny pack with his revolver.

"Scott, don't underestimate him. He's outsmarted us at every turn. We can't let him do it again." Her mouth broke into a half smile. "I've got a wedding to plan."

Scott stood up and stretched. "Yeah, and I've got a honeymoon to enjoy. We better get moving. And, Sarah, today will be different. If he's there, we'll get him. Count on it."

Walking to the car, he asked. "Why didn't you speak up at the meeting, yesterday? We could have already had a trap in place."

"Could've, but it would have been a mistake."

"Why?"

"We know he's been following me, which means he's been to Stone Mountain three weeks in a row. So, not only does he know our routine on Saturday, but he's also had time to observe the park's schedules. We know from his notes, that he's meticulous, so my guess is that he knows types and numbers of employees on duty on Saturday morning and generally, where they're stationed. Any change in that routine, a sudden influx of cops, rangers, whatever we would have disguised our people as, would tip him off, and he'd bolt. And we'd miss our chance to trap him."

"So, you're so intent on setting him up that you're willing to risk your life, knowing there may be holes in our coverage?"

"I'm not stupid, Scott. I'm not risking anything. I've got total confidence in the man setting up the coverage. I'm planning to marry him. He's not going to risk his dowry by letting something happen to me. Are you?"

"When you put it like that, I guess not. How much is that dowry anyway?"

Sarah punched him on the arm. "You're looking at it, buster. Now get a move on."

"What about Jax? You want to leave him here?"

"No! He goes. If he's not with us, it'll break the routine. And I trust Jax's instincts. Remember Macon?"

"Good call." He grabbed his cell phone. "Now I need to make some calls. Let's go." He tossed Sarah the keys to the Suburban.

Jax jumped into the vehicle as soon as Sarah opened the back door. In one swift move, he crossed into the passenger seat and propped his head on the windowsill.

"Whoa, partner, that's my seat." Scott told the dog. Jax didn't budge. He just looked over at Sarah as she buckled up. He barked. She smiled.

"He has a point, Scott. He was here first. Now be a good boy and get in the back." Jax swung his big head around and looked at Scott and grinned.

"Momma's boy," Scott taunted.

"Now children, stop fighting." Jax slurped Sarah's cheek, let out a single bark and then stuck his head out the passenger window. The Springer's thoughts were obvious, "Guess we know whose number one with mom."

Sarah smiled as she reached over and scratched the dog's back. It feels good to laugh; things will get serious soon enough. She backed out of the drive, thinking about what lay ahead. The quest that directed her every move for the past thirteen years was almost over. The high-stakes game that Hawkins started so long ago was about to come to a close. I'm in charge. I'm calling the shots. He'll be there today. I can feel it. As they turned into the park, Scott flipped his phone shut.

"PD's plainclothes and our people will both be here. To blend in, they will either be playing touch football, jogging, or taking leisurely walks, in areas near enough to our route, to keep us in sight without being obvious."

"I hope our guys leave their windbreakers at home."

"Smart Ass!" he chuckled, "Maybe I should call."

Sarah's nervous laughter filled the car. What did Roy say?"

"He thinks we're wasting our time. His lead in south Atlanta panned out. Hawkins was on the tapes from Target. Neighbors identified his photograph. Roy's getting a search warrant for the house. Our people should start filtering into the park any time now. It's going to be okay."

HAWKINS HAD BEEN ONE of the first to drive through the gate when the park opened at seven-thirty. Once inside, he had driven around looking for any indication that he was expected, to be sure the Cops or the Feds weren't planning a surprise party for him. If he had spotted anything unusual or out of the ordinary, he was out of there, pronto, and JJ would have to wait until that night.

I don't see any extra rangers, no dark Suburban with long antennas and there's nobody walking around with wires running out of their ears, talking to their lapel. Its all clear and all that stands between me and JJ is a love-struck FBI Agent and Goofy the hound.

He was parked beside a lake overlooking the third green, passing the time watching the occasional golfers that were beginning to filter by, and admiring his pictures of JJ. At eight-fifty he rolled down his window and sucked in some fresh morning air.

With a dull plop, a ball landed on the green, not more than three feet from the hole. Plop! Plop, plop, plop, three more balls landed on the green. Two carts came up the path and parked. Four golfers got out and grabbed their putters. Hawkins watched as they meticulously lined up their putts. One sank a long one from the edge of the green and the others gave him a high five. Two, two-putted and the fourth, the one who had the shortest putt of the four, missed, his ball rimming the cup and rolling down a slope. A steam of profanities filled the air as he picked up his ball and disgustedly left the green. The foursome climbed into their carts and headed for the number four tee-box.

Laughing at them, Hawkins rolled up his windows, backed out and made another tour of the park. Everything appeared to be okay, no cops and no blue windbreakers. The Feds are so stupid they wear those things even when they're undercover. Either the windbreakers or the caps with FBI over the brim! Satisfied, he drove to the parking area for the jogging trails. There's their SUV. She's here! The old Suburban was in its regular Saturday spot. He began shaking. He could feel her, taste her, and smell her.

He parked beside their Suburban, straddling two spaces. He checked the small dog in his back seat. It had slept the whole morning, and he had almost forgotten it was there. One of the neighbors had shoved it out of their front door just as Hawkins was backing out of his drive. He caught it and stuck it in his car, thinking that walking it around the parking area would throw off suspicion while he waited for JJ and super prick to get back from their run.

He looked at his watch, it was 9:15. He thumbed through the photos until he found his favorite. Sarah framed in the window wearing skimpy black panties and a black top that barely covered her breasts, with her midriff exposed. The photo shook as he brought it to his lips.

Hawkins got out of his car and moved to the back of the Suburban. Using his cell phone he called the number noted on the sticker on the side window.

"Yes, I've locked my keys in my car." He verified Sarah's address and phone number. "My password is Callie, I think. It's been so long since I set up the account, and I've never had to use it." He guessed right.

The door locks popped up. "Yes, it's unlocked. Thank you."

He opened the back and quickly went about his business. Finished, he closed it. Went back to his car, got the dog and his favorite picture of JJ and moved to the park bench to wait.

Enjoy your run, JJ. I think I'll take care of the dog first, and then it'll be Mr. Wrong's turn. Then yours.

He blinked rapidly, his mouth twitched as his shaking hands picked up his favorite photo. He lightly rubbed his fingertips across her image, almost feeling her silky skin. He could hear her whimpers.

This time she will beg. If it wasn't for her, everything would be different. I'd be president of the company and Hawkins Enterprises would be one of the 500. I'd be hob-nobbing with the elite, the money people, and my picture would be on the society and financial pages of all the major newspapers. Instead, my face is plastered all over the FBI's Most Wanted List and the media is haunting me. It's your fault, JJ. Why'd you do this to me? Why did you run out on

302   JIM DAHER

me? Why couldn't you have been like weak little Callie, and done yourself in?

Instead you ran, rejected me, like my mother. She didn't want me. Dad's lied to me all these years, telling me she's dead. I know different. She left me. How could she run out on me? She deserves to die. All of them, Momma, JJ and all the others that walked out on me, deserve to die.

Hawkins shook his head to clear up the confusion in his mind. He checked the time, again. Then he looked at his picture of JJ. *She's so beautiful, so sexy.* He kissed it, and then looked at his watch again. If they stick to their schedule, she'll be in the trunk by eleven.

THE CRISP AIR and light breeze made it seem cooler than the forecasted fifty-three degrees when Sarah and Scott got out of the Suburban. They were sitting on the grass facing each other, legs out straight, feet touching, stretching by bending forward touching their noses to their knees, first one, then the other, rotating from right to left. The grass was deep and soft, and the moisture from the ground was seeping through her thin running shorts sending chills down Sarah's legs and up her spine. She could feel the morning sun on the back of her neck and knew it and the exercise would soon warm her.

"It's almost nine, let's get started." She got up and went to the Suburban, got her FBI T-shirt off the backseat and slipped it over her head. With the door blocking her on one side and Scott on the other, she tucked her back-up weapon, a small Sig-Sauer P230 9mm in the back of her shorts and pulled her T-shirt to conceal it. Stepping away, she strapped on her fanny pack, securing the Sig in her waistband. Her primary weapon, the FBI issued Glock, was in the fanny pack. Scott put on his fanny pack. This was the same routine they had followed for the past three Saturdays, with the only exception being the pistols in their waistbands.

Scott kissed her cheek. "Let's do it. Stay loose. Be ready. Let's alternate running side by side, with me following a little behind."

Sarah nodded, called Jax and started out at a slow pace. "That won't be hard. You can't keep up anyway. Let me know when to slow down so you can catch up."

"Funny, very funny." Scott mumbled.

Jax was a few yards in front of them, head high, alert as if sensing danger — the point man leading his troops into combat. For the first mile the trio stayed in that formation, maintaining a nine-minute pace. A quarter mile later, Jax barked and sprang off to the right. Sarah tensed, broke stride and almost fell as her right hand went to the fanny pack. Beside her, Scott was on one knee with his gun drawn. Ready.

She relaxed and smiled when a rabbit scurried across the trail and into some tall grass, with the big Springer hot on its trail. "Stupid mutt," Scott growled.

Jax disappeared for a few seconds then his head appeared above the top of the grass and turned one-eighty to get his bearings in a split second and then he was lost from sight again.

The two resumed running. The grass and underbrush gave way to a thin line of trees. Jax chased his prey for another fifty yards before tiring of the game and returning to Sarah's side. "Jax, stay alert boy. Hawkins, where are you?" she whispered.

At the three mile mark, Scott slowed his pace and dropped back beside Sarah. "You doing okay?"

Sarah could see the strain in his eyes. The same strain she was feeling. "As okay as I can be until this is over."

Scott was breathing hard from being in the lead.

"I'll take the lead for a while." Lengthening her stride, Sarah increased her pace to just under a seven and a half-minute mile.

Scott fell back, his eyes continually sweeping the terrain ahead.

At the five-mile marker Jax veered off to the left and sprang over a log, landing in a lake running parallel to the path. His head never went under as he began paddling through the water. He came out on the far bank and gave chase to a flock of ducks that had been sunning. Sarah slowed to watch him, allowing Scott to catch up with her.

"That dog is nuts. Maybe he'll keep going."

"Then you'd just have to spend the afternoon using all your FBI skills to find him." They could no longer see him but could hear his excited barking.

"That'll be the day."

"Won't it though?" She smiled, and then turned serious. "You think Roy has gone in yet?"

"No, he hasn't had time yet. He's got to coordinate with the Gwinnett County cops. That will slow him up some. But it shouldn't be long."

Roy had called just as they were pulling through the Park's entrance and told them that there was a van in the garage of the south Atlanta house and that the tag number was a match. A warrant had been issued and a SWAT team was on its way there.

"As far as we know, the van is his only mode of travel so if its here, he must be, and you guys are safe. Okay if I pull some of my people to help out here when we go in?"

"Yeah, I've got enough agents to get the job done here," Scott answered.

"Why don't the two of you come down and be in on the capture?"

Scott told Sarah what Roy thought and asked if she wanted to skip the run and go to Jonesboro.

"No, he's here." And I'll put three bullets in his heart before they get through the door.

SCOTT AND SARAH were running side by side when the parking lot came into view. "This has to be it, be ready for anything," Scott told her.

"I'll go in first, be careful." Sarah picked up her pace. Jax sprang out of nowhere and joined her. Scott followed at a safe distance, keeping an eye out for Hawkins.

She eased to a slow jog for the last twenty yards, eyeing the Suburban and the surrounding area carefully. Six other cars were in the lot and they all appeared to be empty.

By the time she reached the Suburban, Jax was lying beside it, panting. Scott had the keys, so Sarah began stretching to keep her muscles from cramping, and casually scanned the area, again. *Where are you?* She sensed Scott coming into the clearing before she heard his feet pounding on the path. Then she heard the doors unlock. Without taking time to stretch, Scott opened the back of the vehicle and took out the dog's water bowl and filled it from a faucet near the edge of the lot.

While he was tending to Jax, Sarah opened the cooler. She noticed a couple of pieces of ice and a wet spot around it. *Odd. How'd they get there? Why hasn't that ice melted?*

Setting the water bowl down, Scott surveyed the area, looking for Hawkins. He didn't see anything unusual, just an old man walking on the trail with a little dog. Both looked harmless.

Sarah's little voice was screaming in her head, "Don't get careless." She looked around the area again but didn't notice anything unusual. Nothing was disturbed in the car, either, except for the ice. But she wasn't satisfied. Her survival instinct was telling her that she was overlooking something. What? She scanned around the area again, Nothing, just an old man shuffling along, slightly stop shouldered, and a cute little dog. *That dog.*

She took a bottle of water and a PowerAde out of the cooler and handed Scott the water.

"Scott, did you open the cooler?"

He guzzled half the bottle of water. "No. Why?"

Sarah took a small sip of the PowerAde. She never drank too fast after a run, preferring to cool down a bit first. "There's some ice around it. How'd it get there?"

Scott took another long slug of water, still casting his eyes around the area. "I don't know. Did you leave the car unlocked?"

"No. Why would anyone go in the cooler?"

"Maybe he spiked our drinks." Scott laughed at the thought and visually scanned the area again, before looking at the almost empty bottle. "I don't know if the seal was broken on this one. Yours?"

"I don't think so."

"I still don't see anything. Maybe Roy is right and Hawkins is in Jonesboro." His voice was so low it was barely audible. "Why don't we get Jax and head down there?"

"No. Let's give it a minute. He's here! I feel him. He'll show himself."

"Well, he better make his move or we'll be outta here. So far all I've seen is that old guy with the little dog. I've got a good mind to say something to him. He's going to break the pooch's neck, yanking on that leash."

Sarah looked back at the cooler then at the old man. *Something isn't right. What is it? What am I missing? It has to be right in front of me.* Sarah reached into the recesses of her mind. *Think!*

Something was dawning on her, the man and the dog? The cap, the shoes — those white Keds. It was coming together in her mind when Scott diverted her attention.

"Sarah something's wrong. I'm sick, weak — really weak. Never felt like this before. I've got to sit down before my legs go out from under me." His speech was slurred.

Startled, Sarah watched him ease down onto the grass. "What's the matter — cramps?" Sarah dropped her PowerAde and knelt down and looked at Scott. "Your eyes look glassy."

He dropped the almost empty bottle of water. His movements were sluggish.

Oh, no, don't let him be having a heart attack. No, that can't be, he's too young. I'm missing something.

She frantically scanned the area, looking for trouble.

"Get me out of here — to an ER." Scott tried to stand up. Instead he fell to the ground. The empty water bottle was lying on the grass beside him. It caught Sarah's attention as she reached for Scott. The bottle had a purple tint inside it.

That's it. "Scott!" She grabbed his wrist to check the pulse, while yanking her gun out of her fanny pack. "He's drugged you!"

"JJ!" A voice boomed.

Sarah froze.

The old man was standing not more than ten yards away from her. He had on baggy brown trousers and a tan windbreaker. "It's been a long time. But I must say. The years have been good to you. Now be a good girl and drop the gun. Move away from him."

She dropped the gun next to Scott. The man had moved within ten feet of them. He dropped the leash and kicked at the dog. It scurried away. Hawkins took off the large glasses and Georgia Tech cap with his left hand, dropped the glasses on the ground and put the cap under his arm. He pulled off the costume wig with its bald top and gray fringe around his head above his ears and let it fall to the grass. Then he put the cap back on his head. The right hand held a gun, pointed at Sarah.

She looked at Hawkins. Anger coursed through her body. How could she have been so stupid? Of course he'd change his appearance. She had seen him as a woman, she knew Hawkins' face. The old man was his only alternative. What the hell had she been thinking? He'd probably dropped the ice around the cooler on purpose, to divert her attention. She looked down at his shoes.

Those white Keds. How could I have missed them?

"I have to give you credit. I wasn't expecting the disguise — or the Rohypnol."

"Didn't think you would. It's all been so easy — fooling you. You're nothing but a group of imbeciles, and you two are a couple of slaves to habit, following the same routine every Saturday. You always have the PowerAde and he sucks down the water. It was nothing to break into the car, pop the cooler, squirt a double shot of my little purple relaxer into his water and add a dose to your drink. I'm surprised you didn't recognize the dog. He lives across the street from you. Now, if you do anything, any fast move, macho man is dead. Understand?"

Sarah nodded.

"Are you getting a little tired, sugar? Your shot of my purple elixir ought to be kicking in. I didn't give you much. I don't want you all drugged out when I partake of your sweet body." That cold look appeared in his blue eyes, the one that had haunted Sarah.

Sarah looked around for help.

"Scream and he's dead!" He cut his eyes to the prone figure. "Do you believe in De ja vu, JJ?" He had moved beside Scott's prone body and pointed the pistol at his head."

"You hurt him and you're a dead man, asshole."

"Oh, my. Bad language, and tough, too. Is that what screwing an agent does to a woman? Makes her think she's tough? In case you haven't noticed, I'm holding all the cards, again. You're in no position to be giving orders."

I've got to stall him, think of something. "Okay, you're right, just don't hurt him. I'll do whatever you want." Sarah's voice oozed remorse, acceptance.

Where is our backup? They should be here, stopping this, bringing him down. Then she remembered, Roy had shifted his team to the house in south Atlanta.

Don't panic. He doesn't know that I barely sipped the PowerAde before dropping it or that I've got an extra piece.

Stall him, get a grip. He'll make a mistake.

"How did you recognize me? When?" Sarah inched way from Scott.

"Easy. I never forget a good piece of ass." He smiled. "Actually you weren't that good, you know. I'm expecting a lot more this time. What was your question...oh yeah, how did I recognize you? I started watching you after you visited my dad. At first you were just a prissy FBI agent, then I saw you running, and I knew. That stride of yours was a dead giveaway."

Come on guys. Where are you?

"No, Sarah! Shoot him, now!" Scott's voice was raspy, weak.

Hawkins kicked him in the side. "Shut up, prick. I ought to kill you right now. Screwing around with my woman, but you know what? If she behaves, I'll let you live. Let you lay there. You and Goofy can watch me drive away with JJ." He gave Scott another vicious kick. "Where is Goofy?" He shifted his eyes without moving his head, looking for Jax while keeping an eye on Sarah. "A real protector, that dog."

Scott was helpless. The drug was taking its toll. His body felt numb. He could barely speak. "Kill him, Sarah. Do It." He croaked.

Sarah's hand had slipped inside the fanny pack. Her gun wasn't there. It was on the ground.

"Don't be stupid. I'd love to kill him." Hawkins leaned down and pressed the pistol against Scott's head.

Sarah's hand froze and she slowly pulled it out of the pouch, empty. "You win." *Gotta let him think he's in charge. Get him to relax, let his guard down.*

Sarah was sweating from the run. Using it to her favor she wiped her brow. "I don't feel so good." She leaned against the park bench for support, and then she lowered herself to her knees, moving inches away from Scott.

Hawkins eyes widened in alarm, he stepped away. "No funny business, bitch." Using his left hand Hawkins took a key ring out of his pocket and pushed the remote keypad. Sarah heard a noise behind her. She slowly turned her head, feigning weakness. She glanced over her shoulder and saw a large car sitting a short distance away with its trunk open — a Lincoln.

"I got it just for you — same model, same year — for old times sake." His eyes hardened. "I believe you know the drill. Now get moving before I have to carry you. Then I'll have to kill him for sure."

This can't be happening. Where are they? She glanced around wildly. *I need a diversion.*

"Look at you, JJ. Just like the first time. Eyes wide, looking for help and nobody's there. You're just a frightened little girl instead of the big, bad FBI agent.

"Wait a minute. While you're down there take off his fanny pack and throw it over here, then yours. I wouldn't want either of you playing with guns, all drugged out. That's not safe you know. Someone could get hurt."

That laugh again, Sarah cringed and did as she was told. *If only Scott wasn't down, I'd risk it all and go for the bastard. He's probably never fired that thing. I can't risk it.*

She reached over to Scott and slowly unfastened his fanny pack and pulled it out from under his body.

Scott's eyes pleaded with Sarah, silently telling her to kill Hawkins.

Her eyes met Scott's. "Hang in there. It's not over till it's over," She whispered.

"Watch it. No secret messages. Throw it over here."

"I love you, Scott," She said loudly. Sarah threw the fanny pack toward Hawkins. It landed near his feet.

"How sweet. Tell you what, Macho Man, I'll take a few pictures and leave them for you, with her body." He laughed at the pained look on Scott's face. "Now your fanny pack, sweet pants."

"I'd like to rip your throat out," Scott managed to say.

Sarah stood up, purposely unsteady and wobbly. She

slowly undid the clasp on her fanny pack, pretending to struggle with it. She let it fall from her hips. It landed at her feet.

"Not good enough. Throw it over here. You're not as tough as I thought. I only gave you a small dose and you're weak as a kitten."

Sarah bent down and retrieved the fanny pack. She pretended to lose her balance and pretended to stumble, moving another few steps away from Scott. Got to get Scott out of the line of fire.

Then she threw the pack over to Hawkins. It landed inches away from Scott's. She straightened up and focused on Hawkins. *To hell with the backup, I'll do it myself.*

She wasn't helpless. Not unless she got in that trunk, and that wasn't going to happen.

"We can't wait any longer, over to the trunk. We've got a long night ahead of us and I'm anxious to get started."

Time seemed to stand still. She remembered another time, the little town in North Carolina, another Lincoln and two innocent teenagers — the confining trunk, the stifling air inside it. *Not this time.* She focused on the present. She smelled the fresh cut grass, heard the birds chirping, some squirrels chattering and Jax splashing in a nearby pond. Stay there, Jax, please.

"Look what I got you." Hawkins held up a Victoria's Secret shopping bag he had retrieved from the trunk. "All black and lacy, I hope they fit."

Sarah jiggled her body, her fingers, little, slight movements to be sure the blood was flowing, that she was loose. She glanced back and forth, cutting her eyes from side to side rather than moving her head, looking for an opening, an edge, anything.

She saw several men jogging down a hill toward them, she recognized the agents. They were a couple of hundred yards away. From his angle Hawkins couldn't see them.

"I see that look. The same one you had in the bathroom

that day. I've learned my lesson, no more Mister Nice Guy. We keep our distance and you do as you're told or your lover gets a bullet in the head. Got it?

Sarah nodded. The agents had closed the gap they were less than a hundred yards away.

If I wait they might take him, might. Can I risk it? Do I want to let them? If he sees them, will he resist? Or will he give it up?

She looked up the hill again. *Fifty yards, it's now or never. I've got to decide. Arrested or dead, do I want the bastard in hell or jail? If he'd just quit pointing that gun at Scott's head.*

WHAT IS THIS CRAZY BITCH thinking? That look in her eyes, she's not scared, why not? I've got a gun pointed at her lover's head and she has to know I won't hesitate to kill him. She has no weapon. It's hopeless, what's she thinking? I'm too far away for her to jump me. But that look in her eyes, she's planning something. She's got a way out. What, what have I missed?

Hawkins felt a sense of panic. Was he losing control? Had she outfoxed him? He couldn't take his eyes off her. That was his mistake before. Thinking she had given up, that she was beaten.

Maybe I ought to just kill Justice right now. That will take all the fight out of her. No, no it won't either. She's a survivor. She proved that before. Besides if I kill him now, she may think she has nothing to live for and try something dumb. Then I'd have to kill her. No, I can't do that. She's almost mine. I've got to have her!

He clutched the Victoria's Secret sack in his left hand. He loved the feel of the black silk. He couldn't wait to see her in the outfit. He knew she'd look great.

"Move it JJ. We need to get going. I'll let him live if you

do what you're told."

Sarah took a couple of more steps away from Scott, moving toward the Lincoln.

THAT'S ENOUGH, Scott's out of the line of fire. Sarah jiggled some more to stay loose. She couldn't let her muscles stiffen from the run. She wiped her hands on her shorts. Got to keep my hands dry, I have to have a good grip on my gun. I'll only get one chance...decision time.

Do I let them take Hawkins, or do it myself? The options ran through her mind. Hell or Jail—Hell or Jail?

Sarah eyes met Scott's. He was pleading with her. He mouthed. "Don't go. Kill him. He turned his head toward Hawkins. "I'll get you," Scott croaked in a faint whisper.

Laughter erupted from deep within Hawkins throat. "Sure you will. Wait till you find her, and see what I do to your girl." He turned the pistol on Sarah. "I'm tired of waiting. Get in the trunk!"

She stared into the barrel of the pistol. Something, anything, distract him. All I need is a split second. It's now or never! Just give me a break.

A ferocious bark broke the silence. Jax came charging in from the pond, eyes glaring and droplets of water flying off his shiny coat. When he was ten feet from Hawkins, Jax launched himself into the air — teeth bared, growling, ready for the kill.

Hawkins didn't hesitate. He turned his arm and fired, then side stepped. The dog flew past him. Sarah heard a yelp of pain and a thud.

"No!" Sarah screamed.

Jax hit the ground, rolled over and immediately regained his footing, blood pouring from his chest, his coat covered with dirt. He gathered his strength ready to launch another attack.

It wasn't necessary. He had given Sarah the break she needed. In one fluid motion Sarah dropped to her right knee, simultaneously pulling her back-up weapon out of the small of her back.

She leveled the 9mm Sig-Sauer in a two handed grip and pulled the trigger three times in rapid succession. Each time the gun discharged, she said a name.

"Callie." "Jessica." "Theresa."

Three red holes formed a circle no bigger than a quarter in the center of Hawkins chest. His eyes flamed with shock.

"And this is for me and Jax." The gun spat a fourth time and a small hole appeared between Hawkins' dead blue eyes.

CHAPTER 26

JAX STRUGGLED TO SARAH, positioning himself between her and Hawkins prone body. Sarah knelt down. "Jax." She cried, tears streaming down her cheeks. She pulled off her T-shirt and used it to try to stop the bleeding. She pulled him along the ground until they were beside Scott.

The agents arrived and immediately took charge. First they verified that Hawkins was no longer a menace to anyone. "He's dead!" one announced. Another was checking on Scott.

"Call an ambulance." Sarah shouted. "He's been drugged. I've got to get my dog to a vet. Hurry! Please!"

Hawkins' bullet had gone through Jax's shoulder. After the veterinarian finished cleaning and stitching up the wound, she assured Sarah that the Springer would be okay. "No muscle or cartilage was permanently damaged. He'll be good as new in a few weeks, but I would like to keep him here for a few days."

The ER Doctors pumped Scott's stomach and flushed his system with IV's to dilute the effects of the Rohypnol. "Agent Justice will be fine. There will be no permanent after effects of the drug. I suggest he stay here overnight for observation, just as a precaution."

After seeing to the health of the two males in her life, Sarah asked to be allowed to go home to clean up before being questioned about the shooting. Two agents took her home, one driving her and the other driving the Suburban.

As soon as she walked through her front door, Sarah began shivering uncontrollably. She walked through the house taking off her clothes and got in the shower. With the water flowing over her body she leaned her head against the wall and cried, watching Jax's blood flowing down the drain.

I almost lost them both. He almost won. Oh, God, what would I have done if he had gotten Scott, or if Jax had died? I don't want to be here tonight, not by myself.

Representatives of both the Bureau and Atlanta Homicide attended the inquiry session. Sarah spent five hours answering their questions. She outlined the sequence of events leading up to the shooting. Hawkins had stalked her. He had made harassing phone calls to her home. Hawkins had broken into her house and stolen personal items. And, he had managed to elude surveillance in order to take pictures of her and to put together a file detailing her daily schedules.

After covering that, she was asked about the shooting itself. The questions repeatedly focused on the fact that if she had waited another couple of minutes, backup could have interceded and perhaps Hawkins could have been taken into custody. Sarah was adamant that she acted as a last resort. She did not have any time left. No options, she had to act if Agent Justice was to remain alive. Testimony from the agents supported Sarah's story and verified that Hawkins had fired the first shot. A favorable ruling was passed on to the Review Board.

Two days later, the Review Board ruled that the shooting was in the line of duty, justified and in self-defense—a "Righteous Kill."

EPILOGUE

JAX AND SCOTT WATCHED from the car as Sarah knelt on the grass and placed a bouquet of fresh flowers next to the gravestone.

"It's over, Callie." Tears streamed down her cheeks. "It took me a while but I kept my promise. He'll never hurt anyone again."

She bowed her head and said a silent prayer asking God to forgive her and to let Callie and all the others rest in peace. Then she sat down and began talking.

"Callie, I miss you so much. I wish you were here. We could talk about Scott and whoever you'd be dating or married to, your kids, what we plan for the future." She wiped her eyes with her sleeve.

"We could plan the wedding. Mom might even let us decide something. Callie, you'd really like Scott — he's cool and thoughtful and knows how to make me feel good. You could be my maid of honor. I'm trying to convince Scott to let Jax be the ring-bearer. Isn't that a hoot?"

Sarah went on talking to her friend just like old times, when they used to sit on their beds and stay up all night. She told her stories about Scott and Jax, her wedding and honeymoon plans, and her new job.

She and Scott agreed that it was best if she resigned from the Bureau.

She couldn't stay in the Atlanta office after they were married, and transferring wasn't an option. When it came, unexpectedly, the solution to their dilemma seemed almost too good to be true. Management Illusions, a company that investigated corporate crime, where Stella David worked, made Sarah an offer she couldn't refuse. Sarah would be doing the same thing she had at the Bureau at three times the salary. A professional PI without any sleazy assignments and out of harms way.

When she finished she stood up, smiled and looked down.

"I love you Callie."

THE NEW ORLEANS REDHEAD was located and couldn't believe that the man she spent a weekend with was a serial killer. After the FBI told her Hawkins' history, the woman was grateful to be alive.

But not as much as Sarah James, who was not only alive, but also free. Finally.